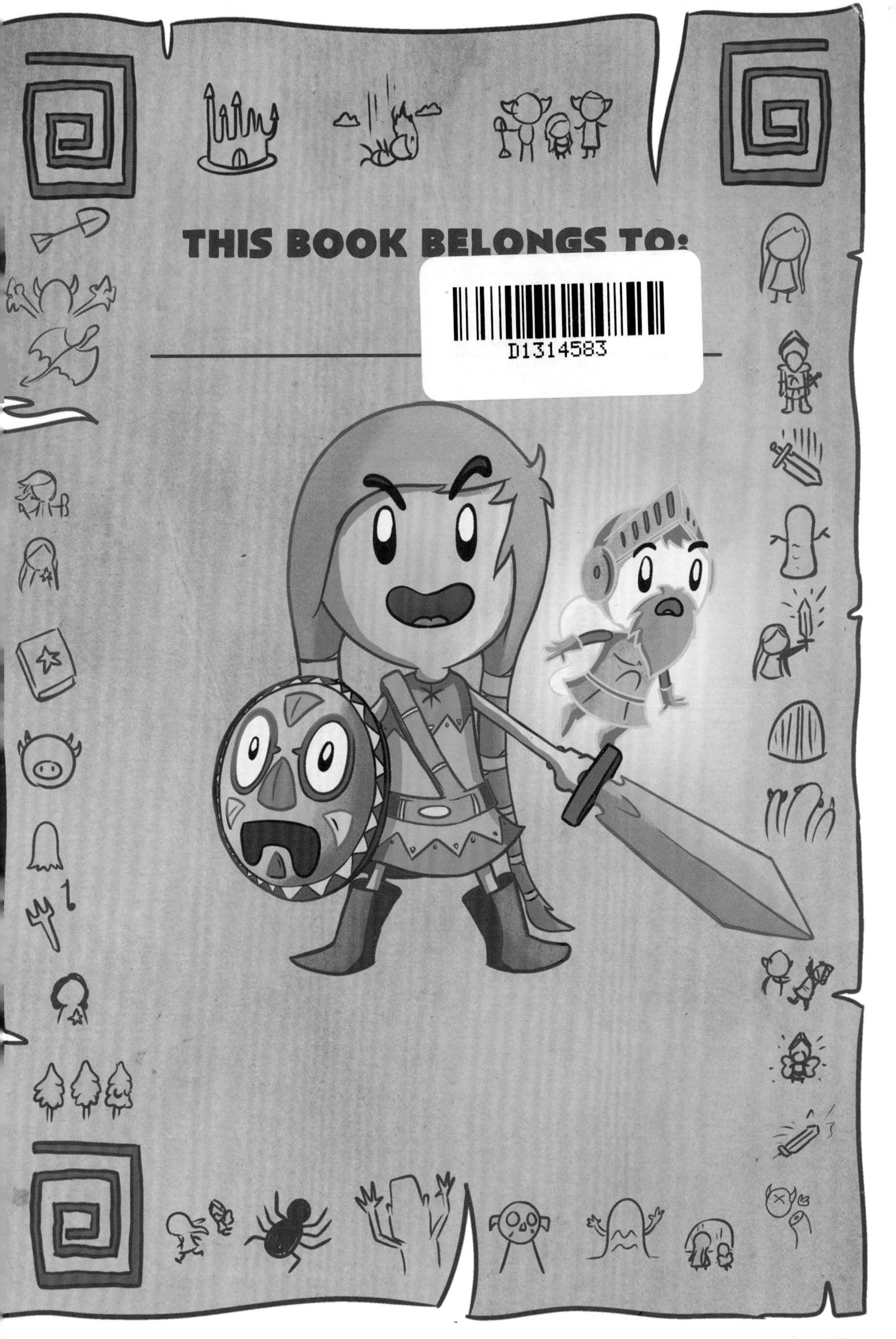
THIS BOOK BELONGS TO:

WRITTEN AND LETTERED BY
COLIN BELL

ART AND COLOURS BY
NEIL SLORANCE

ADDITIONAL COLOURS
DAVID B. COOPER

COLOUR ASSISTS
**DAVID B. COOPER, LISA MURPHY
AND HOLLEY McKEND**

DUNGEON FUN CREATED BY BELL & SLORANCE

FIRST PRINTING 2019. PUBLISHED IN GLASGOW BY BHP COMICS

ISBN: 9781910775226

MADE IN SCOTLAND.

A CIP CATALOGUE REFERENCE FOR THIS BOOK IS AVAILABLE FROM THE BRITISH LIBRARY

ASK YOUR LOCAL COMIC OR BOOK SHOP TO STOCK BHP COMICS.

VISIT **BHPCOMICS.COM** FOR MORE INFO.

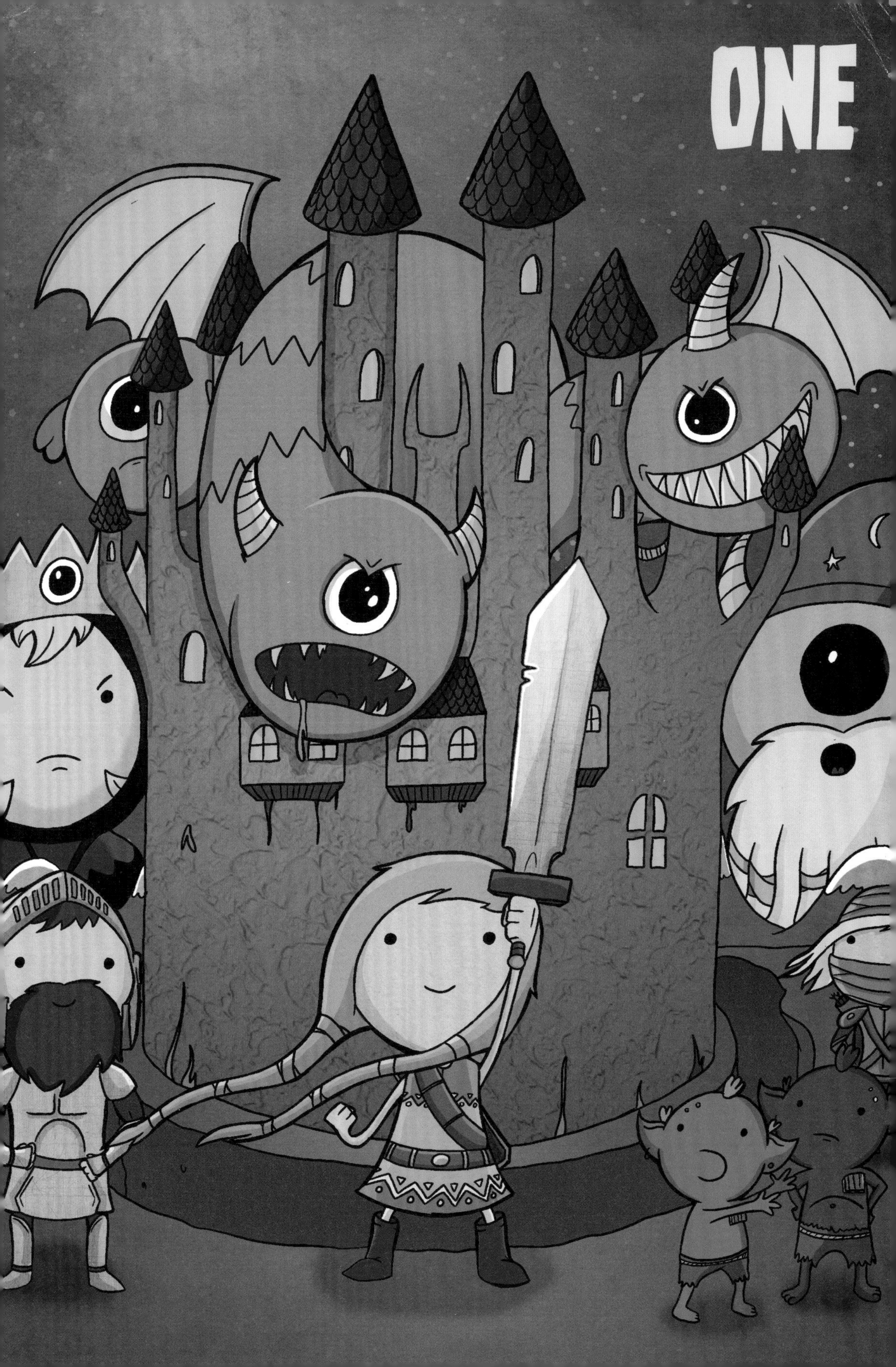
ONE

"THIS IS THE STORY OF A GIRL AND HER SWORD."

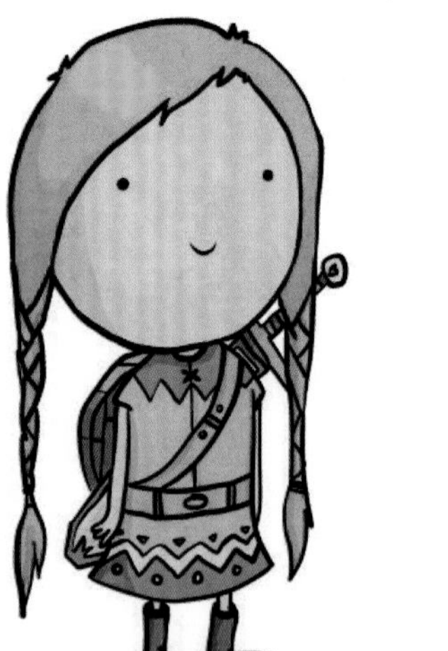

neil slorance

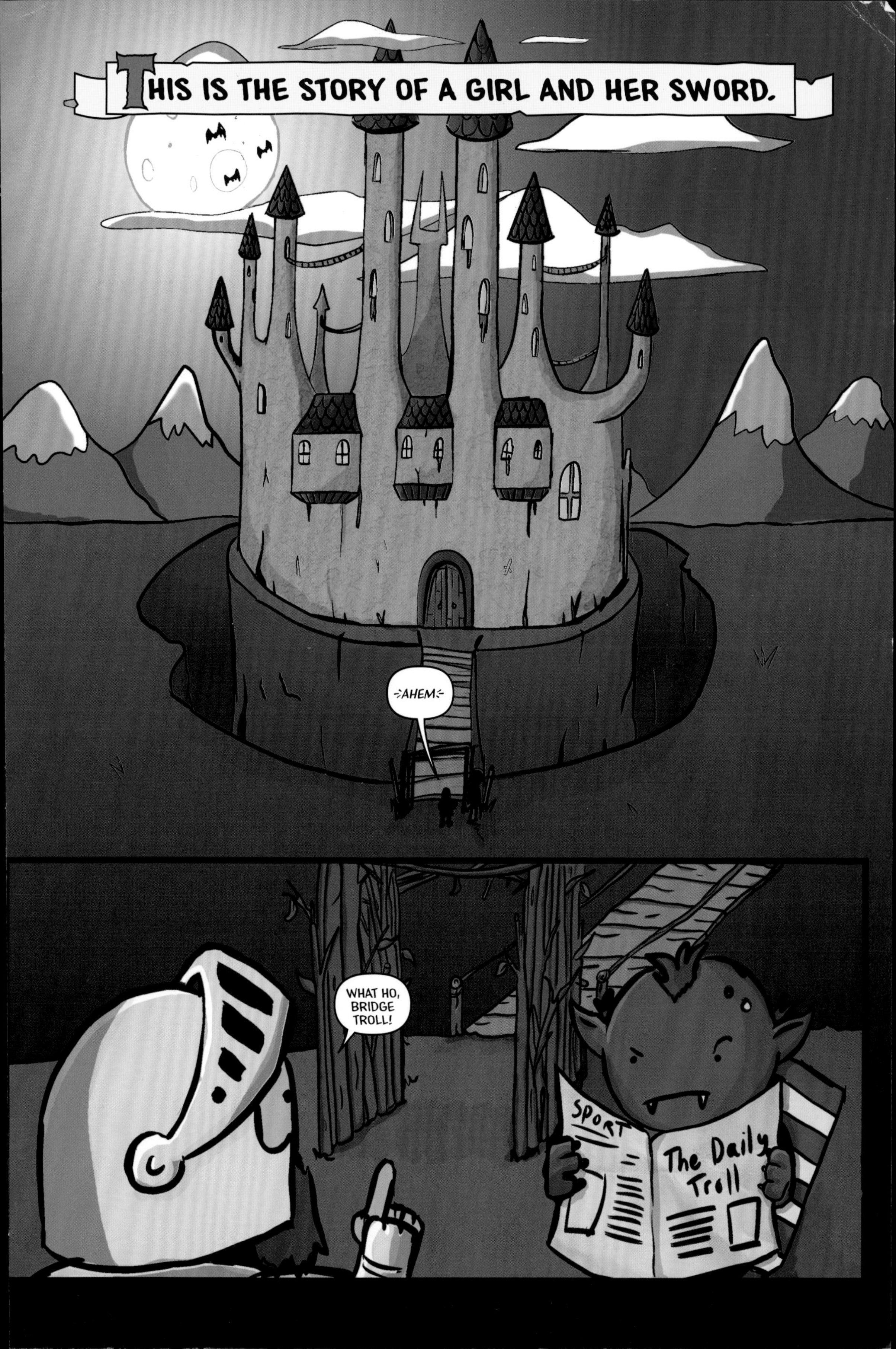
THIS IS THE STORY OF A GIRL AND HER SWORD.
AHEM
WHAT HO, BRIDGE TROLL!
SPORT
The Daily Troll

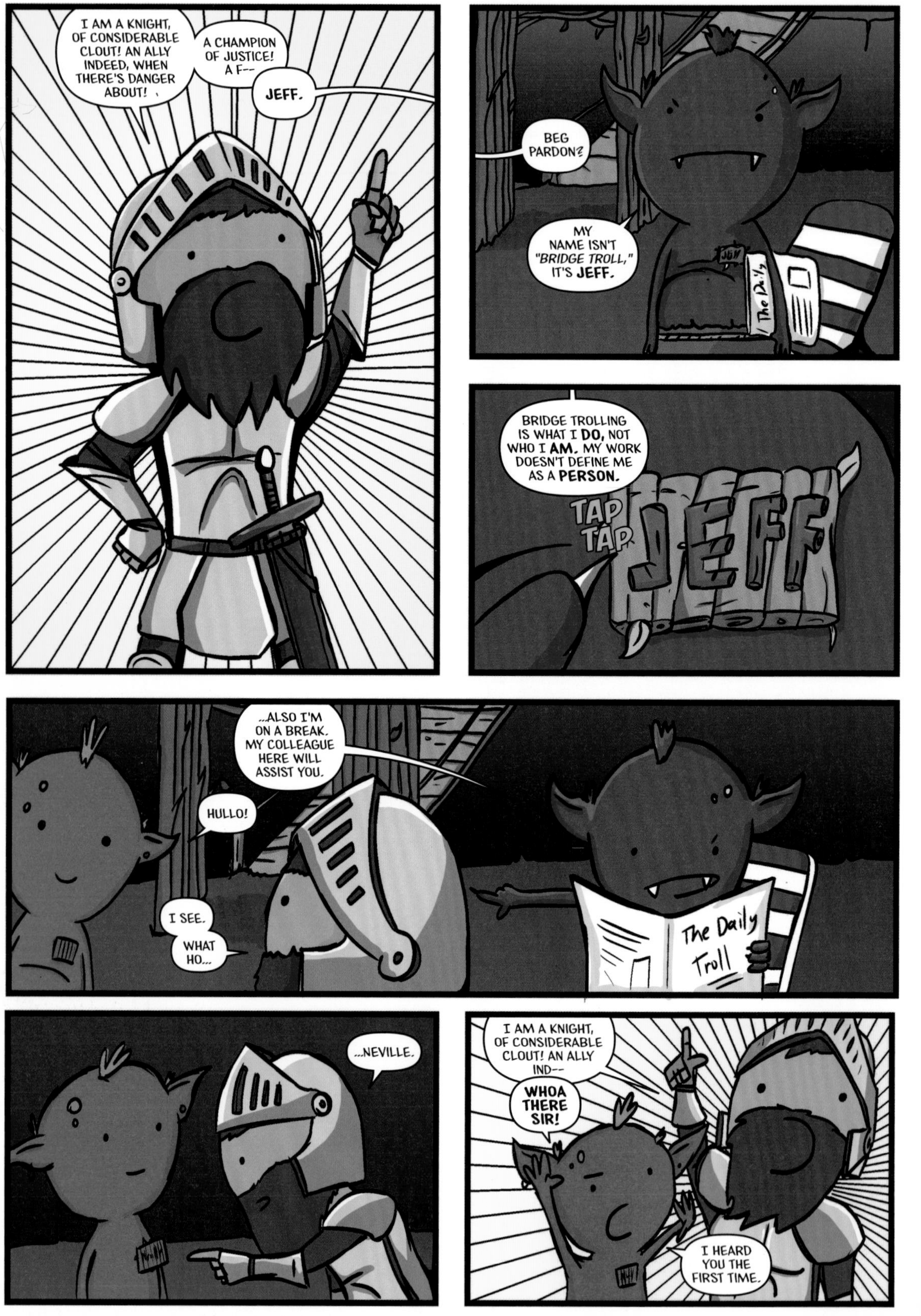
I AM A KNIGHT, OF CONSIDERABLE CLOUT! AN ALLY INDEED, WHEN THERE'S DANGER ABOUT!
A CHAMPION OF JUSTICE! A F--
JEFF.
BEG PARDON?
MY NAME ISN'T "BRIDGE TROLL," IT'S JEFF.
JEFF
The Daily
BRIDGE TROLLING IS WHAT I DO, NOT WHO I AM. MY WORK DOESN'T DEFINE ME AS A PERSON.
TAP TAP
JEFF
...ALSO I'M ON A BREAK. MY COLLEAGUE HERE WILL ASSIST YOU.
HULLO!
I SEE.
WHAT HO...
The Daily Troll
...NEVILLE.
I AM A KNIGHT, OF CONSIDERABLE CLOUT! AN ALLY IND--
WHOA THERE SIR!
I HEARD YOU THE FIRST TIME.

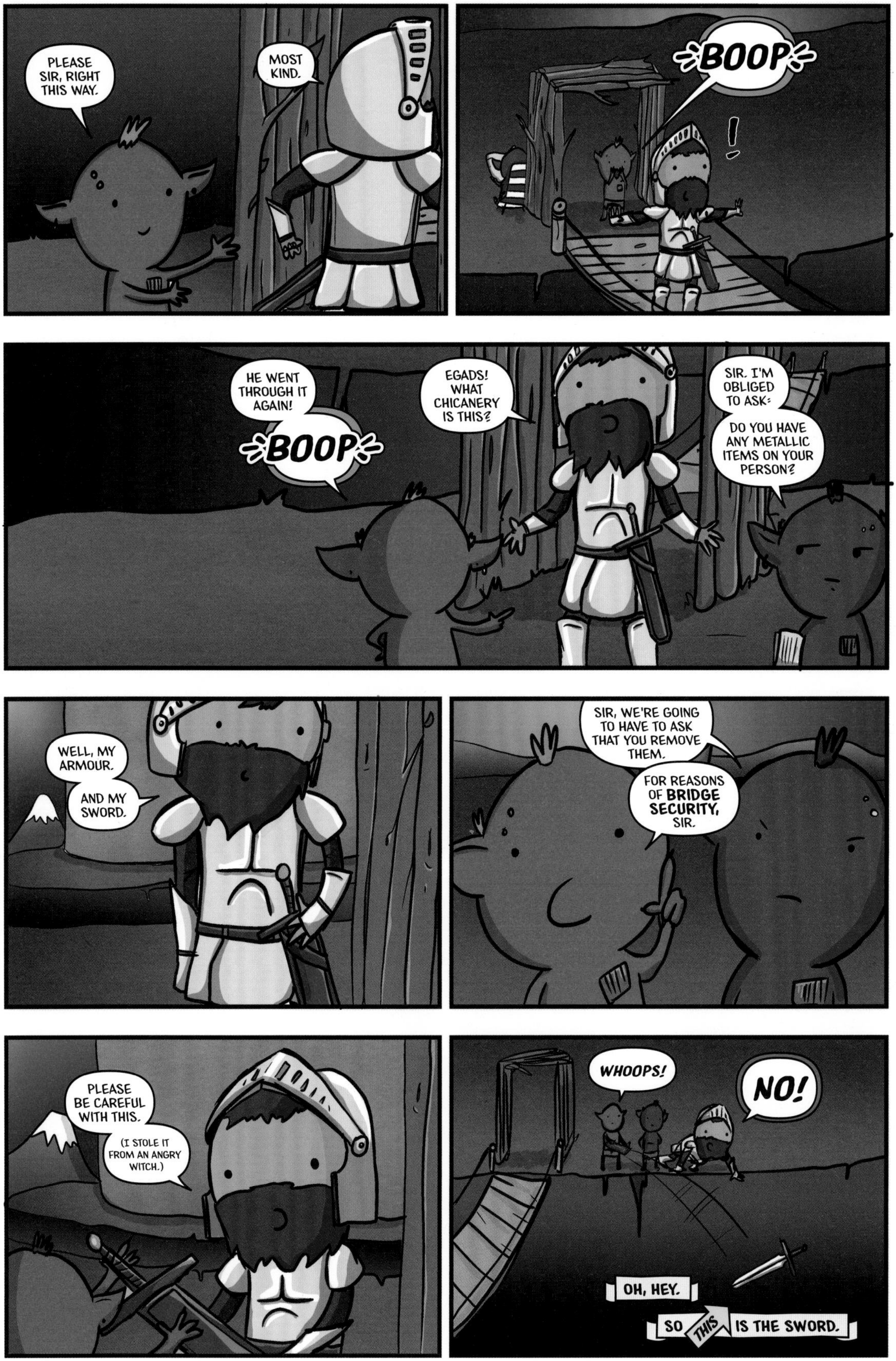
PLEASE SIR, RIGHT THIS WAY.
MOST KIND.
BOOP
!
HE WENT THROUGH IT AGAIN!
BOOP
EGADS! WHAT CHICANERY IS THIS?
SIR. I'M OBLIGED TO ASK:
DO YOU HAVE ANY METALLIC ITEMS ON YOUR PERSON?
WELL, MY ARMOUR.
AND MY SWORD.
SIR, WE'RE GOING TO HAVE TO ASK THAT YOU REMOVE THEM.
FOR REASONS OF BRIDGE SECURITY, SIR.
PLEASE BE CAREFUL WITH THIS.
(I STOLE IT FROM AN ANGRY WITCH.)
WHOOPS!
NO!
OH, HEY.
SO THIS IS THE SWORD.

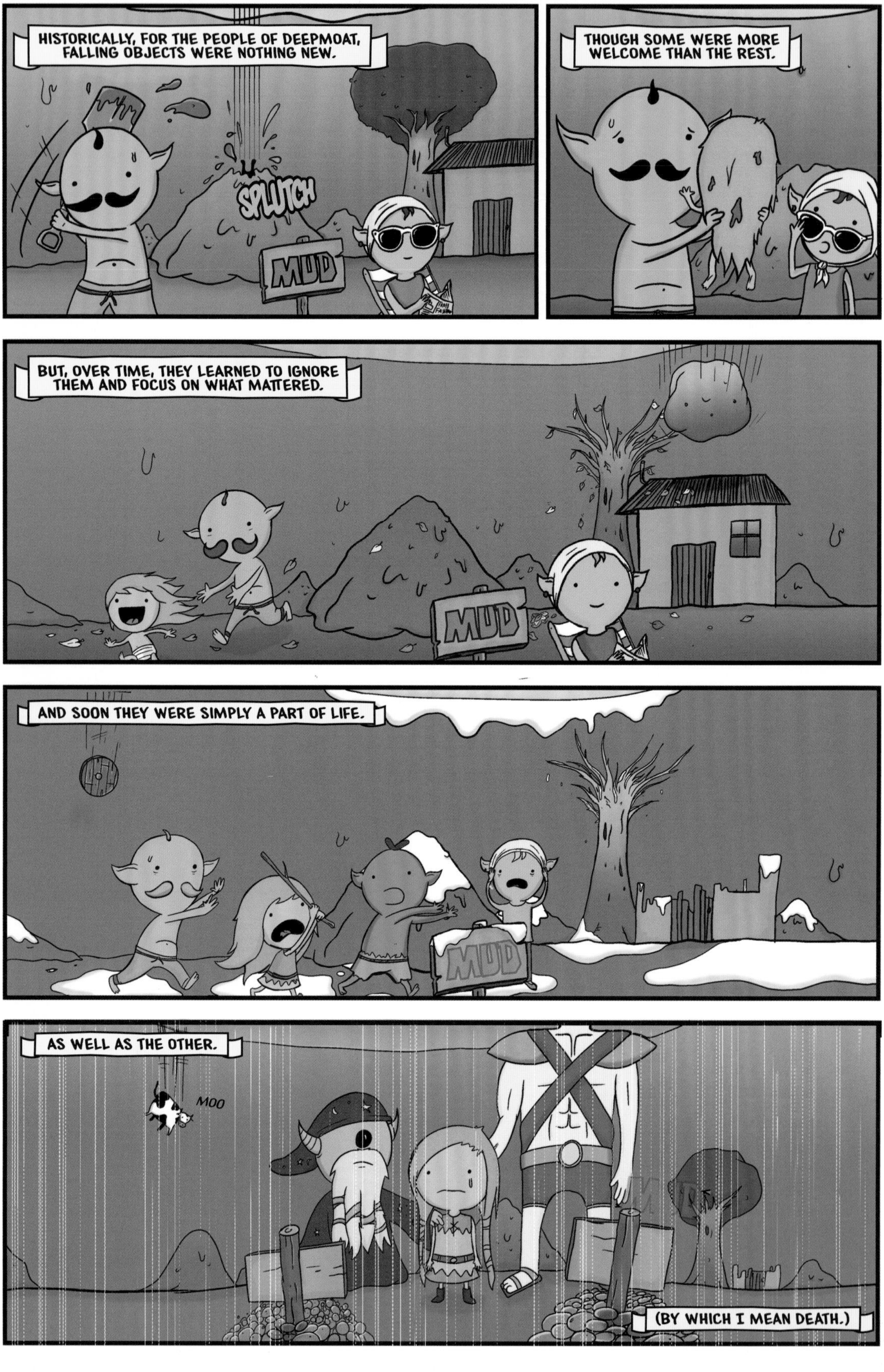
HISTORICALLY, FOR THE PEOPLE OF DEEPMOAT, FALLING OBJECTS WERE NOTHING NEW.
SPLUTCH
MUD
THOUGH SOME WERE MORE WELCOME THAN THE REST.
BUT, OVER TIME, THEY LEARNED TO IGNORE THEM AND FOCUS ON WHAT MATTERED.
MUD
AND SOON THEY WERE SIMPLY A PART OF LIFE.
MUD
AS WELL AS THE OTHER.
MOO
(BY WHICH I MEAN DEATH.)

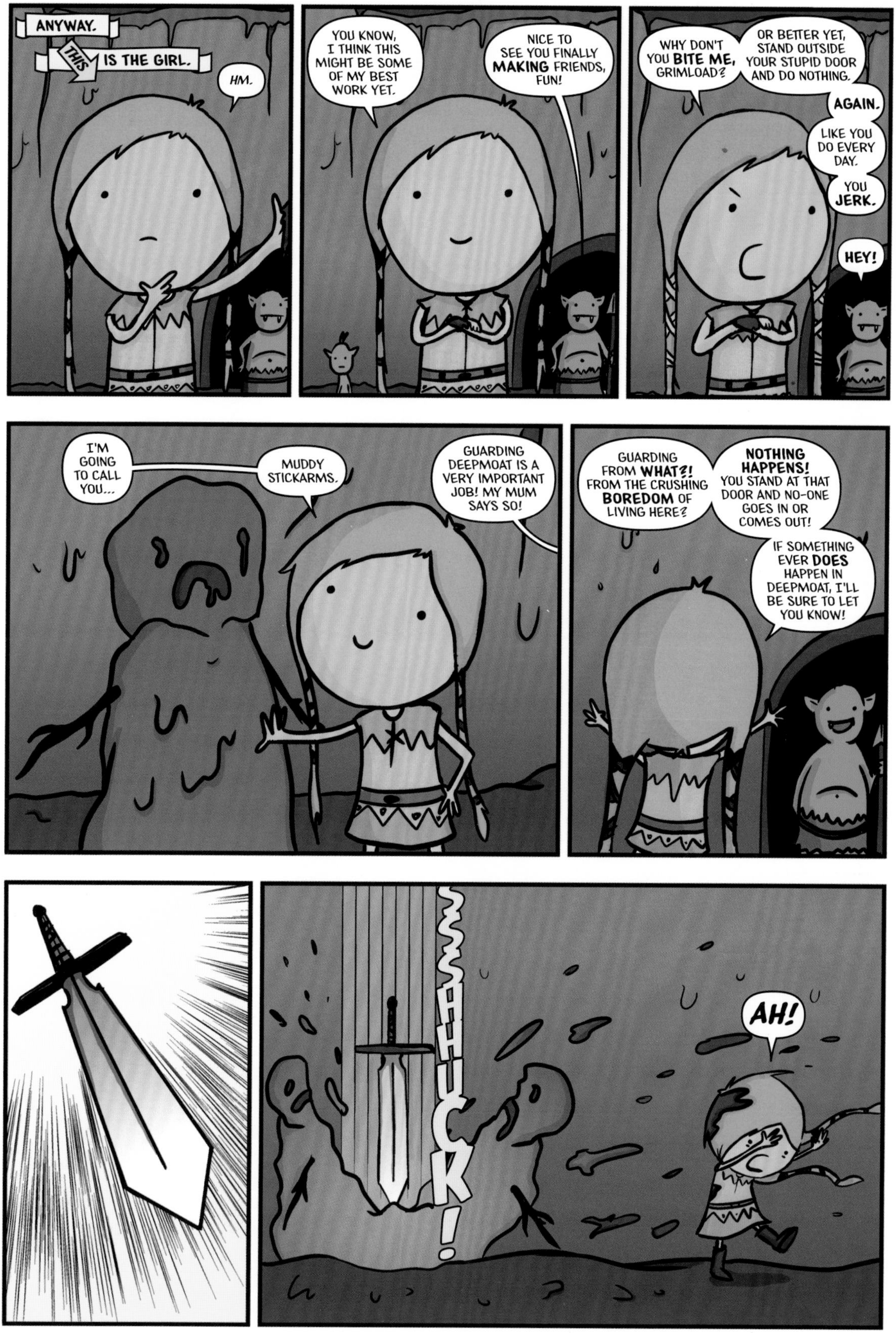
ANYWAY.
THIS IS THE GIRL.
HM.
YOU KNOW, I THINK THIS MIGHT BE SOME OF MY BEST WORK YET.
NICE TO SEE YOU FINALLY MAKING FRIENDS, FUN!
WHY DON'T YOU BITE ME, GRIMLOAD?
OR BETTER YET, STAND OUTSIDE YOUR STUPID DOOR AND DO NOTHING.
AGAIN.
LIKE YOU DO EVERY DAY.
YOU JERK.
HEY!
I'M GOING TO CALL YOU...
MUDDY STICKARMS.
GUARDING DEEPMOAT IS A VERY IMPORTANT JOB! MY MUM SAYS SO!
GUARDING FROM WHAT?! FROM THE CRUSHING BOREDOM OF LIVING HERE?
NOTHING HAPPENS! YOU STAND AT THAT DOOR AND NO-ONE GOES IN OR COMES OUT!
IF SOMETHING EVER DOES HAPPEN IN DEEPMOAT, I'LL BE SURE TO LET YOU KNOW!
SSSHHUCK!
AH!

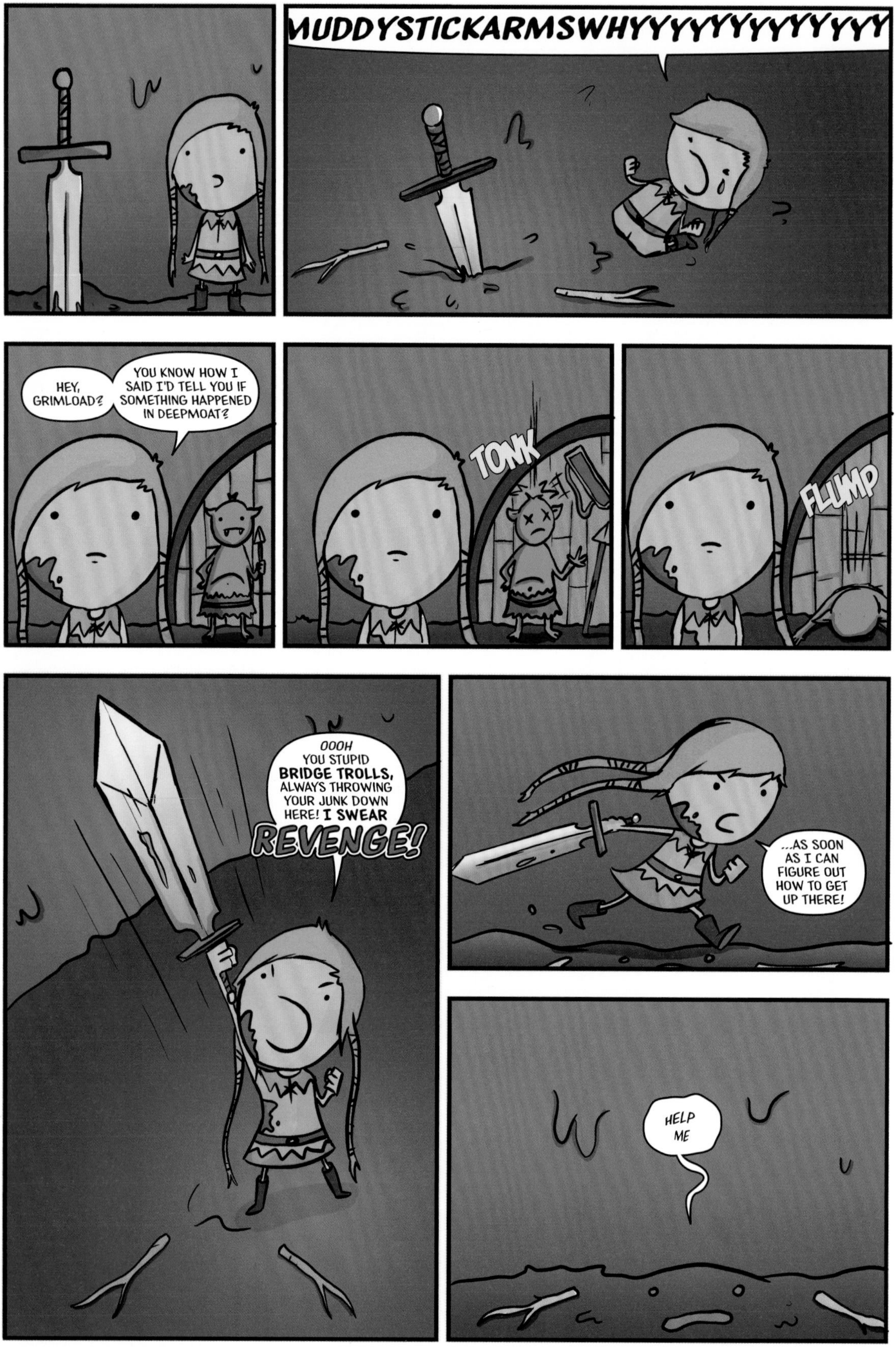

MUDDYSTICKARMSWHYYYYYYYYYYY
HEY, GRIMLOAD?
YOU KNOW HOW I SAID I'D TELL YOU IF SOMETHING HAPPENED IN DEEPMOAT?
TONK
FLUMP
OOOH YOU STUPID BRIDGE TROLLS, ALWAYS THROWING YOUR JUNK DOWN HERE! I SWEAR REVENGE!
...AS SOON AS I CAN FIGURE OUT HOW TO GET UP THERE!
HELP ME

BRONAN!

OUT OF MY WAY, PEOPLE!

BRONAN, LOOKIT! THOSE STUPID BRIDGE TROLLS THREW MORE JUNK DOWN HERE! I NEED TO GO TELL THEM WHAT FOR!

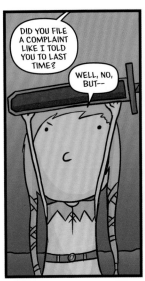

DID YOU FILE A COMPLAINT LIKE I TOLD YOU TO LAST TIME?

WELL, NO, BUT--

SSH.

I KNEW YOU WOULDN'T.

SO I FILED ONE ON YOUR BEHALF.

YOU'RE WELCOME!

BRONAN. THANK YOU.

I STILL NEED TO SEE HIM.

I'M SORRY, FUN, BUT YOU KNOW THE RULE:

NO ONE SEES MISTER ELLISEYE UNLESS HE SUMMONS

"NO ONE SEES ELLISEYE UNLESS HE SUMMONS THEM."

HALT.

...IT'S OKAY, BRONAN. I KNEW THIS DAY WOULD COME.

FOR IT WAS WRITTEN.

IN THIS BOOK.

OF PROPHECIES.

THAT I WROTE.

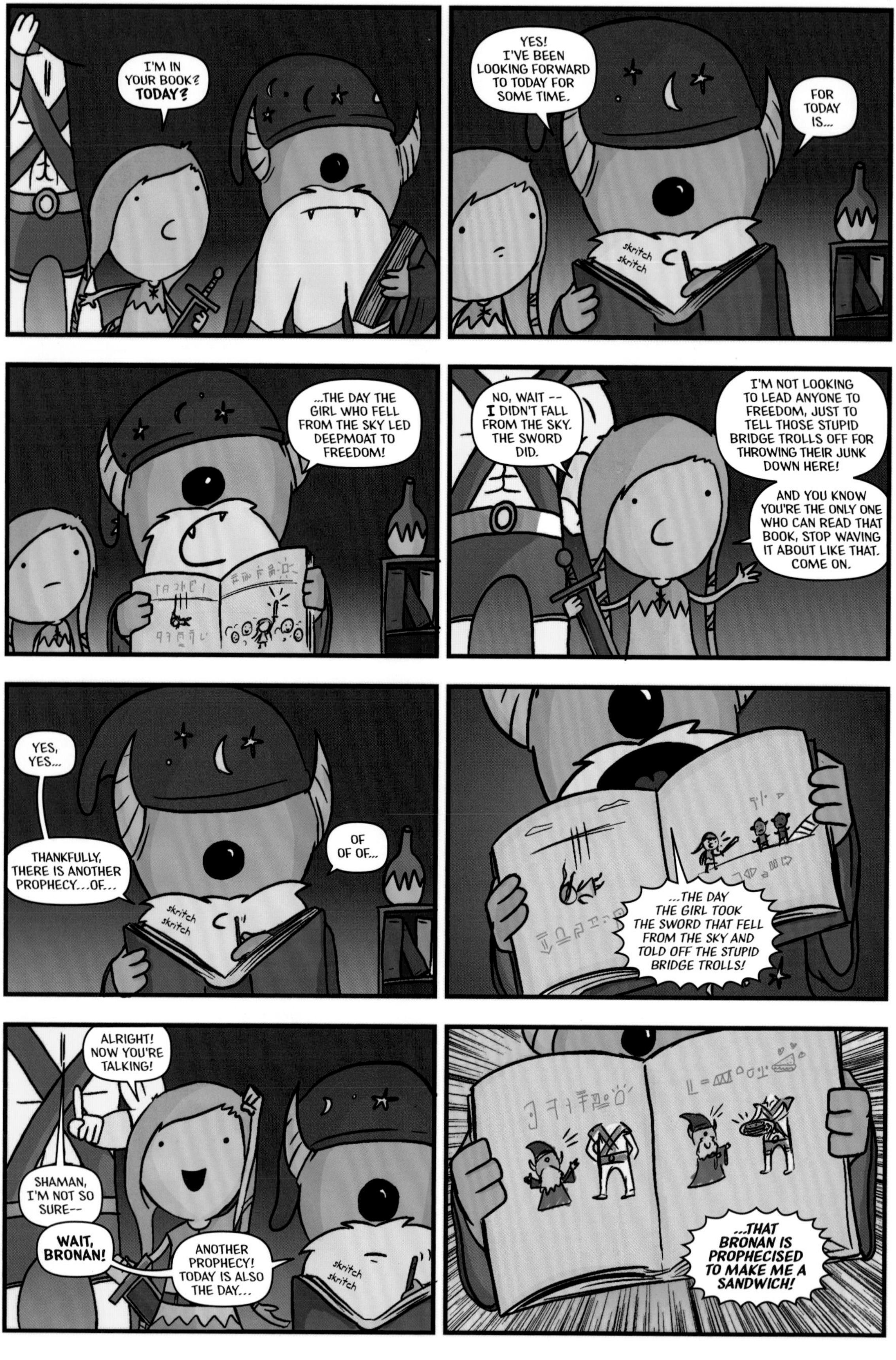
I'M IN YOUR BOOK? TODAY?
YES! I'VE BEEN LOOKING FORWARD TO TODAY FOR SOME TIME.
FOR TODAY IS...
skritch skritch
...THE DAY THE GIRL WHO FELL FROM THE SKY LED DEEPMOAT TO FREEDOM!
NO, WAIT -- I DIDN'T FALL FROM THE SKY. THE SWORD DID.
I'M NOT LOOKING TO LEAD ANYONE TO FREEDOM, JUST TO TELL THOSE STUPID BRIDGE TROLLS OFF FOR THROWING THEIR JUNK DOWN HERE!
AND YOU KNOW YOU'RE THE ONLY ONE WHO CAN READ THAT BOOK, STOP WAVING IT ABOUT LIKE THAT. COME ON.
YES, YES...
THANKFULLY, THERE IS ANOTHER PROPHECY...OF...
skritch skritch
OF OF OF...
...THE DAY THE GIRL TOOK THE SWORD THAT FELL FROM THE SKY AND TOLD OFF THE STUPID BRIDGE TROLLS!
ALRIGHT! NOW YOU'RE TALKING!
SHAMAN, I'M NOT SO SURE--
WAIT, BRONAN!
ANOTHER PROPHECY! TODAY IS ALSO THE DAY...
skritch skritch
...THAT BRONAN IS PROPHECISED TO MAKE ME A SANDWICH!

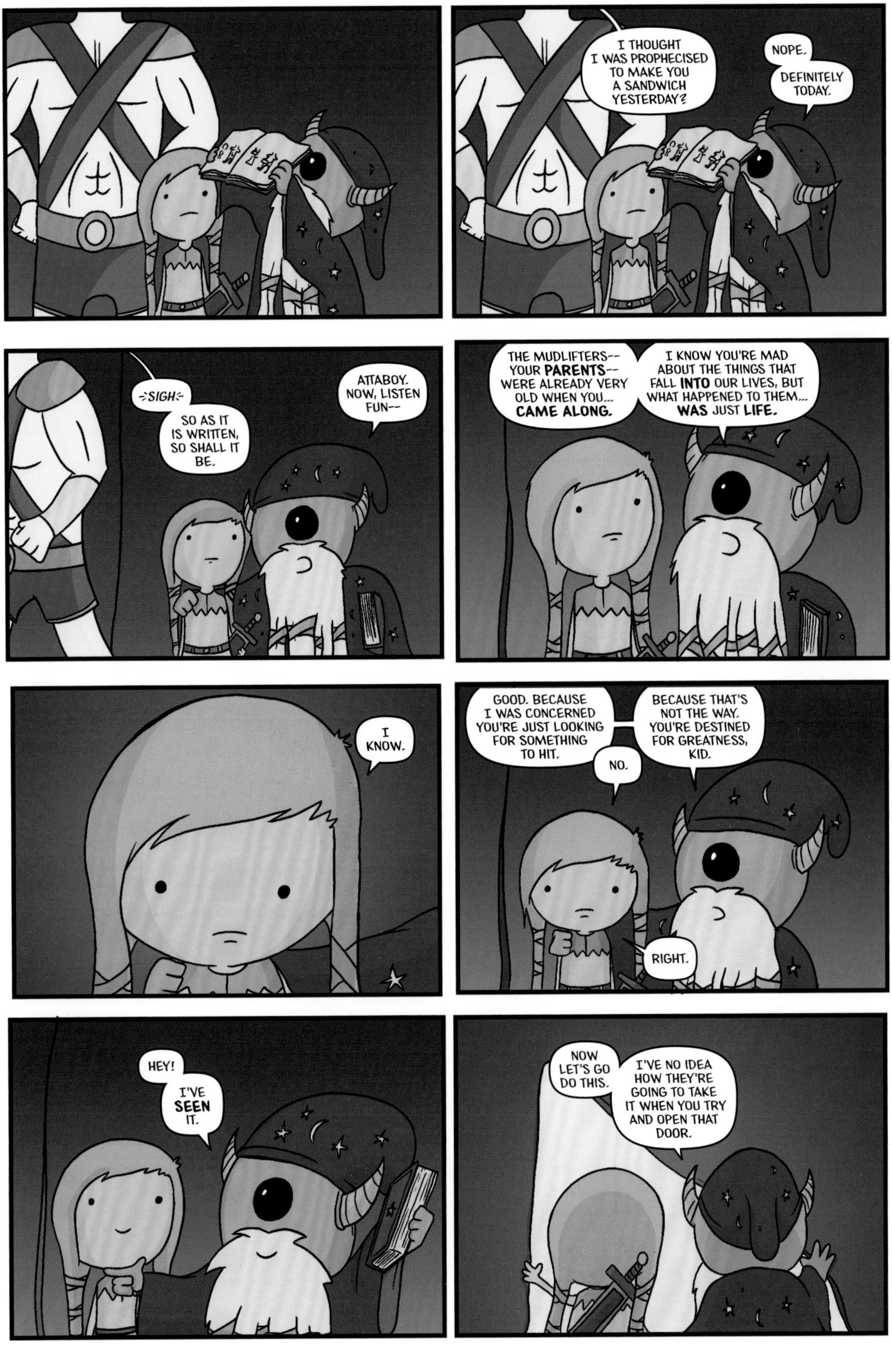

I THOUGHT I WAS PROPHECISED TO MAKE YOU A SANDWICH YESTERDAY?
NOPE.
DEFINITELY TODAY.
SIGH
SO AS IT IS WRITTEN, SO SHALL IT BE.
ATTABOY. NOW, LISTEN FUN--
THE MUDLIFTERS-- YOUR PARENTS-- WERE ALREADY VERY OLD WHEN YOU... CAME ALONG.
I KNOW YOU'RE MAD ABOUT THE THINGS THAT FALL INTO OUR LIVES, BUT WHAT HAPPENED TO THEM... WAS JUST LIFE.
I KNOW.
GOOD. BECAUSE I WAS CONCERNED YOU'RE JUST LOOKING FOR SOMETHING TO HIT.
NO.
BECAUSE THAT'S NOT THE WAY. YOU'RE DESTINED FOR GREATNESS, KID.
RIGHT.
HEY!
I'VE SEEN IT.
NOW LET'S GO DO THIS.
I'VE NO IDEA HOW THEY'RE GOING TO TAKE IT WHEN YOU TRY AND OPEN THAT DOOR.

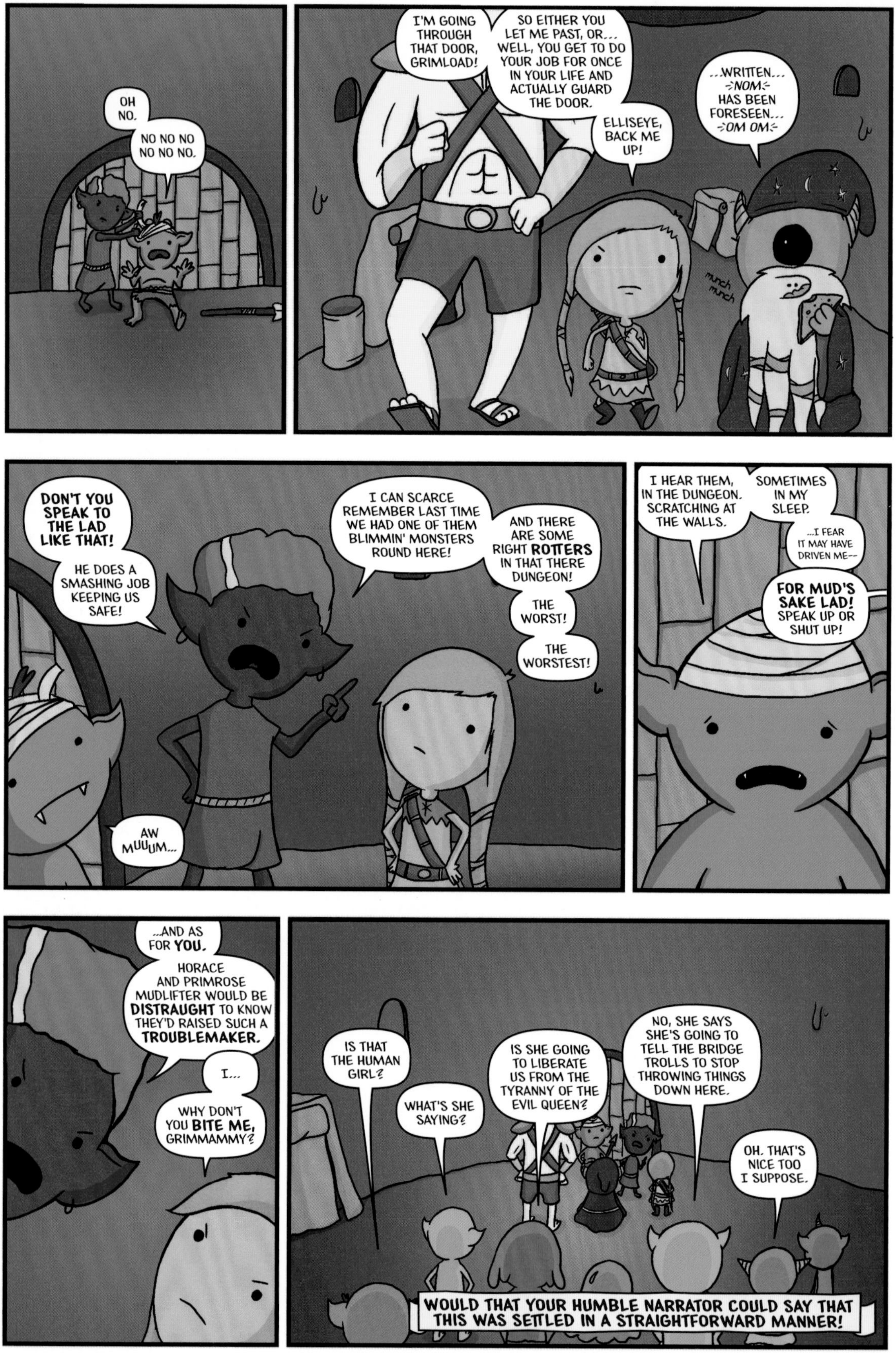
OH NO.
NO NO NO NO NO NO.
I'M GOING THROUGH THAT DOOR, GRIMLOAD!
SO EITHER YOU LET ME PAST, OR... WELL, YOU GET TO DO YOUR JOB FOR ONCE IN YOUR LIFE AND ACTUALLY GUARD THE DOOR.
ELLISEYE, BACK ME UP!
...WRITTEN... NOM HAS BEEN FORESEEN... OM OM
munch munch
DON'T YOU SPEAK TO THE LAD LIKE THAT!
HE DOES A SMASHING JOB KEEPING US SAFE!
I CAN SCARCE REMEMBER LAST TIME WE HAD ONE OF THEM BLIMMIN' MONSTERS ROUND HERE!
AND THERE ARE SOME RIGHT ROTTERS IN THAT THERE DUNGEON!
THE WORST!
THE WORSTEST!
AW MUUUM...
I HEAR THEM, IN THE DUNGEON. SCRATCHING AT THE WALLS.
SOMETIMES IN MY SLEEP.
...I FEAR IT MAY HAVE DRIVEN ME--
FOR MUD'S SAKE LAD! SPEAK UP OR SHUT UP!
...AND AS FOR YOU.
HORACE AND PRIMROSE MUDLIFTER WOULD BE DISTRAUGHT TO KNOW THEY'D RAISED SUCH A TROUBLEMAKER.
I...
WHY DON'T YOU BITE ME, GRIMMAMMY?
IS THAT THE HUMAN GIRL?
WHAT'S SHE SAYING?
IS SHE GOING TO LIBERATE US FROM THE TYRANNY OF THE EVIL QUEEN?
NO, SHE SAYS SHE'S GOING TO TELL THE BRIDGE TROLLS TO STOP THROWING THINGS DOWN HERE.
OH. THAT'S NICE TOO I SUPPOSE.
WOULD THAT YOUR HUMBLE NARRATOR COULD SAY THAT THIS WAS SETTLED IN A STRAIGHTFORWARD MANNER!

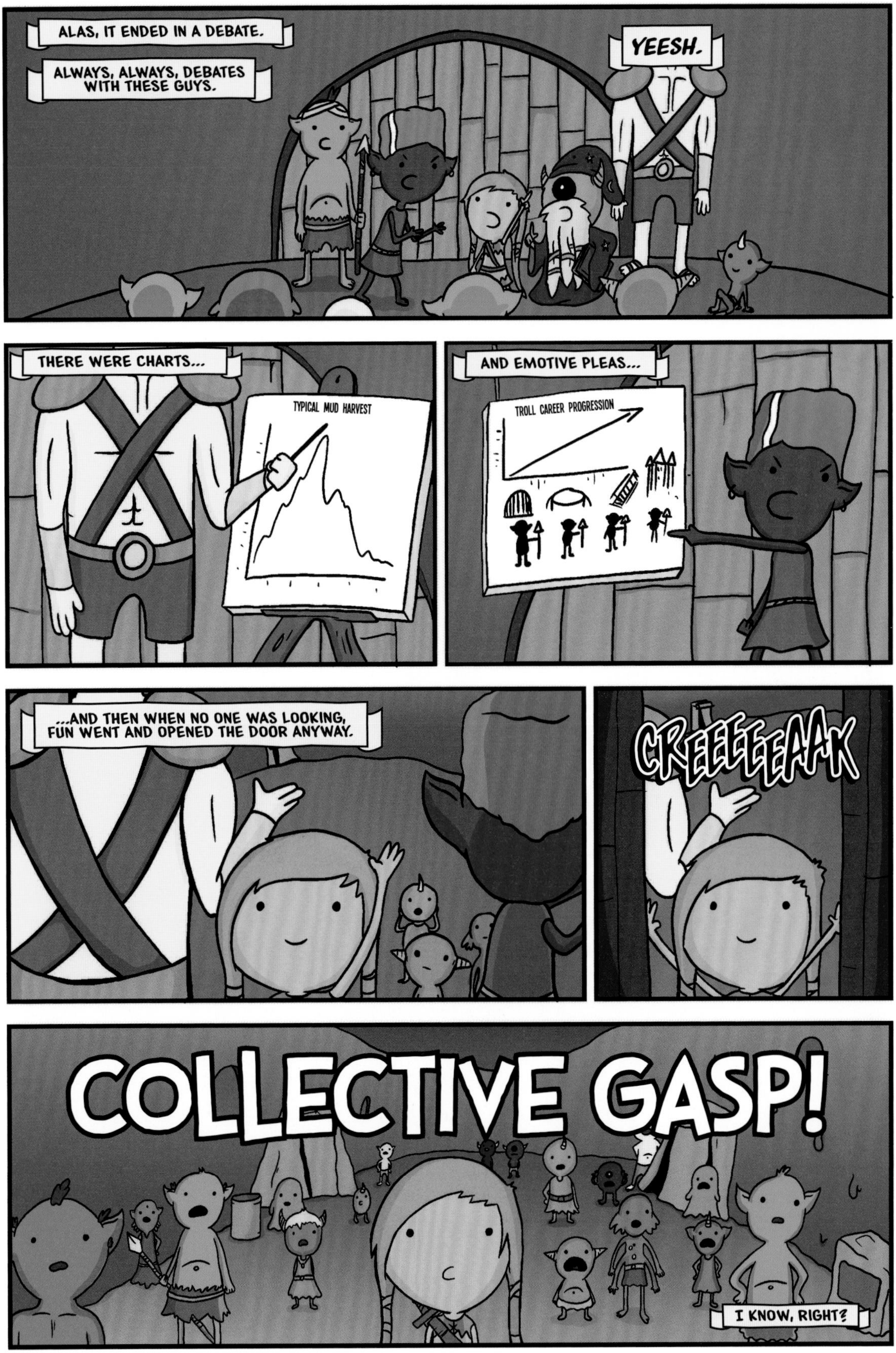

ALAS, IT ENDED IN A DEBATE.
ALWAYS, ALWAYS, DEBATES WITH THESE GUYS.
YEESH.
THERE WERE CHARTS...
TYPICAL MUD HARVEST
AND EMOTIVE PLEAS...
TROLL CAREER PROGRESSION
...AND THEN WHEN NO ONE WAS LOOKING, FUN WENT AND OPENED THE DOOR ANYWAY.
CREEEEEAAK
COLLECTIVE GASP!
I KNOW, RIGHT?

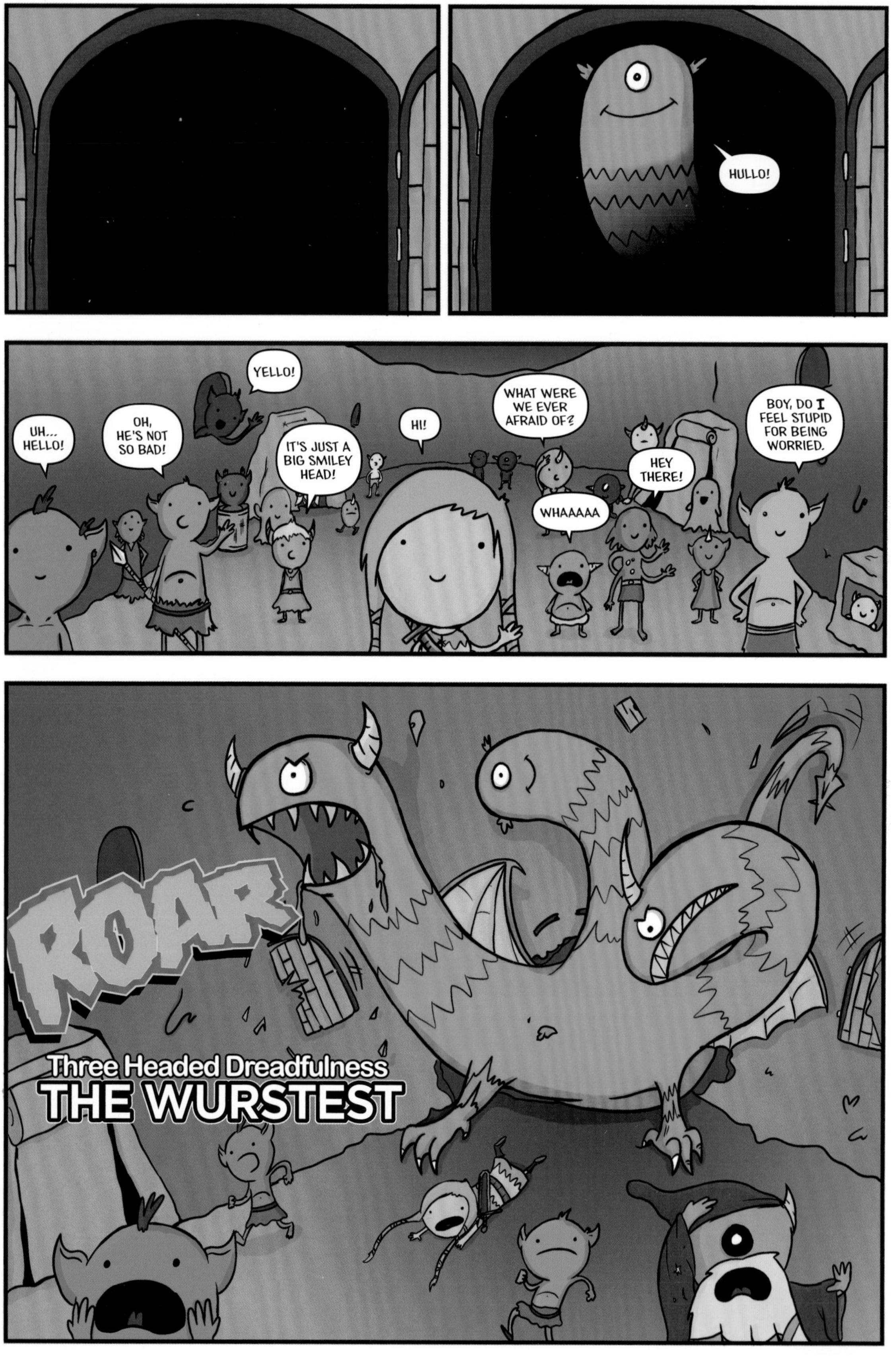
HULLO!
UH... HELLO!
OH, HE'S NOT SO BAD!
YELLO!
IT'S JUST A BIG SMILEY HEAD!
HI!
WHAT WERE WE EVER AFRAID OF?
WHAAAAA
HEY THERE!
BOY, DO I FEEL STUPID FOR BEING WORRIED.
ROAR
Three Headed Dreadfulness
THE WURSTEST

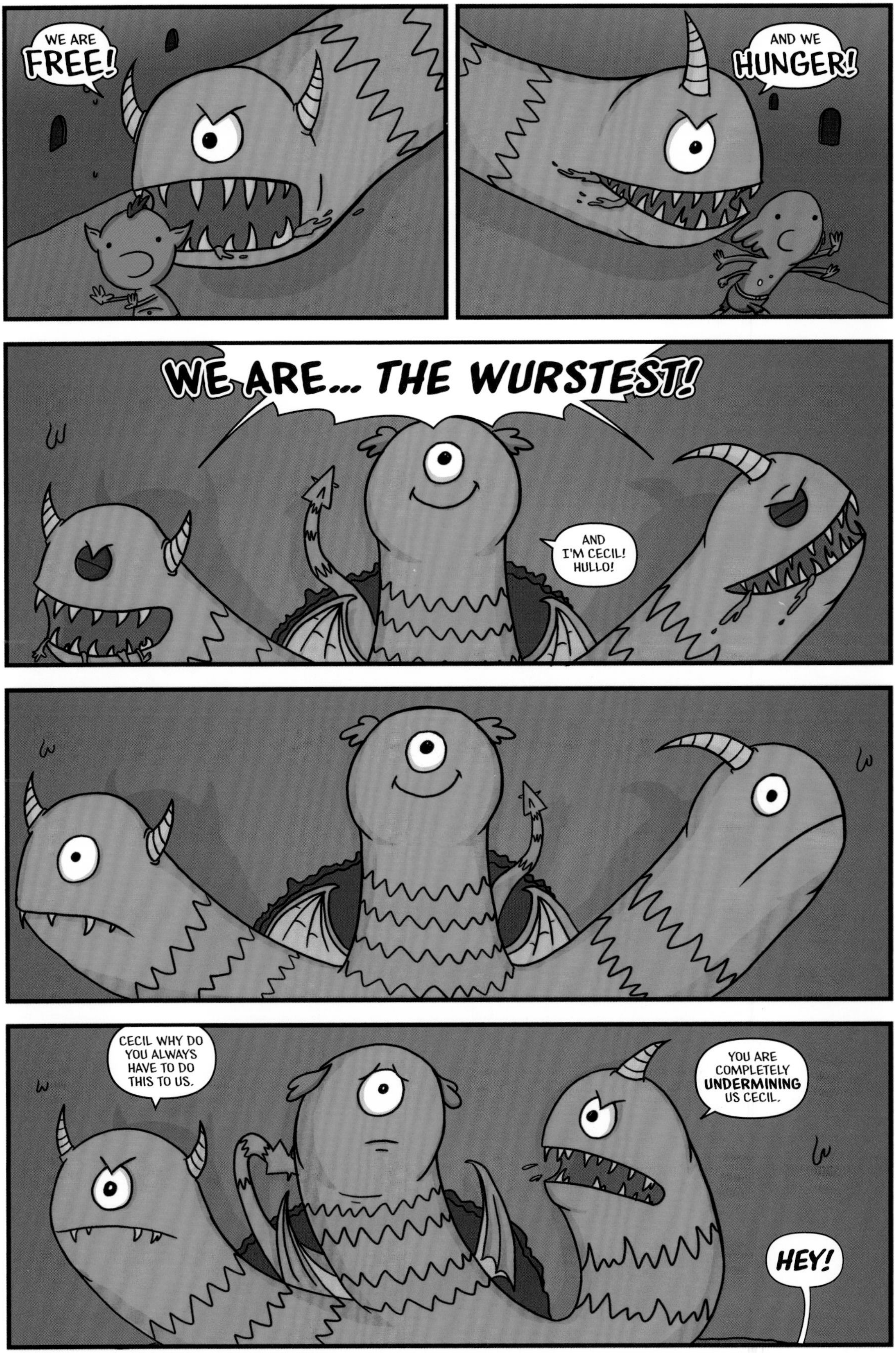
WE ARE FREE!
AND WE HUNGER!
WE ARE... THE WURSTEST!
AND I'M CECIL! HULLO!
CECIL WHY DO YOU ALWAYS HAVE TO DO THIS TO US.
YOU ARE COMPLETELY UNDERMINING US CECIL.
HEY!

WHY DON'T YOU **WHOA!** **FUN!** JAM IT UP **LANGUAGE!** FALLS OFF?

(APOLOGIES FOR ANY OFFENCE CAUSED)

A HUMAN! WHAT'S A HUMAN DOING DOWN HERE?

ALSO, DO YOU KISS YOUR MOTHER WITH THAT MOUTH?

YOU EAT IT, CECIL!

GUUUYS, YOU KNOW I'M ALLERGIC TO HUMANS!

I SAY WE VOTE! ALL IN FAVOUR OF CECIL EATING THE HUMAN? WHAT SAY YOU, WURSTEST?

AYE! WHAT SAY YOU, WURSTEST?

AYE!

MOTION CARRIED!

VETO!

YOU USED YOUR VETO LAST WEEK!

OH FOR CRYING OUT LOUD...

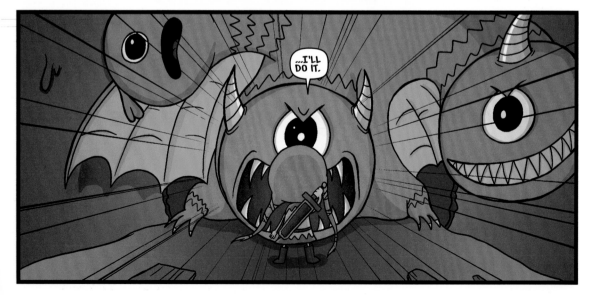

...I'LL DO IT.

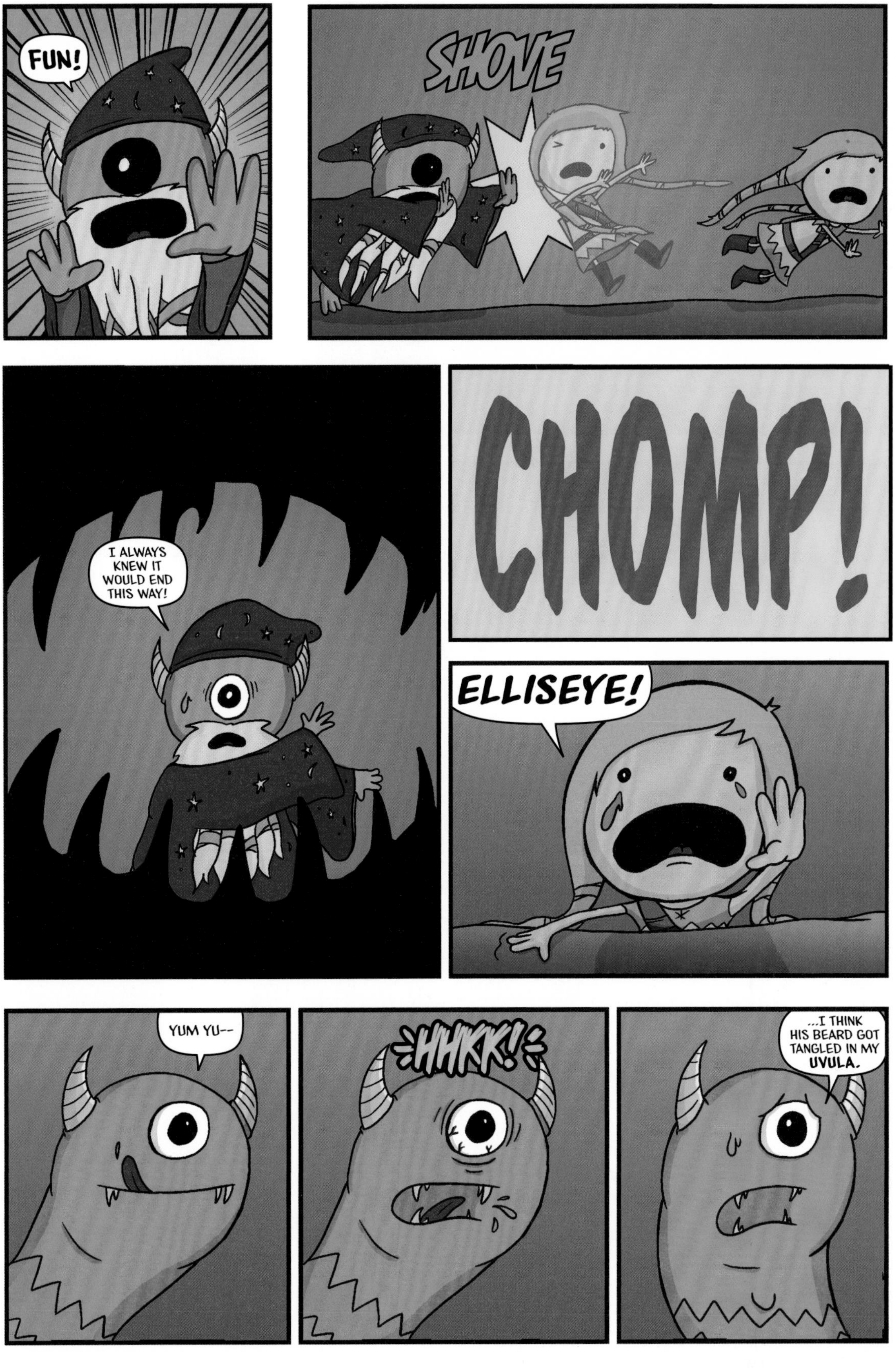

FUN!
SHOVE
I ALWAYS KNEW IT WOULD END THIS WAY!
CHOMP!
ELLISEYE!
YUM YU--
HHKK!
...I THINK HIS BEARD GOT TANGLED IN MY **UVULA.**

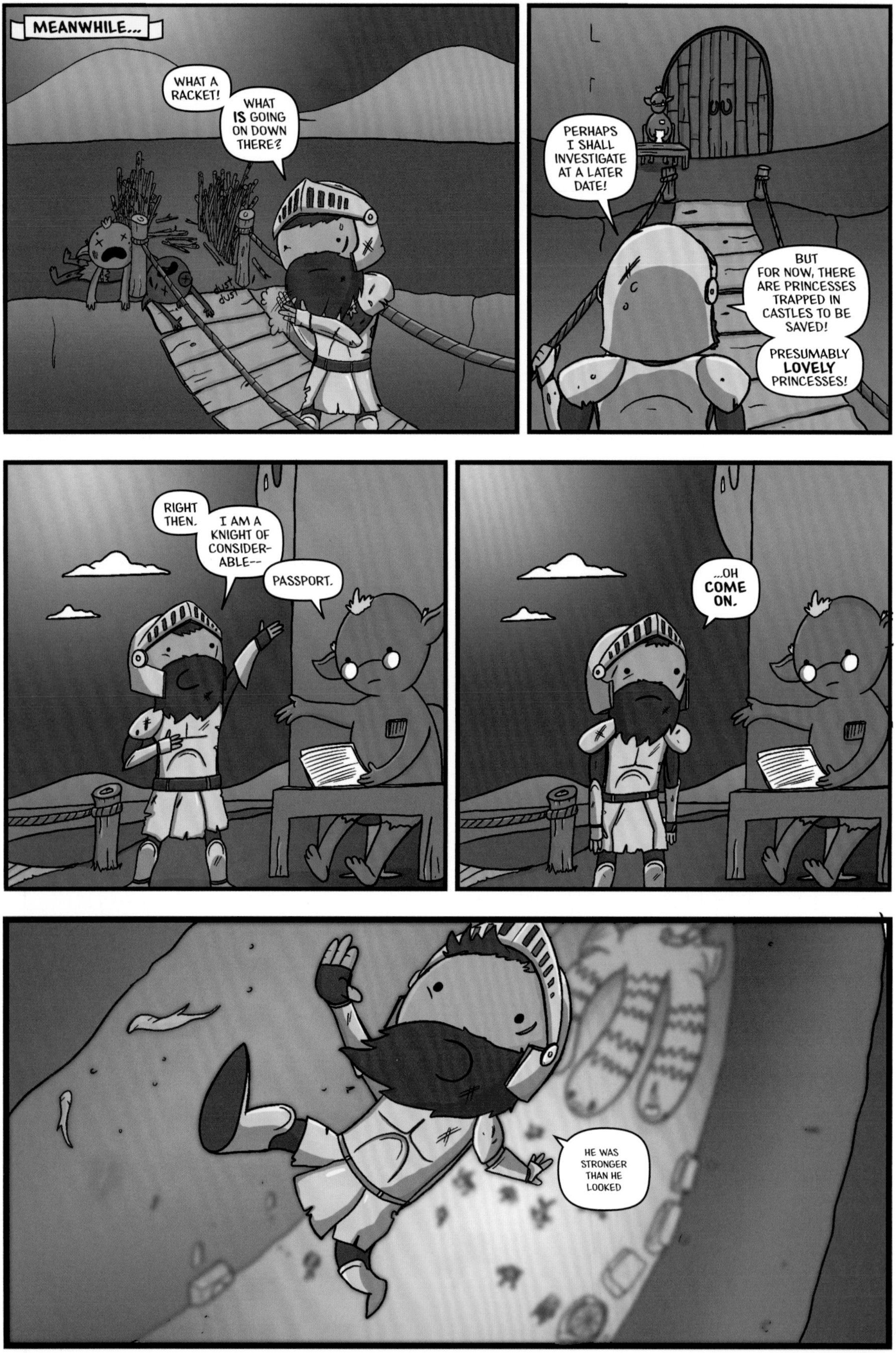
MEANWHILE...
WHAT A RACKET!
WHAT IS GOING ON DOWN THERE?
dust dust
PERHAPS I SHALL INVESTIGATE AT A LATER DATE!
BUT FOR NOW, THERE ARE PRINCESSES TRAPPED IN CASTLES TO BE SAVED!
PRESUMABLY LOVELY PRINCESSES!
RIGHT THEN.
I AM A KNIGHT OF CONSIDER-ABLE--
PASSPORT.
...OH COME ON.
HE WAS STRONGER THAN HE LOOKED

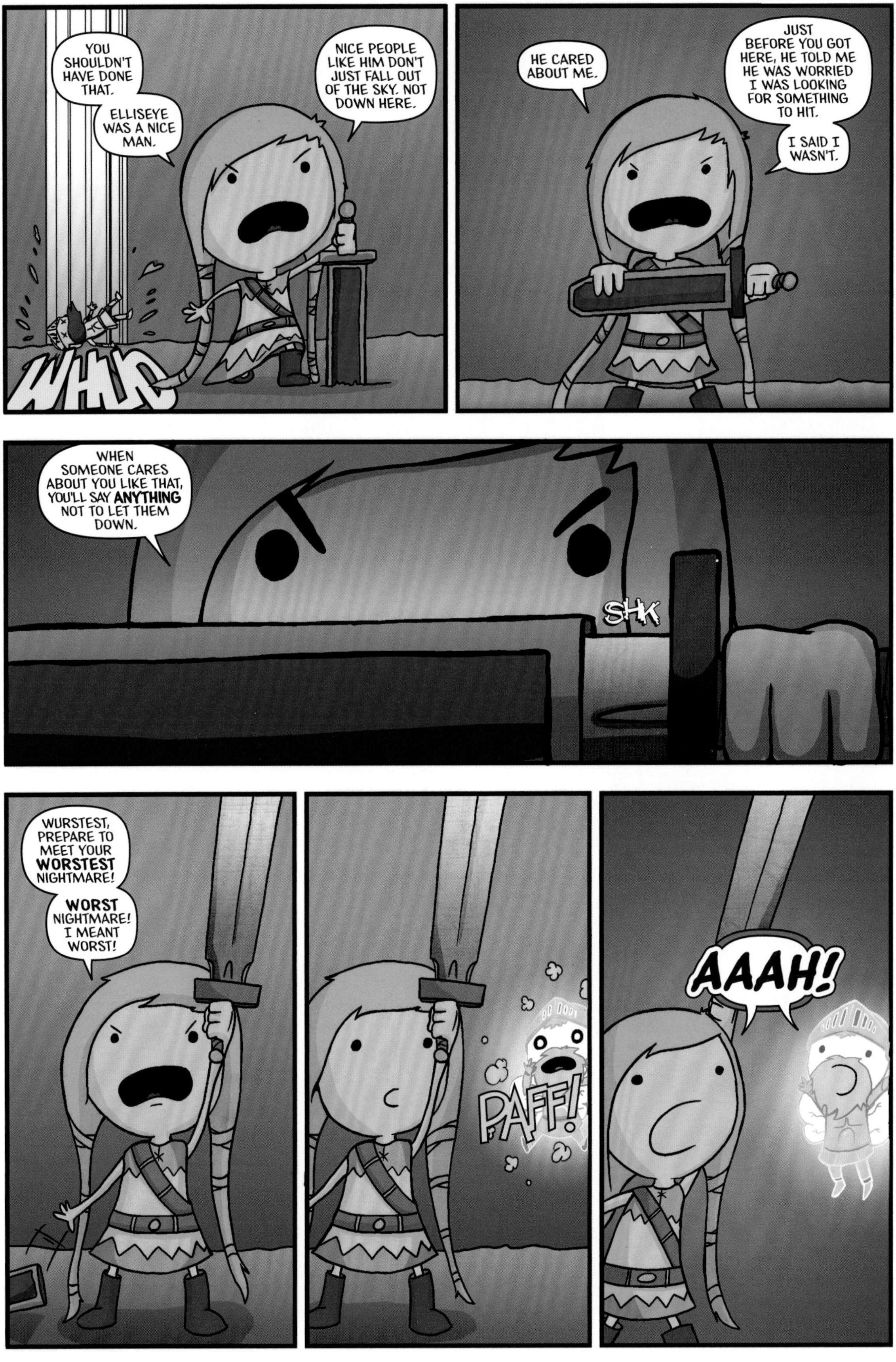
YOU SHOULDN'T HAVE DONE THAT.
ELLISEYE WAS A NICE MAN.
NICE PEOPLE LIKE HIM DON'T JUST FALL OUT OF THE SKY. NOT DOWN HERE.
WHD
HE CARED ABOUT ME.
JUST BEFORE YOU GOT HERE, HE TOLD ME HE WAS WORRIED I WAS LOOKING FOR SOMETHING TO HIT.
I SAID I WASN'T.
WHEN SOMEONE CARES ABOUT YOU LIKE THAT, YOU'LL SAY ANYTHING NOT TO LET THEM DOWN.
SHK
WURSTEST, PREPARE TO MEET YOUR WORSTEST NIGHTMARE!
WORST NIGHTMARE! I MEANT WORST!
PAFF!
AAAH!

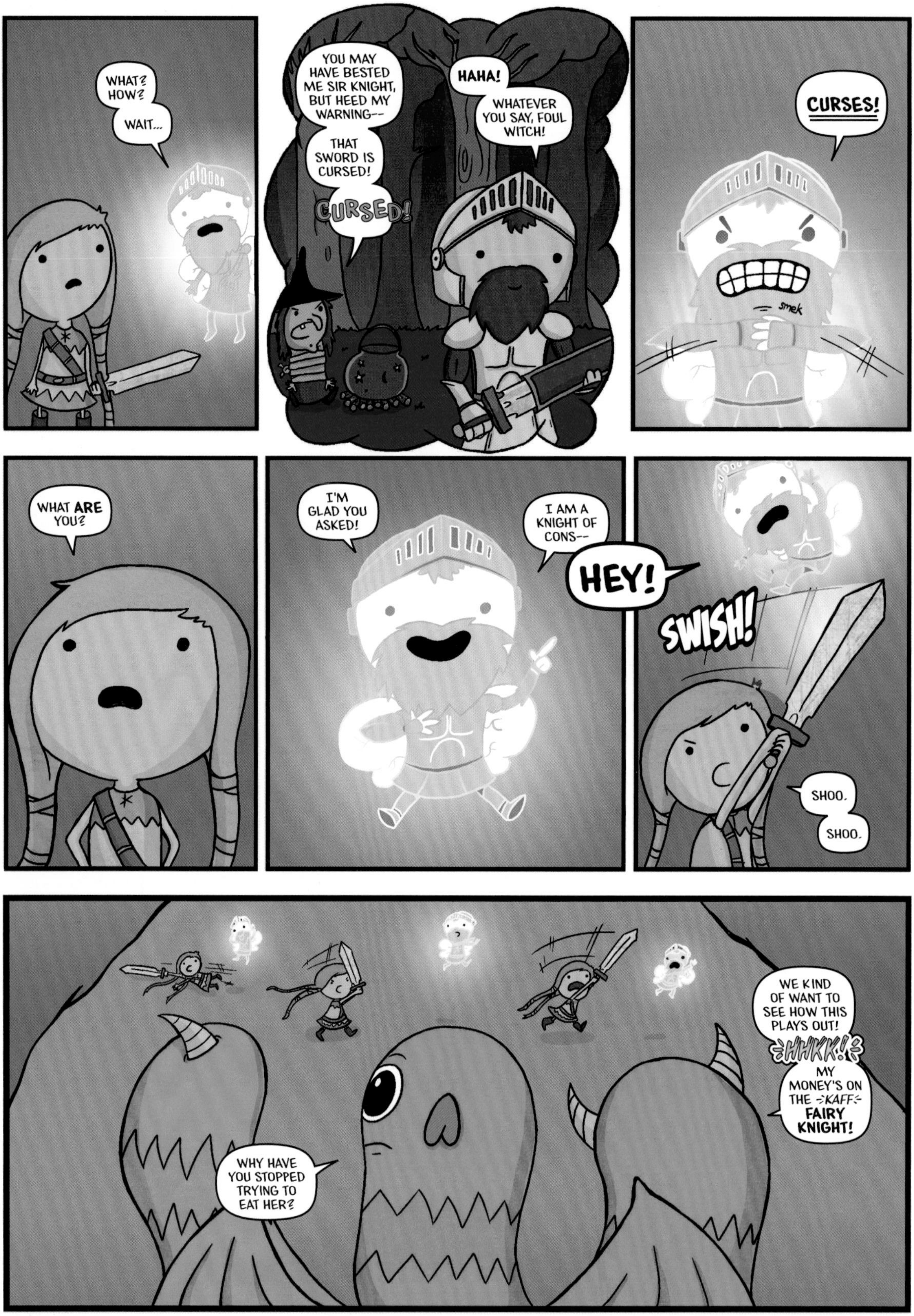
WHAT? HOW?
WAIT...
YOU MAY HAVE BESTED ME SIR KNIGHT, BUT HEED MY WARNING--
THAT SWORD IS CURSED!
CURSED!
HAHA!
WHATEVER YOU SAY, FOUL WITCH!
CURSES!
smek
WHAT ARE YOU?
I'M GLAD YOU ASKED!
I AM A KNIGHT OF CONS--
HEY!
SWISH!
SHOO.
SHOO.
WE KIND OF WANT TO SEE HOW THIS PLAYS OUT!
HHKK!
MY MONEY'S ON THE KAFF FAIRY KNIGHT!
WHY HAVE YOU STOPPED TRYING TO EAT HER?

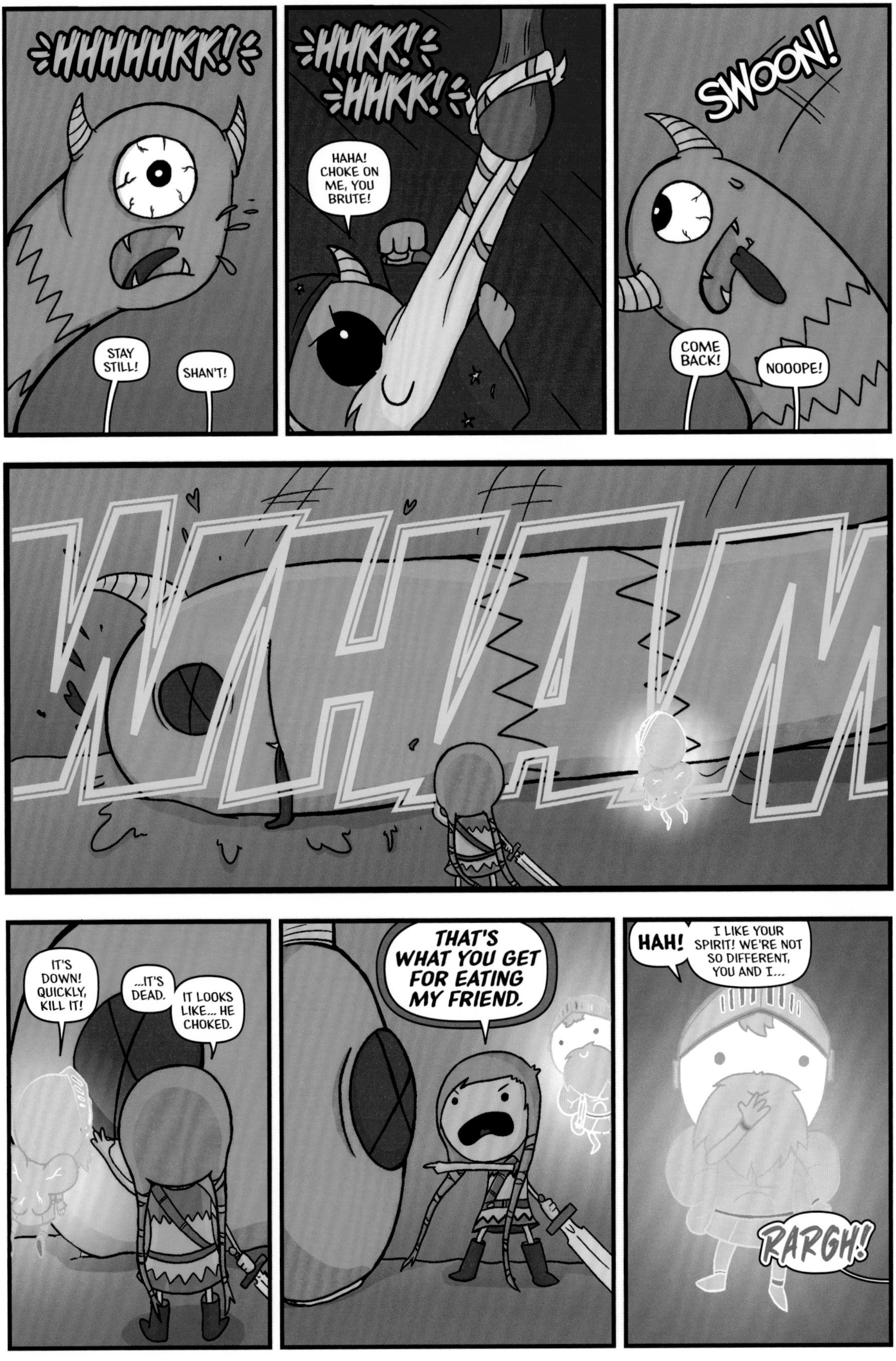
HHHHHKK!
STAY STILL!
SHAN'T!
HHKK! HHKK!
HAHA! CHOKE ON ME, YOU BRUTE!
SWOON!
COME BACK!
NOOOPE!
WHAM
IT'S DOWN! QUICKLY, KILL IT!
...IT'S DEAD.
IT LOOKS LIKE... HE CHOKED.
THAT'S WHAT YOU GET FOR EATING MY FRIEND.
HAH!
I LIKE YOUR SPIRIT! WE'RE NOT SO DIFFERENT, YOU AND I...
RARGH!

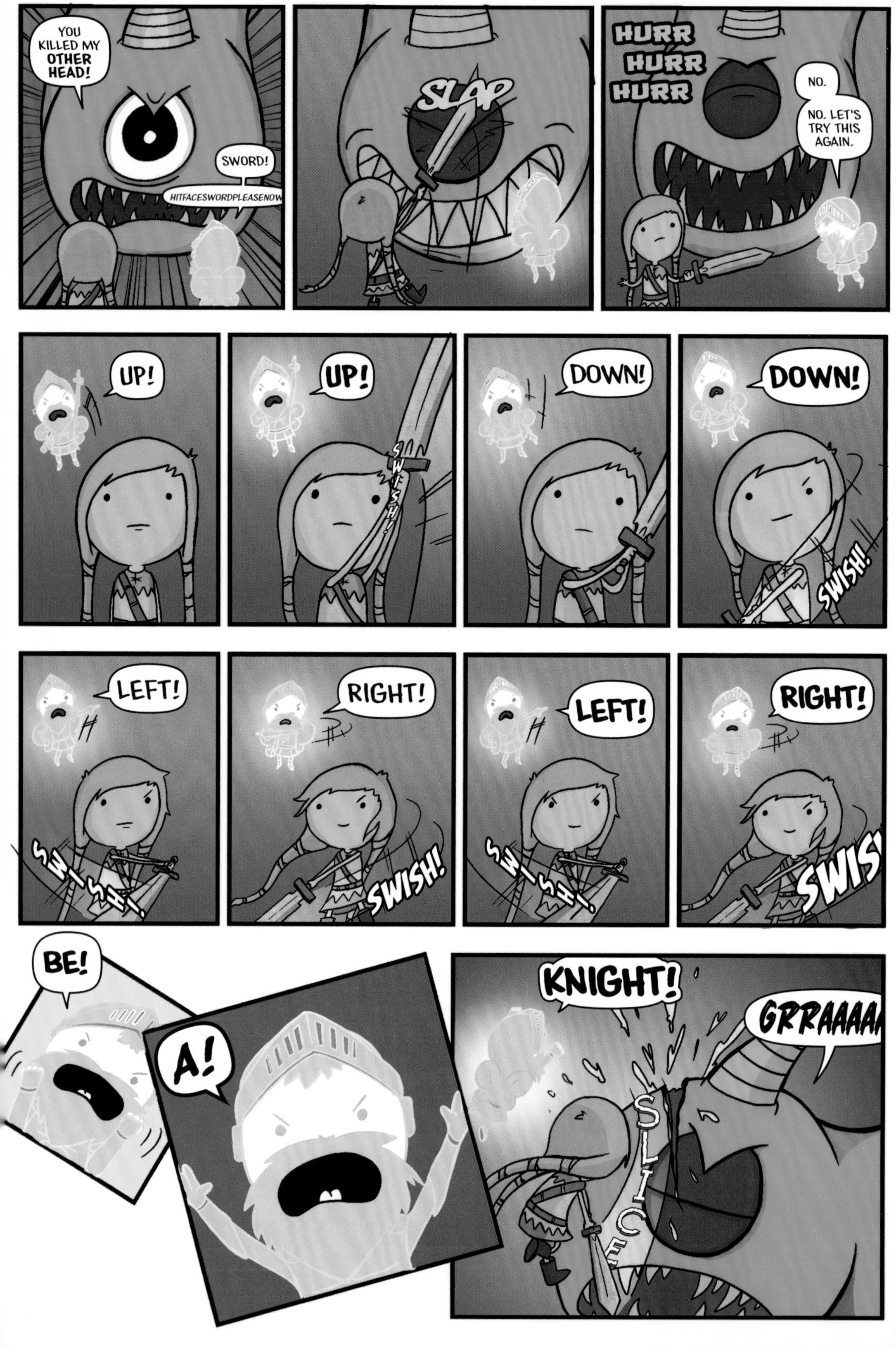
YOU KILLED MY OTHER HEAD!
SWORD!
HITFACESWORDPLEASENOW
SLAP
HURR HURR HURR
NO.
NO. LET'S TRY THIS AGAIN.
UP!
UP!
SWISH!
DOWN!
DOWN!
SWISH!
LEFT!
SWISH!
RIGHT!
SWISH!
LEFT!
SWISH!
RIGHT!
BE!
A!
KNIGHT!
GRRAAAA
SLICE

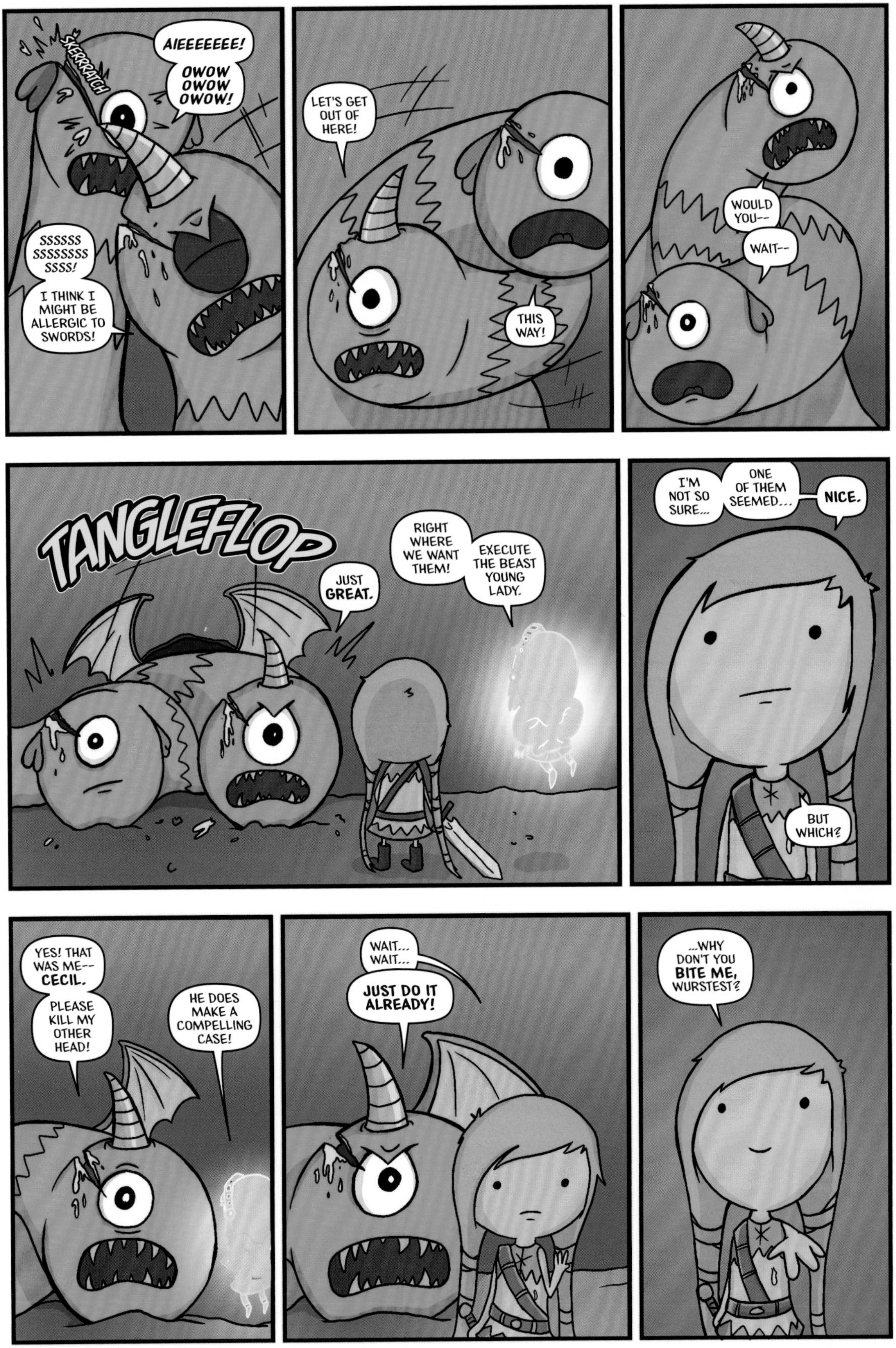
SKERRATCH
AIEEEEEEE!
OWOW OWOW OWOW!
SSSSSS SSSSSSSS SSSS!
I THINK I MIGHT BE ALLERGIC TO SWORDS!
LET'S GET OUT OF HERE!
THIS WAY!
WOULD YOU--
WAIT--
TANGLEFLOP
JUST GREAT.
RIGHT WHERE WE WANT THEM!
EXECUTE THE BEAST YOUNG LADY.
I'M NOT SO SURE...
ONE OF THEM SEEMED...
NICE.
BUT WHICH?
YES! THAT WAS ME-- CECIL.
PLEASE KILL MY OTHER HEAD!
HE DOES MAKE A COMPELLING CASE!
WAIT... WAIT...
JUST DO IT ALREADY!
...WHY DON'T YOU BITE ME, WURSTEST?

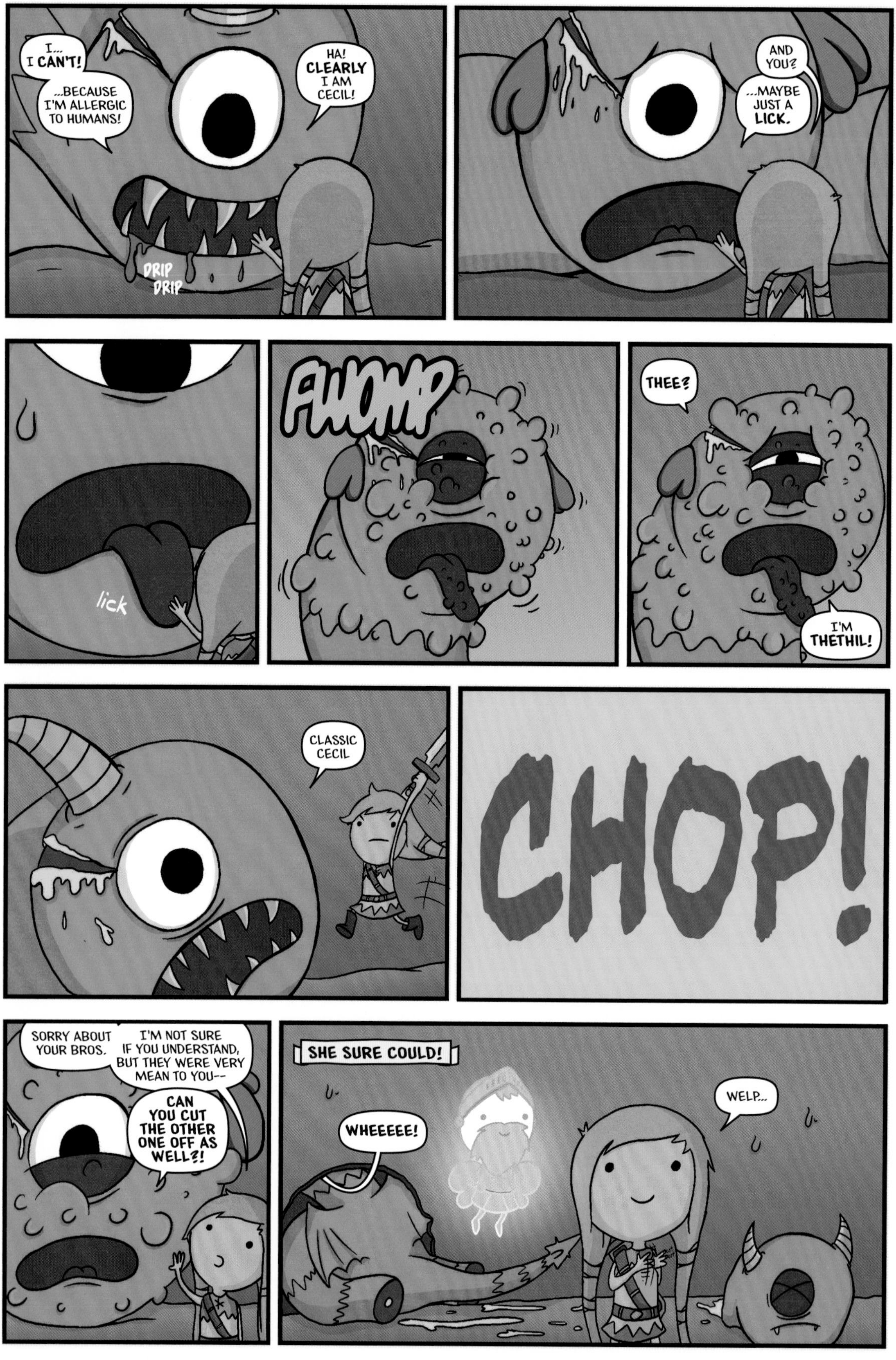

I... I CAN'T!
...BECAUSE I'M ALLERGIC TO HUMANS!
HA! CLEARLY I AM CECIL!
DRIP DRIP
AND YOU?
...MAYBE JUST A LICK.
lick
FWOMP
THEE?
I'M THETHIL!
CLASSIC CECIL
CHOP!
SORRY ABOUT YOUR BROS.
I'M NOT SURE IF YOU UNDERSTAND, BUT THEY WERE VERY MEAN TO YOU--
CAN YOU CUT THE OTHER ONE OFF AS WELL?!
SHE SURE COULD!
WHEEEEE!
WELP...

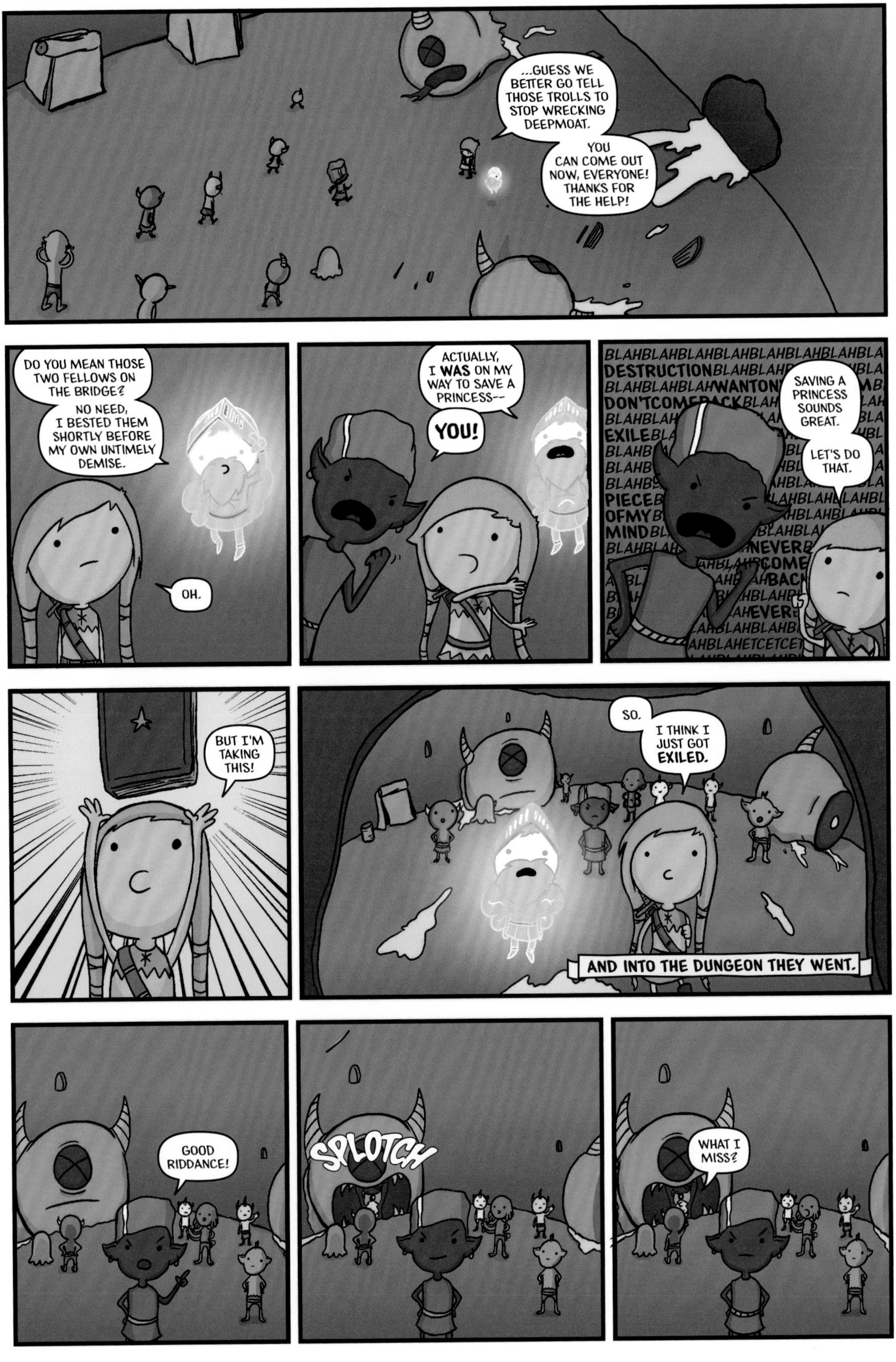
...GUESS WE BETTER GO TELL THOSE TROLLS TO STOP WRECKING DEEPMOAT.
YOU CAN COME OUT NOW, EVERYONE! THANKS FOR THE HELP!
DO YOU MEAN THOSE TWO FELLOWS ON THE BRIDGE?
NO NEED, I BESTED THEM SHORTLY BEFORE MY OWN UNTIMELY DEMISE.
OH.
ACTUALLY, I WAS ON MY WAY TO SAVE A PRINCESS--
YOU!
DESTRUCTION
WANTON
DON'TCOMEBACK
EXILE
PIECE
OFMY
MIND
NEVER
COME
BACK
EVER
SAVING A PRINCESS SOUNDS GREAT.
LET'S DO THAT.
BUT I'M TAKING THIS!
SO.
I THINK I JUST GOT EXILED.
AND INTO THE DUNGEON THEY WENT.
GOOD RIDDANCE!
SPLOTCH
WHAT I MISS?

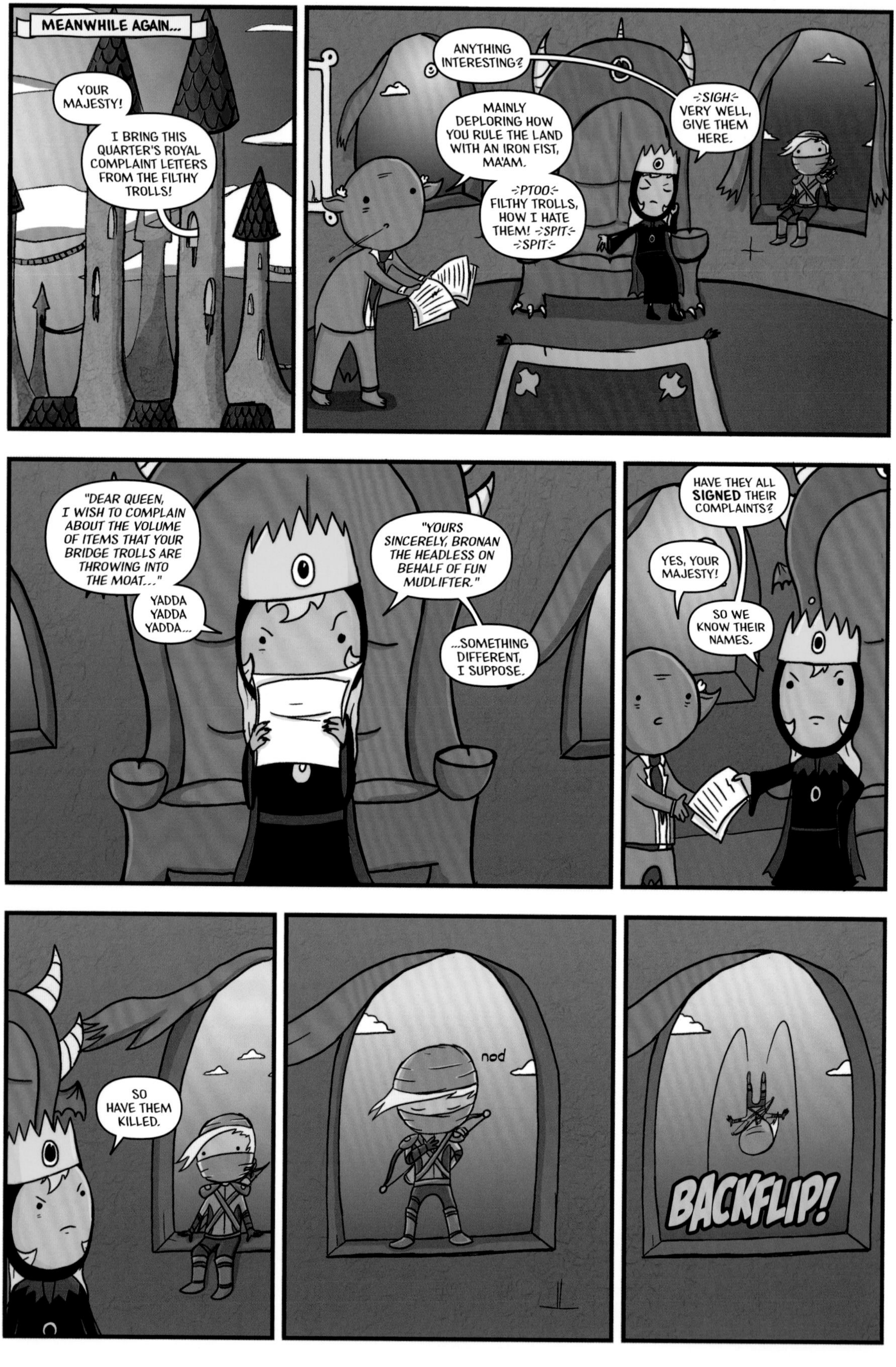
MEANWHILE AGAIN...
YOUR MAJESTY!
I BRING THIS QUARTER'S ROYAL COMPLAINT LETTERS FROM THE FILTHY TROLLS!
ANYTHING INTERESTING?
MAINLY DEPLORING HOW YOU RULE THE LAND WITH AN IRON FIST, MA'AM.
-PTOO- FILTHY TROLLS, HOW I HATE THEM! -SPIT- -SPIT-
-SIGH- VERY WELL, GIVE THEM HERE.
"DEAR QUEEN, I WISH TO COMPLAIN ABOUT THE VOLUME OF ITEMS THAT YOUR BRIDGE TROLLS ARE THROWING INTO THE MOAT..."
YADDA YADDA YADDA...
"YOURS SINCERELY, BRONAN THE HEADLESS ON BEHALF OF FUN MUDLIFTER."
...SOMETHING DIFFERENT, I SUPPOSE.
HAVE THEY ALL SIGNED THEIR COMPLAINTS?
YES, YOUR MAJESTY!
SO WE KNOW THEIR NAMES.
SO HAVE THEM KILLED.
nod
BACKFLIP!

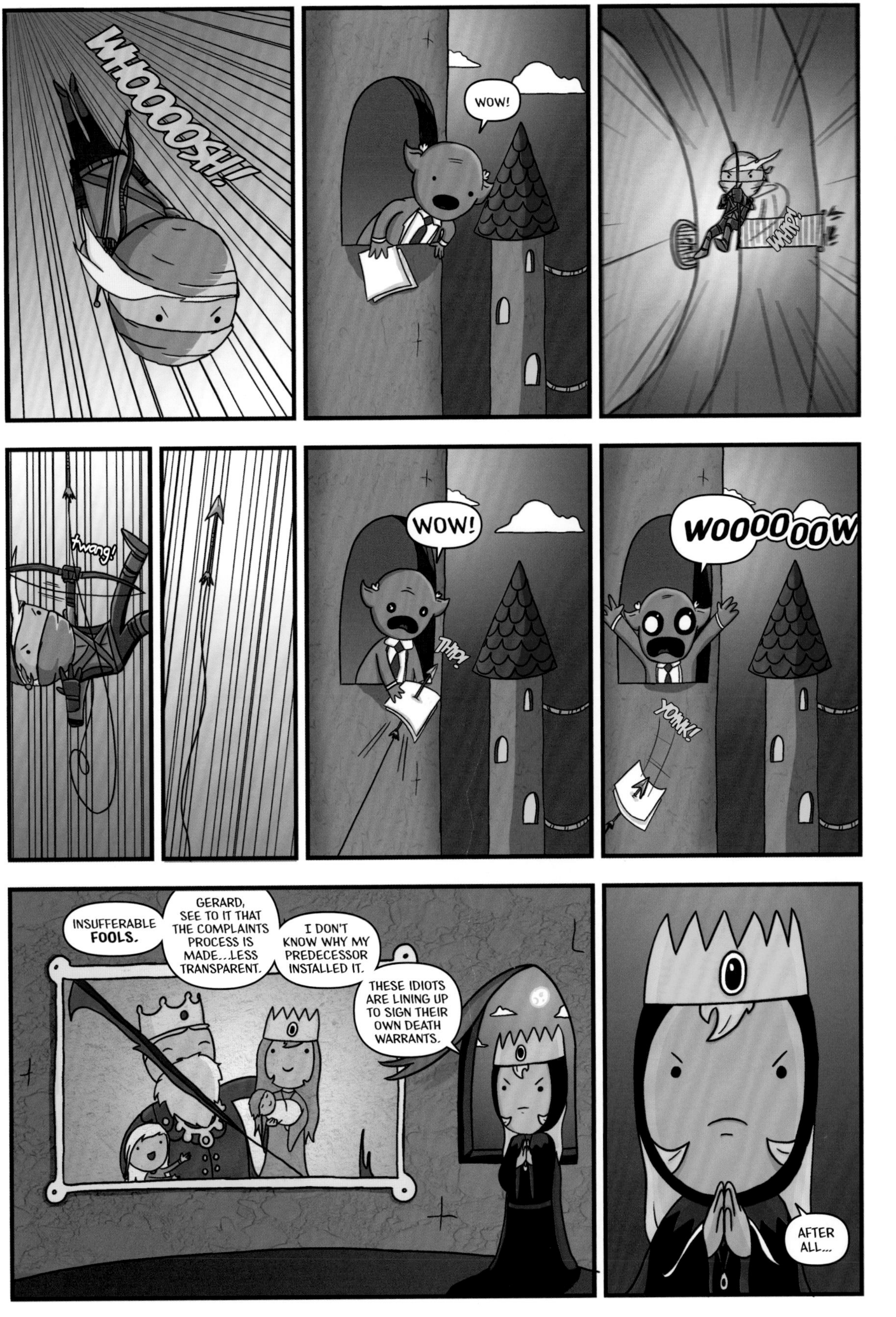
WHOOOOSH!!
WOW!
WHIP!
twang!
WOW!
THIP!
WOOOOOOW
YOINK!
INSUFFERABLE FOOLS.
GERARD, SEE TO IT THAT THE COMPLAINTS PROCESS IS MADE...LESS TRANSPARENT.
I DON'T KNOW WHY MY PREDECESSOR INSTALLED IT.
THESE IDIOTS ARE LINING UP TO SIGN THEIR OWN DEATH WARRANTS.
AFTER ALL...

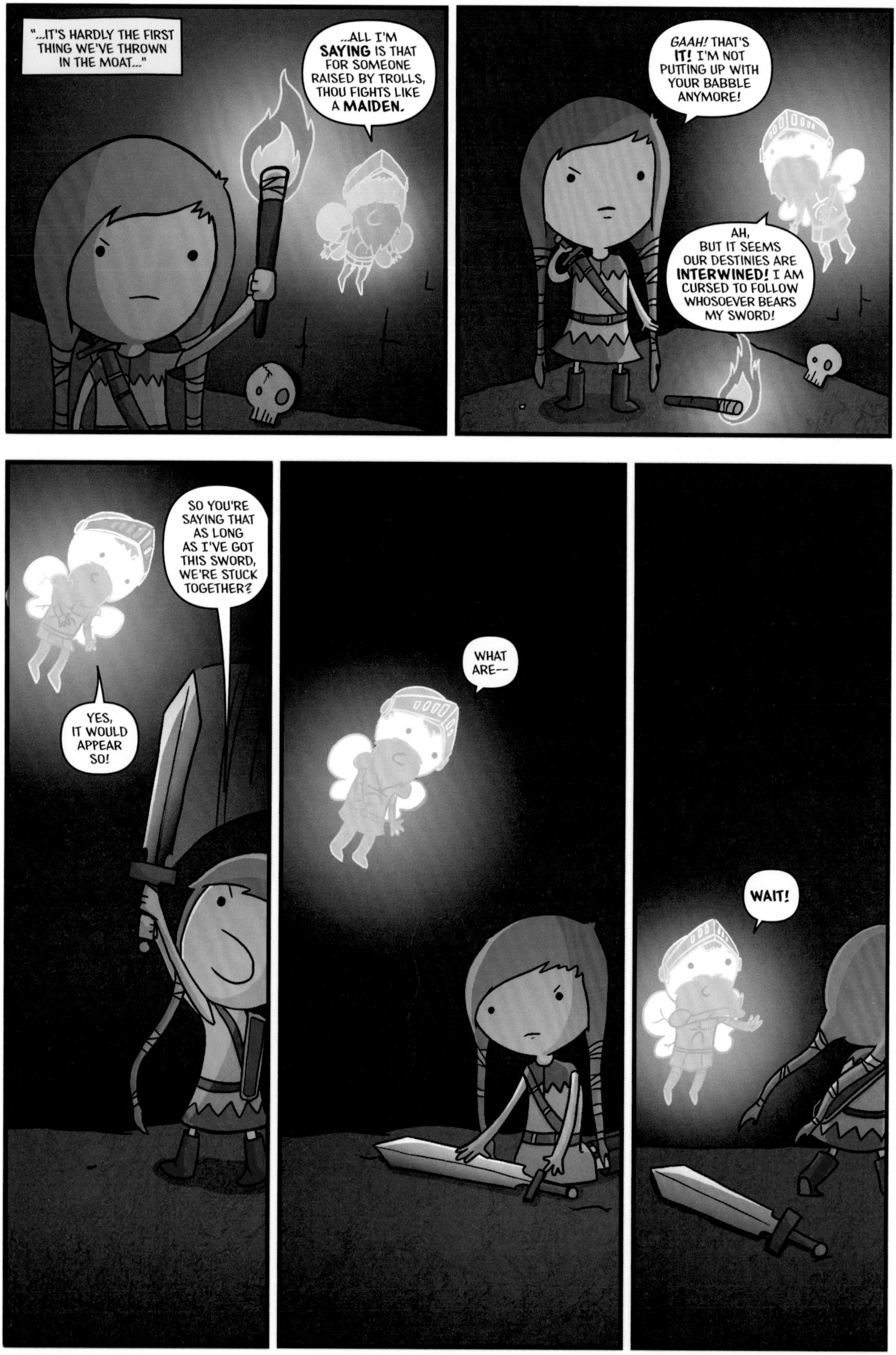

"...IT'S HARDLY THE FIRST THING WE'VE THROWN IN THE MOAT..."
...ALL I'M SAYING IS THAT FOR SOMEONE RAISED BY TROLLS, THOU FIGHTS LIKE A MAIDEN.
GAAH! THAT'S IT! I'M NOT PUTTING UP WITH YOUR BABBLE ANYMORE!
AH, BUT IT SEEMS OUR DESTINIES ARE INTERWINED! I AM CURSED TO FOLLOW WHOSOEVER BEARS MY SWORD!
SO YOU'RE SAYING THAT AS LONG AS I'VE GOT THIS SWORD, WE'RE STUCK TOGETHER?
YES, IT WOULD APPEAR SO!
WHAT ARE--
WAIT!

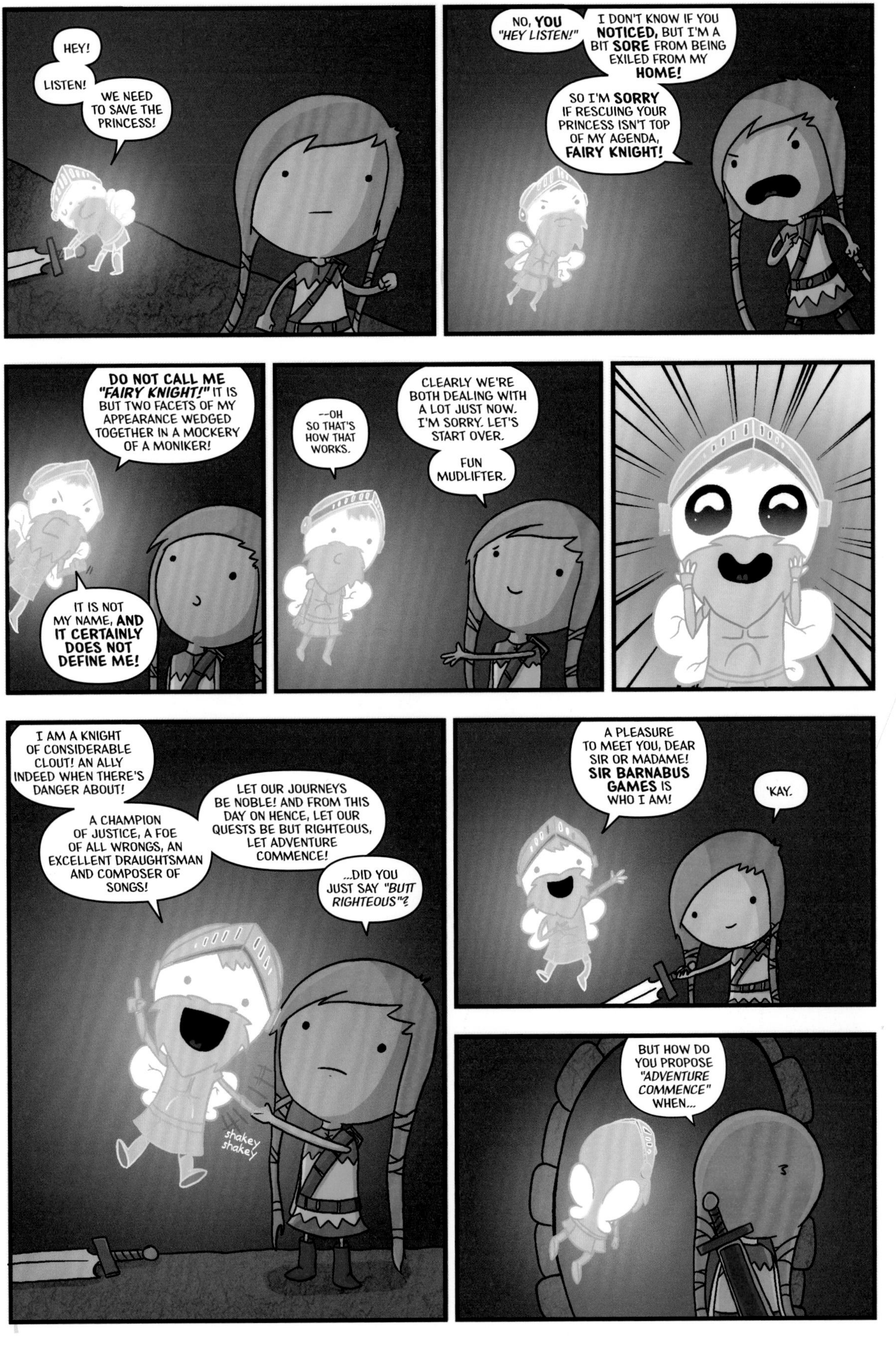
HEY!
LISTEN!
WE NEED TO SAVE THE PRINCESS!
NO, YOU "HEY LISTEN!"
I DON'T KNOW IF YOU NOTICED, BUT I'M A BIT SORE FROM BEING EXILED FROM MY HOME!
SO I'M SORRY IF RESCUING YOUR PRINCESS ISN'T TOP OF MY AGENDA, FAIRY KNIGHT!
DO NOT CALL ME "FAIRY KNIGHT!" IT IS BUT TWO FACETS OF MY APPEARANCE WEDGED TOGETHER IN A MOCKERY OF A MONIKER!
IT IS NOT MY NAME, AND IT CERTAINLY DOES NOT DEFINE ME!
--OH SO THAT'S HOW THAT WORKS.
CLEARLY WE'RE BOTH DEALING WITH A LOT JUST NOW. I'M SORRY. LET'S START OVER.
FUN MUDLIFTER.
I AM A KNIGHT OF CONSIDERABLE CLOUT! AN ALLY INDEED WHEN THERE'S DANGER ABOUT!
A CHAMPION OF JUSTICE, A FOE OF ALL WRONGS, AN EXCELLENT DRAUGHTSMAN AND COMPOSER OF SONGS!
LET OUR JOURNEYS BE NOBLE! AND FROM THIS DAY ON HENCE, LET OUR QUESTS BE BUT RIGHTEOUS, LET ADVENTURE COMMENCE!
...DID YOU JUST SAY "BUTT RIGHTEOUS"?
shakey shakey
A PLEASURE TO MEET YOU, DEAR SIR OR MADAME! SIR BARNABUS GAMES IS WHO I AM!
'KAY.
BUT HOW DO YOU PROPOSE "ADVENTURE COMMENCE" WHEN...

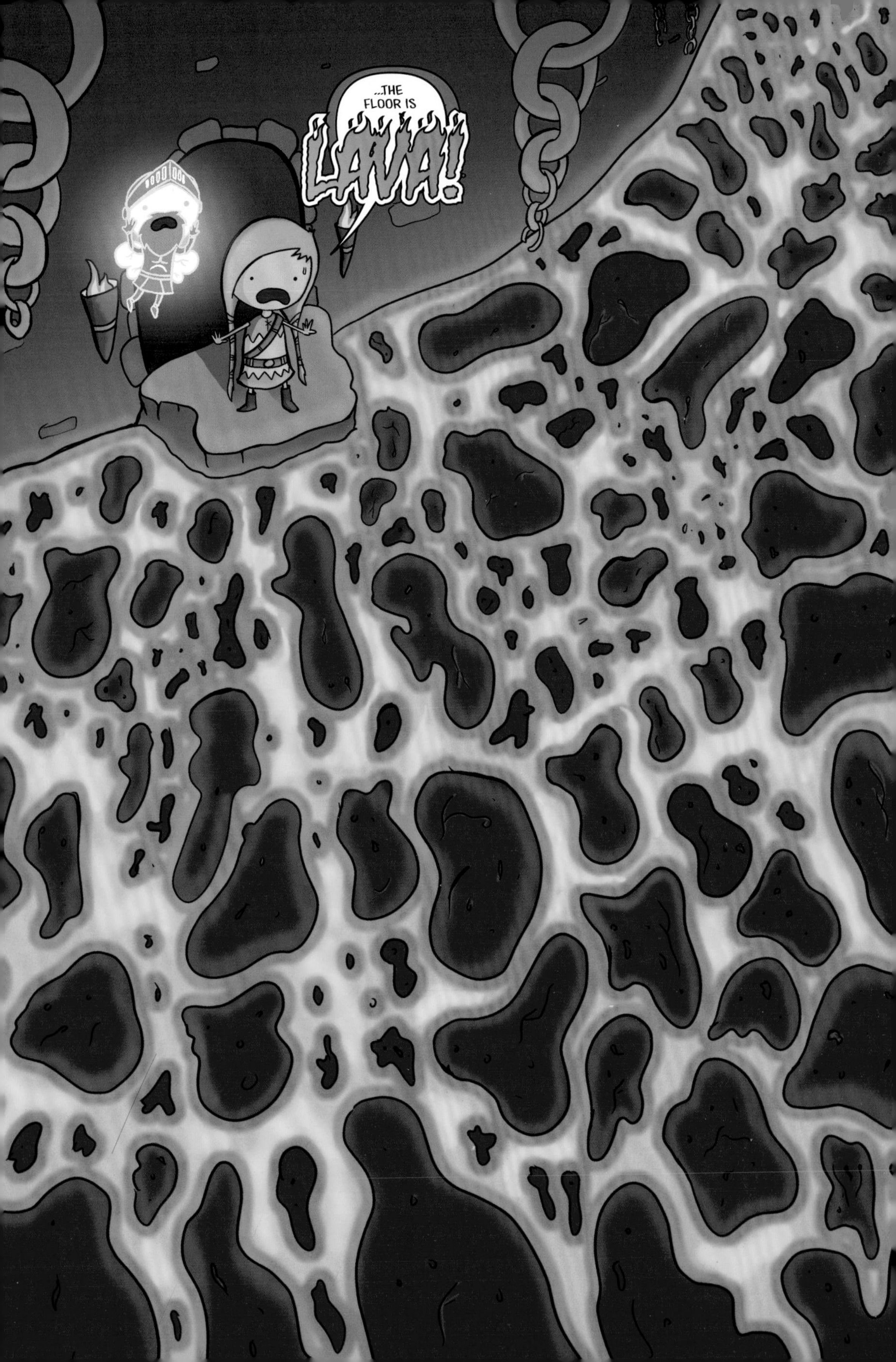
...THE FLOOR IS
LAVA!

TWO

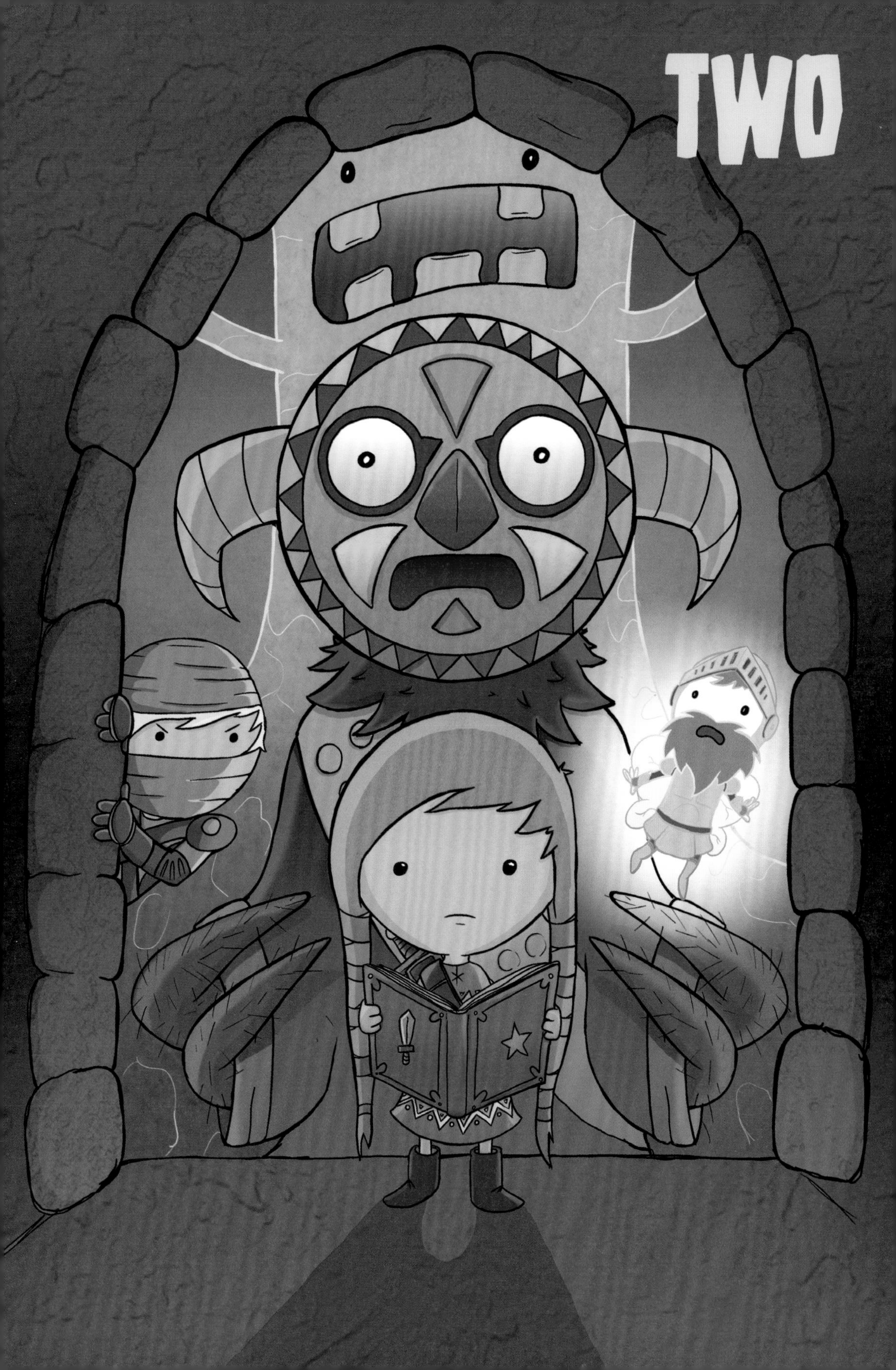

"I AM A KNIGHT OF CONSIDERABLE CLOUT!"

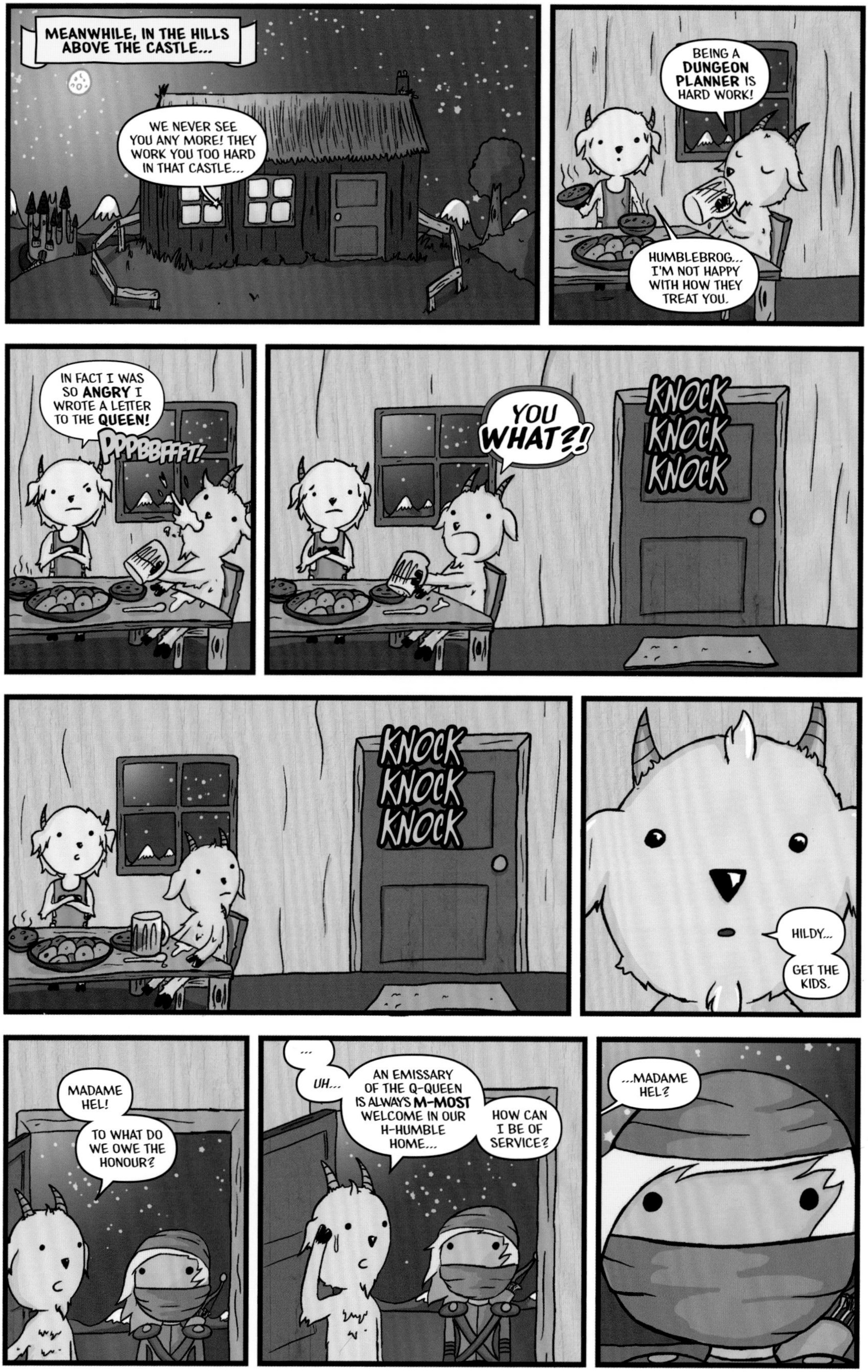
MEANWHILE, IN THE HILLS ABOVE THE CASTLE...
WE NEVER SEE YOU ANY MORE! THEY WORK YOU TOO HARD IN THAT CASTLE...
BEING A DUNGEON PLANNER IS HARD WORK!
HUMBLEBROG... I'M NOT HAPPY WITH HOW THEY TREAT YOU.
IN FACT I WAS SO ANGRY I WROTE A LETTER TO THE QUEEN!
PPPBBFFFT!
YOU WHAT?!
KNOCK KNOCK KNOCK
KNOCK KNOCK KNOCK
HILDY...
GET THE KIDS.
MADAME HEL!
TO WHAT DO WE OWE THE HONOUR?
...
UH...
AN EMISSARY OF THE Q-QUEEN IS ALWAYS M-MOST WELCOME IN OUR H-HUMBLE HOME...
HOW CAN I BE OF SERVICE?
...MADAME HEL?

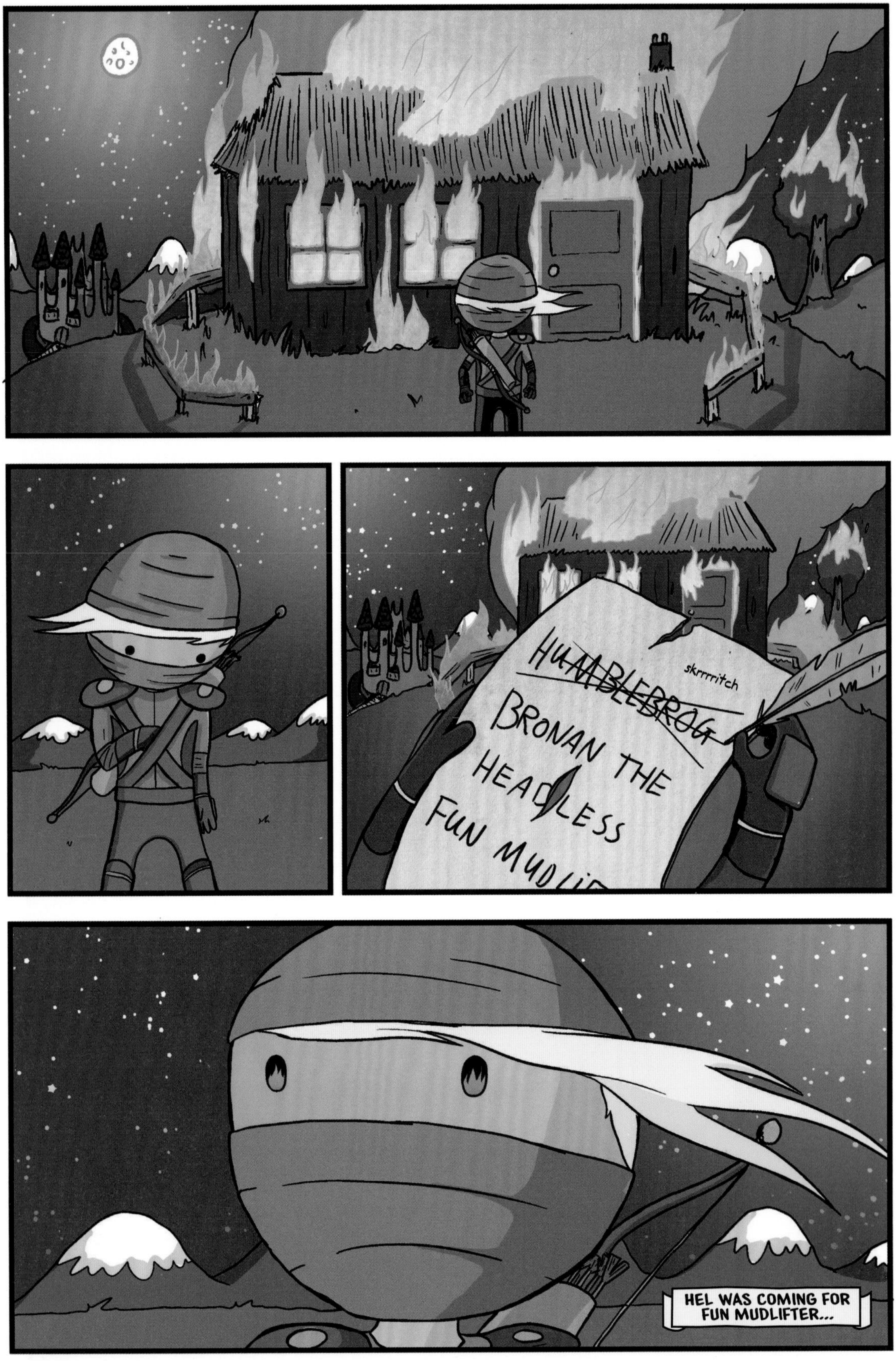

~~HUMBLEBROG~~
skrrrritch
BRONAN THE
HEADLESS
FUN
HEL WAS COMING FOR FUN MUDLIFTER...

...EVEN IF SHE DIDN'T KNOW IT YET.

SO...

THE FLOOR IS LAVA.

OKAY. MAYBE THIS IS A SIGN.

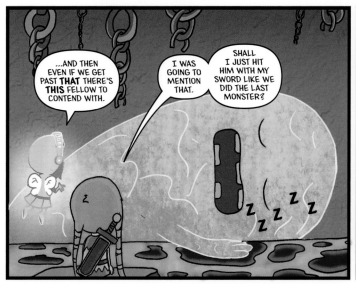

...AND THEN EVEN IF WE GET PAST **THAT** THERE'S **THIS** FELLOW TO CONTEND WITH.

I WAS GOING TO MENTION THAT.

SHALL I JUST HIT HIM WITH MY SWORD LIKE WE DID THE LAST MONSTER?

ZZZZ

DON'T BE **BARBARIC,** CHILD! THE CREATURE IS CLEARLY ASLEEP!

SO?

SO, I CAN FLY OVER, SNEAK CLOSE, AND FIND A **WEAK SPOT** TO JAM OUR SWORD IN!

RESEARCH! THAT IS A MANNER MORE BEFITTING OF A **KNIGHT!**

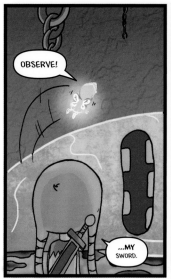

OBSERVE!

...MY SWORD.

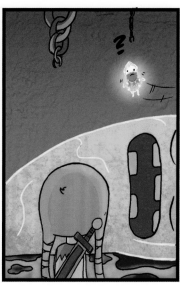

?

NO I DON'T THINK I CAN SEE ANYTHING

!

smek

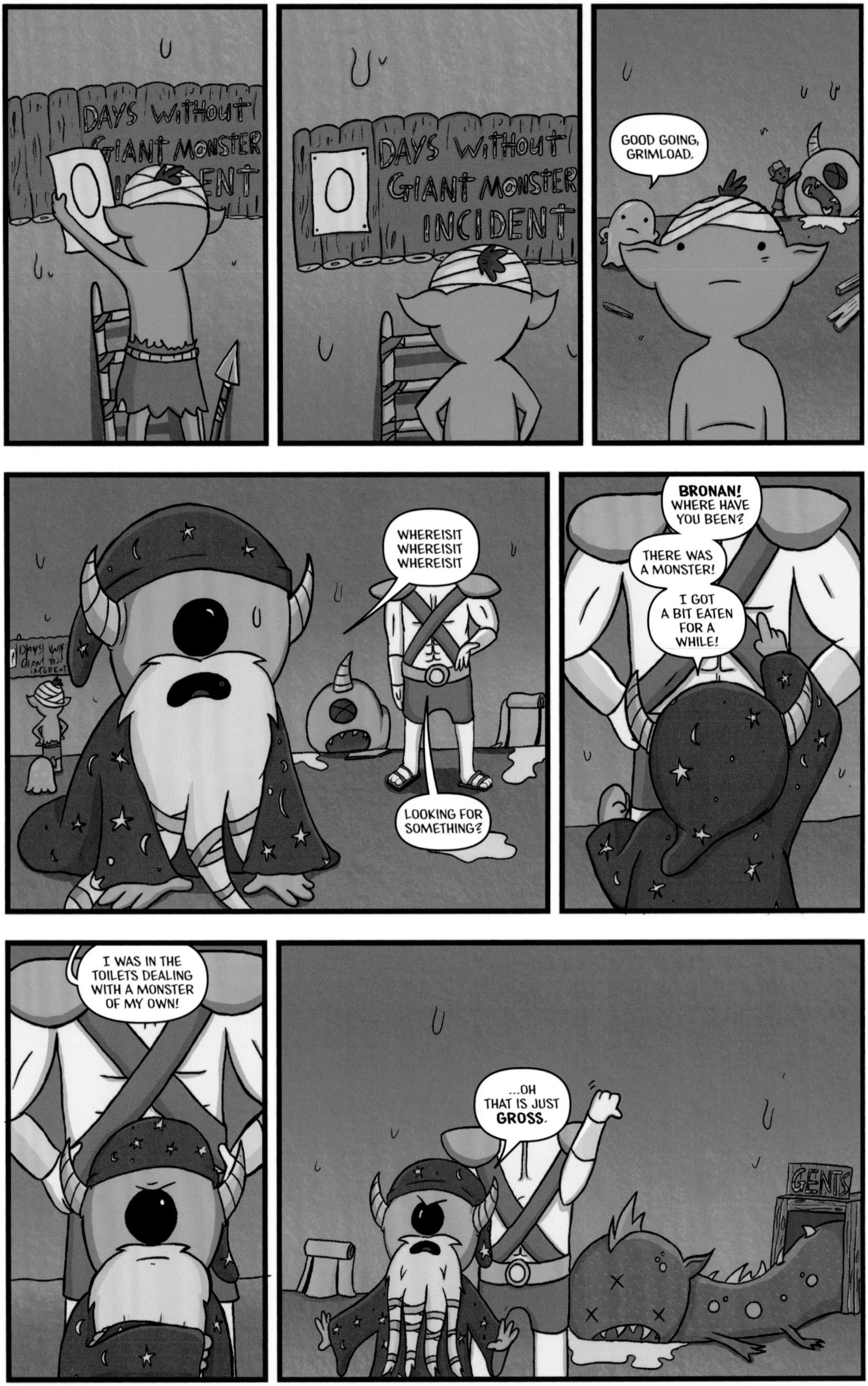
DAYS WITHOUT GIANT MONSTER INCIDENT
0
DAYS WITHOUT GIANT MONSTER INCIDENT
GOOD GOING, GRIMLOAD.
WHEREISIT WHEREISIT WHEREISIT
LOOKING FOR SOMETHING?
BRONAN! WHERE HAVE YOU BEEN?
THERE WAS A MONSTER!
I GOT A BIT EATEN FOR A WHILE!
I WAS IN THE TOILETS DEALING WITH A MONSTER OF MY OWN!
...OH THAT IS JUST **GROSS**.
GENTS

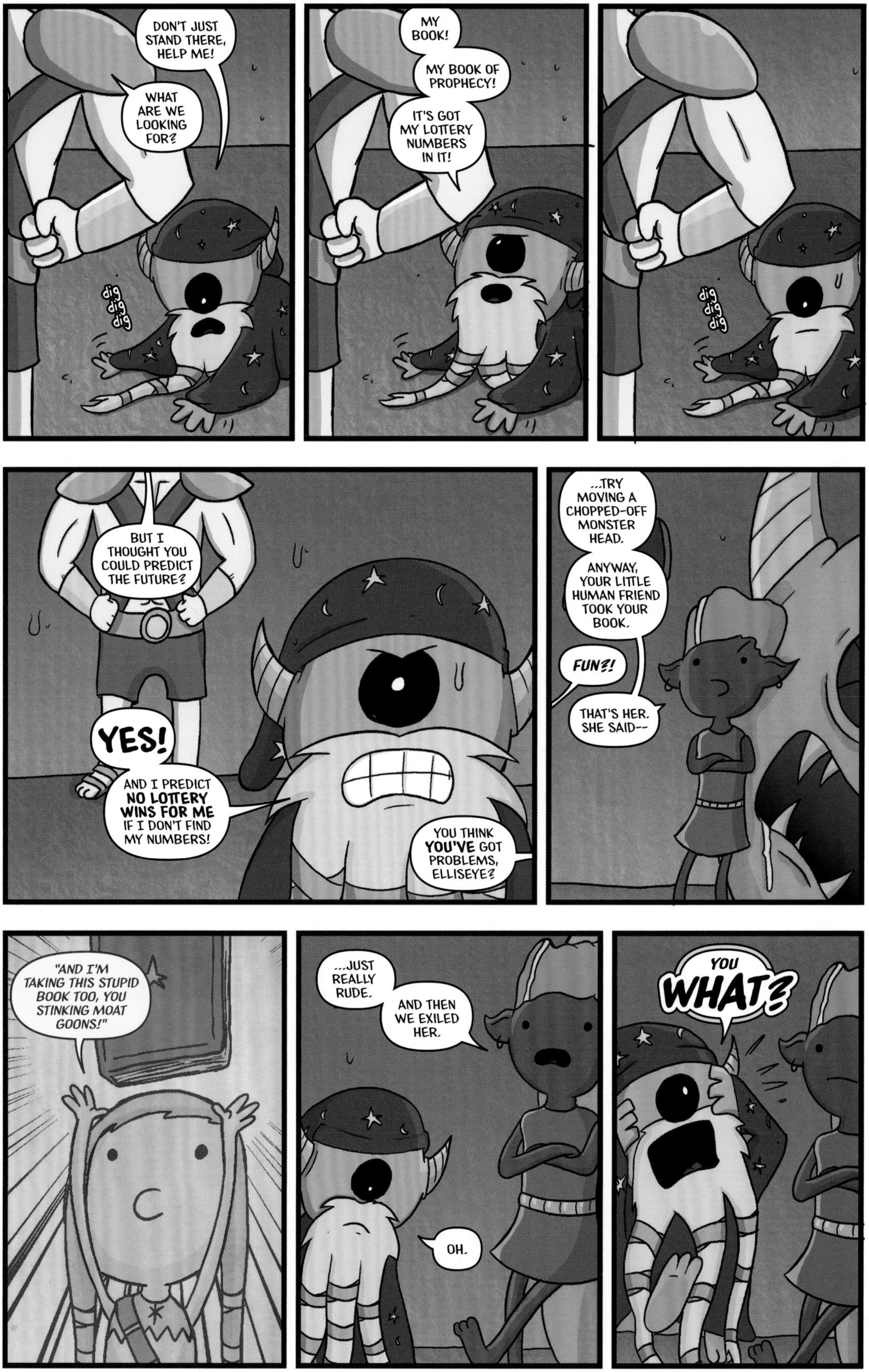
DON'T JUST STAND THERE, HELP ME!
WHAT ARE WE LOOKING FOR?
dig dig dig
MY BOOK!
MY BOOK OF PROPHECY!
IT'S GOT MY LOTTERY NUMBERS IN IT!
dig dig dig
BUT I THOUGHT YOU COULD PREDICT THE FUTURE?
YES!
AND I PREDICT **NO LOTTERY WINS FOR ME** IF I DON'T FIND MY NUMBERS!
YOU THINK **YOU'VE** GOT PROBLEMS, ELLISEYE?
...TRY MOVING A CHOPPED-OFF MONSTER HEAD.
ANYWAY, YOUR LITTLE HUMAN FRIEND TOOK YOUR BOOK.
THAT'S HER. SHE SAID--
FUN?!
"AND I'M TAKING THIS STUPID BOOK TOO, YOU STINKING MOAT GOONS!"
...JUST REALLY RUDE.
AND THEN WE EXILED HER.
OH.
YOU WHAT?

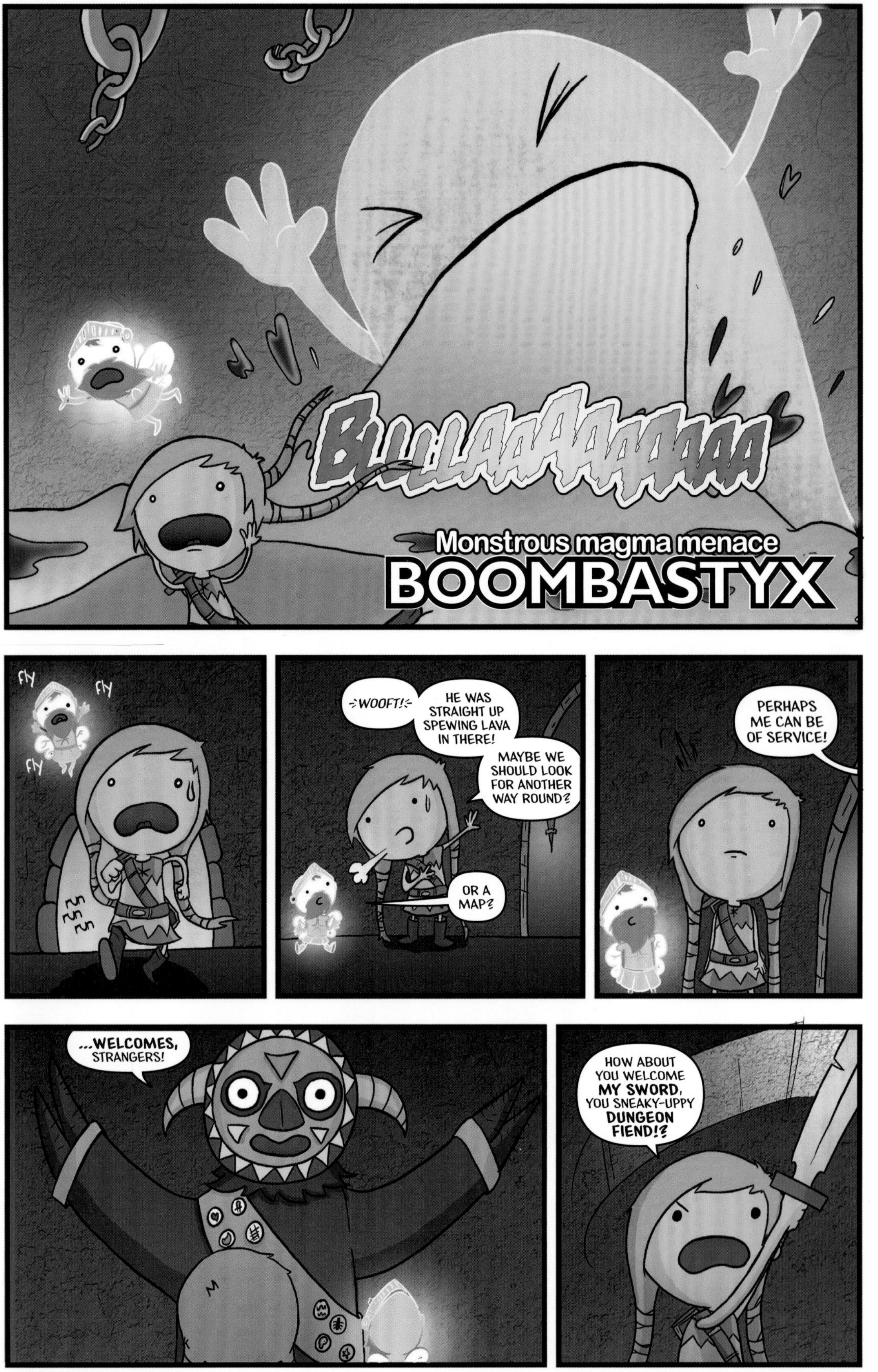
BLLLLAAAAAAAAAA
Monstrous magma menace
BOOMBASTYX
FLY
FLY
FLY
RUN RUN RUN
WOOFT!
HE WAS STRAIGHT UP SPEWING LAVA IN THERE!
MAYBE WE SHOULD LOOK FOR ANOTHER WAY ROUND?
OR A MAP?
PERHAPS ME CAN BE OF SERVICE!
...WELCOMES, STRANGERS!
HOW ABOUT YOU WELCOME MY SWORD, YOU SNEAKY-UPPY DUNGEON FIEND!?

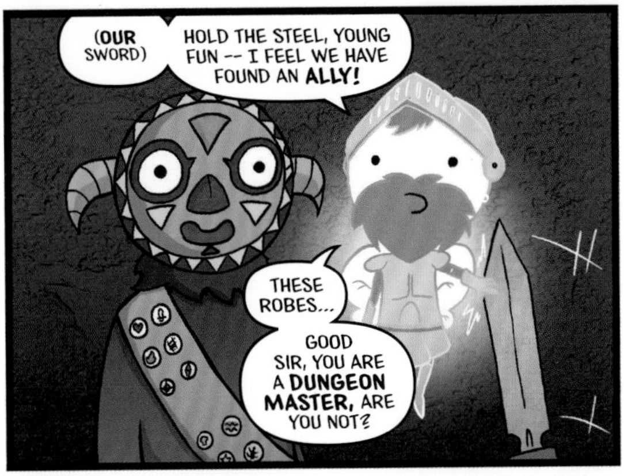
(OUR SWORD)
HOLD THE STEEL, YOUNG FUN -- I FEEL WE HAVE FOUND AN ALLY!
THESE ROBES...
GOOD SIR, YOU ARE A DUNGEON MASTER, ARE YOU NOT?

ANY DUNGEON WORTH ITS SALT HAS A DUNGEON MASTER!

DUNGEON MASTER

ˈdʌndʒən ˈmɑːstə(r)

DUNGEON MASTERS ARE OATH-BOUND TO MAINTAIN THE ORDER OF A DUNGEON AND PROVIDE INFORMATION TO INHABITANTS AND VISITORS ALIKE!

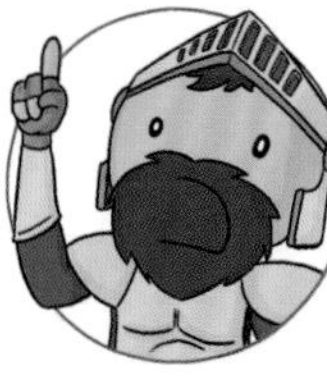

SO, WE CAN ASK HIM ANYTHING AND HE HAS TO TELL US! LIKE, HOW DO WE GET ROUND THIS LAVA BEAST, FOR INSTANCE?

GOSH LET'S FIND OUT!

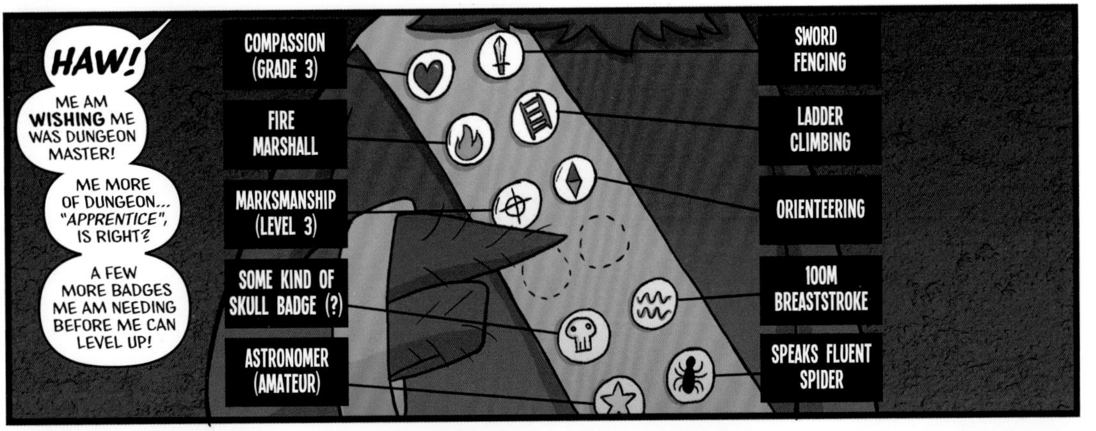
HAW!
ME AM WISHING ME WAS DUNGEON MASTER!
ME MORE OF DUNGEON... "APPRENTICE", IS RIGHT?
A FEW MORE BADGES ME AM NEEDING BEFORE ME CAN LEVEL UP!
COMPASSION (GRADE 3)
FIRE MARSHALL
MARKSMANSHIP (LEVEL 3)
SOME KIND OF SKULL BADGE (?)
ASTRONOMER (AMATEUR)
SWORD FENCING
LADDER CLIMBING
ORIENTEERING
100M BREASTSTROKE
SPEAKS FLUENT SPIDER

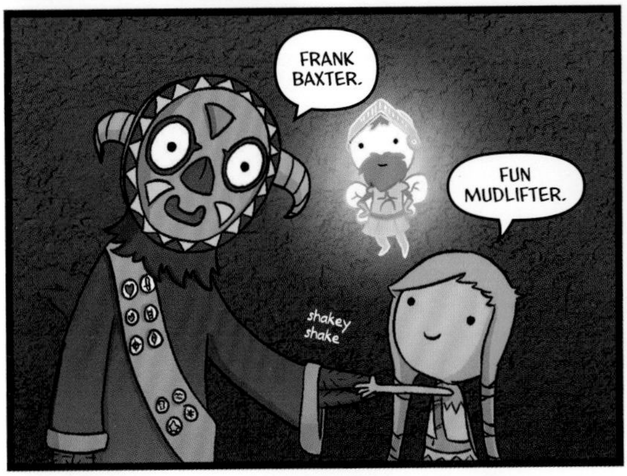
FRANK BAXTER.
FUN MUDLIFTER.
shakey shake

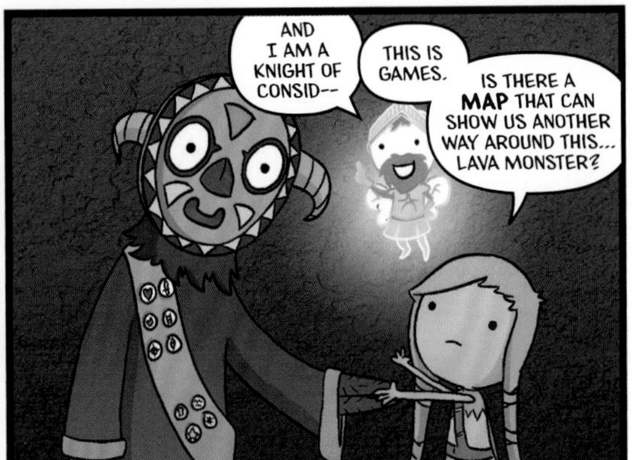
AND I AM A KNIGHT OF CONSID--
THIS IS GAMES.
IS THERE A MAP THAT CAN SHOW US ANOTHER WAY AROUND THIS... LAVA MONSTER?

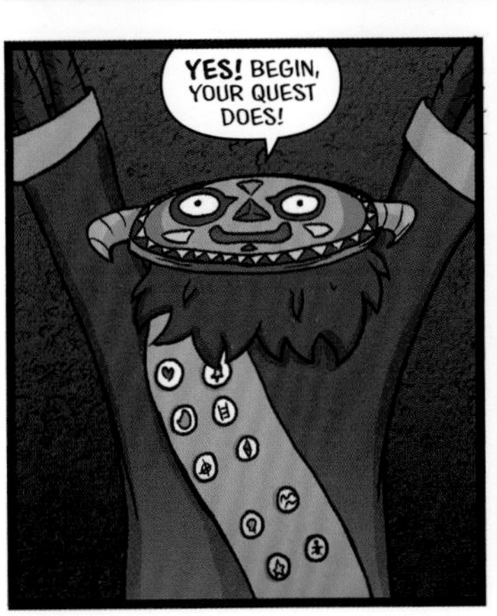
YES! BEGIN, YOUR QUEST DOES!

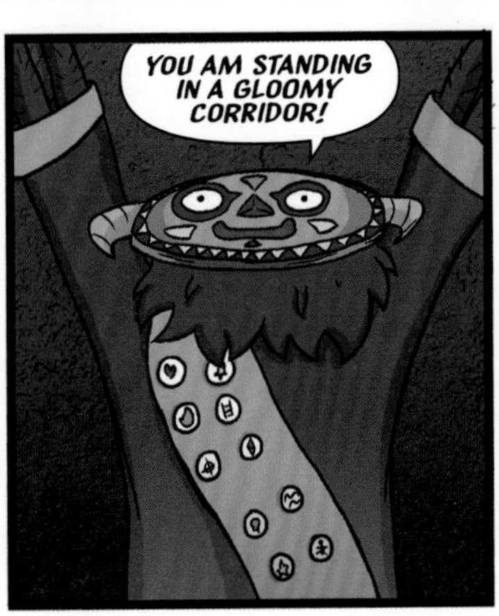
YOU AM STANDING IN A GLOOMY CORRIDOR!

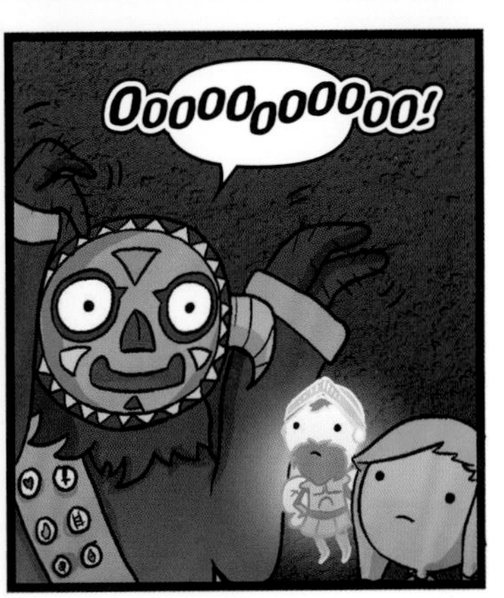
Oooooooooooo!

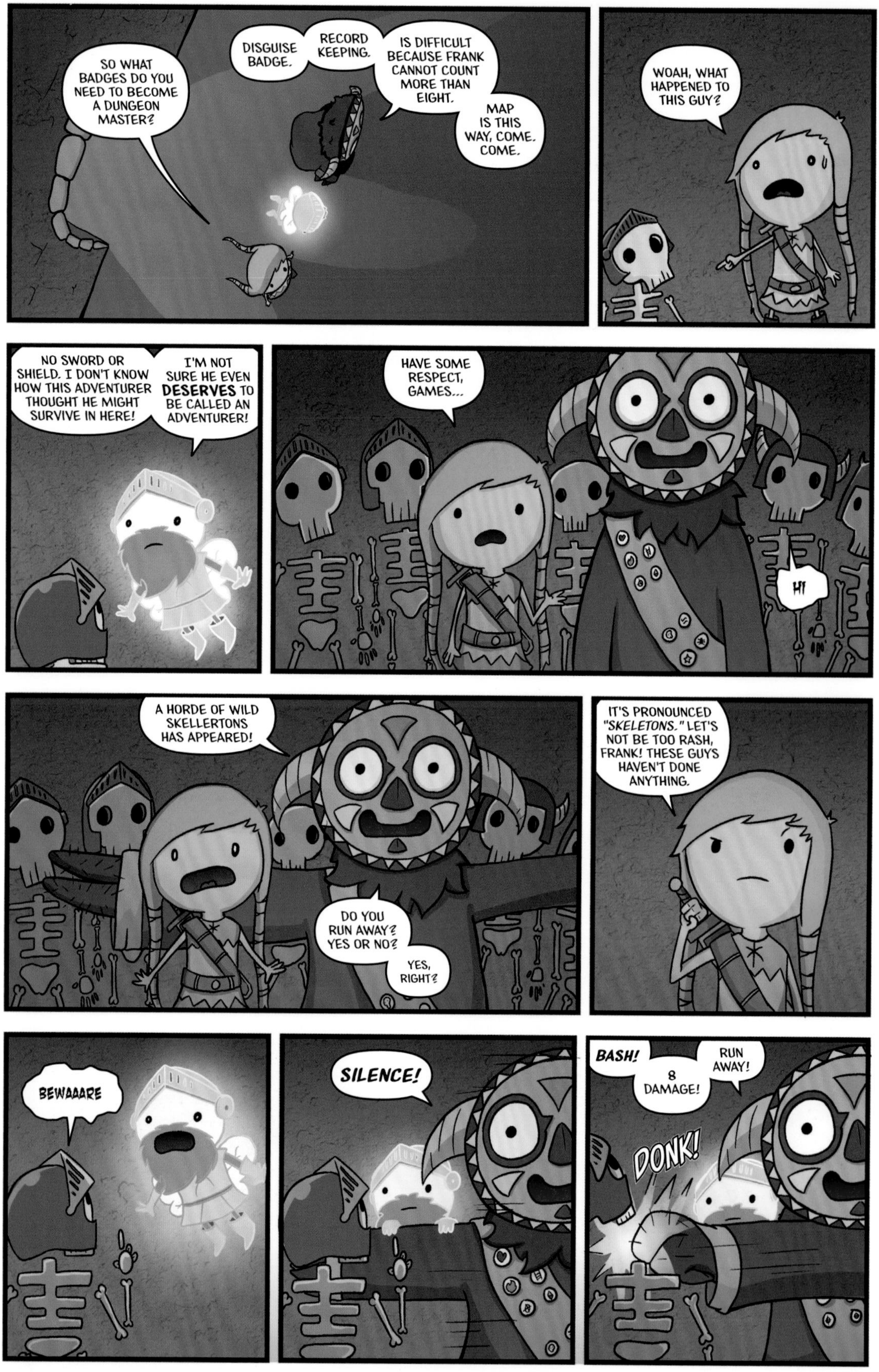
SO WHAT BADGES DO YOU NEED TO BECOME A DUNGEON MASTER?
DISGUISE BADGE.
RECORD KEEPING.
IS DIFFICULT BECAUSE FRANK CANNOT COUNT MORE THAN EIGHT.
MAP IS THIS WAY, COME. COME.
WOAH, WHAT HAPPENED TO THIS GUY?
NO SWORD OR SHIELD. I DON'T KNOW HOW THIS ADVENTURER THOUGHT HE MIGHT SURVIVE IN HERE!
I'M NOT SURE HE EVEN **DESERVES** TO BE CALLED AN ADVENTURER!
HAVE SOME RESPECT, GAMES...
HI
A HORDE OF WILD SKELLERTONS HAS APPEARED!
DO YOU RUN AWAY? YES OR NO?
YES, RIGHT?
IT'S PRONOUNCED *"SKELETONS."* LET'S NOT BE TOO RASH, FRANK! THESE GUYS HAVEN'T DONE ANYTHING.
BEWAAARE
SILENCE!
BASH!
8 DAMAGE!
RUN AWAY!
DONK!

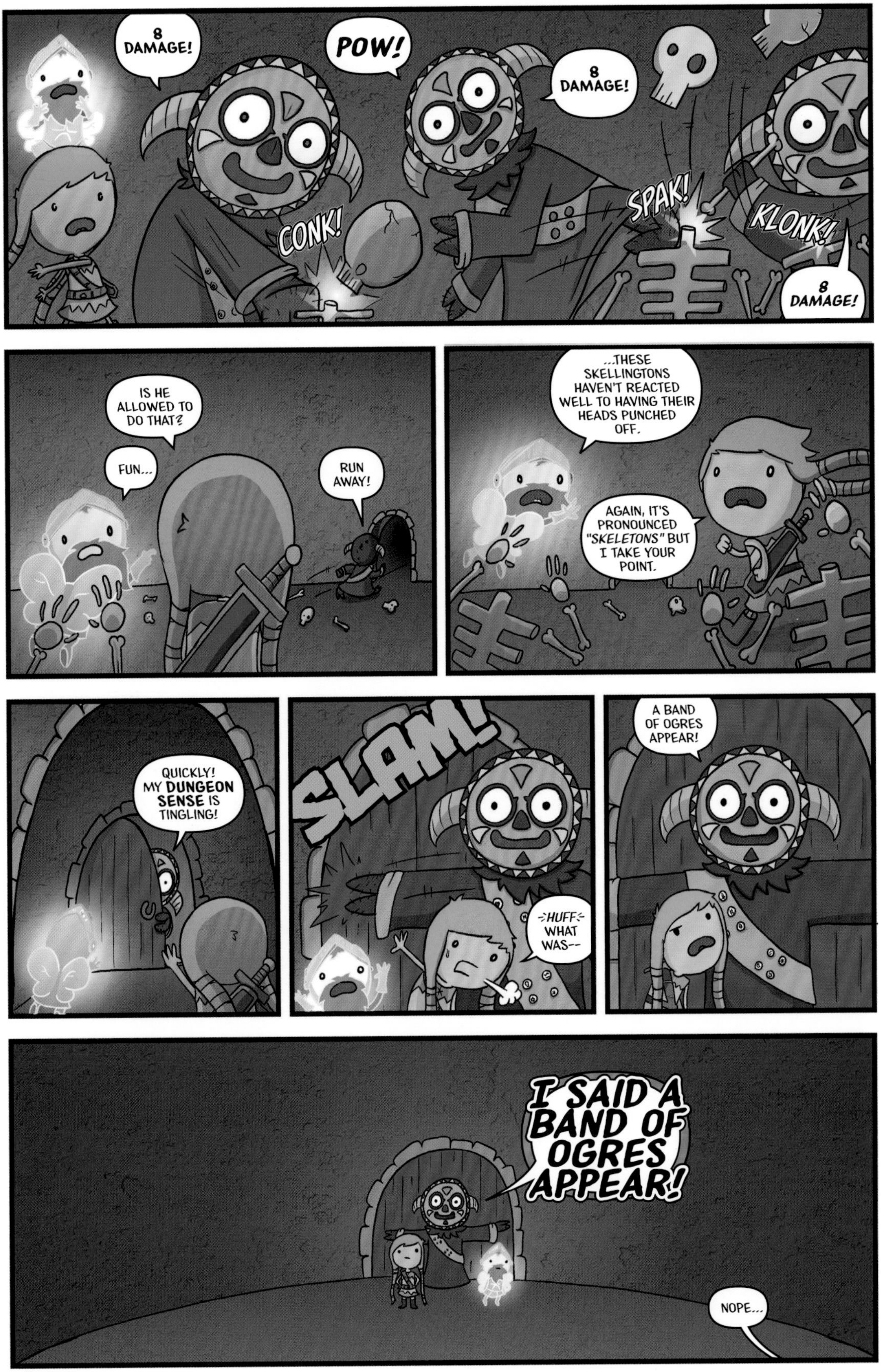

8 DAMAGE!
POW!
8 DAMAGE!
CONK!
SPAK!
KLONK!
8 DAMAGE!
IS HE ALLOWED TO DO THAT?
FUN...
RUN AWAY!
...THESE SKELLINGTONS HAVEN'T REACTED WELL TO HAVING THEIR HEADS PUNCHED OFF.
AGAIN, IT'S PRONOUNCED "SKELETONS" BUT I TAKE YOUR POINT.
QUICKLY! MY DUNGEON SENSE IS TINGLING!
SLAM!
HUFF WHAT WAS--
A BAND OF OGRES APPEAR!
I SAID A BAND OF OGRES APPEAR!
NOPE...

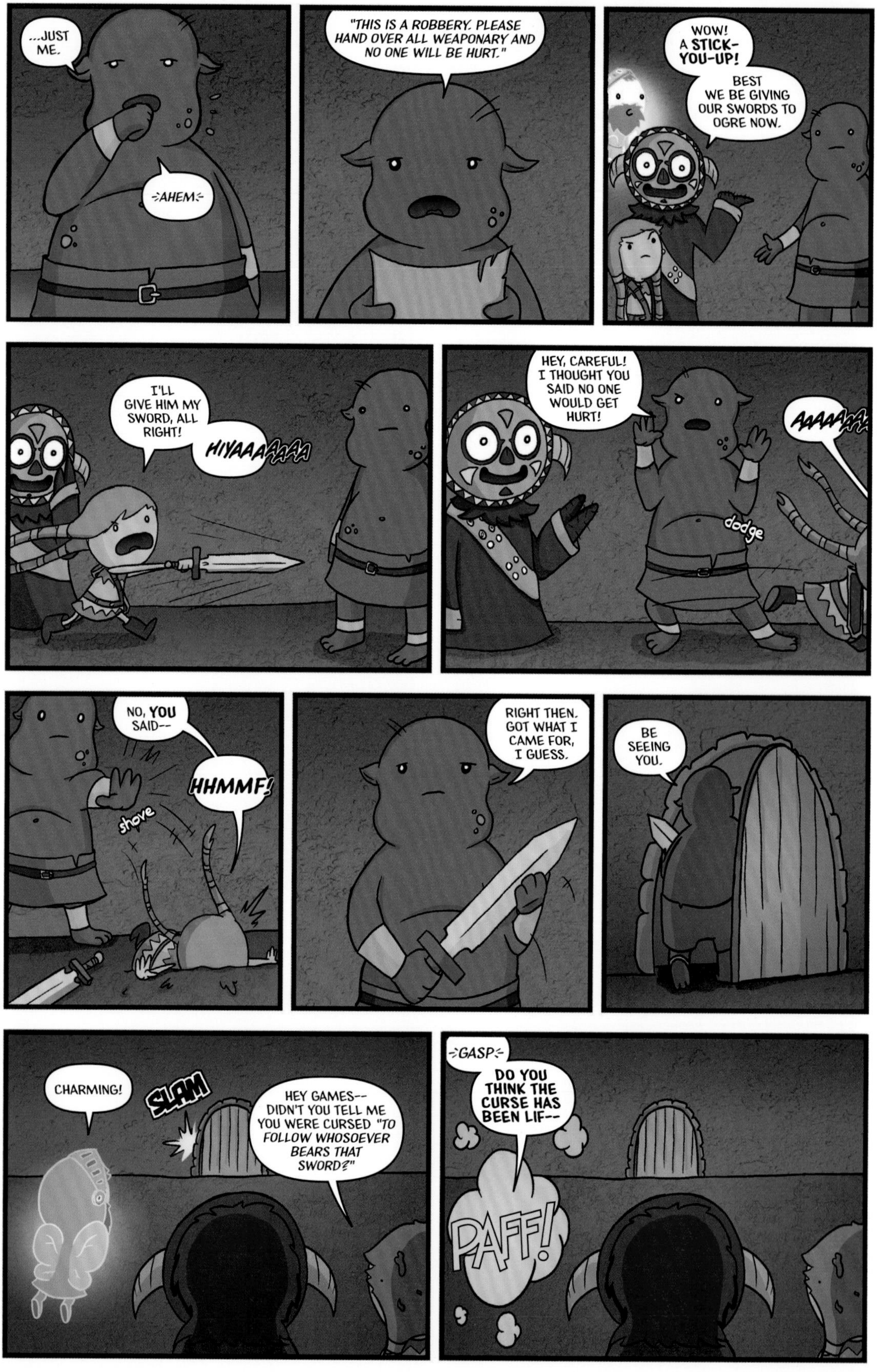
...JUST ME.
AHEM
"THIS IS A ROBBERY. PLEASE HAND OVER ALL WEAPONARY AND NO ONE WILL BE HURT."
WOW! A STICK-YOU-UP!
BEST WE BE GIVING OUR SWORDS TO OGRE NOW.
I'LL GIVE HIM MY SWORD, ALL RIGHT!
HIYAAAAAAA
HEY, CAREFUL! I THOUGHT YOU SAID NO ONE WOULD GET HURT!
dodge
NO, YOU SAID--
HHMMF!
shove
RIGHT THEN. GOT WHAT I CAME FOR, I GUESS.
BE SEEING YOU.
CHARMING!
SLAM
HEY GAMES-- DIDN'T YOU TELL ME YOU WERE CURSED "TO FOLLOW WHOSOEVER BEARS THAT SWORD?"
GASP
DO YOU THINK THE CURSE HAS BEEN LIF--
PAFF!

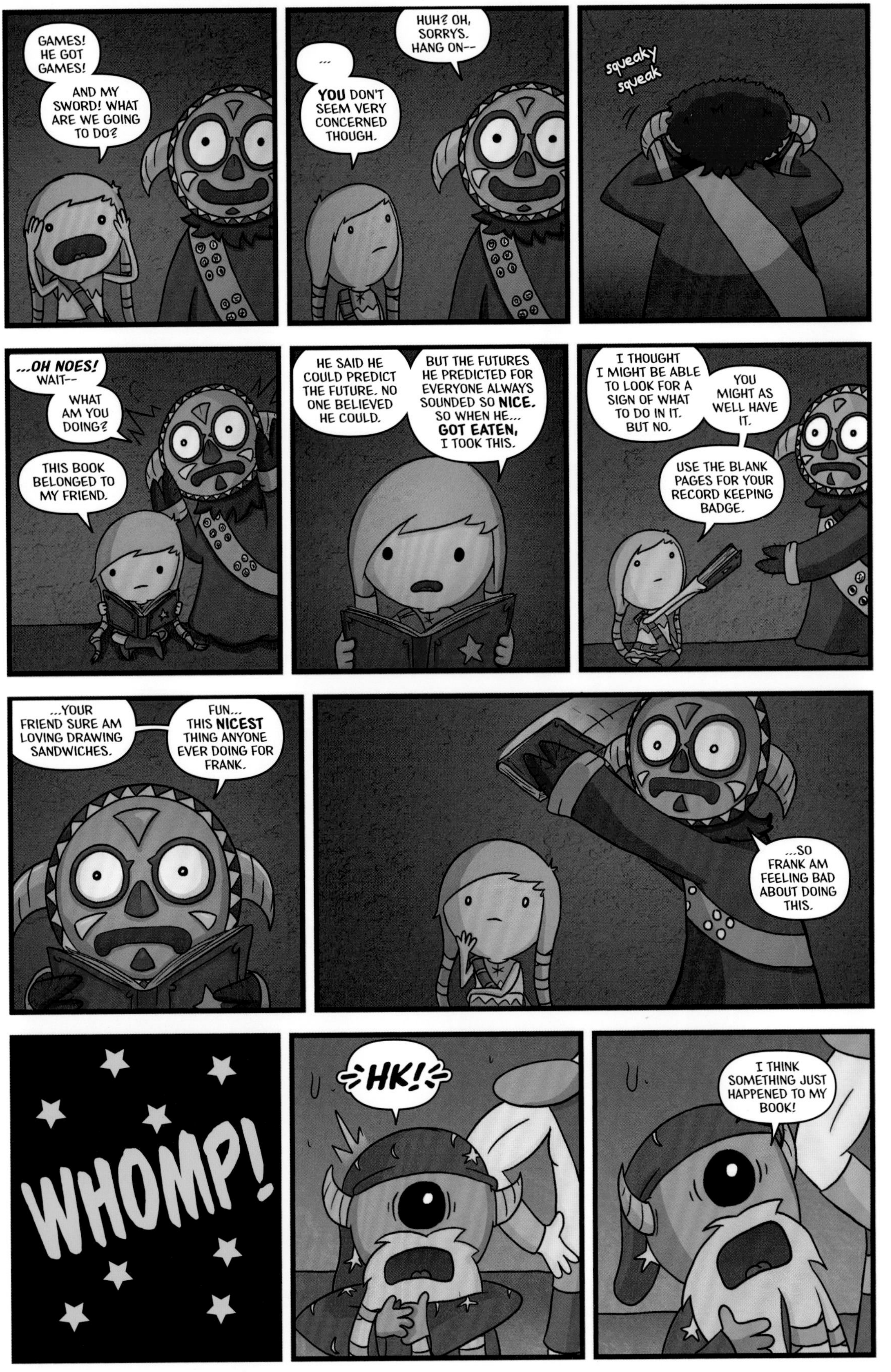

GAMES! HE GOT GAMES!
AND MY SWORD! WHAT ARE WE GOING TO DO?
...
YOU DON'T SEEM VERY CONCERNED THOUGH.
HUH? OH, SORRYS. HANG ON--
squeaky squeak
...OH NOES! WAIT--
WHAT AM YOU DOING?
THIS BOOK BELONGED TO MY FRIEND.
HE SAID HE COULD PREDICT THE FUTURE. NO ONE BELIEVED HE COULD.
BUT THE FUTURES HE PREDICTED FOR EVERYONE ALWAYS SOUNDED SO NICE. SO WHEN HE... GOT EATEN, I TOOK THIS.
I THOUGHT I MIGHT BE ABLE TO LOOK FOR A SIGN OF WHAT TO DO IN IT. BUT NO.
YOU MIGHT AS WELL HAVE IT.
USE THE BLANK PAGES FOR YOUR RECORD KEEPING BADGE.
...YOUR FRIEND SURE AM LOVING DRAWING SANDWICHES.
FUN... THIS NICEST THING ANYONE EVER DOING FOR FRANK.
...SO FRANK AM FEELING BAD ABOUT DOING THIS.
WHOMP!
HK!
I THINK SOMETHING JUST HAPPENED TO MY BOOK!

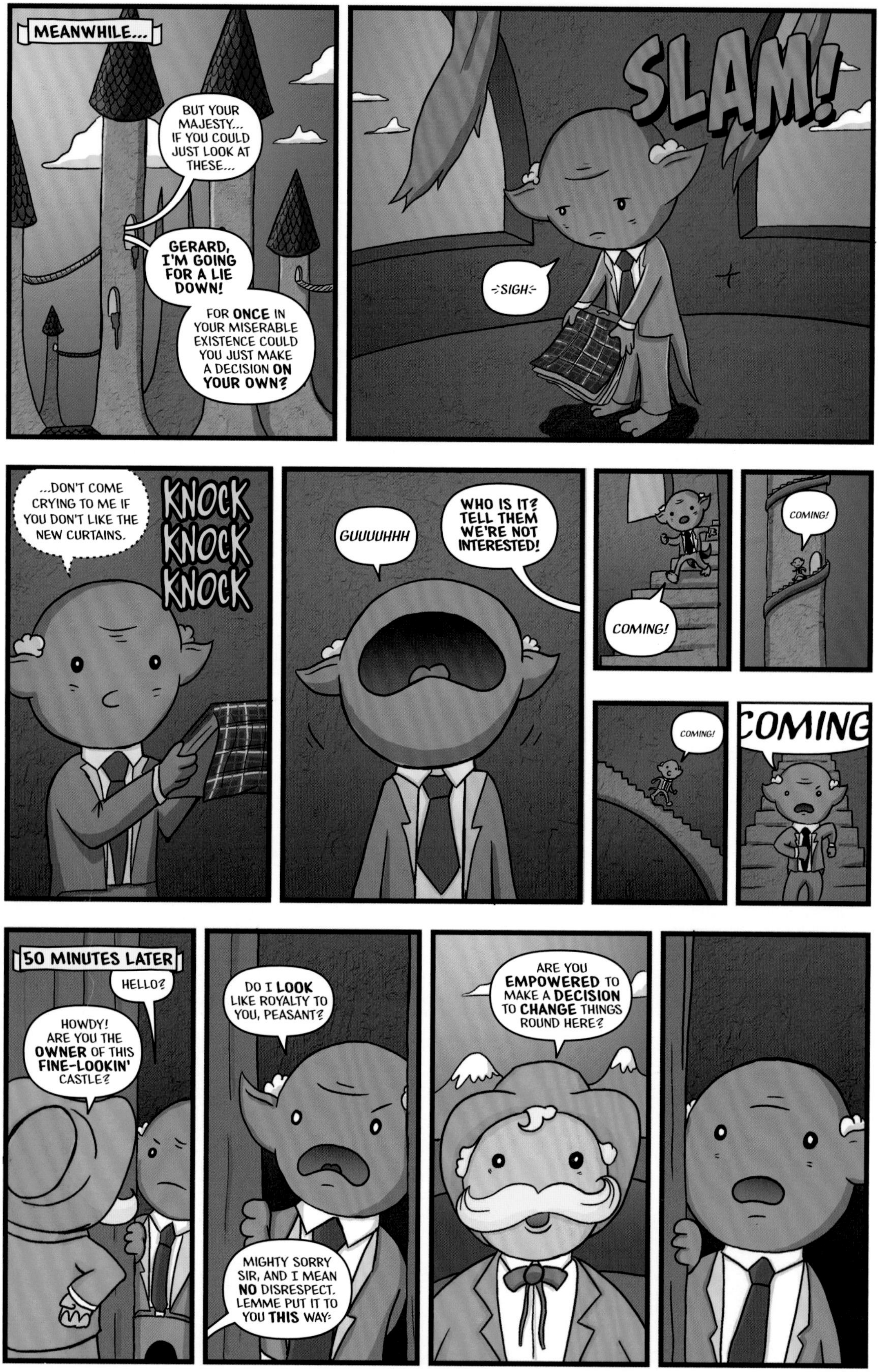
MEANWHILE...
BUT YOUR MAJESTY... IF YOU COULD JUST LOOK AT THESE...
GERARD, I'M GOING FOR A LIE DOWN!
FOR ONCE IN YOUR MISERABLE EXISTENCE COULD YOU JUST MAKE A DECISION ON YOUR OWN?
SLAM!
-SIGH-
...DON'T COME CRYING TO ME IF YOU DON'T LIKE THE NEW CURTAINS.
KNOCK KNOCK KNOCK
GUUUUHHH
WHO IS IT? TELL THEM WE'RE NOT INTERESTED!
COMING!
COMING!
COMING!
COMING
50 MINUTES LATER
HELLO?
HOWDY! ARE YOU THE OWNER OF THIS FINE-LOOKIN' CASTLE?
DO I LOOK LIKE ROYALTY TO YOU, PEASANT?
MIGHTY SORRY SIR, AND I MEAN NO DISRESPECT. LEMME PUT IT TO YOU THIS WAY:
ARE YOU EMPOWERED TO MAKE A DECISION TO CHANGE THINGS ROUND HERE?

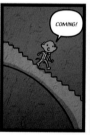

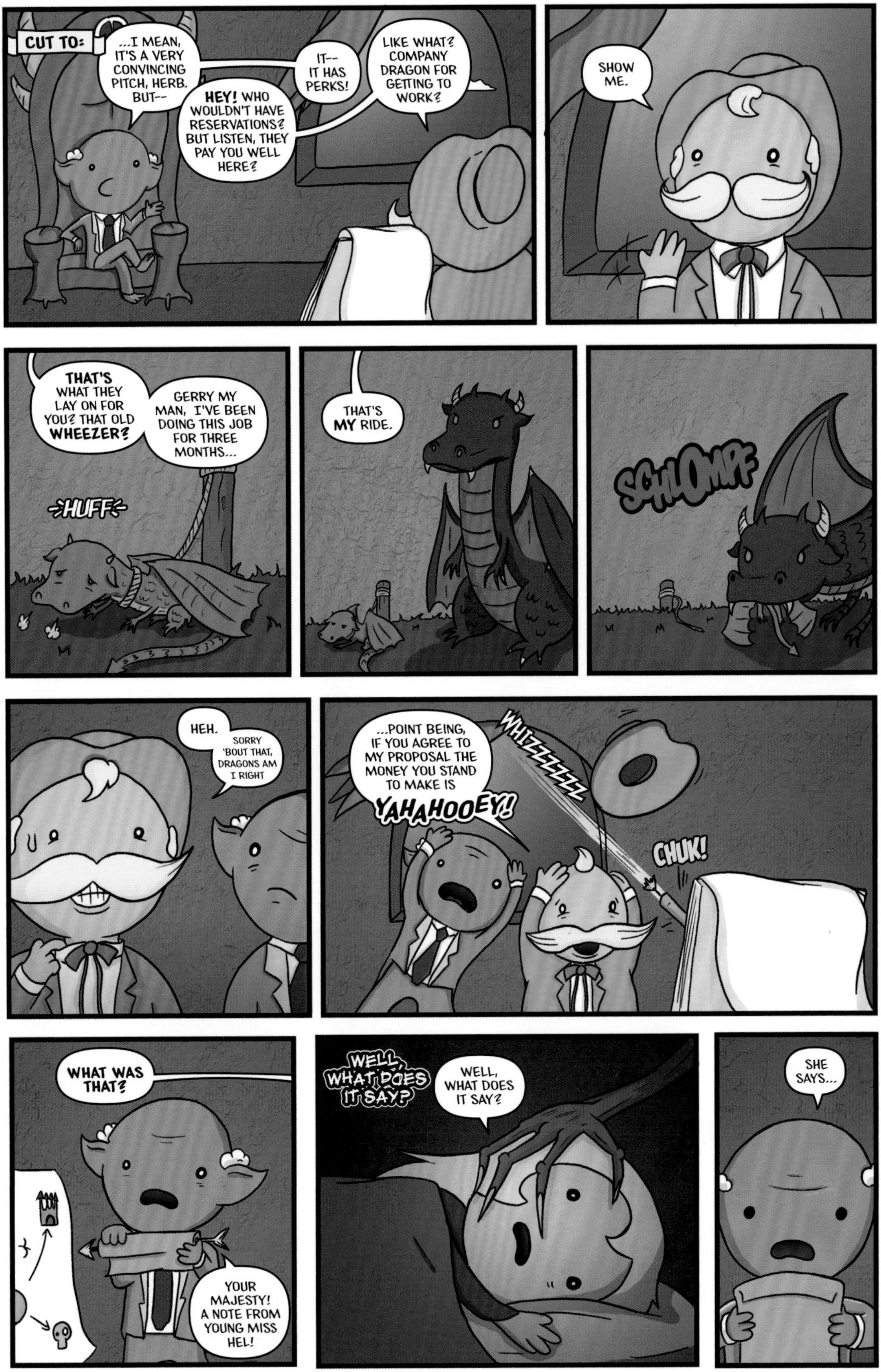
CUT TO:
...I MEAN, IT'S A VERY CONVINCING PITCH, HERB. BUT--
HEY! WHO WOULDN'T HAVE RESERVATIONS? BUT LISTEN, THEY PAY YOU WELL HERE?
IT-- IT HAS PERKS!
LIKE WHAT? COMPANY DRAGON FOR GETTING TO WORK?
SHOW ME.
THAT'S WHAT THEY LAY ON FOR YOU? THAT OLD WHEEZER?
GERRY MY MAN, I'VE BEEN DOING THIS JOB FOR THREE MONTHS...
HUFF
THAT'S MY RIDE.
SCHLOMPF
HEH.
SORRY 'BOUT THAT, DRAGONS AM I RIGHT
...POINT BEING, IF YOU AGREE TO MY PROPOSAL THE MONEY YOU STAND TO MAKE IS YAHAHOOEY!
WHIZZZZZZZ
CHUK!
WHAT WAS THAT?
YOUR MAJESTY! A NOTE FROM YOUNG MISS HEL!
WELL, WHAT DOES IT SAY?
WELL, WHAT DOES IT SAY?
SHE SAYS...

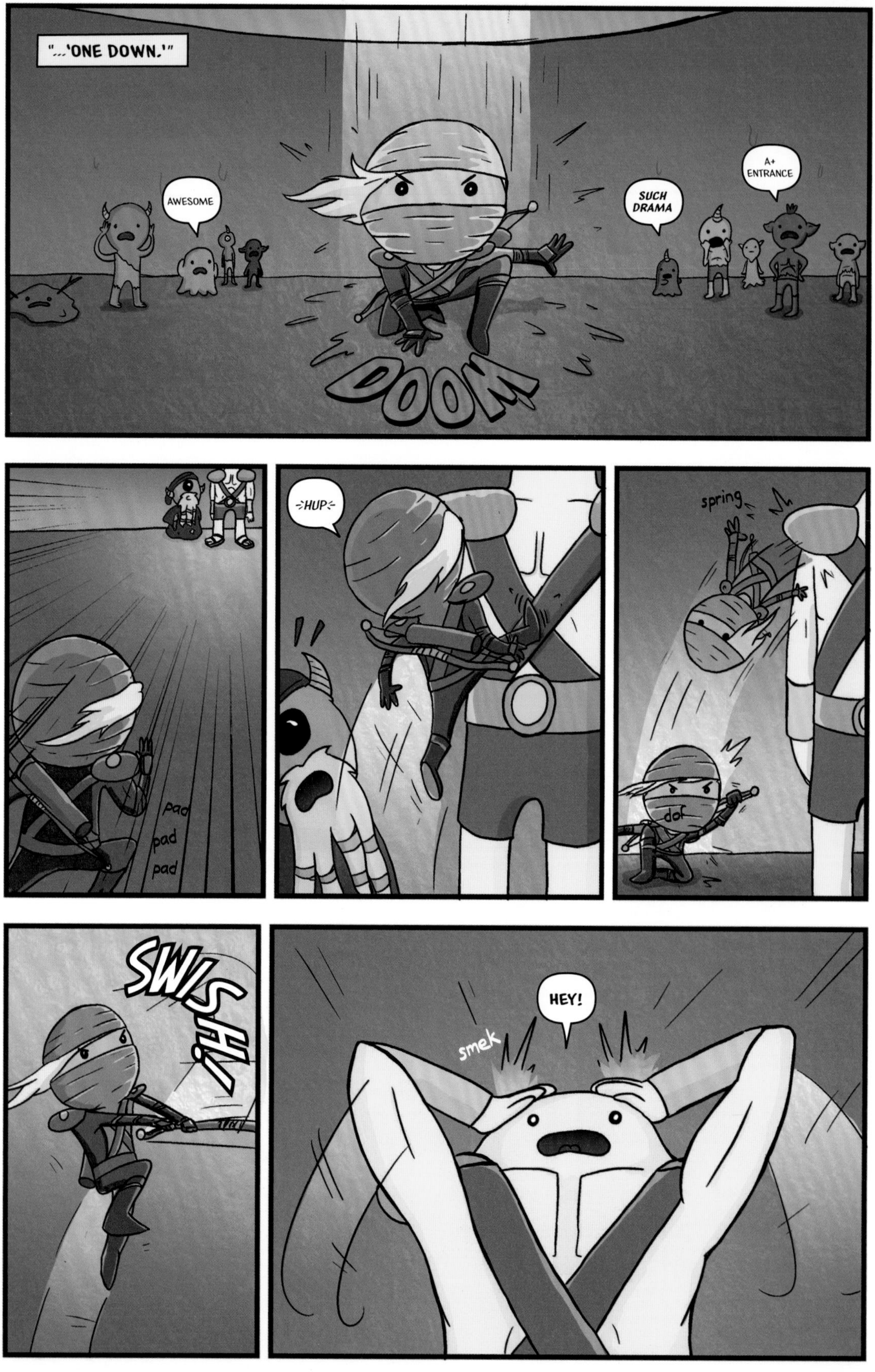
"...'ONE DOWN.'"
AWESOME
SUCH DRAMA
A+ ENTRANCE
DOOM
pad
pad
pad
HUP
spring
dof
SWISH!
HEY!
smek

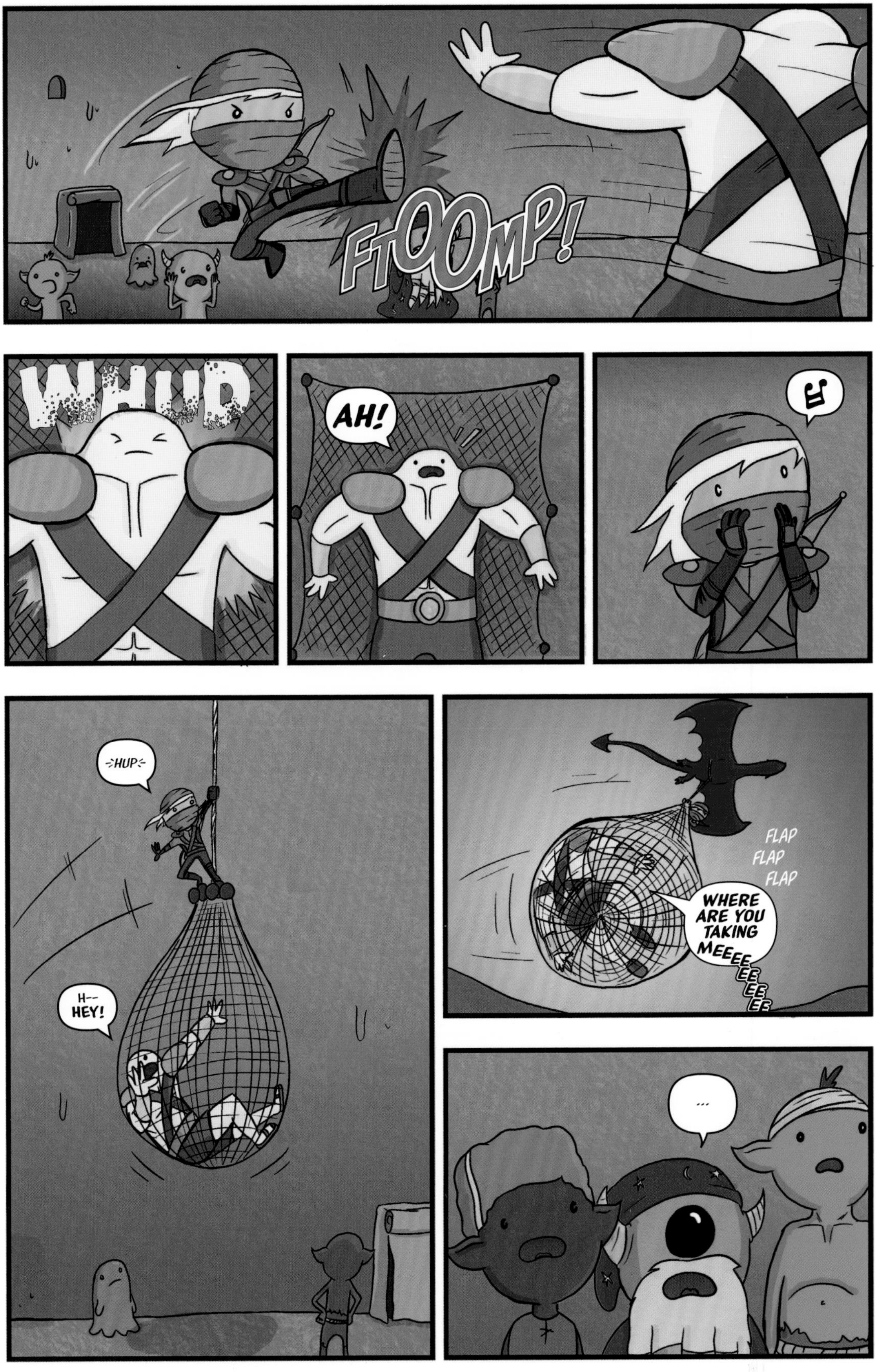
FTOOMP!
WHUD
AH!
HUP
H--
HEY!
FLAP
FLAP
FLAP
WHERE ARE YOU TAKING MEEEEEEE
...

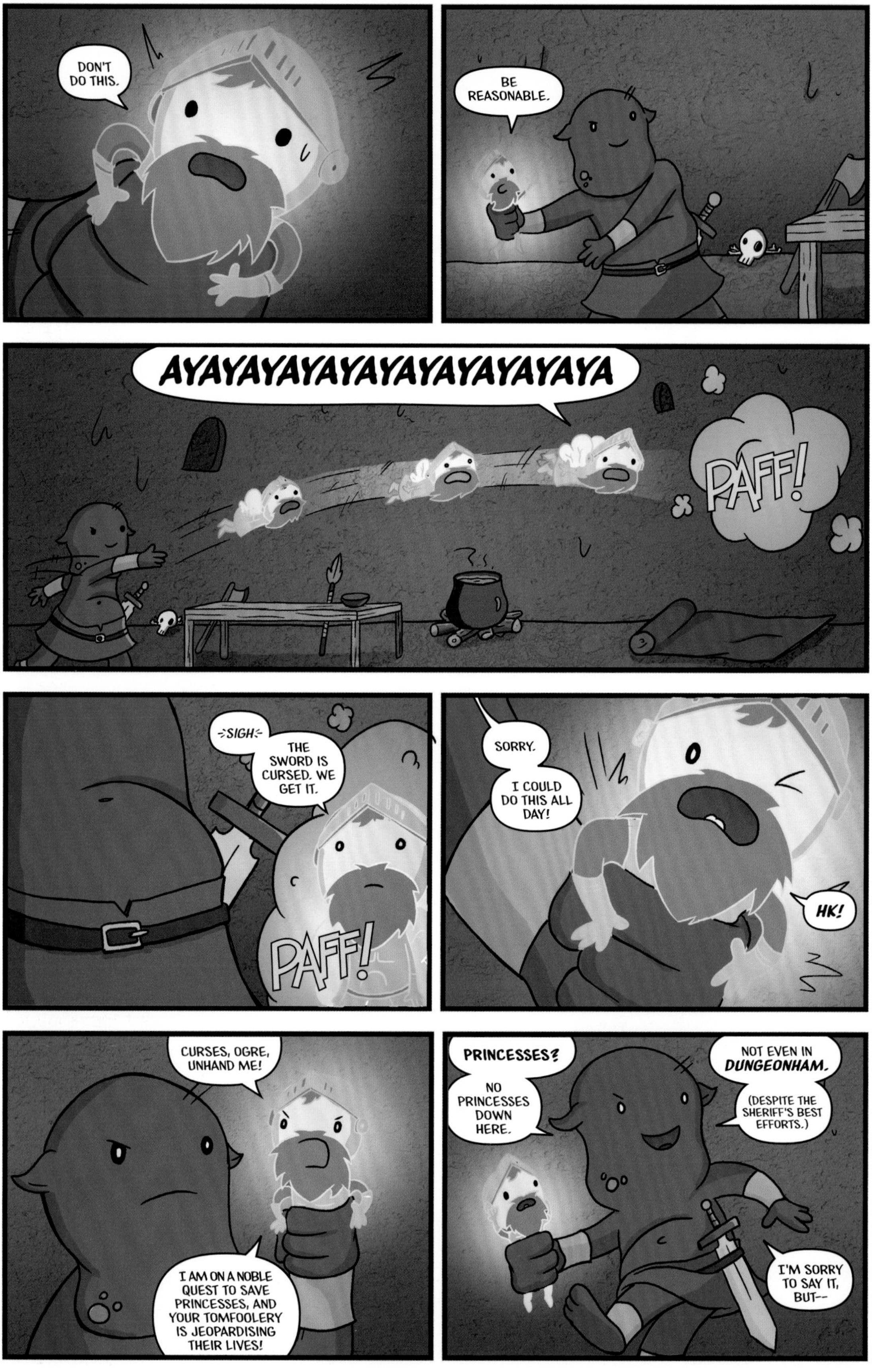
DON'T DO THIS.
BE REASONABLE.
AYAYAYAYAYAYAYAYAYAYAYAYA
PAFF!
-SIGH-
THE SWORD IS CURSED. WE GET IT.
PAFF!
SORRY.
I COULD DO THIS ALL DAY!
HK!
CURSES, OGRE, UNHAND ME!
I AM ON A NOBLE QUEST TO SAVE PRINCESSES, AND YOUR TOMFOOLERY IS JEOPARDISING THEIR LIVES!
PRINCESSES?
NO PRINCESSES DOWN HERE.
NOT EVEN IN DUNGEONHAM.
(DESPITE THE SHERIFF'S BEST EFFORTS.)
I'M SORRY TO SAY IT, BUT--

"...YOUR PRINCESSES ARE IN ANOTHER CASTLE!"

HMMMF

YI!

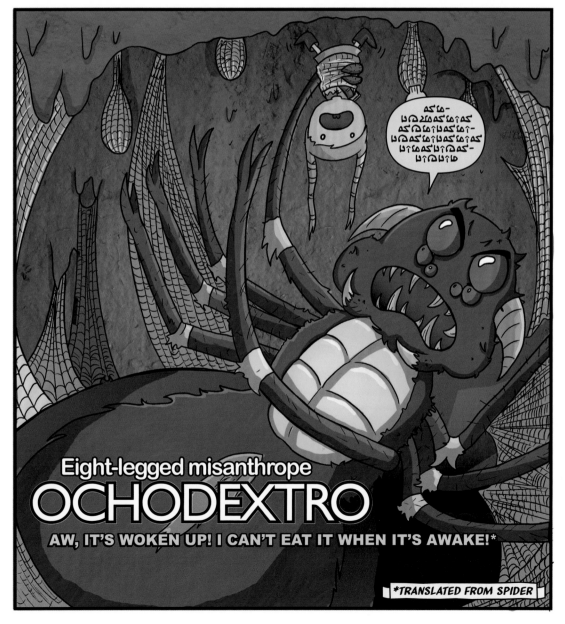

Eight-legged misanthrope

OCHODEXTRO

AW, IT'S WOKEN UP! I CAN'T EAT IT WHEN IT'S AWAKE!*

*TRANSLATED FROM SPIDER

FRNKBXTR!

MUM, YOU'RE NOT GOING TO BELIEVE THIS.

THIS BOOK... SHE SAID IT WAS WRITTEN BY A FOOL...

SO? JUST KNOCK HER OUT AGAIN SO I CAN EAT HER!

NO! WAIT!

SHE'S ACTUALLY REALLY NICE. I KNOW YOU NEED ME TO BRING YOU FOOD, BUT I'D FEEL AWFUL IF YOU ATE THIS ONE.

I WAS JUST PRETENDING TO BE A DUNGEON MASTER AT FIRST. BUT MUM, I'M REALLY GOOD AT IT. AND SHE WANTED TO HELP ME.

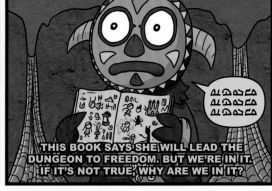

THIS BOOK SAYS SHE WILL LEAD THE DUNGEON TO FREEDOM. BUT WE'RE IN IT. IF IT'S NOT TRUE, WHY ARE WE IN IT?

HMM. I LIKE THIS DUNGEON. BUT I ALWAYS FANCIED SOMETHING BESIDE THE SEA.

...MAYBE WITH A TENNIS COURT.

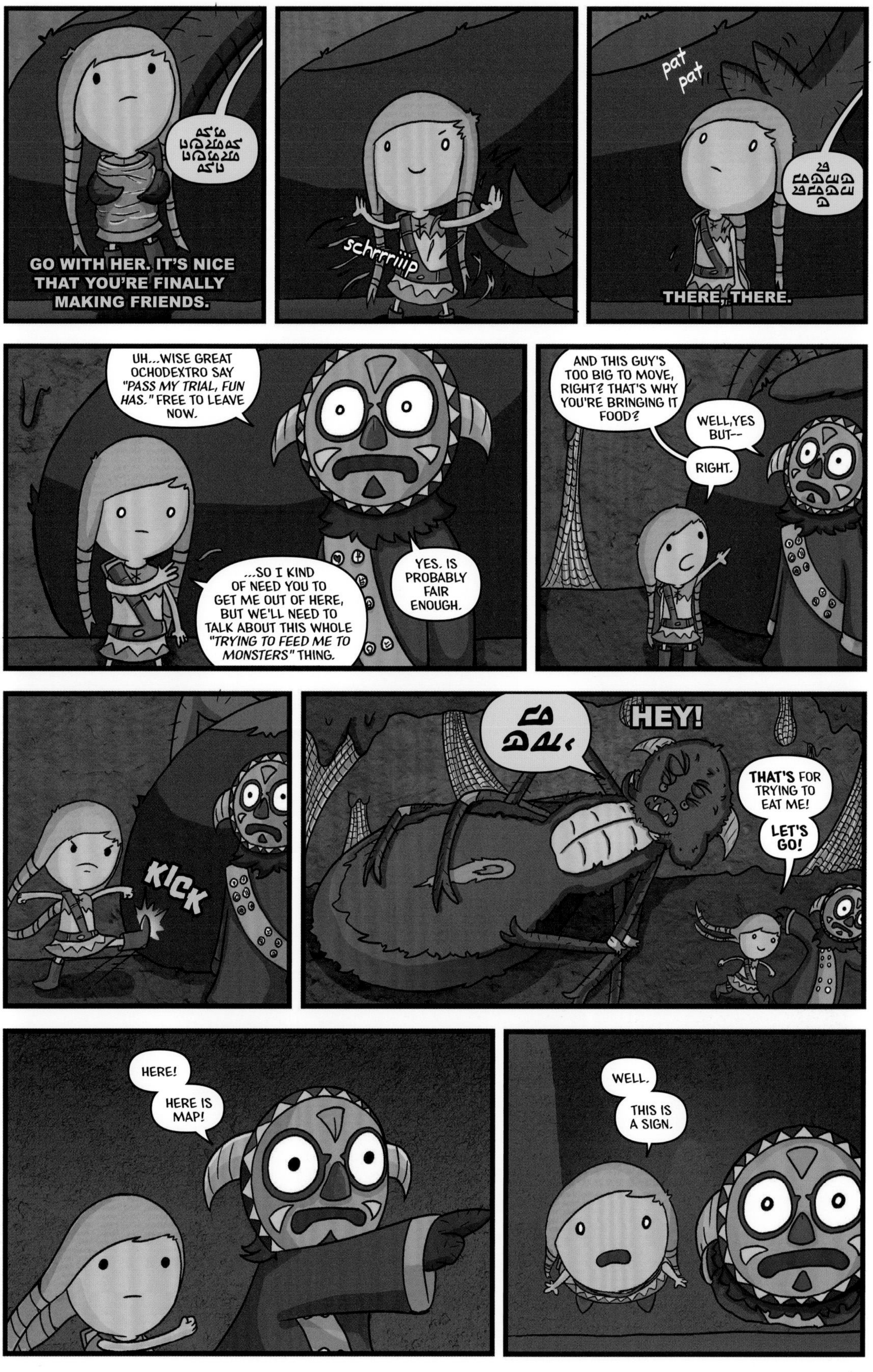
GO WITH HER. IT'S NICE THAT YOU'RE FINALLY MAKING FRIENDS.
schrrriiip
pat pat
THERE, THERE.
UH...WISE GREAT OCHODEXTRO SAY "PASS MY TRIAL, FUN HAS." FREE TO LEAVE NOW.
...SO I KIND OF NEED YOU TO GET ME OUT OF HERE, BUT WE'LL NEED TO TALK ABOUT THIS WHOLE "TRYING TO FEED ME TO MONSTERS" THING.
YES. IS PROBABLY FAIR ENOUGH.
AND THIS GUY'S TOO BIG TO MOVE, RIGHT? THAT'S WHY YOU'RE BRINGING IT FOOD?
WELL, YES BUT--
RIGHT.
KICK
HEY!
THAT'S FOR TRYING TO EAT ME!
LET'S GO!
HERE!
HERE IS MAP!
WELL.
THIS IS A SIGN.

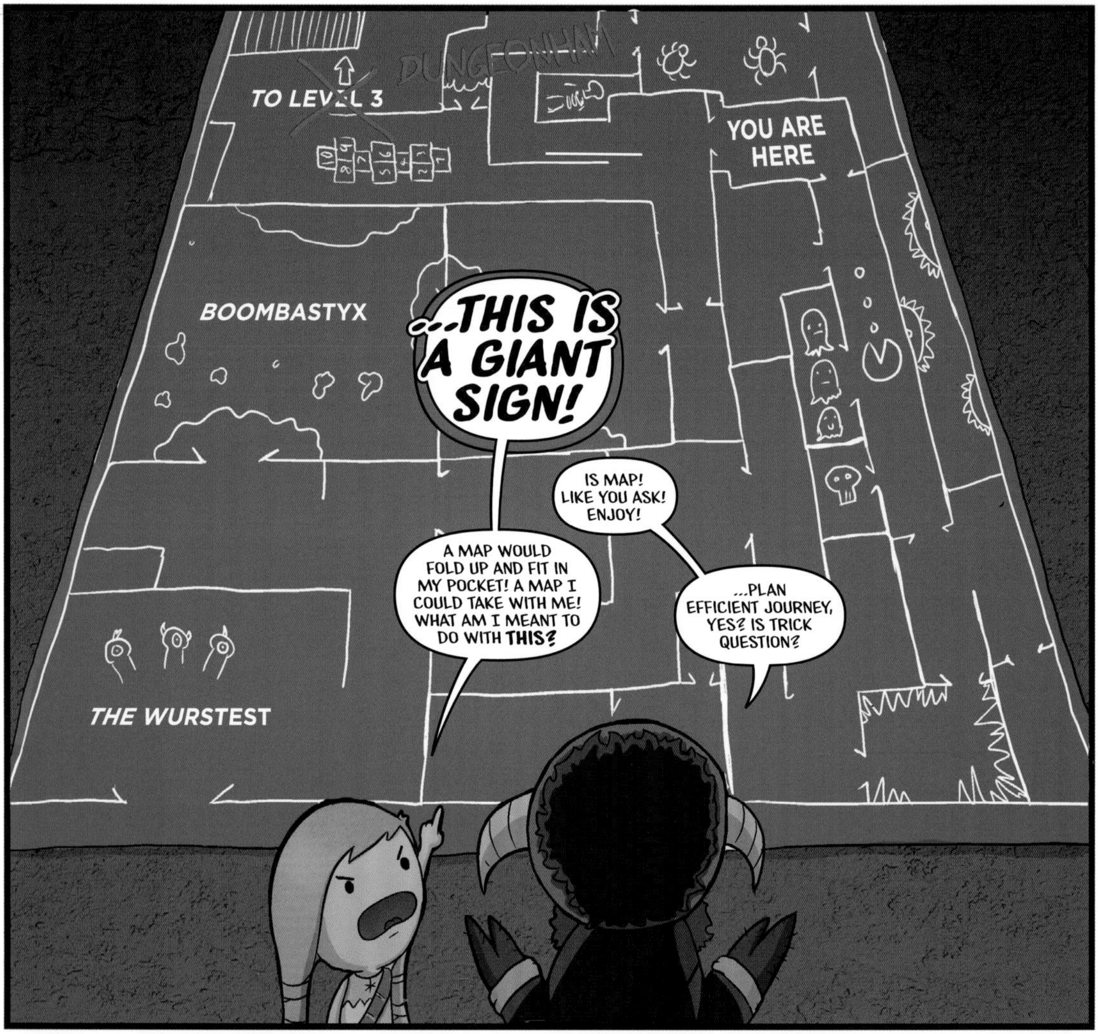
TO LEVEL 3
DUNGEONHAM
YOU ARE HERE
BOOMBASTYX
THE WURSTEST
...THIS IS A GIANT SIGN!
A MAP WOULD FOLD UP AND FIT IN MY POCKET! A MAP I COULD TAKE WITH ME! WHAT AM I MEANT TO DO WITH THIS?
IS MAP! LIKE YOU ASK! ENJOY!
...PLAN EFFICIENT JOURNEY, YES? IS TRICK QUESTION?

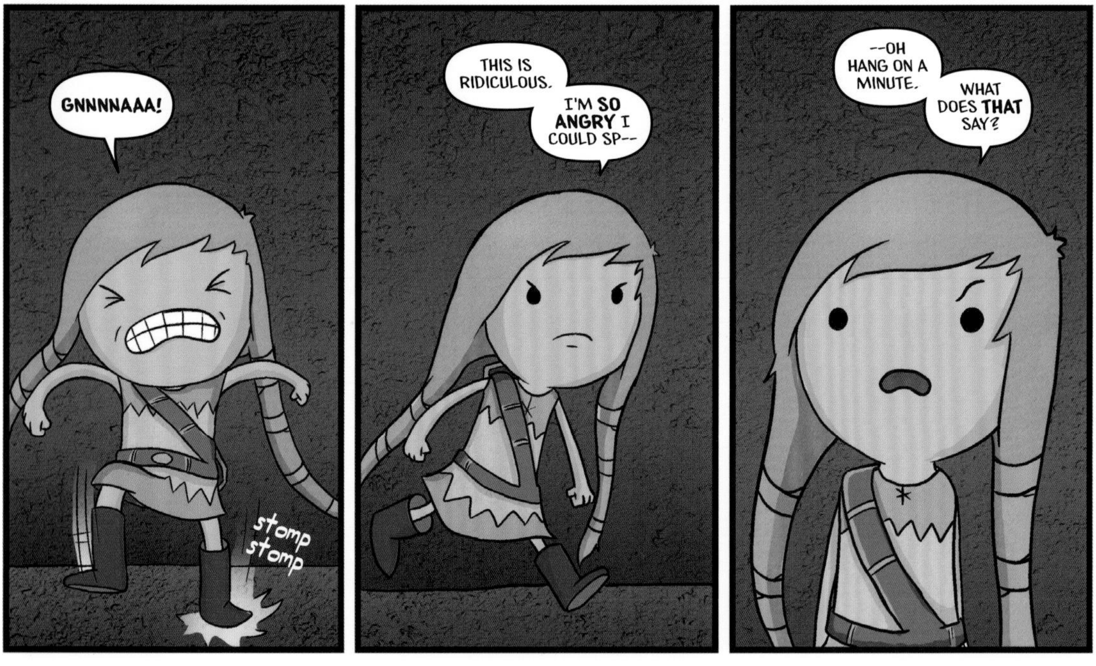
GNNNNAAA!
stomp stomp
THIS IS RIDICULOUS.
I'M SO ANGRY I COULD SP--
--OH HANG ON A MINUTE.
WHAT DOES THAT SAY?

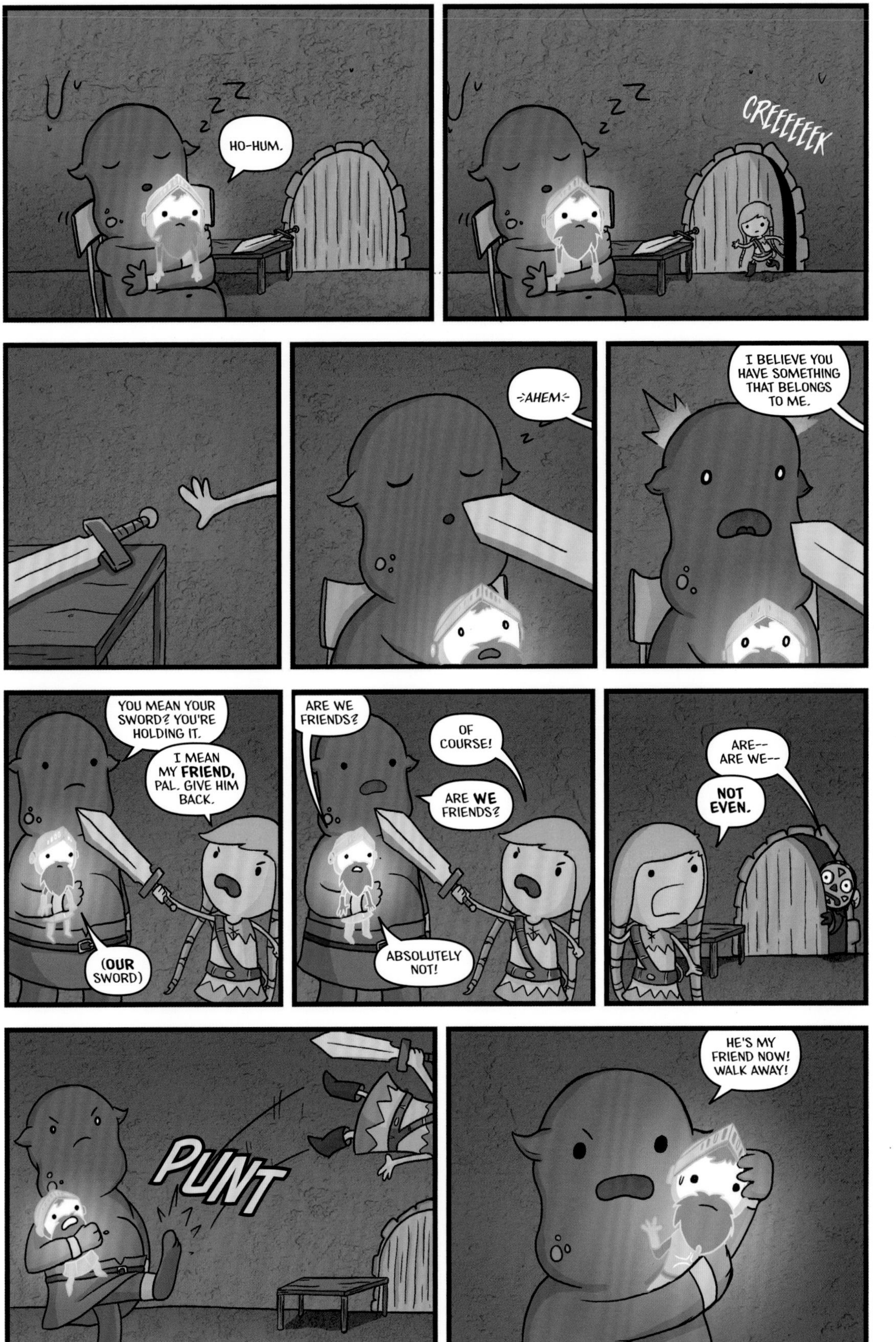

HO-HUM.
CREEEEEEK
-AHEM-
I BELIEVE YOU HAVE SOMETHING THAT BELONGS TO ME.
YOU MEAN YOUR SWORD? YOU'RE HOLDING IT.
I MEAN MY **FRIEND,** PAL. GIVE HIM BACK.
(**OUR** SWORD)
ARE WE FRIENDS?
OF COURSE!
ARE **WE** FRIENDS?
ABSOLUTELY NOT!
ARE-- ARE WE--
NOT EVEN.
PUNT
HE'S MY FRIEND NOW! WALK AWAY!

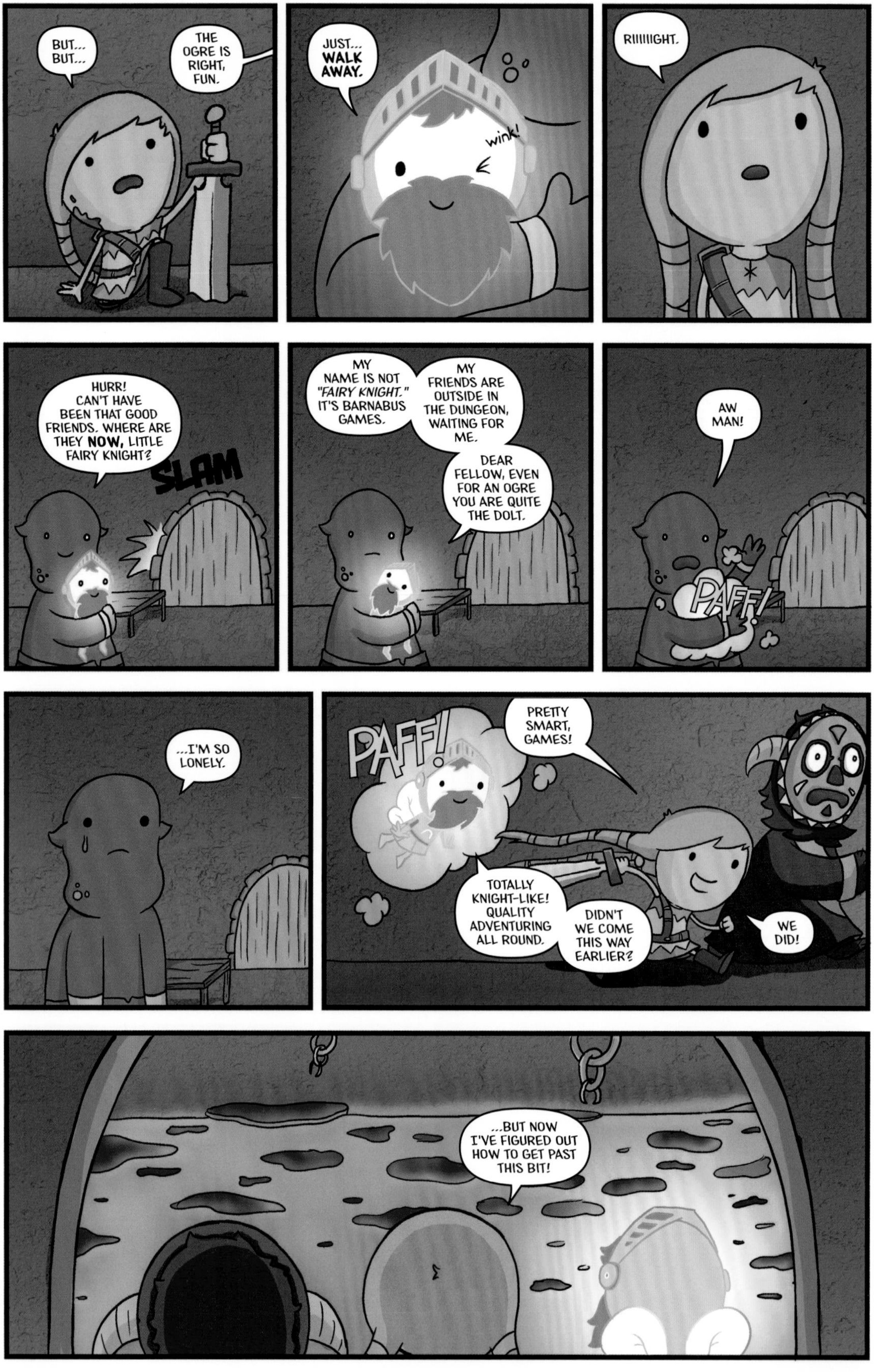
BUT...
BUT...
THE OGRE IS RIGHT, FUN.
JUST... WALK AWAY.
wink!
RIIIIIIGHT.
HURR! CAN'T HAVE BEEN THAT GOOD FRIENDS. WHERE ARE THEY NOW, LITTLE FAIRY KNIGHT?
SLAM
MY NAME IS NOT "FAIRY KNIGHT." IT'S BARNABUS GAMES.
MY FRIENDS ARE OUTSIDE IN THE DUNGEON, WAITING FOR ME.
DEAR FELLOW, EVEN FOR AN OGRE YOU ARE QUITE THE DOLT.
AW MAN!
PAFF!
...I'M SO LONELY.
PAFF!
PRETTY SMART, GAMES!
TOTALLY KNIGHT-LIKE! QUALITY ADVENTURING ALL ROUND.
DIDN'T WE COME THIS WAY EARLIER?
WE DID!
...BUT NOW I'VE FIGURED OUT HOW TO GET PAST THIS BIT!

SO, GAMES, YOU'LL DISTRACT THE MONSTER WHILE FRANK GETS US OVER TO THE OTHER SIDE.

HOW WILL I DISTRACT IT?

YOU KNOW HOW.

AH YES!

COO-EE!

MISTER LAVALAVA!

AND HOW IS FRANK GETTING YOU OVER?

YOU. KNOW. HOW.

THIS WAY! THIS WAY! NOTSCARED NOTSCARED WAWAWAWA

THWIP

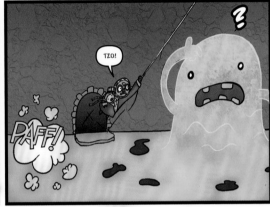

TZO!

PAFF!

WHERE DID THE ROPE COME FROM?

PAFF!

YOU DON'T WANT TO KNOW.

HUP

CAUTION TEAM!

SO HERE'S THE THING I FIGURED.

YOUR LAVA MONSTER ISN'T TRYING TO ATTACK US....

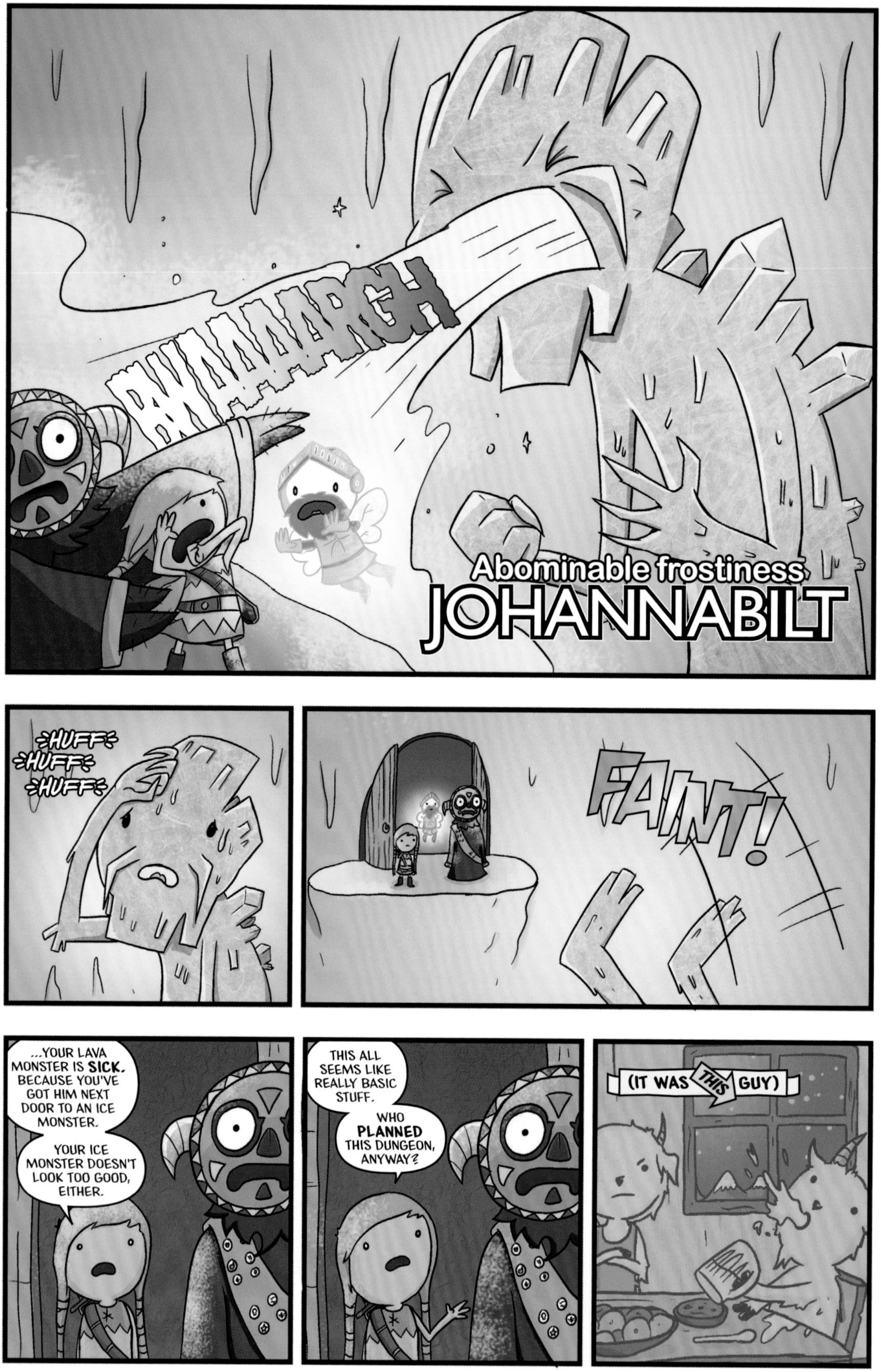
BWAAARGH
Abominable frostiness
JOHANNABILT
HUFF
HUFF
HUFF
FAINT!
...YOUR LAVA MONSTER IS **SICK.** BECAUSE YOU'VE GOT HIM NEXT DOOR TO AN ICE MONSTER.
YOUR ICE MONSTER DOESN'T LOOK TOO GOOD, EITHER.
THIS ALL SEEMS LIKE REALLY BASIC STUFF.
WHO **PLANNED** THIS DUNGEON, ANYWAY?
(IT WAS THIS GUY)

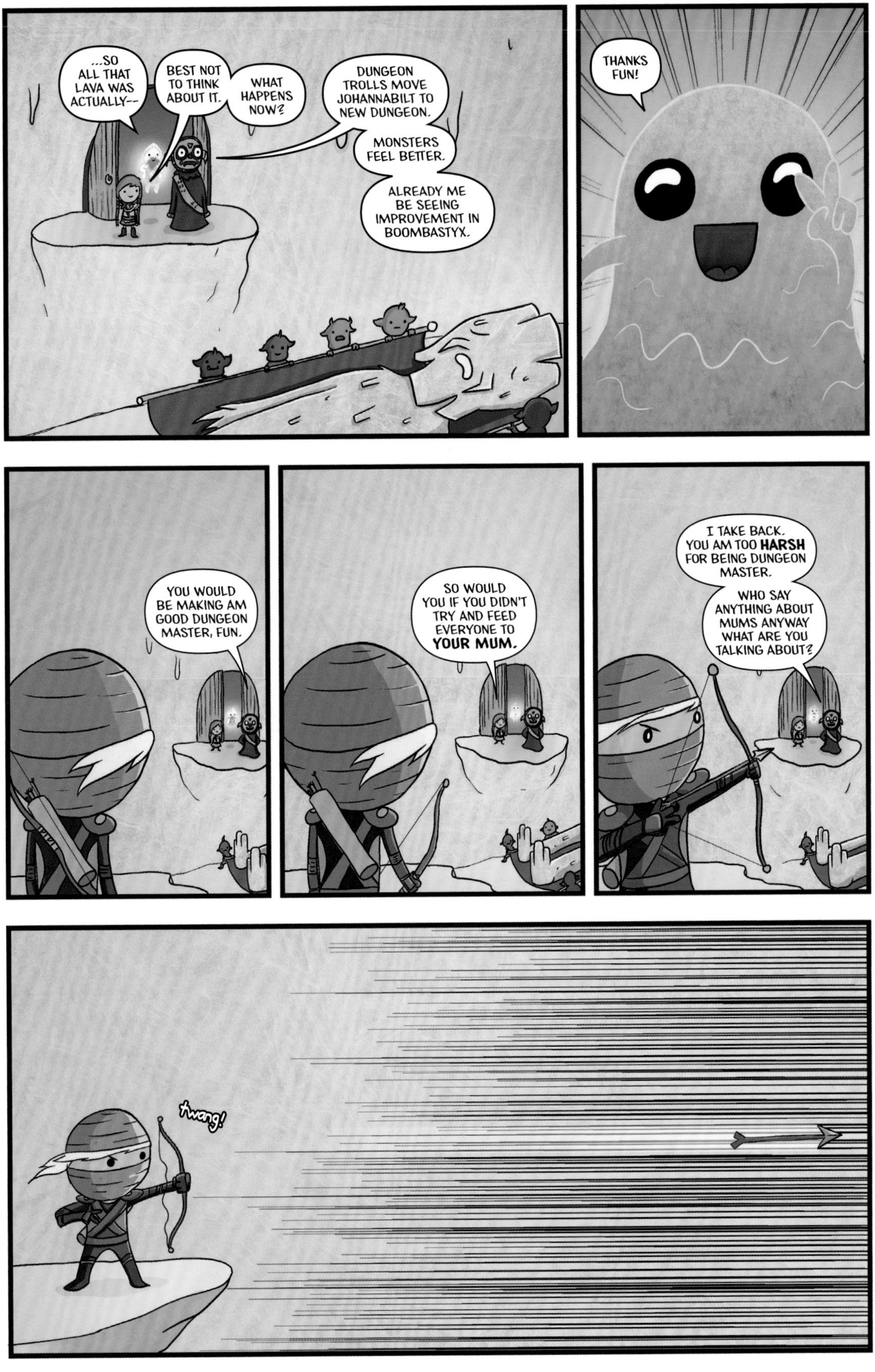
...SO ALL THAT LAVA WAS ACTUALLY--
BEST NOT TO THINK ABOUT IT.
WHAT HAPPENS NOW?
DUNGEON TROLLS MOVE JOHANNABILT TO NEW DUNGEON.
MONSTERS FEEL BETTER.
ALREADY ME BE SEEING IMPROVEMENT IN BOOMBASTYX.
THANKS FUN!
YOU WOULD BE MAKING AM GOOD DUNGEON MASTER, FUN.
SO WOULD YOU IF YOU DIDN'T TRY AND FEED EVERYONE TO **YOUR MUM.**
I TAKE BACK. YOU AM TOO **HARSH** FOR BEING DUNGEON MASTER.
WHO SAY ANYTHING ABOUT MUMS ANYWAY WHAT ARE YOU TALKING ABOUT?
twang!

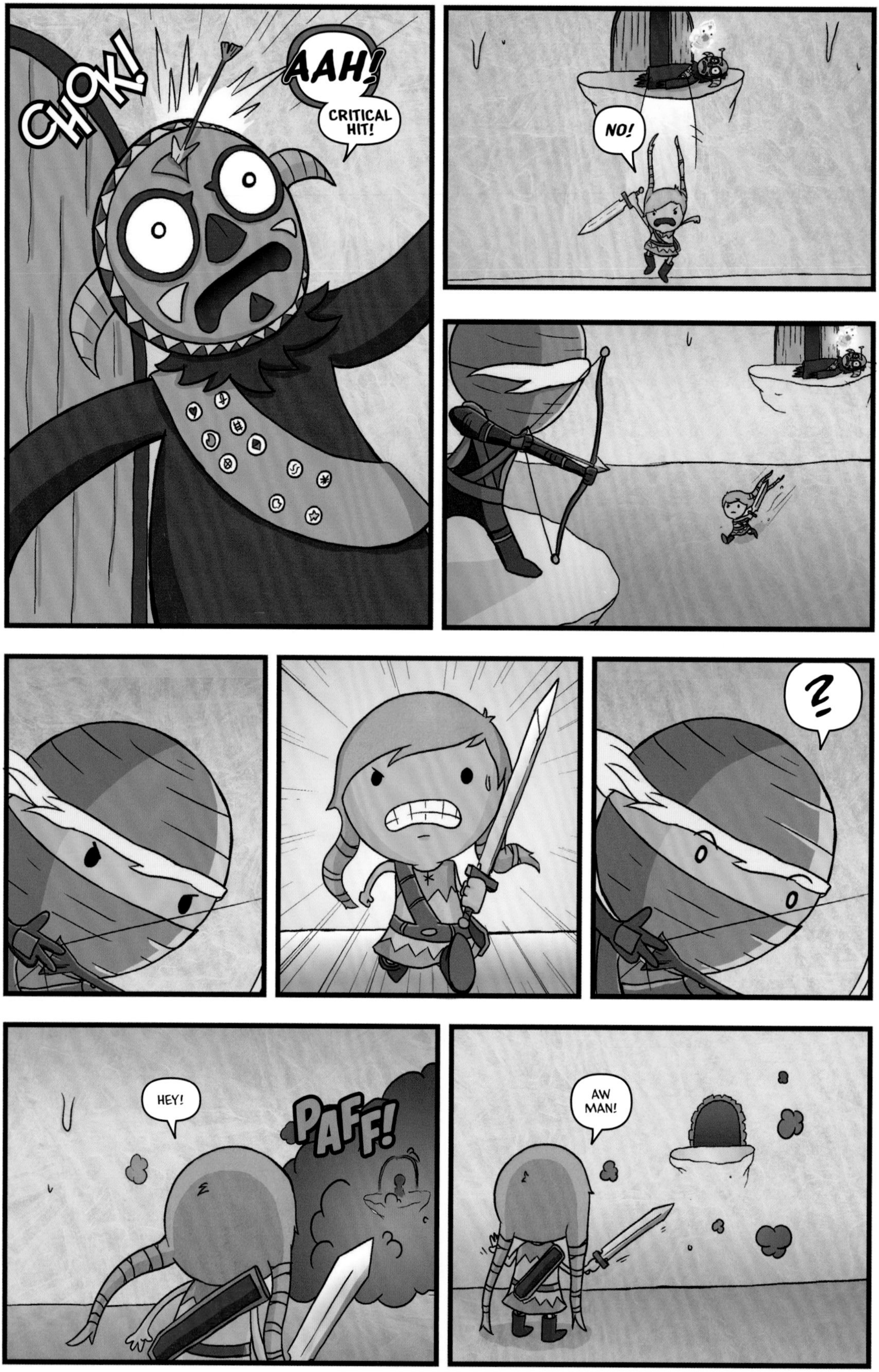
CHOK!
AAH!
CRITICAL HIT!
NO!
?
HEY!
PAFF!
AW MAN!

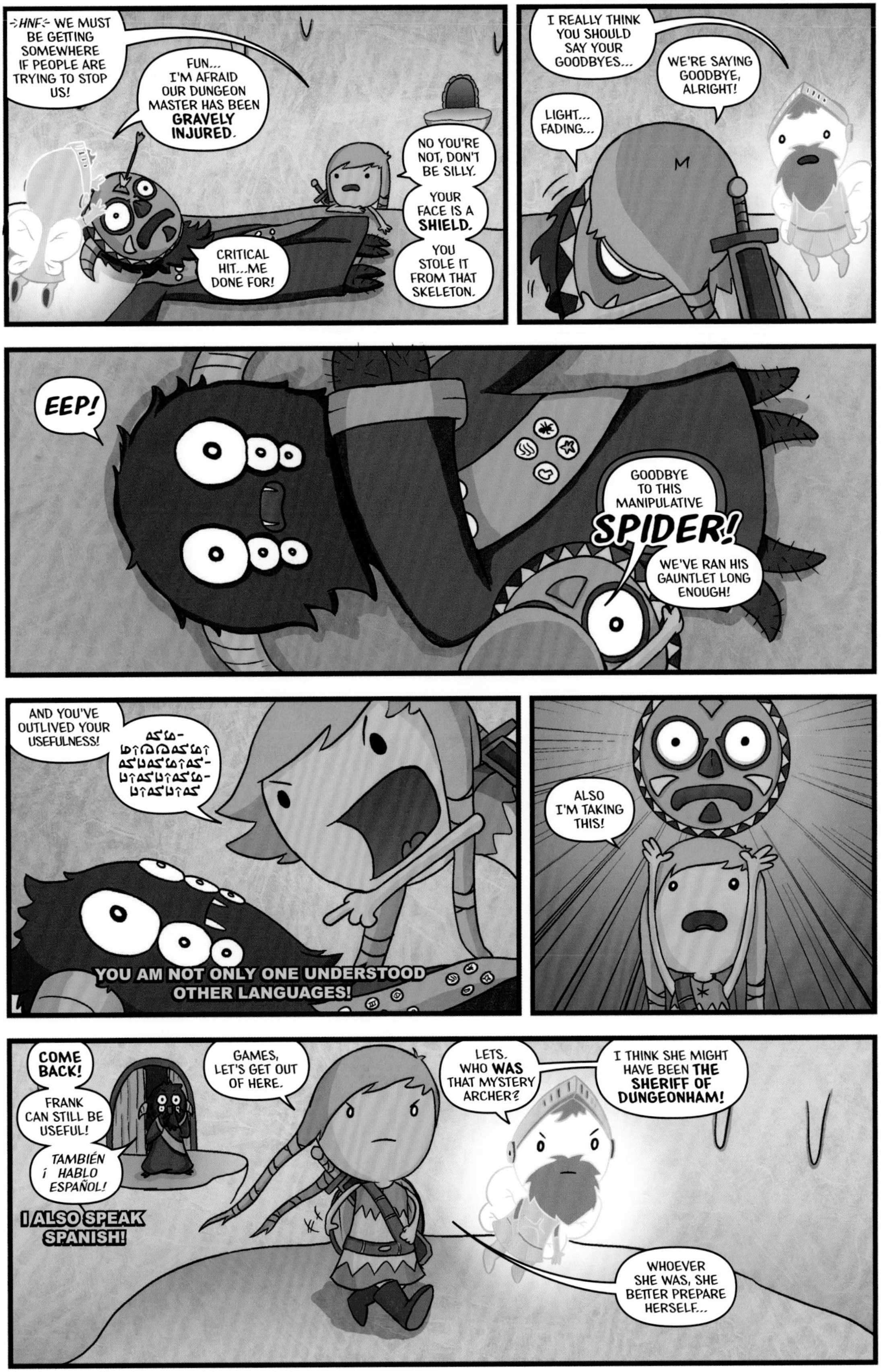

HNF WE MUST BE GETTING SOMEWHERE IF PEOPLE ARE TRYING TO STOP US!
FUN... I'M AFRAID OUR DUNGEON MASTER HAS BEEN **GRAVELY INJURED**.
NO YOU'RE NOT, DON'T BE SILLY.
YOUR FACE IS A **SHIELD**.
YOU STOLE IT FROM THAT SKELETON.
CRITICAL HIT...ME DONE FOR!
I REALLY THINK YOU SHOULD SAY YOUR GOODBYES...
WE'RE SAYING GOODBYE, ALRIGHT!
LIGHT... FADING...
EEP!
GOODBYE TO THIS MANIPULATIVE **SPIDER!**
WE'VE RAN HIS GAUNTLET LONG ENOUGH!
AND YOU'VE OUTLIVED YOUR USEFULNESS!
YOU AM NOT ONLY ONE UNDERSTOOD OTHER LANGUAGES!
ALSO I'M TAKING THIS!
COME BACK!
FRANK CAN STILL BE USEFUL!
TAMBIÉN HABLO ESPAÑOL!
I ALSO SPEAK SPANISH!
GAMES, LET'S GET OUT OF HERE.
LETS. WHO **WAS** THAT MYSTERY ARCHER?
I THINK SHE MIGHT HAVE BEEN **THE SHERIFF OF DUNGEONHAM!**
WHOEVER SHE WAS, SHE BETTER PREPARE HERSELF...

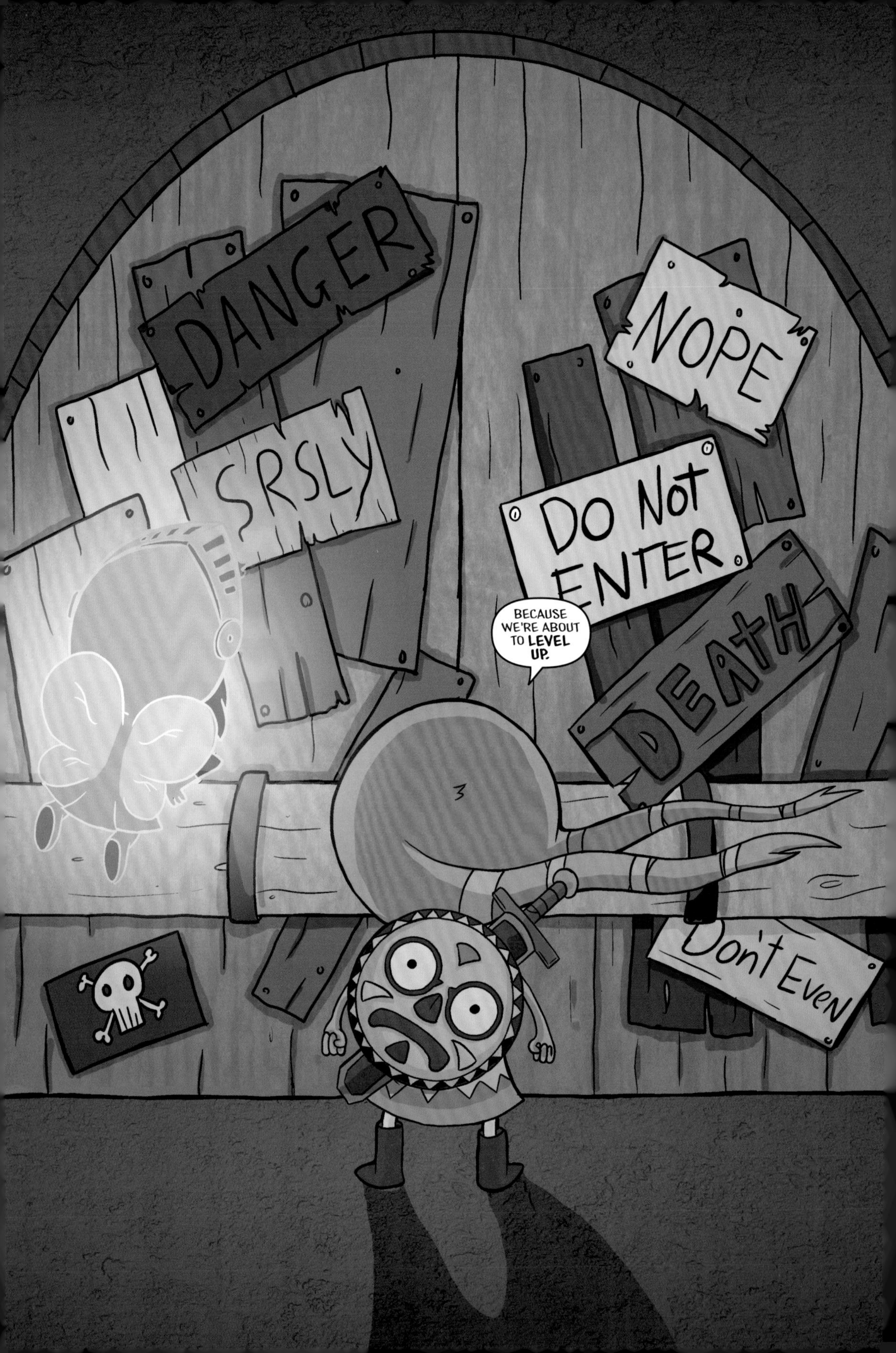
DANGER
NOPE
SRSLY
DO NOT ENTER
BECAUSE WE'RE ABOUT TO LEVEL UP.
DEATH
Don't Even

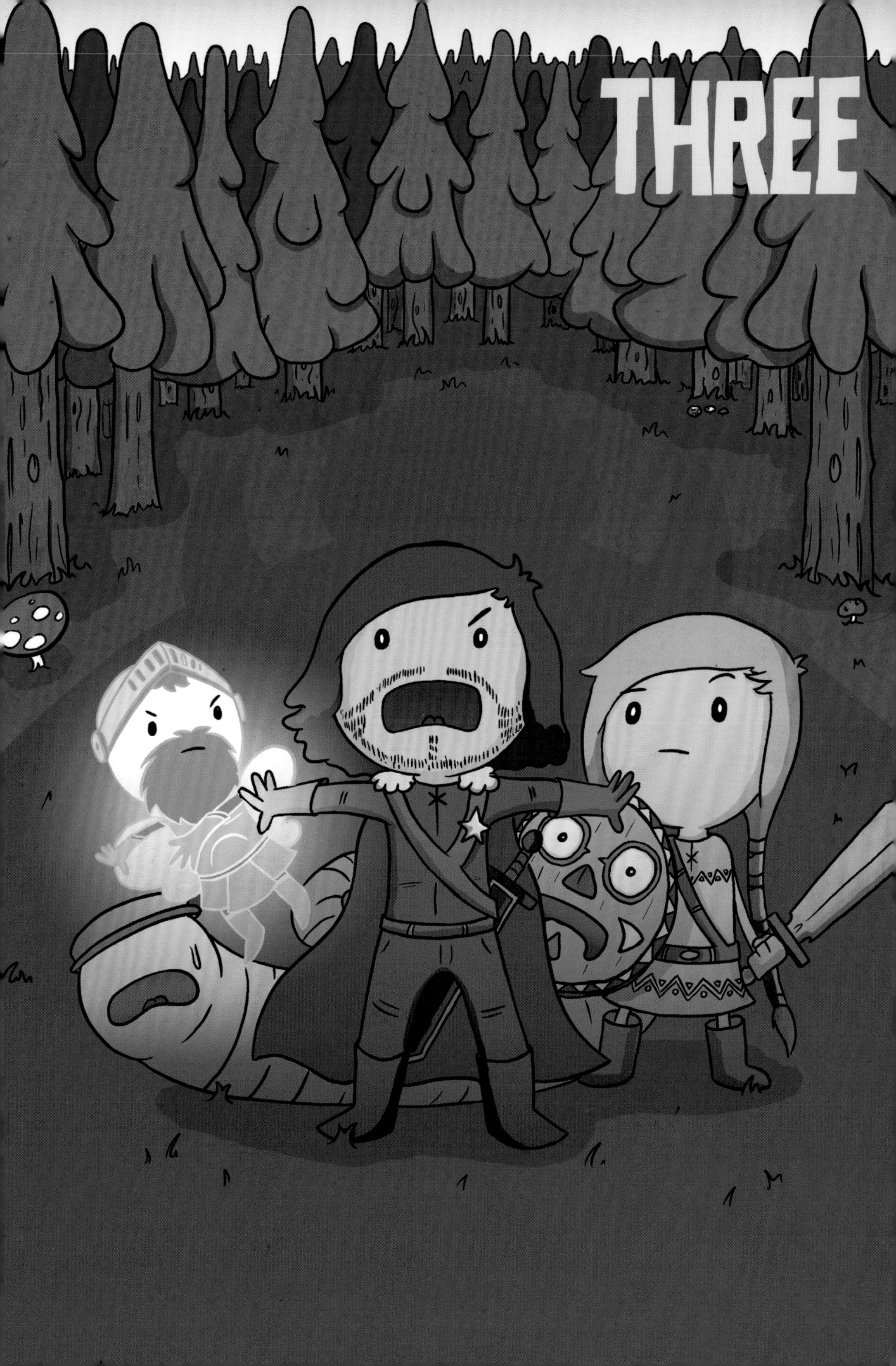
THREE

"MY DUNGEON SENSE IS TINGLING!"

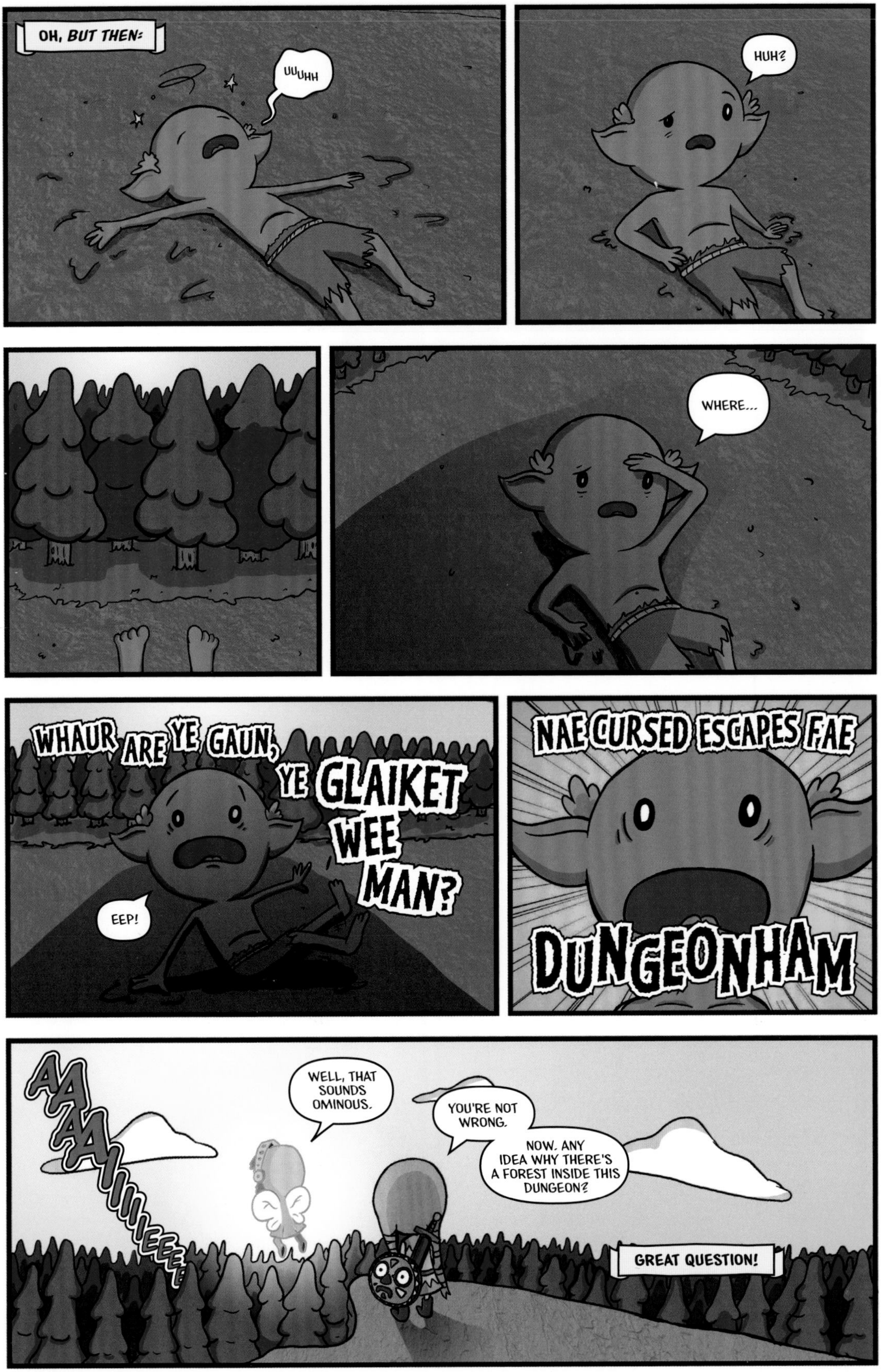
OH, BUT THEN:
UUUHH
HUH?
WHERE...
WHAUR ARE YE GAUN, YE GLAIKET WEE MAN?
EEP!
NAE CURSED ESCAPES FAE DUNGEONHAM
AAAAIIIIIEEEE
WELL, THAT SOUNDS OMINOUS.
YOU'RE NOT WRONG.
NOW, ANY IDEA WHY THERE'S A FOREST INSIDE THIS DUNGEON?
GREAT QUESTION!

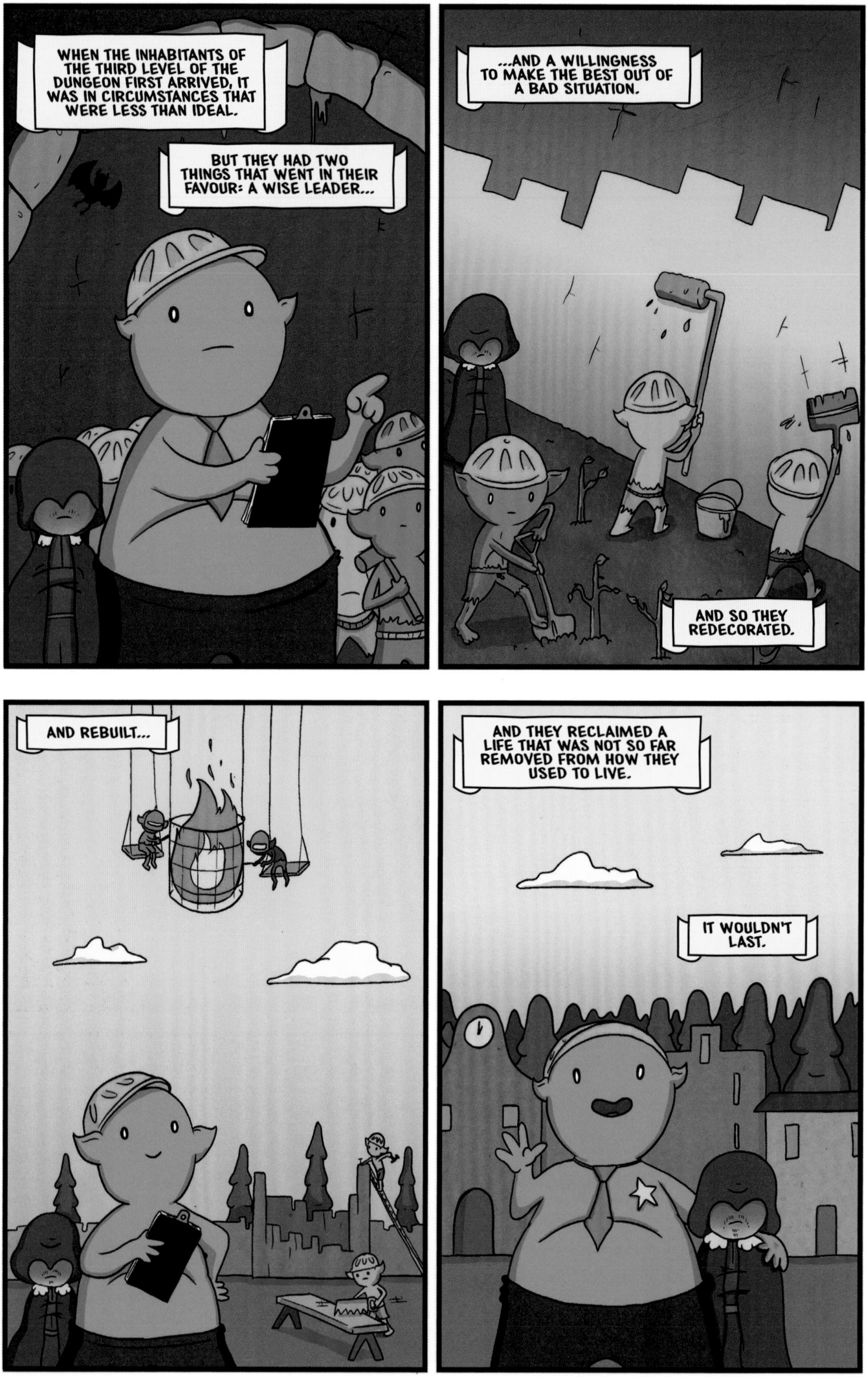
WHEN THE INHABITANTS OF THE THIRD LEVEL OF THE DUNGEON FIRST ARRIVED, IT WAS IN CIRCUMSTANCES THAT WERE LESS THAN IDEAL.
BUT THEY HAD TWO THINGS THAT WENT IN THEIR FAVOUR: A WISE LEADER...
...AND A WILLINGNESS TO MAKE THE BEST OUT OF A BAD SITUATION.
AND SO THEY REDECORATED.
AND REBUILT...
AND THEY RECLAIMED A LIFE THAT WAS NOT SO FAR REMOVED FROM HOW THEY USED TO LIVE.
IT WOULDN'T LAST.

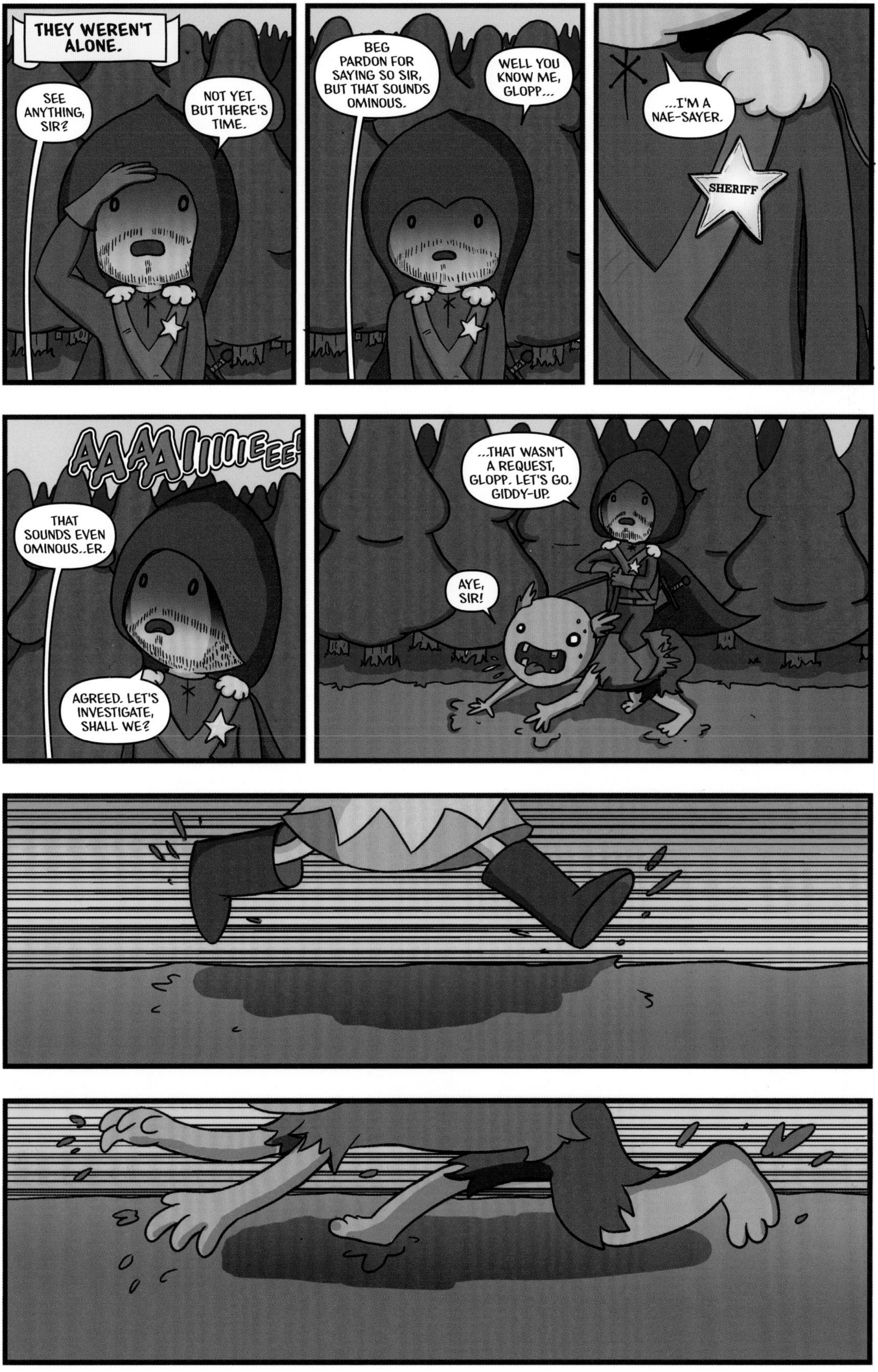
THEY WEREN'T ALONE.
SEE ANYTHING, SIR?
NOT YET. BUT THERE'S TIME.
BEG PARDON FOR SAYING SO SIR, BUT THAT SOUNDS OMINOUS.
WELL YOU KNOW ME, GLOPP...
...I'M A NAE-SAYER.
SHERIFF
AAAAIIIIIEEE
THAT SOUNDS EVEN OMINOUS..ER.
AGREED. LET'S INVESTIGATE, SHALL WE?
...THAT WASN'T A REQUEST, GLOPP. LET'S GO. GIDDY-UP.
AYE, SIR!

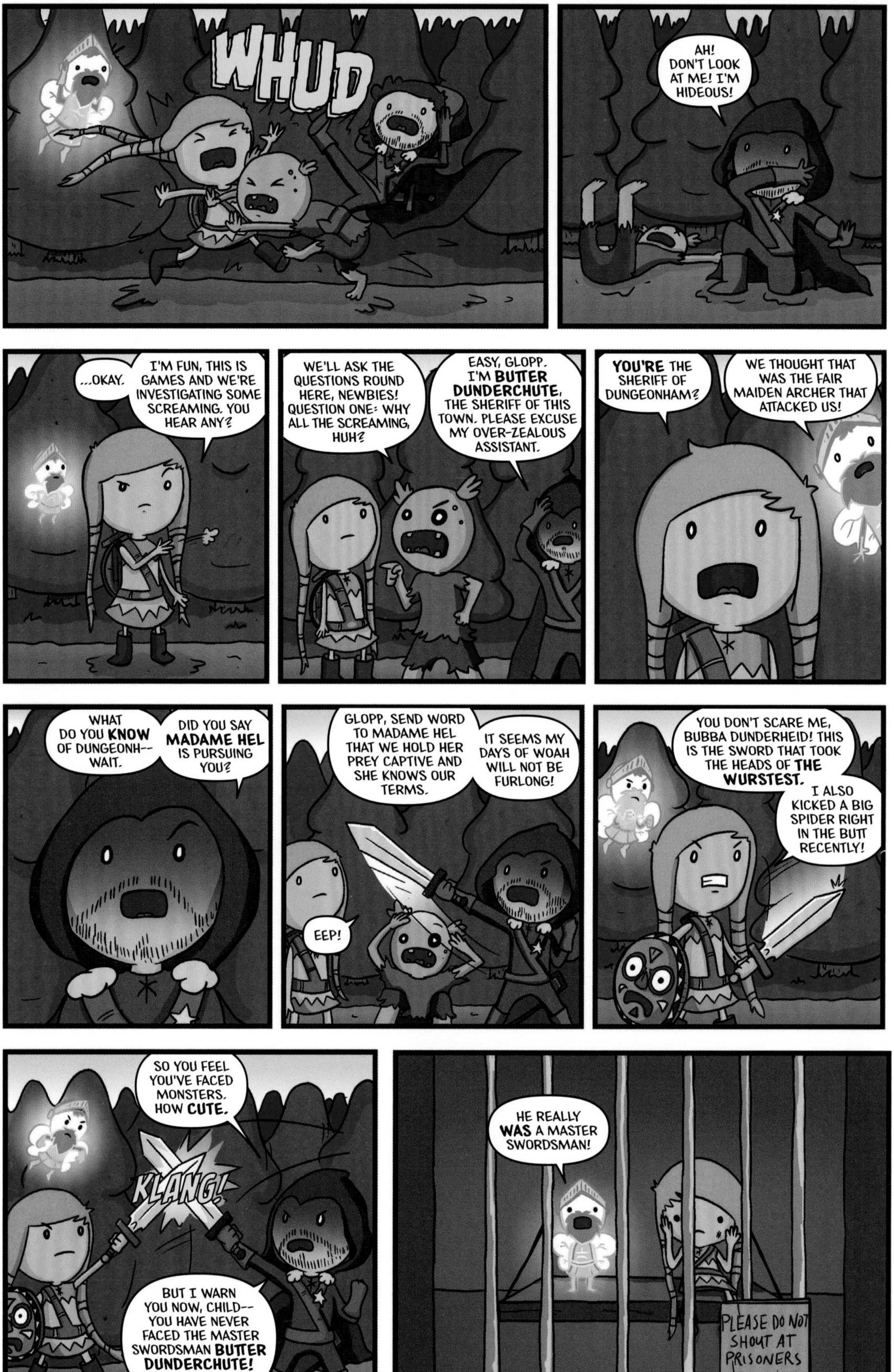
WHUD
AH! DON'T LOOK AT ME! I'M HIDEOUS!
...OKAY.
I'M FUN, THIS IS GAMES AND WE'RE INVESTIGATING SOME SCREAMING. YOU HEAR ANY?
WE'LL ASK THE QUESTIONS ROUND HERE, NEWBIES! QUESTION ONE: WHY ALL THE SCREAMING, HUH?
EASY, GLOPP. I'M **BUTTER DUNDERCHUTE**, THE SHERIFF OF THIS TOWN. PLEASE EXCUSE MY OVER-ZEALOUS ASSISTANT.
YOU'RE THE SHERIFF OF DUNGEONHAM?
WE THOUGHT THAT WAS THE FAIR MAIDEN ARCHER THAT ATTACKED US!
WHAT DO YOU **KNOW** OF DUNGEONH-- WAIT.
DID YOU SAY **MADAME HEL** IS PURSUING YOU?
GLOPP, SEND WORD TO MADAME HEL THAT WE HOLD HER PREY CAPTIVE AND SHE KNOWS OUR TERMS.
IT SEEMS MY DAYS OF WOAH WILL NOT BE FURLONG!
EEP!
YOU DON'T SCARE ME, BUBBA DUNDERHEID! THIS IS THE SWORD THAT TOOK THE HEADS OF **THE WURSTEST.**
I ALSO KICKED A BIG SPIDER RIGHT IN THE BUTT RECENTLY!
SO YOU FEEL YOU'VE FACED MONSTERS. HOW **CUTE.**
KLANG!
BUT I WARN YOU NOW, CHILD-- YOU HAVE NEVER FACED THE MASTER SWORDSMAN **BUTTER DUNDERCHUTE!**
HE REALLY **WAS** A MASTER SWORDSMAN!
PLEASE DO NOT SHOUT AT PRISONERS

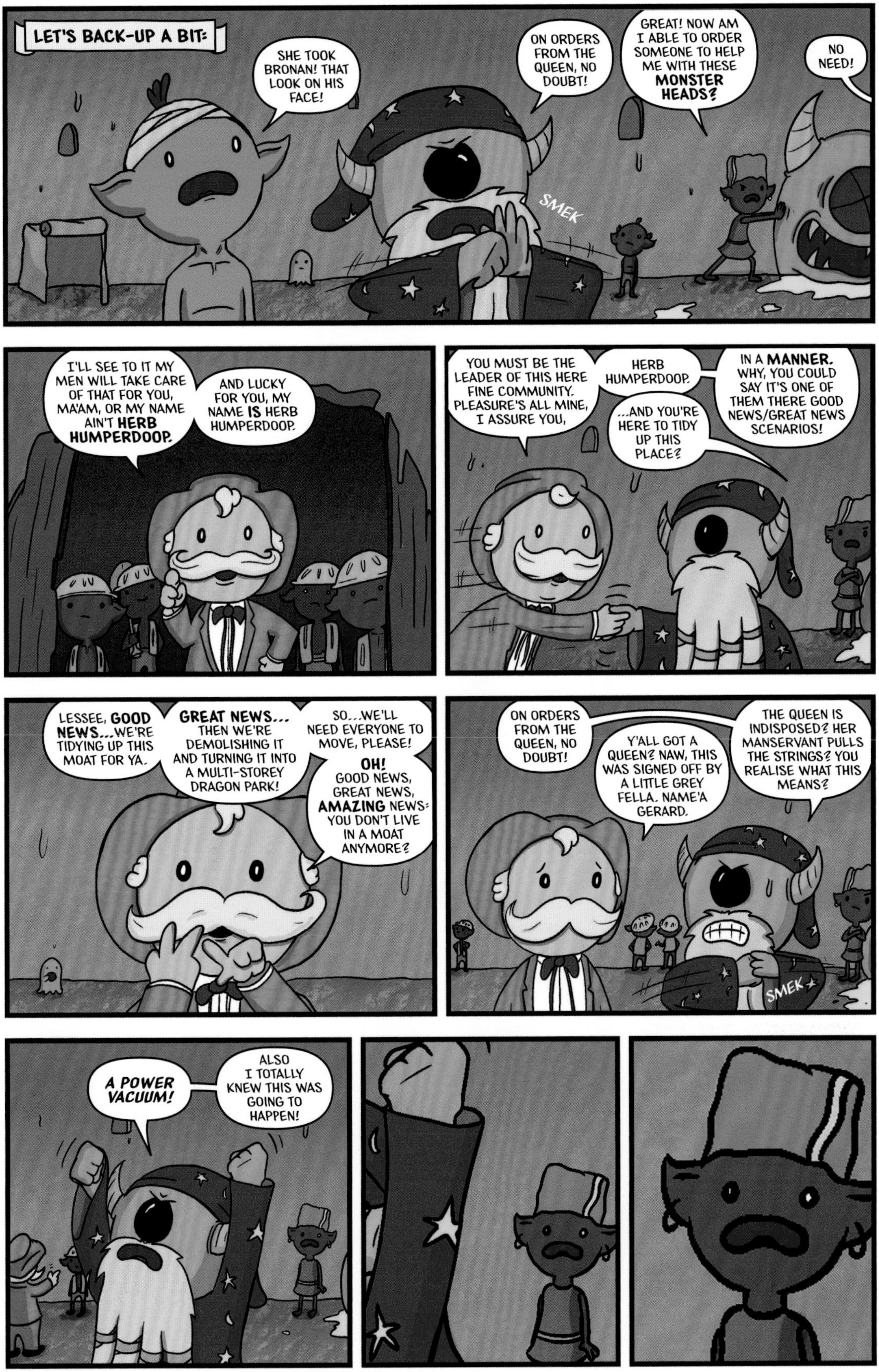
LET'S BACK-UP A BIT:
SHE TOOK BRONAN! THAT LOOK ON HIS FACE!
ON ORDERS FROM THE QUEEN, NO DOUBT!
GREAT! NOW AM I ABLE TO ORDER SOMEONE TO HELP ME WITH THESE **MONSTER HEADS?**
NO NEED!
SMEK
I'LL SEE TO IT MY MEN WILL TAKE CARE OF THAT FOR YOU, MA'AM, OR MY NAME AIN'T **HERB HUMPERDOOP.**
AND LUCKY FOR YOU, MY NAME **IS** HERB HUMPERDOOP.
YOU MUST BE THE LEADER OF THIS HERE FINE COMMUNITY. PLEASURE'S ALL MINE, I ASSURE YOU,
HERB HUMPERDOOP.
...AND YOU'RE HERE TO TIDY UP THIS PLACE?
IN A **MANNER.** WHY, YOU COULD SAY IT'S ONE OF THEM THERE GOOD NEWS/GREAT NEWS SCENARIOS!
LESSEE, **GOOD NEWS...** WE'RE TIDYING UP THIS MOAT FOR YA.
GREAT NEWS... THEN WE'RE DEMOLISHING IT AND TURNING IT INTO A MULTI-STOREY DRAGON PARK!
SO...WE'LL NEED EVERYONE TO MOVE, PLEASE!
OH! GOOD NEWS, GREAT NEWS, **AMAZING** NEWS: YOU DON'T LIVE IN A MOAT ANYMORE?
ON ORDERS FROM THE QUEEN, NO DOUBT!
Y'ALL GOT A QUEEN? NAW, THIS WAS SIGNED OFF BY A LITTLE GREY FELLA. NAME'A GERARD.
THE QUEEN IS INDISPOSED? HER MANSERVANT PULLS THE STRINGS? YOU REALISE WHAT THIS MEANS?
SMEK
A POWER VACUUM!
ALSO I TOTALLY KNEW THIS WAS GOING TO HAPPEN!

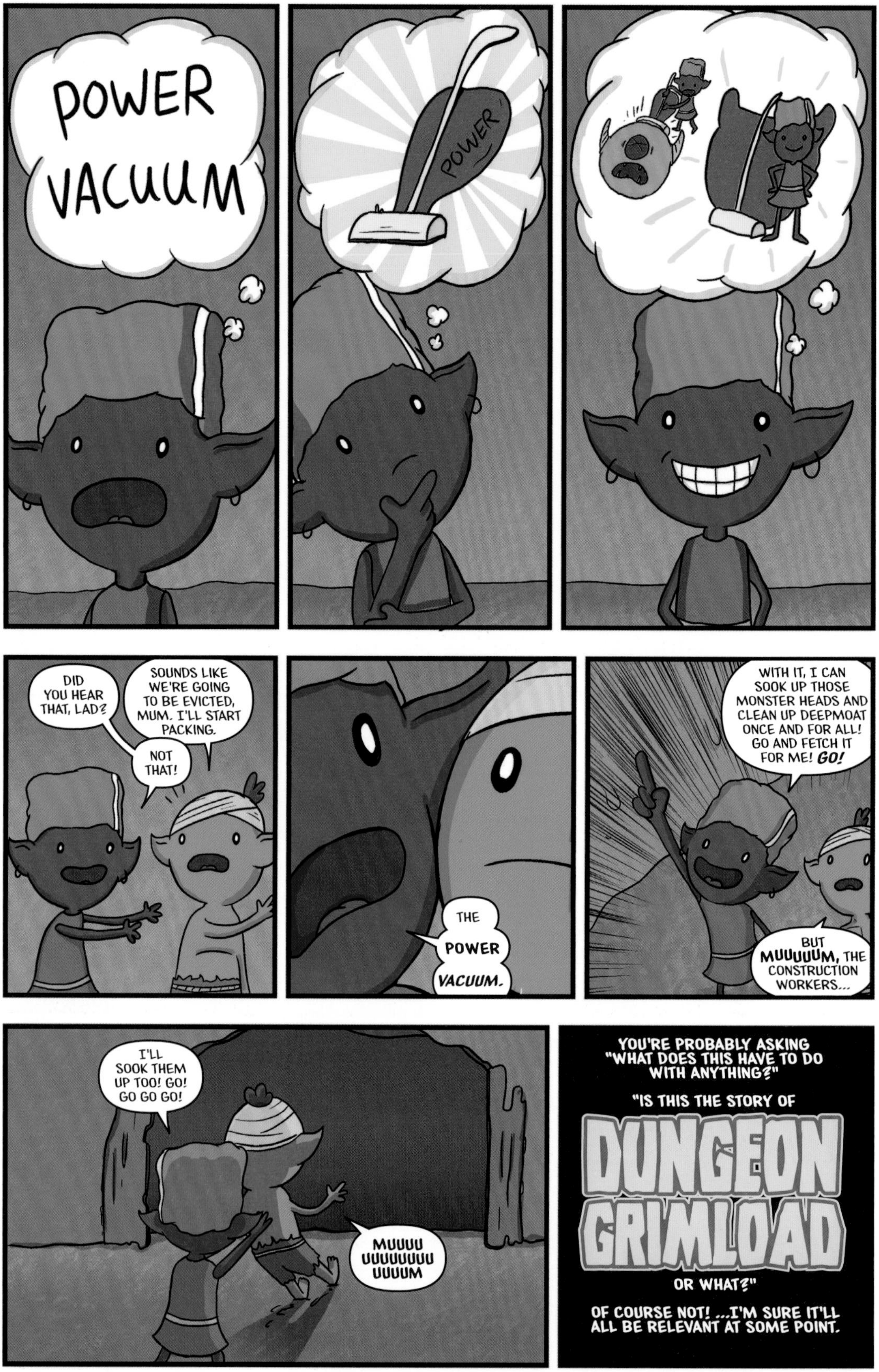
POWER VACUUM
POWER
DID YOU HEAR THAT, LAD?
SOUNDS LIKE WE'RE GOING TO BE EVICTED, MUM. I'LL START PACKING.
NOT THAT!
THE POWER VACUUM.
WITH IT, I CAN SOOK UP THOSE MONSTER HEADS AND CLEAN UP DEEPMOAT ONCE AND FOR ALL! GO AND FETCH IT FOR ME! GO!
BUT MUUUUUM, THE CONSTRUCTION WORKERS...
I'LL SOOK THEM UP TOO! GO! GO GO GO!
MUUUU UUUUUUUU UUUUM
YOU'RE PROBABLY ASKING "WHAT DOES THIS HAVE TO DO WITH ANYTHING?"
"IS THIS THE STORY OF
DUNGEON GRIMLOAD
OR WHAT?"
OF COURSE NOT! ...I'M SURE IT'LL ALL BE RELEVANT AT SOME POINT.

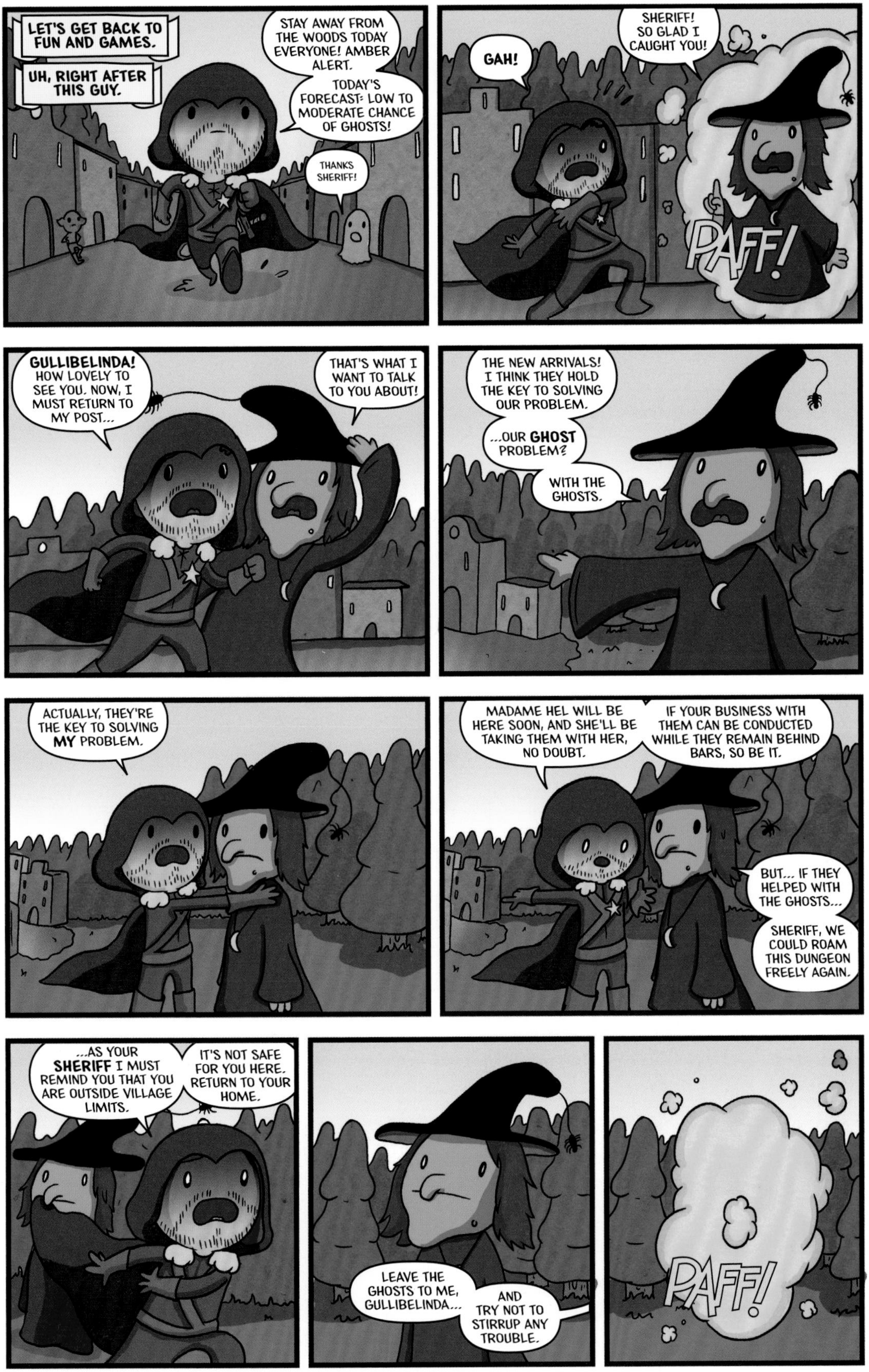
LET'S GET BACK TO FUN AND GAMES.
UH, RIGHT AFTER THIS GUY.
STAY AWAY FROM THE WOODS TODAY EVERYONE! AMBER ALERT.
TODAY'S FORECAST: LOW TO MODERATE CHANCE OF GHOSTS!
THANKS SHERIFF!
SHERIFF! SO GLAD I CAUGHT YOU!
GAH!
PAFF!
GULLIBELINDA! HOW LOVELY TO SEE YOU. NOW, I MUST RETURN TO MY POST...
THAT'S WHAT I WANT TO TALK TO YOU ABOUT!
THE NEW ARRIVALS! I THINK THEY HOLD THE KEY TO SOLVING OUR PROBLEM.
...OUR GHOST PROBLEM?
WITH THE GHOSTS.
ACTUALLY, THEY'RE THE KEY TO SOLVING MY PROBLEM.
MADAME HEL WILL BE HERE SOON, AND SHE'LL BE TAKING THEM WITH HER, NO DOUBT.
IF YOUR BUSINESS WITH THEM CAN BE CONDUCTED WHILE THEY REMAIN BEHIND BARS, SO BE IT.
BUT... IF THEY HELPED WITH THE GHOSTS...
SHERIFF, WE COULD ROAM THIS DUNGEON FREELY AGAIN.
...AS YOUR SHERIFF I MUST REMIND YOU THAT YOU ARE OUTSIDE VILLAGE LIMITS.
IT'S NOT SAFE FOR YOU HERE. RETURN TO YOUR HOME.
LEAVE THE GHOSTS TO ME, GULLIBELINDA...
AND TRY NOT TO STIRRUP ANY TROUBLE.
PAFF!

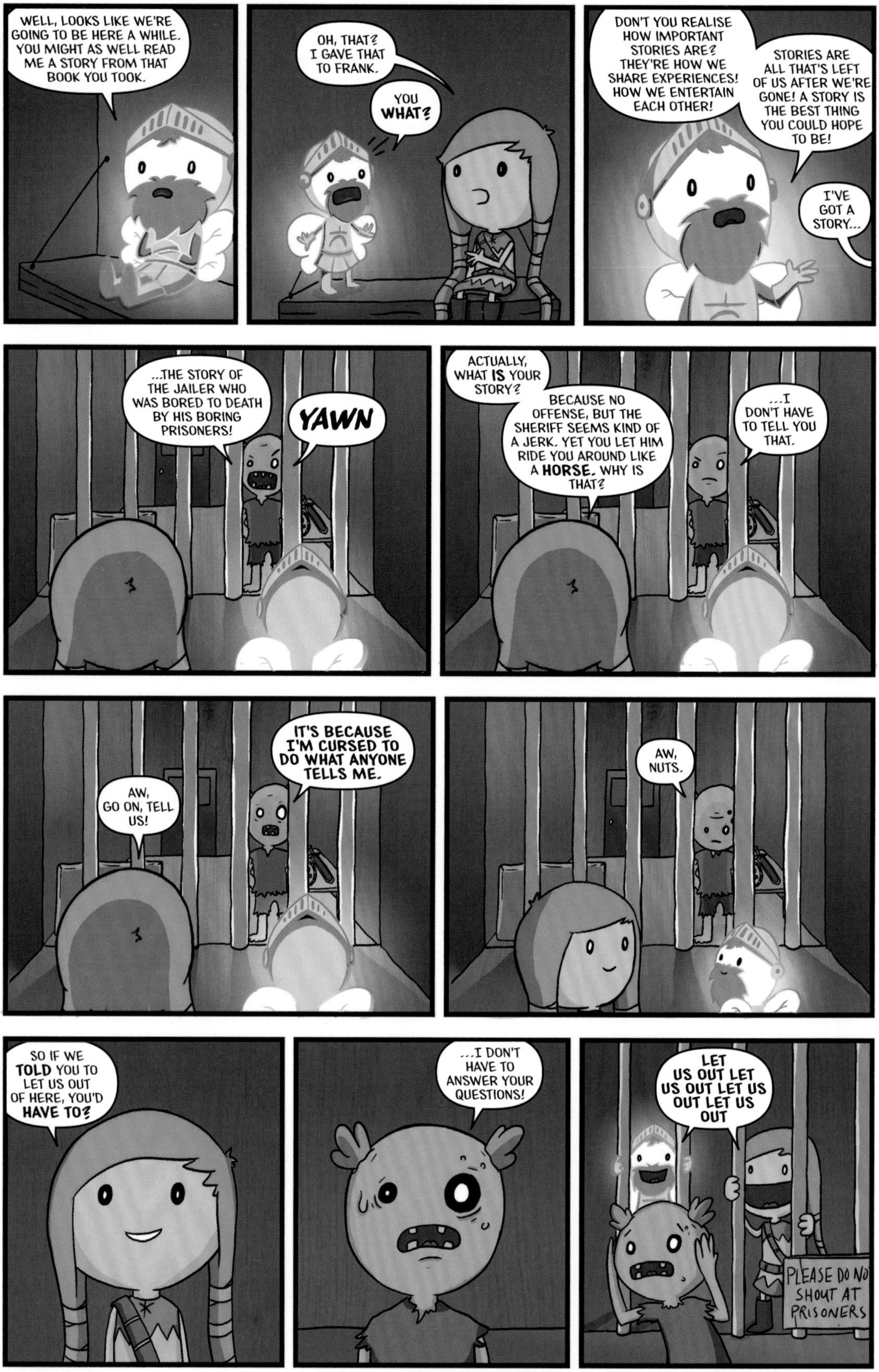
WELL, LOOKS LIKE WE'RE GOING TO BE HERE A WHILE. YOU MIGHT AS WELL READ ME A STORY FROM THAT BOOK YOU TOOK.
OH, THAT? I GAVE THAT TO FRANK.
YOU WHAT?
DON'T YOU REALISE HOW IMPORTANT STORIES ARE? THEY'RE HOW WE SHARE EXPERIENCES! HOW WE ENTERTAIN EACH OTHER!
STORIES ARE ALL THAT'S LEFT OF US AFTER WE'RE GONE! A STORY IS THE BEST THING YOU COULD HOPE TO BE!
I'VE GOT A STORY...
...THE STORY OF THE JAILER WHO WAS BORED TO DEATH BY HIS BORING PRISONERS!
YAWN
ACTUALLY, WHAT IS YOUR STORY?
BECAUSE NO OFFENSE, BUT THE SHERIFF SEEMS KIND OF A JERK. YET YOU LET HIM RIDE YOU AROUND LIKE A HORSE. WHY IS THAT?
...I DON'T HAVE TO TELL YOU THAT.
AW, GO ON, TELL US!
IT'S BECAUSE I'M CURSED TO DO WHAT ANYONE TELLS ME.
AW, NUTS.
SO IF WE TOLD YOU TO LET US OUT OF HERE, YOU'D HAVE TO?
...I DON'T HAVE TO ANSWER YOUR QUESTIONS!
LET US OUT LET US OUT LET US OUT LET US OUT
PLEASE DO NO SHOUT AT PRISONERS

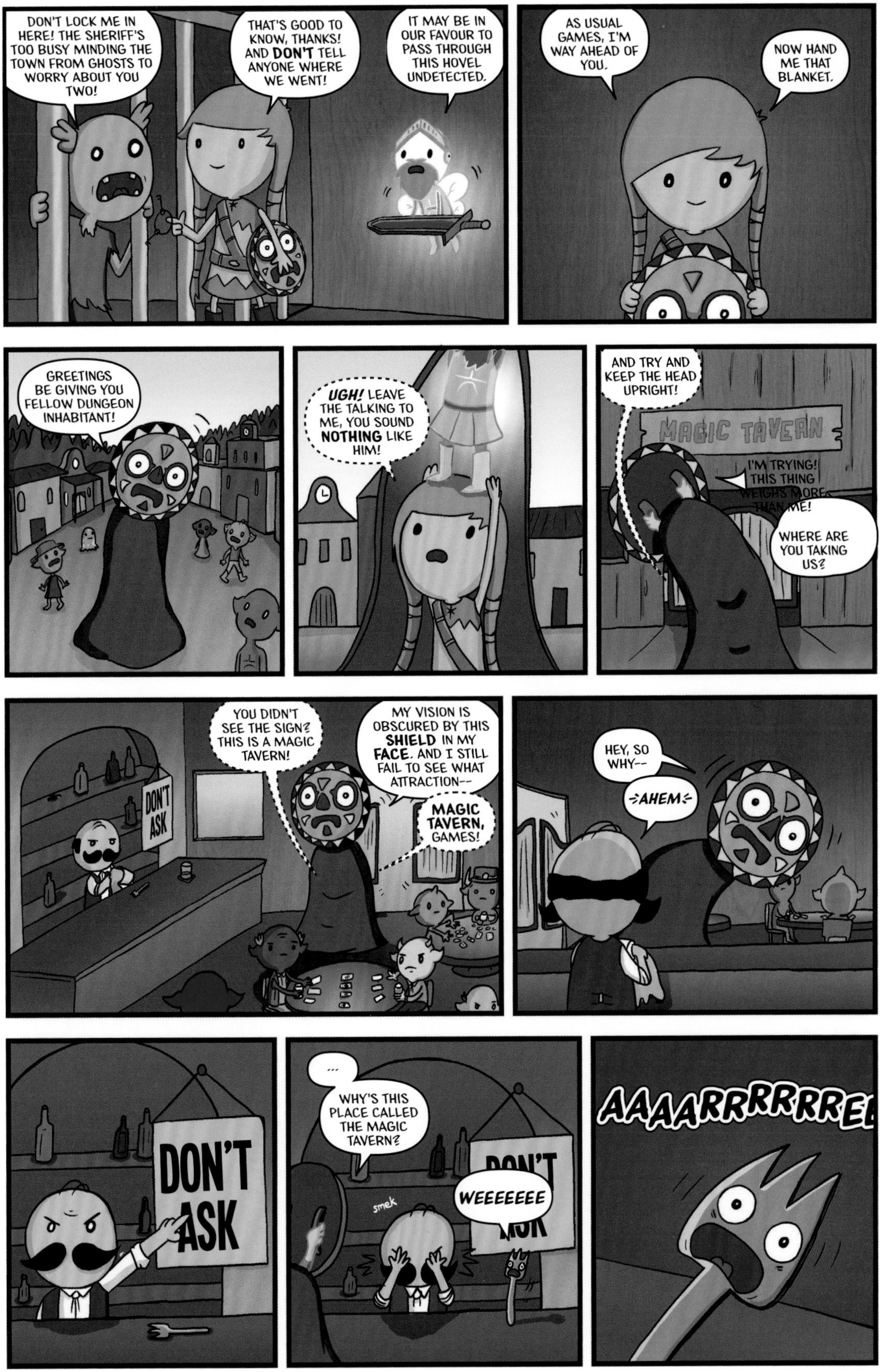
DON'T LOCK ME IN HERE! THE SHERIFF'S TOO BUSY MINDING THE TOWN FROM GHOSTS TO WORRY ABOUT YOU TWO!
THAT'S GOOD TO KNOW, THANKS! AND DON'T TELL ANYONE WHERE WE WENT!
IT MAY BE IN OUR FAVOUR TO PASS THROUGH THIS HOVEL UNDETECTED.
AS USUAL GAMES, I'M WAY AHEAD OF YOU.
NOW HAND ME THAT BLANKET.
GREETINGS BE GIVING YOU FELLOW DUNGEON INHABITANT!
UGH! LEAVE THE TALKING TO ME, YOU SOUND NOTHING LIKE HIM!
AND TRY AND KEEP THE HEAD UPRIGHT!
MAGIC TAVERN
I'M TRYING! THIS THING WEIGHS MORE THAN ME!
WHERE ARE YOU TAKING US?
DON'T ASK
YOU DIDN'T SEE THE SIGN? THIS IS A MAGIC TAVERN!
MY VISION IS OBSCURED BY THIS SHIELD IN MY FACE. AND I STILL FAIL TO SEE WHAT ATTRACTION--
MAGIC TAVERN, GAMES!
HEY, SO WHY--
AHEM
DON'T ASK
...
WHY'S THIS PLACE CALLED THE MAGIC TAVERN?
smek
WEEEEEEE
AAAARRRRRRE

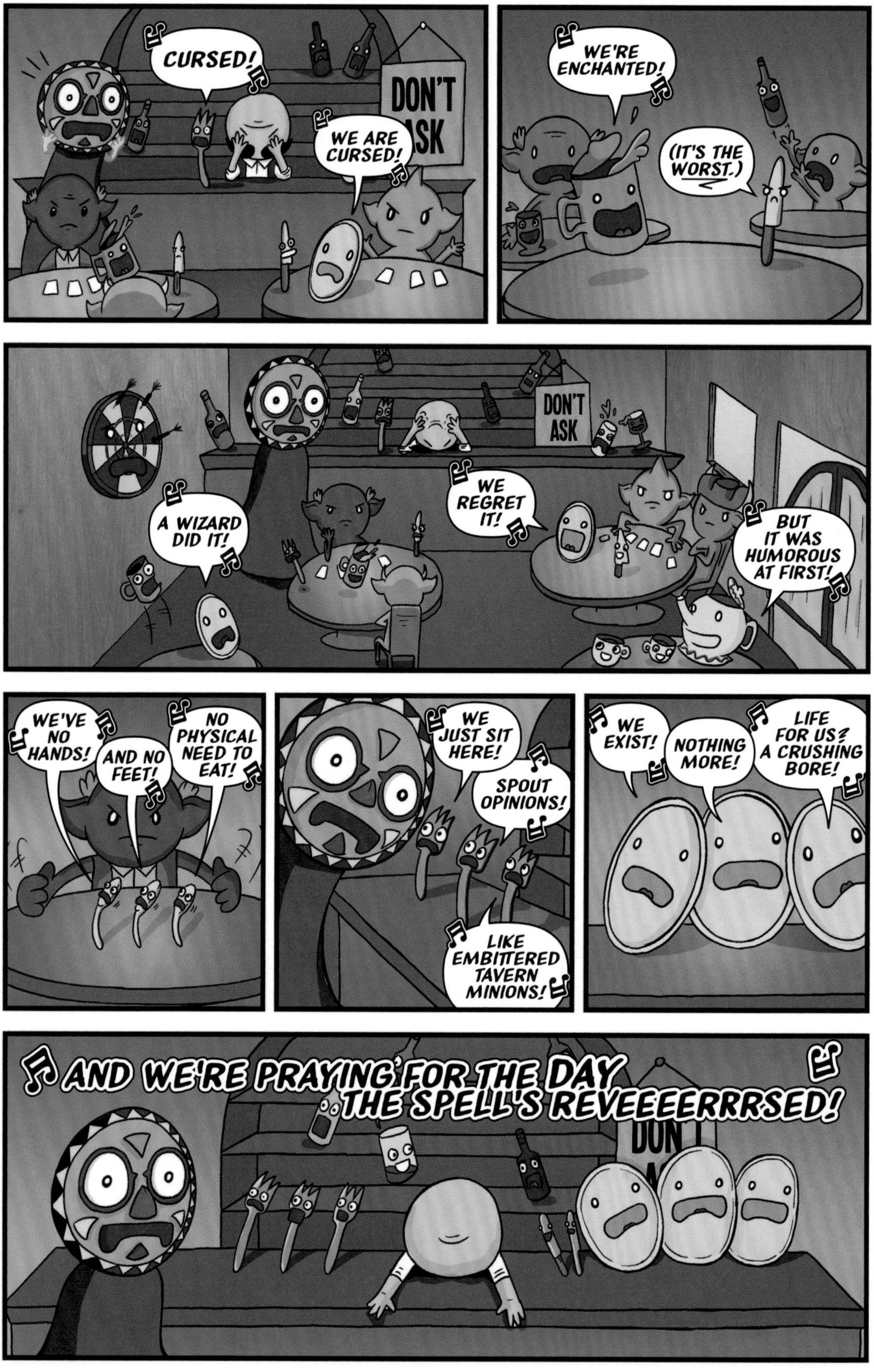
CURSED!
DON'T ASK
WE ARE CURSED!
WE'RE ENCHANTED!
(IT'S THE WORST.)
DON'T ASK
A WIZARD DID IT!
WE REGRET IT!
BUT IT WAS HUMOROUS AT FIRST!
WE'VE NO HANDS!
AND NO FEET!
NO PHYSICAL NEED TO EAT!
WE JUST SIT HERE!
SPOUT OPINIONS!
LIKE EMBITTERED TAVERN MINIONS!
WE EXIST!
NOTHING MORE!
LIFE FOR US? A CRUSHING BORE!
AND WE'RE PRAYING FOR THE DAY THE SPELL'S REVEEEERRRRSED!

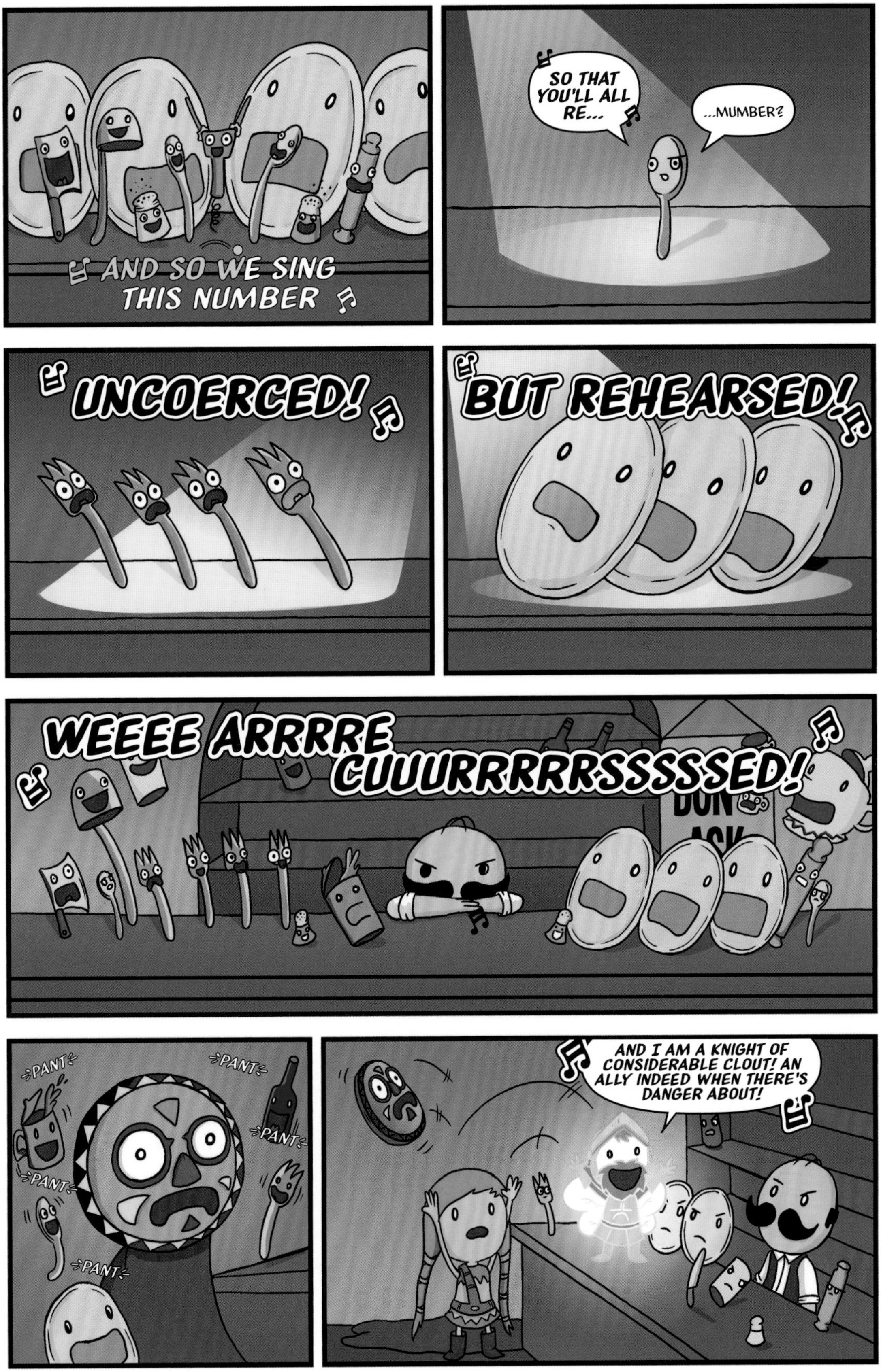
AND SO WE SING THIS NUMBER
SO THAT YOU'LL ALL RE...
...MUMBER?
UNCOERCED!
BUT REHEARSED!
WEEEE ARRRRE CUUURRRRRRSSSSSED!
PANT
PANT
PANT
PANT
PANT
AND I AM A KNIGHT OF CONSIDERABLE CLOUT! AN ALLY INDEED WHEN THERE'S DANGER ABOUT!

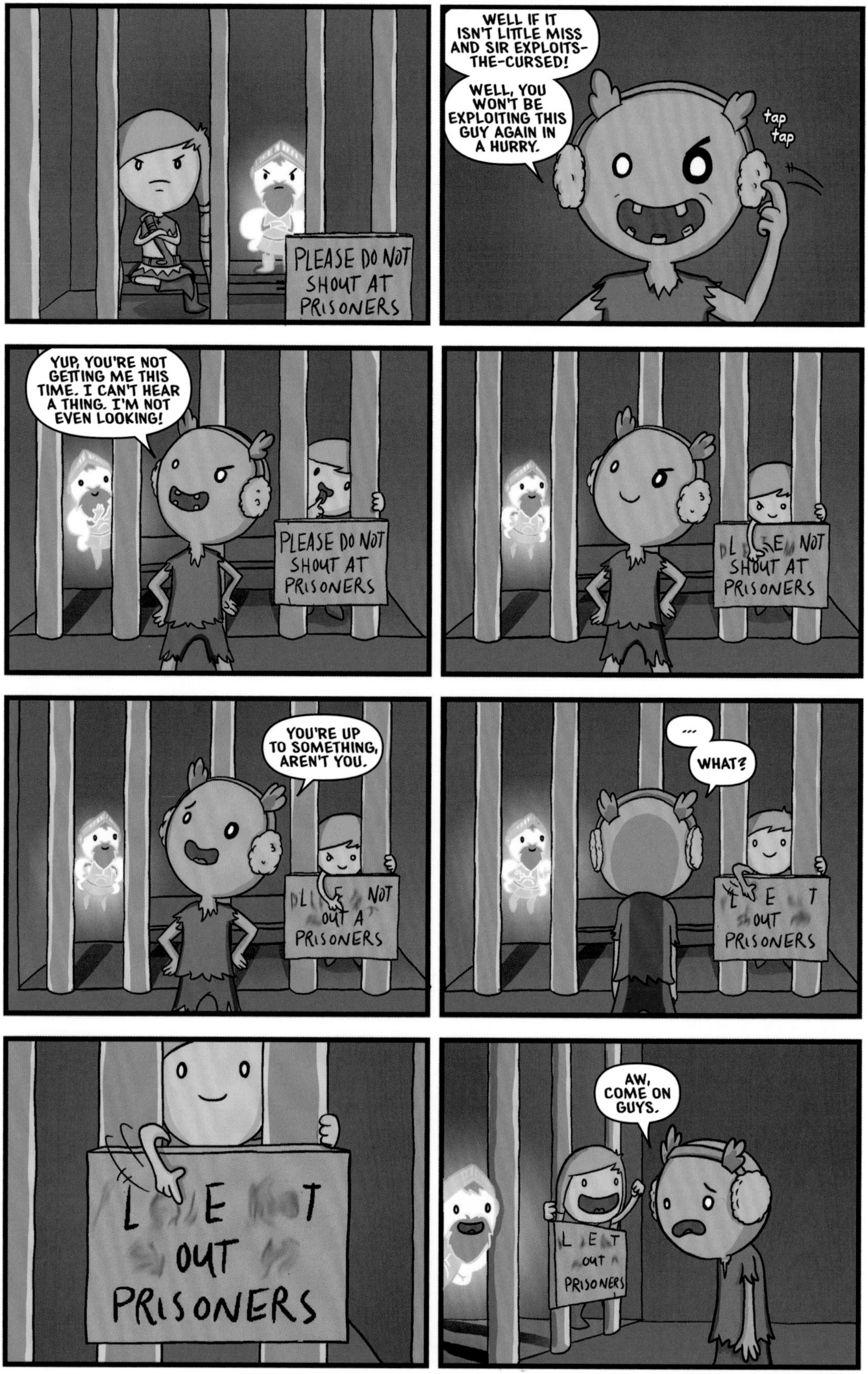
PLEASE DO NOT SHOUT AT PRISONERS
WELL IF IT ISN'T LITTLE MISS AND SIR EXPLOITS-THE-CURSED!
WELL, YOU WON'T BE EXPLOITING THIS GUY AGAIN IN A HURRY.
tap tap
YUP, YOU'RE NOT GETTING ME THIS TIME. I CAN'T HEAR A THING. I'M NOT EVEN LOOKING!
PLEASE DO NOT SHOUT AT PRISONERS
YOU'RE UP TO SOMETHING, AREN'T YOU.
...
WHAT?
L E T OUT PRISONERS
AW, COME ON GUYS.

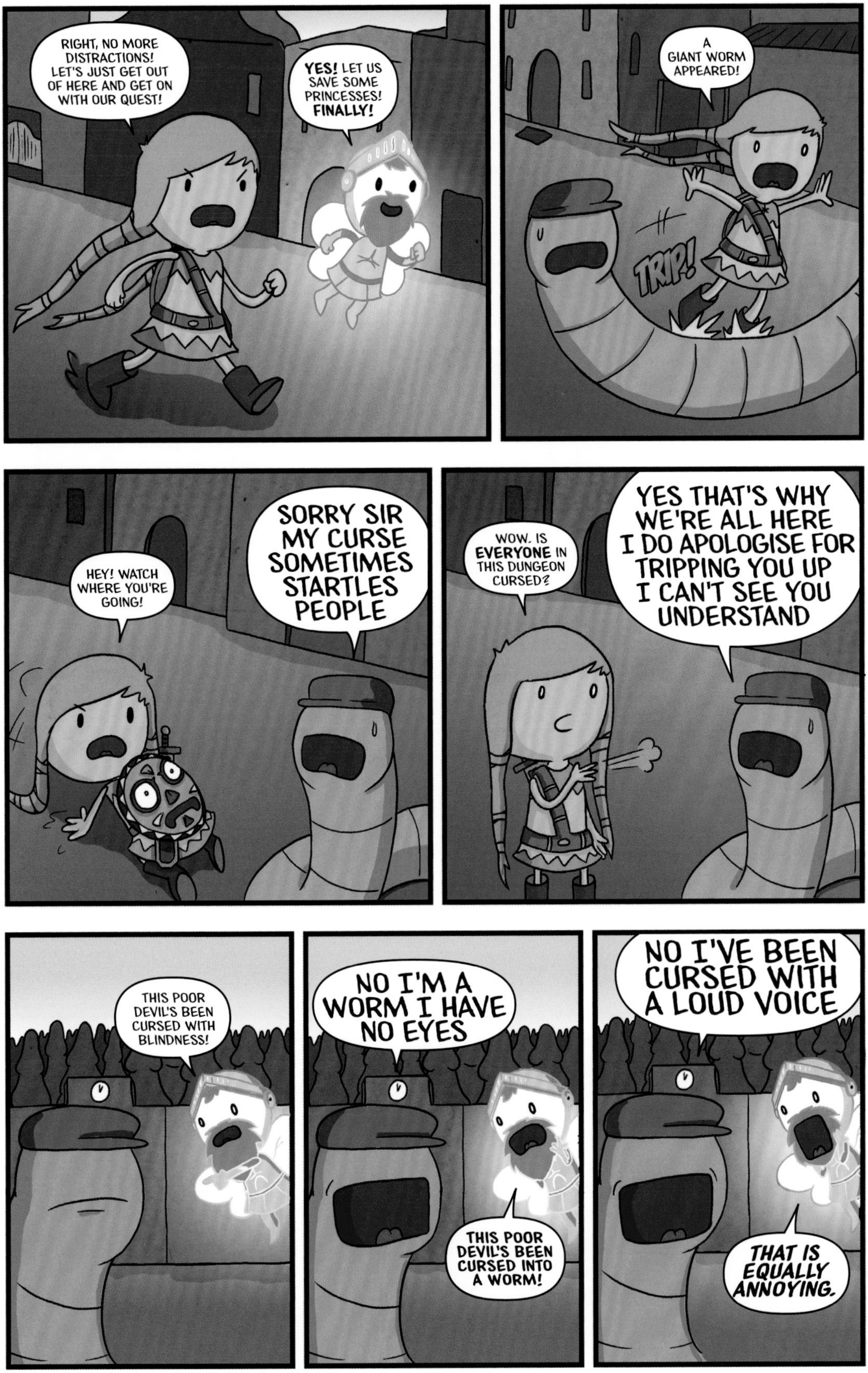

RIGHT, NO MORE DISTRACTIONS! LET'S JUST GET OUT OF HERE AND GET ON WITH OUR QUEST!
YES! LET US SAVE SOME PRINCESSES! FINALLY!
A GIANT WORM APPEARED!
TRIP!
HEY! WATCH WHERE YOU'RE GOING!
SORRY SIR MY CURSE SOMETIMES STARTLES PEOPLE
WOW. IS EVERYONE IN THIS DUNGEON CURSED?
YES THAT'S WHY WE'RE ALL HERE I DO APOLOGISE FOR TRIPPING YOU UP I CAN'T SEE YOU UNDERSTAND
THIS POOR DEVIL'S BEEN CURSED WITH BLINDNESS!
NO I'M A WORM I HAVE NO EYES
THIS POOR DEVIL'S BEEN CURSED INTO A WORM!
NO I'VE BEEN CURSED WITH A LOUD VOICE
THAT IS EQUALLY ANNOYING.

SORRY, DID YOU SAY YOU WERE HERE **BECAUSE** YOU WERE CURSED?

YES

"I WAS ONCE CURSED BY A WIZARD WHO WAS JEALOUS OF MY HAT."

"THIS MADE ME VERY UNPOPULAR. YOU CAN HEAR ME, YOU UNDERSTAND.

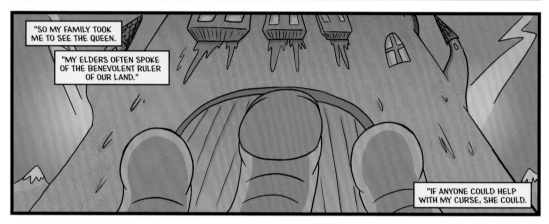

"SO MY FAMILY TOOK ME TO SEE THE QUEEN.

"MY ELDERS OFTEN SPOKE OF THE BENEVOLENT RULER OF OUR LAND."

"IF ANYONE COULD HELP WITH MY CURSE, SHE COULD.

"WELL, SHE COULDN'T.

"OR WOULDN'T.

"I DON'T THINK SHE WAS EVEN LISTENING."

BUT ANOTHER VOICE SPOKE

I COULDN'T SEE IT BUT I FELT A PRESENCE IN THE ROOM

IT JUST SAID

SEND IT TO DUNGEONHAM

AND THEN I WOKE UP HERE

NOW **THAT'S** A STORY!

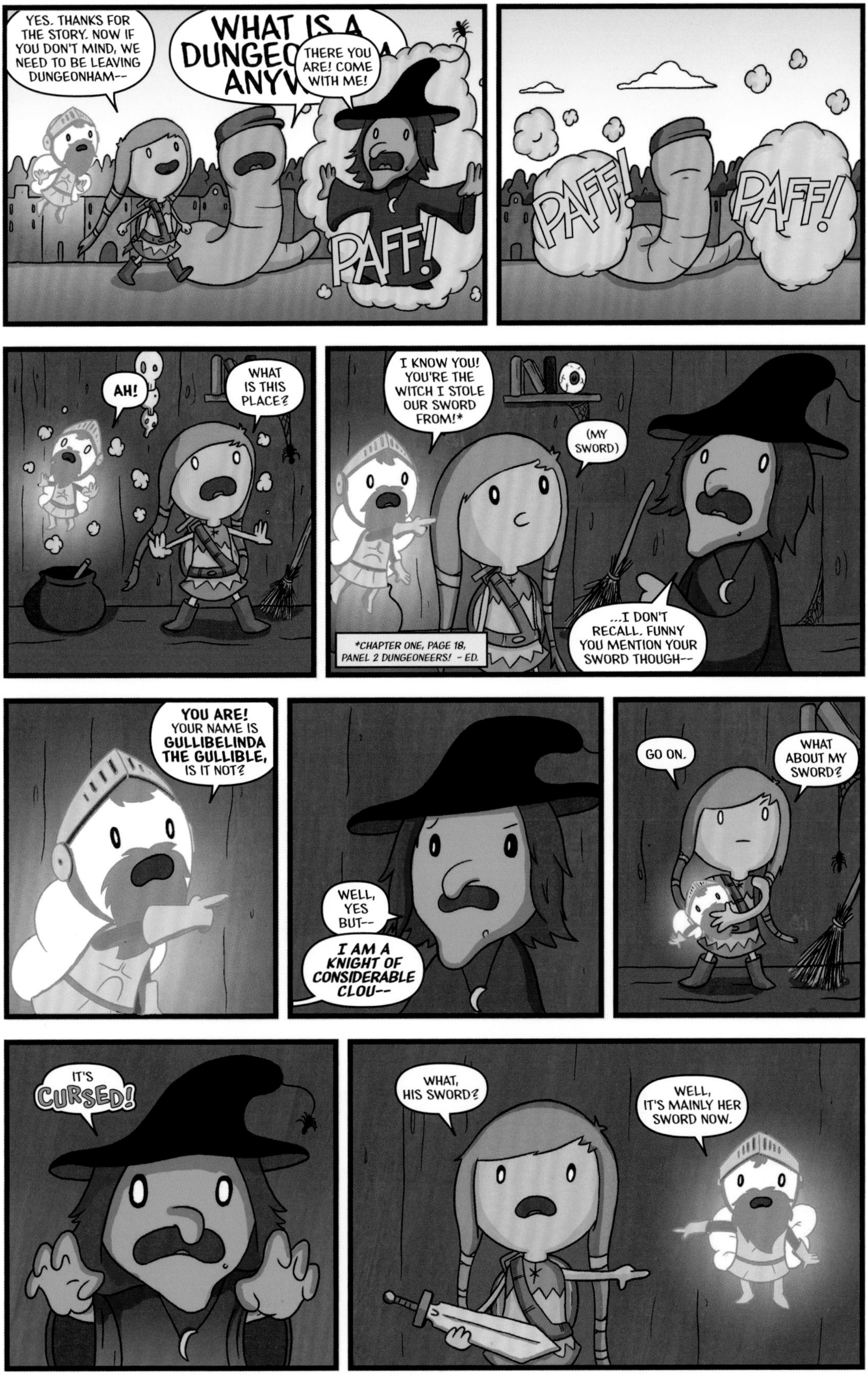
YES. THANKS FOR THE STORY. NOW IF YOU DON'T MIND, WE NEED TO BE LEAVING DUNGEONHAM--
WHAT IS A DUNGEO A ANYW
THERE YOU ARE! COME WITH ME!
PAFF!
PAFF!
PAFF!
AH!
WHAT IS THIS PLACE?
I KNOW YOU! YOU'RE THE WITCH I STOLE OUR SWORD FROM!*
(MY SWORD)
...I DON'T RECALL. FUNNY YOU MENTION YOUR SWORD THOUGH--
*CHAPTER ONE, PAGE 18, PANEL 2 DUNGEONEERS! - ED.
YOU ARE! YOUR NAME IS GULLIBELINDA THE GULLIBLE, IS IT NOT?
WELL, YES BUT--
I AM A KNIGHT OF CONSIDERABLE CLOU--
GO ON.
WHAT ABOUT MY SWORD?
IT'S CURSED!
WHAT, HIS SWORD?
WELL, IT'S MAINLY HER SWORD NOW.

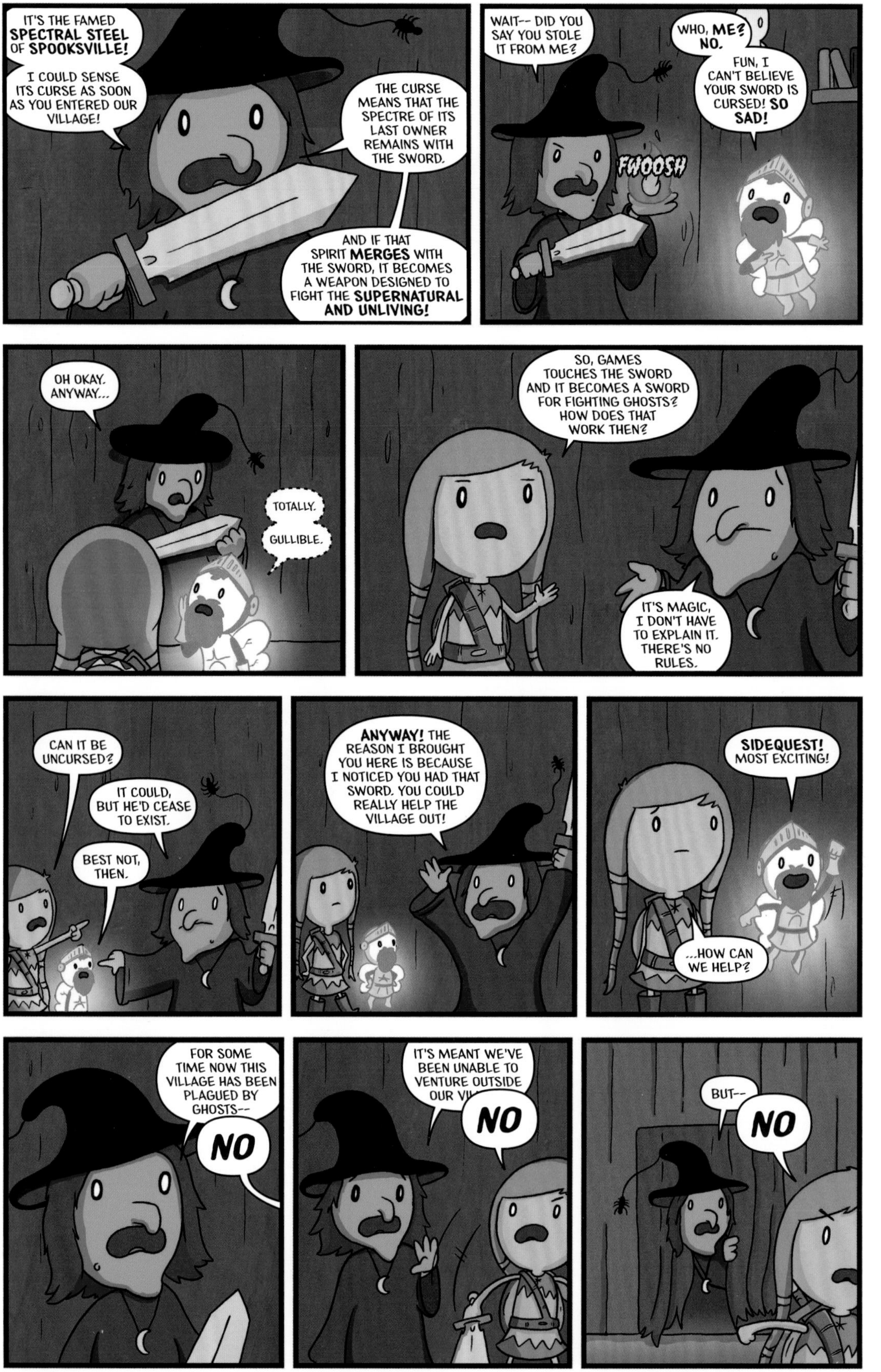
IT'S THE FAMED SPECTRAL STEEL OF SPOOKSVILLE!
I COULD SENSE ITS CURSE AS SOON AS YOU ENTERED OUR VILLAGE!
THE CURSE MEANS THAT THE SPECTRE OF ITS LAST OWNER REMAINS WITH THE SWORD.
AND IF THAT SPIRIT MERGES WITH THE SWORD, IT BECOMES A WEAPON DESIGNED TO FIGHT THE SUPERNATURAL AND UNLIVING!
WAIT-- DID YOU SAY YOU STOLE IT FROM ME?
WHO, ME? NO.
FUN, I CAN'T BELIEVE YOUR SWORD IS CURSED! SO SAD!
FWOOSH
OH OKAY. ANYWAY...
TOTALLY.
GULLIBLE.
SO, GAMES TOUCHES THE SWORD AND IT BECOMES A SWORD FOR FIGHTING GHOSTS? HOW DOES THAT WORK THEN?
IT'S MAGIC, I DON'T HAVE TO EXPLAIN IT. THERE'S NO RULES.
CAN IT BE UNCURSED?
IT COULD, BUT HE'D CEASE TO EXIST.
BEST NOT, THEN.
ANYWAY! THE REASON I BROUGHT YOU HERE IS BECAUSE I NOTICED YOU HAD THAT SWORD. YOU COULD REALLY HELP THE VILLAGE OUT!
SIDEQUEST! MOST EXCITING!
...HOW CAN WE HELP?
FOR SOME TIME NOW THIS VILLAGE HAS BEEN PLAGUED BY GHOSTS--
NO
IT'S MEANT WE'VE BEEN UNABLE TO VENTURE OUTSIDE OUR VI
NO
BUT--
NO

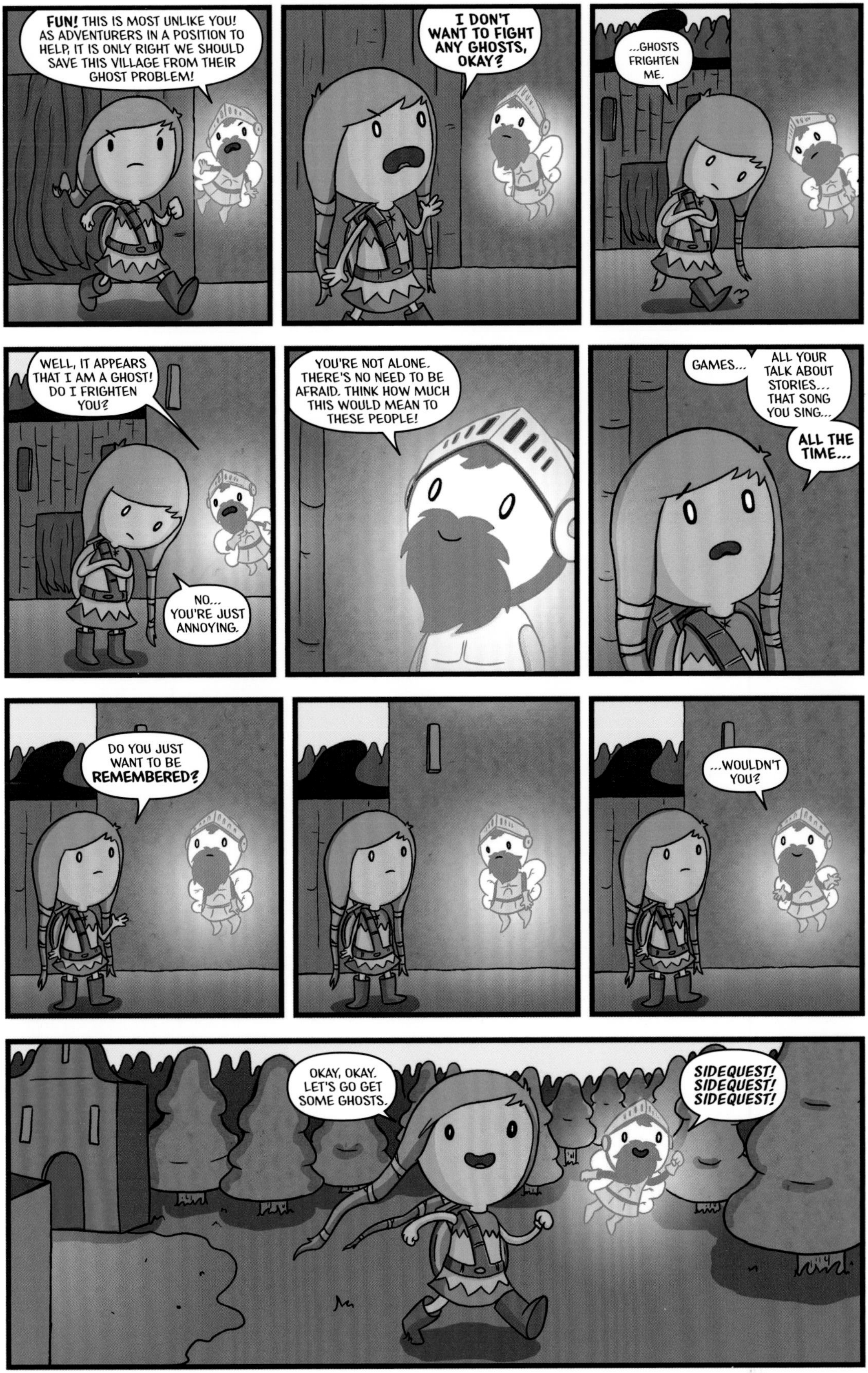
FUN! THIS IS MOST UNLIKE YOU! AS ADVENTURERS IN A POSITION TO HELP, IT IS ONLY RIGHT WE SHOULD SAVE THIS VILLAGE FROM THEIR GHOST PROBLEM!
I DON'T WANT TO FIGHT ANY GHOSTS, OKAY?
...GHOSTS FRIGHTEN ME.
WELL, IT APPEARS THAT I AM A GHOST! DO I FRIGHTEN YOU?
NO... YOU'RE JUST ANNOYING.
YOU'RE NOT ALONE. THERE'S NO NEED TO BE AFRAID. THINK HOW MUCH THIS WOULD MEAN TO THESE PEOPLE!
GAMES...
ALL YOUR TALK ABOUT STORIES... THAT SONG YOU SING...
ALL THE TIME...
DO YOU JUST WANT TO BE REMEMBERED?
...WOULDN'T YOU?
OKAY, OKAY. LET'S GO GET SOME GHOSTS.
SIDEQUEST! SIDEQUEST! SIDEQUEST!

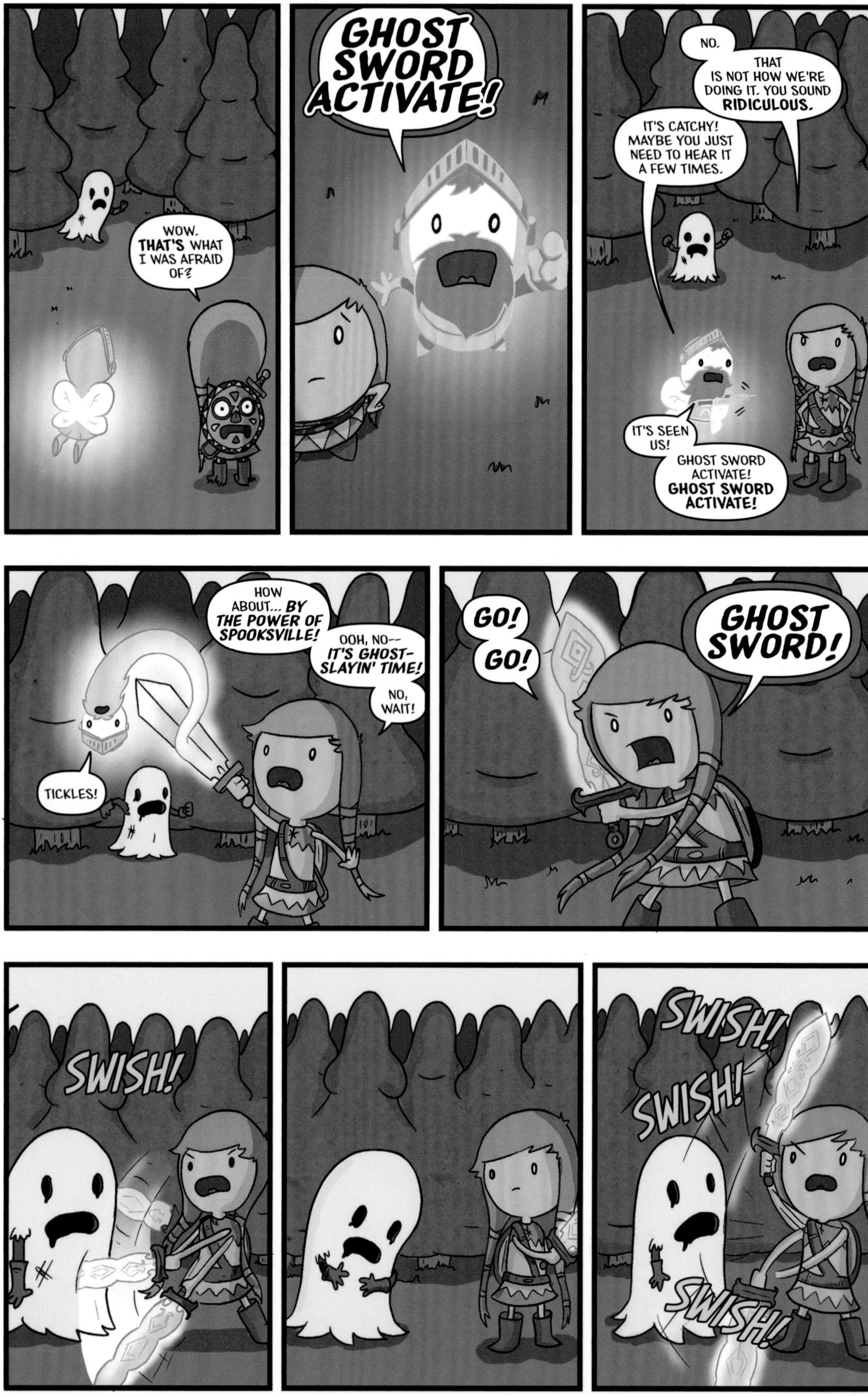

WOW. THAT'S WHAT I WAS AFRAID OF?
GHOST SWORD ACTIVATE!
NO.
THAT IS NOT HOW WE'RE DOING IT. YOU SOUND RIDICULOUS.
IT'S CATCHY! MAYBE YOU JUST NEED TO HEAR IT A FEW TIMES.
IT'S SEEN US!
GHOST SWORD ACTIVATE! GHOST SWORD ACTIVATE!
HOW ABOUT... BY THE POWER OF SPOOKSVILLE!
OOH, NO-- IT'S GHOST-SLAYIN' TIME!
NO, WAIT!
TICKLES!
GO! GO!
GHOST SWORD!
SWISH!
SWISH!
SWISH!
SWISH!

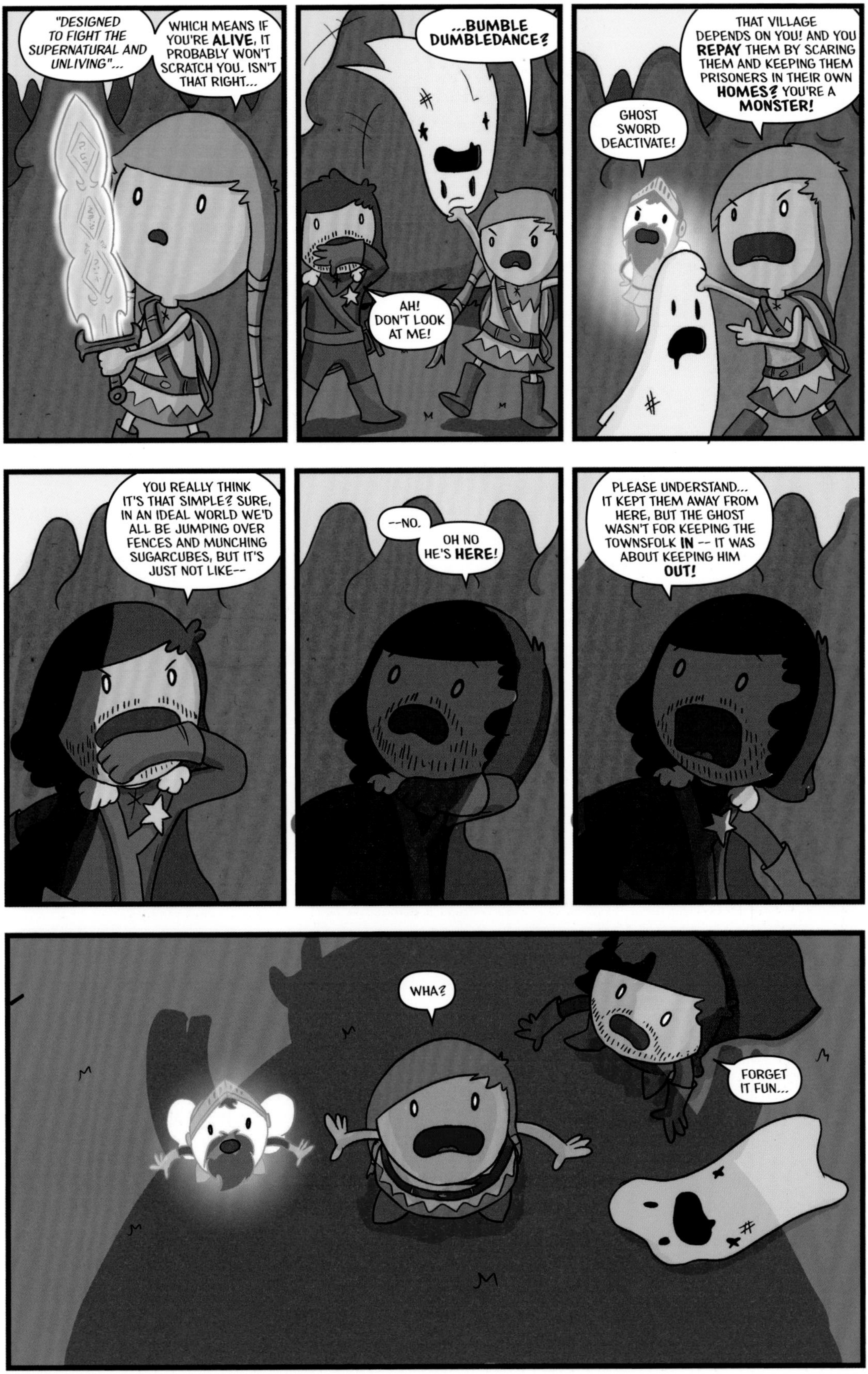
"DESIGNED TO FIGHT THE SUPERNATURAL AND UNLIVING"...
WHICH MEANS IF YOU'RE ALIVE, IT PROBABLY WON'T SCRATCH YOU. ISN'T THAT RIGHT...
...BUMBLE DUMBLEDANCE?
AH! DON'T LOOK AT ME!
GHOST SWORD DEACTIVATE!
THAT VILLAGE DEPENDS ON YOU! AND YOU REPAY THEM BY SCARING THEM AND KEEPING THEM PRISONERS IN THEIR OWN HOMES? YOU'RE A MONSTER!
YOU REALLY THINK IT'S THAT SIMPLE? SURE, IN AN IDEAL WORLD WE'D ALL BE JUMPING OVER FENCES AND MUNCHING SUGARCUBES, BUT IT'S JUST NOT LIKE--
--NO.
OH NO HE'S HERE!
PLEASE UNDERSTAND... IT KEPT THEM AWAY FROM HERE, BUT THE GHOST WASN'T FOR KEEPING THE TOWNSFOLK IN -- IT WAS ABOUT KEEPING HIM OUT!
WHA?
FORGET IT FUN...

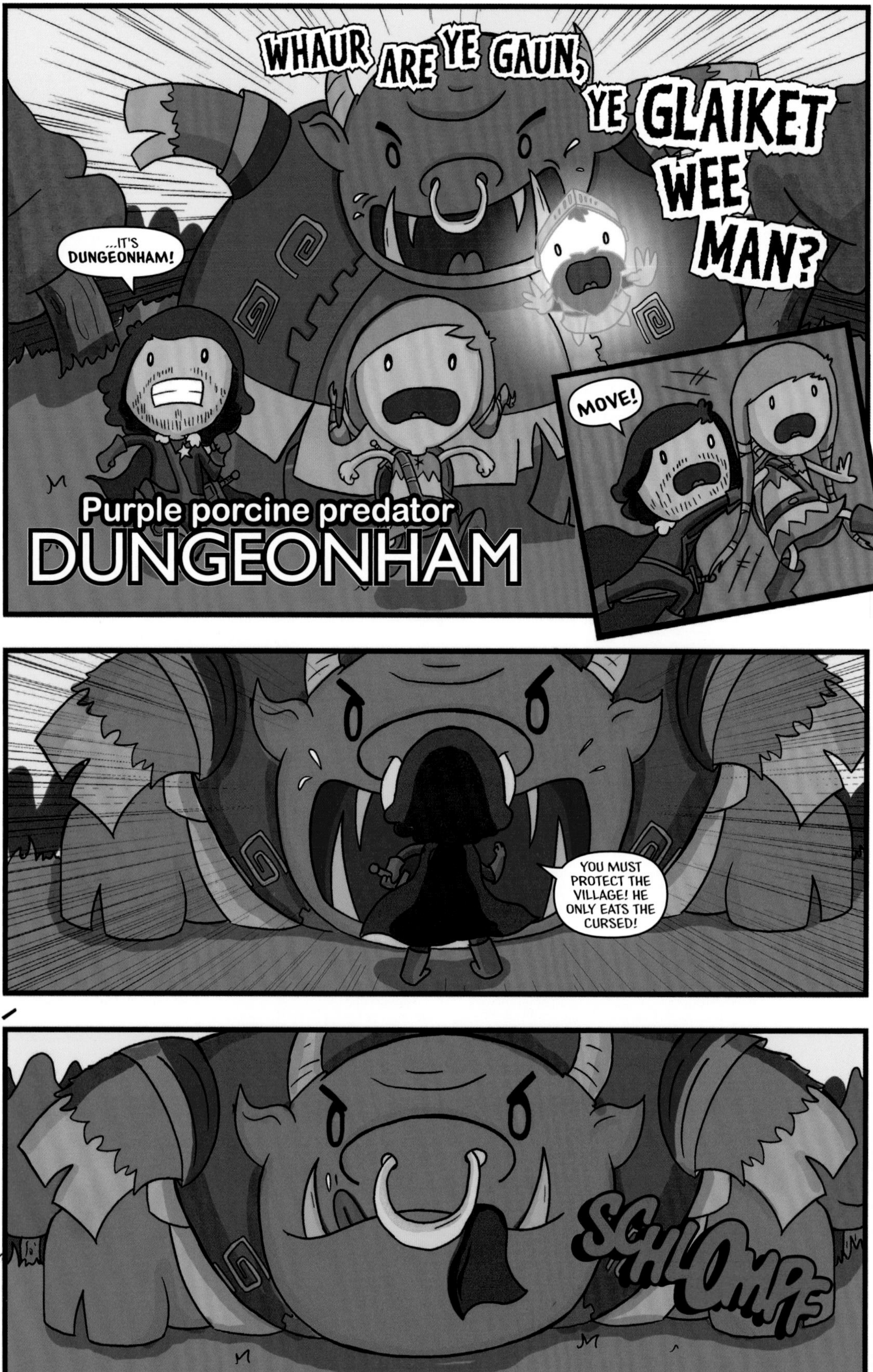
WHAUR ARE YE GAUN, YE GLAIKET WEE MAN?
...IT'S DUNGEONHAM!
Purple porcine predator
DUNGEONHAM
MOVE!
YOU MUST PROTECT THE VILLAGE! HE ONLY EATS THE CURSED!
SCHLOMP

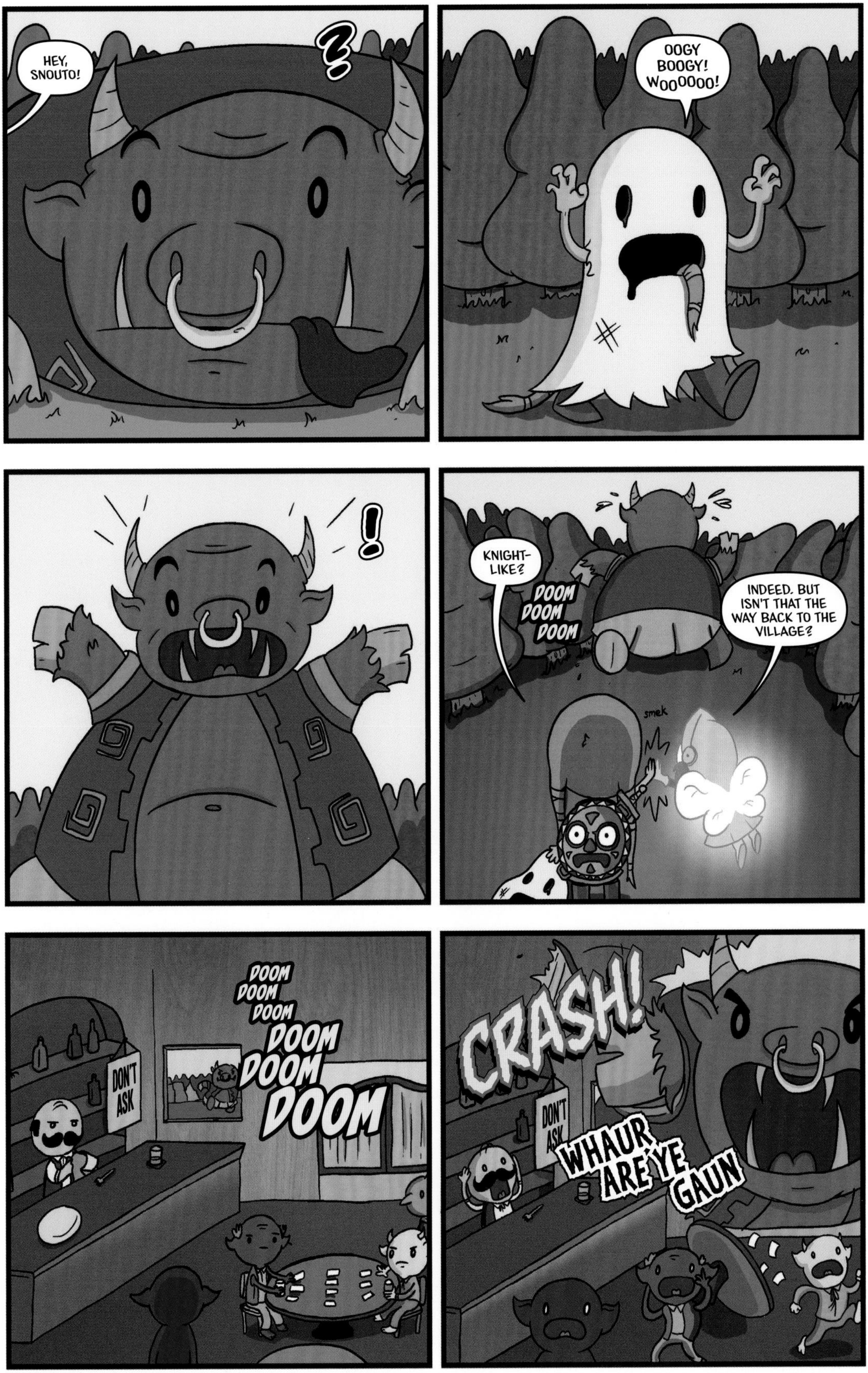
HEY, SNOUTO!
?
OOGY BOOGY! WOOOOOO!
!
KNIGHT-LIKE?
DOOM DOOM DOOM
INDEED. BUT ISN'T THAT THE WAY BACK TO THE VILLAGE?
smek
DON'T ASK
DOOM DOOM DOOM DOOM DOOM DOOM
CRASH!
DON'T ASK
WHAUR ARE YE GAUN

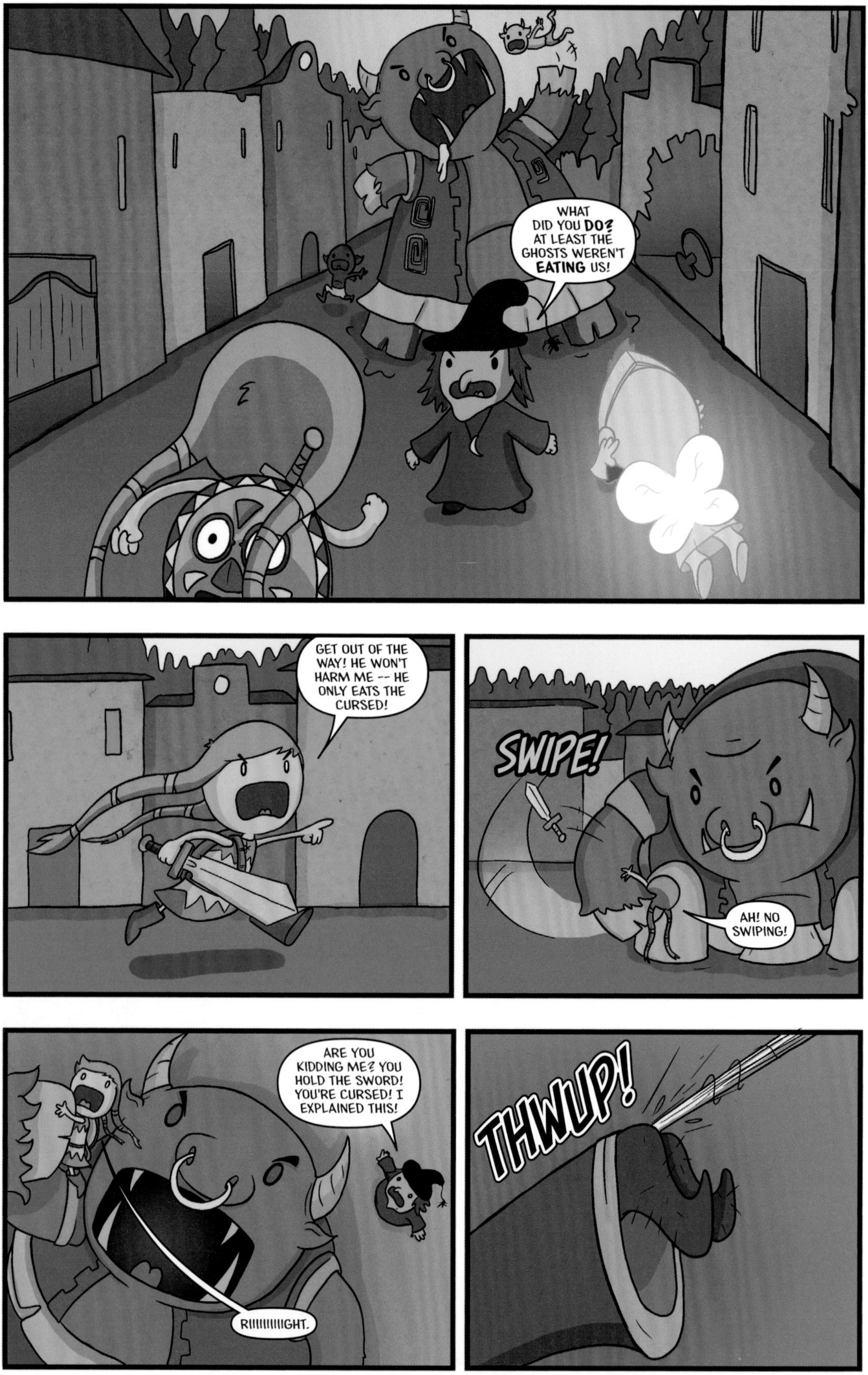
WHAT DID YOU **DO?** AT LEAST THE GHOSTS WEREN'T **EATING** US!
GET OUT OF THE WAY! HE WON'T HARM ME -- HE ONLY EATS THE CURSED!
SWIPE!
AH! NO SWIPING!
ARE YOU KIDDING ME? YOU HOLD THE SWORD! YOU'RE CURSED! I EXPLAINED THIS!
RIIIIIIIIIGHT.
THWUP!

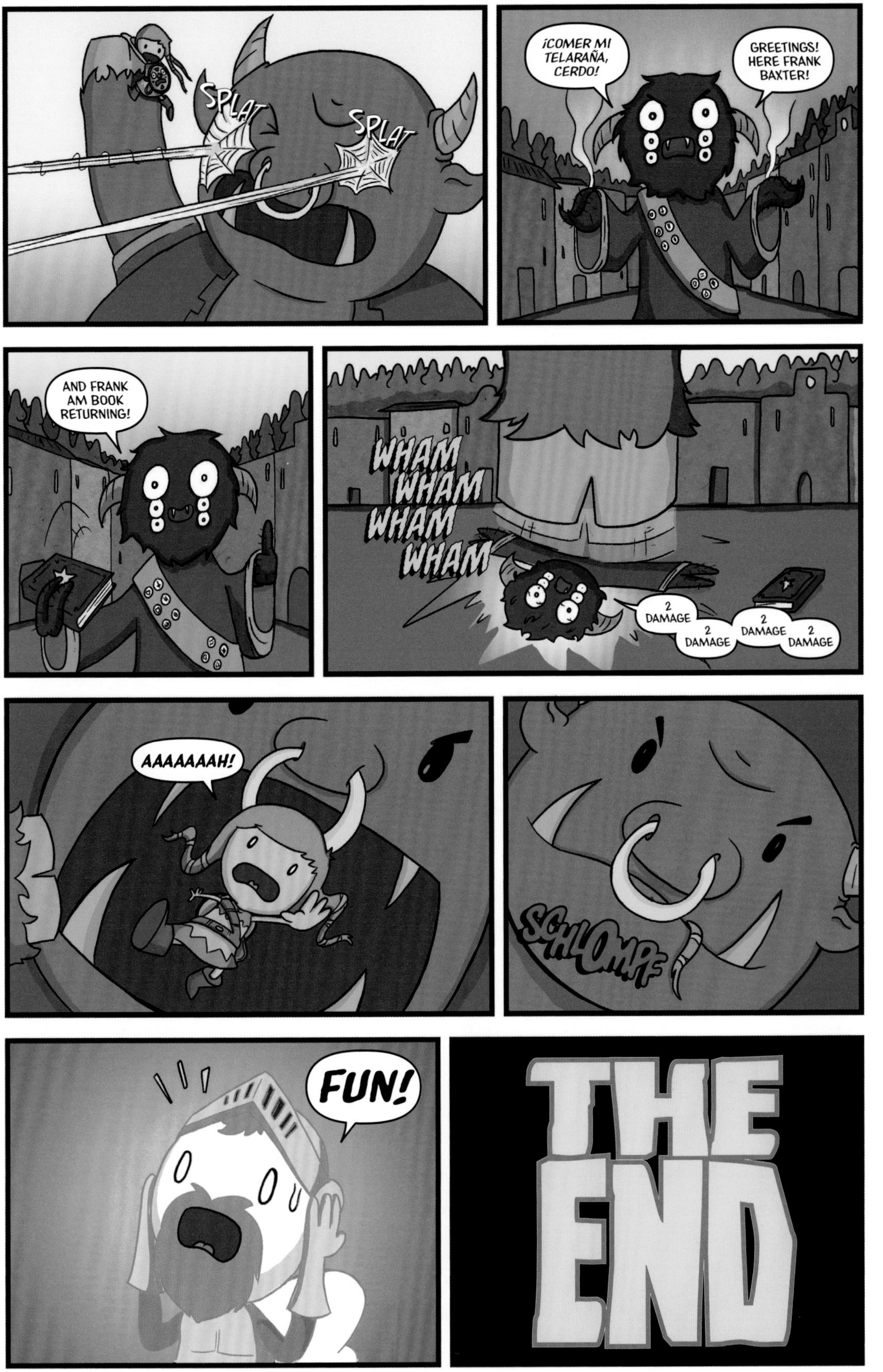
SPLAT
SPLAT
¡COMER MI TELARAÑA, CERDO!
GREETINGS! HERE FRANK BAXTER!
AND FRANK AM BOOK RETURNING!
WHAM
WHAM
WHAM
WHAM
2 DAMAGE
2 DAMAGE
2 DAMAGE
2 DAMAGE
AAAAAAAH!
SCHLOMPF
FUN!
THE END

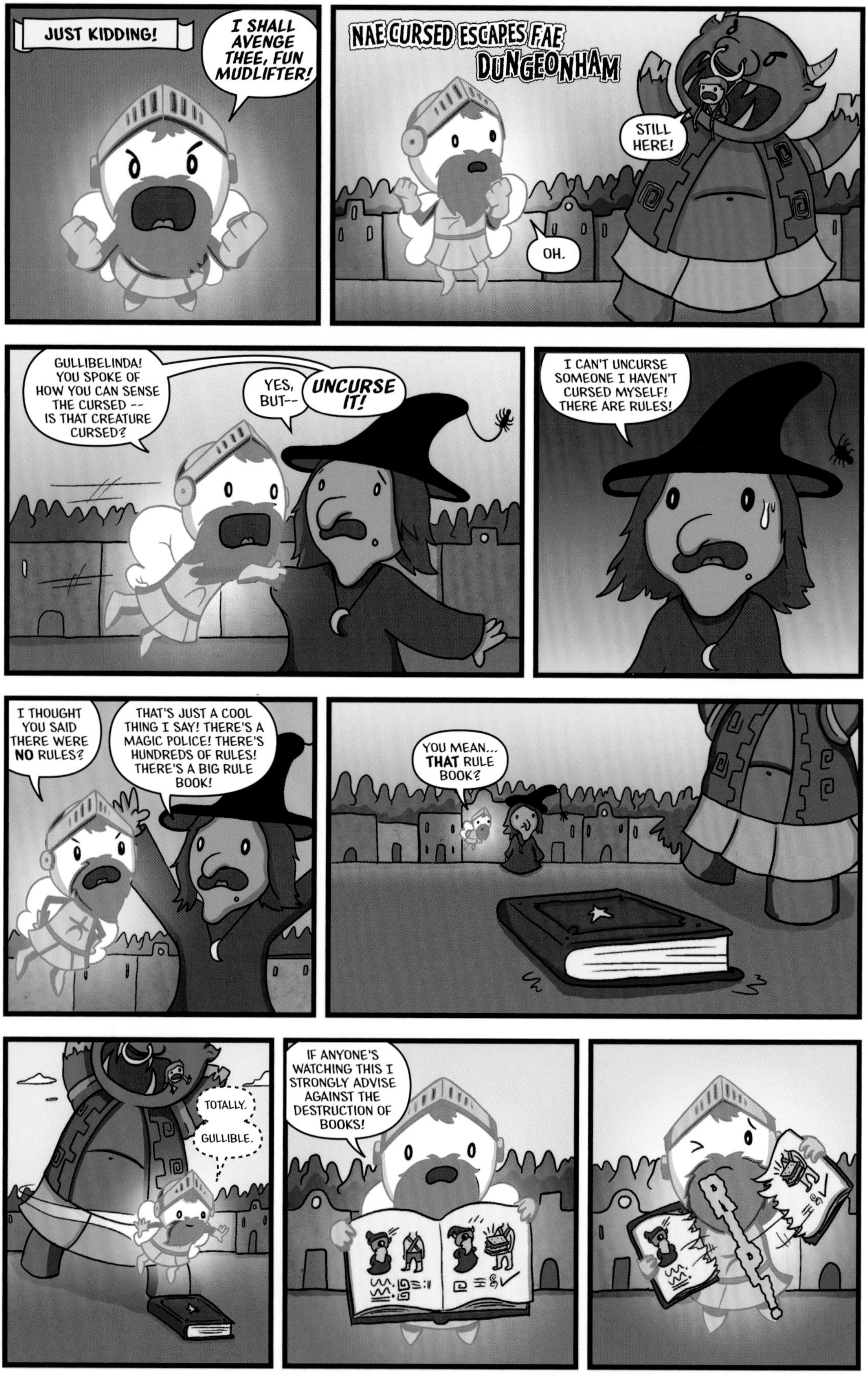
JUST KIDDING!
I SHALL AVENGE THEE, FUN MUDLIFTER!
NAE CURSED ESCAPES FAE DUNGEONHAM
STILL HERE!
OH.
GULLIBELINDA! YOU SPOKE OF HOW YOU CAN SENSE THE CURSED -- IS THAT CREATURE CURSED?
YES, BUT--
UNCURSE IT!
I CAN'T UNCURSE SOMEONE I HAVEN'T CURSED MYSELF! THERE ARE RULES!
I THOUGHT YOU SAID THERE WERE NO RULES?
THAT'S JUST A COOL THING I SAY! THERE'S A MAGIC POLICE! THERE'S HUNDREDS OF RULES! THERE'S A BIG RULE BOOK!
YOU MEAN... THAT RULE BOOK?
TOTALLY.
GULLIBLE.
IF ANYONE'S WATCHING THIS I STRONGLY ADVISE AGAINST THE DESTRUCTION OF BOOKS!

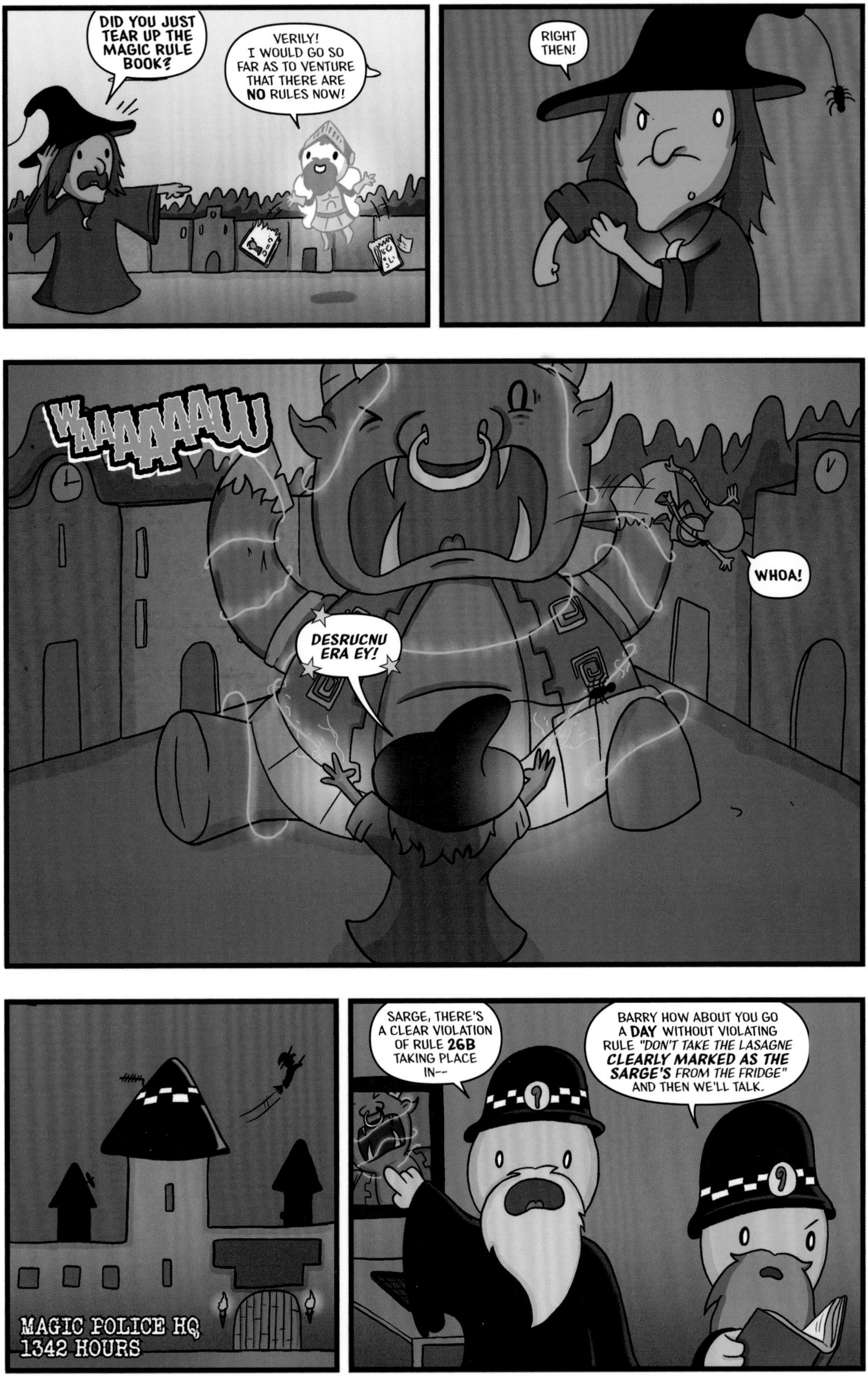

DID YOU JUST TEAR UP THE MAGIC RULE BOOK?
VERILY! I WOULD GO SO FAR AS TO VENTURE THAT THERE ARE NO RULES NOW!
RIGHT THEN!
WAAAAAAUU
DESRUCNU ERA EY!
WHOA!
MAGIC POLICE HQ 1342 HOURS
SARGE, THERE'S A CLEAR VIOLATION OF RULE 26B TAKING PLACE IN--
BARRY HOW ABOUT YOU GO A DAY WITHOUT VIOLATING RULE "DON'T TAKE THE LASAGNE CLEARLY MARKED AS THE SARGE'S FROM THE FRIDGE" AND THEN WE'LL TALK.

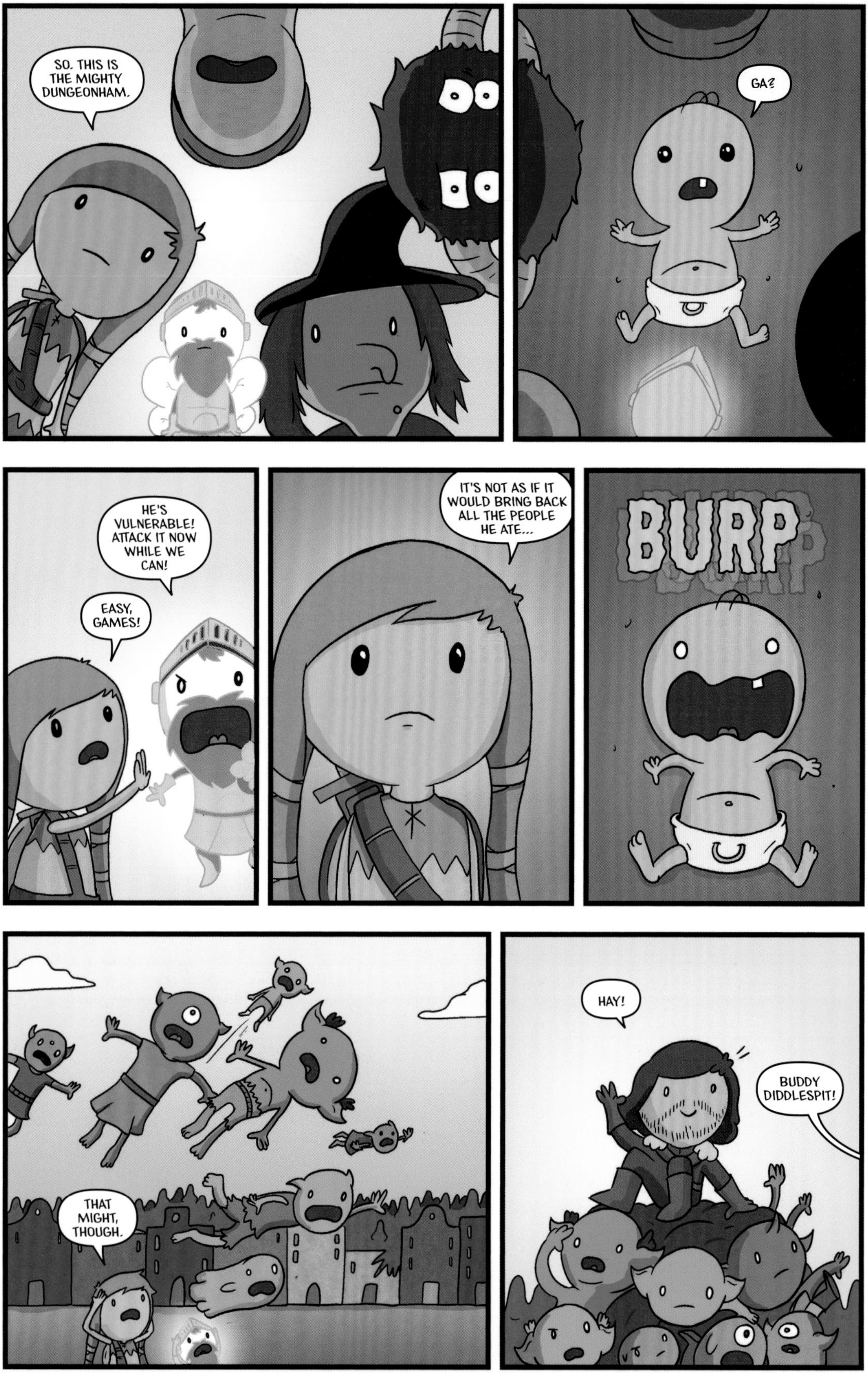
SO. THIS IS THE MIGHTY DUNGEONHAM.
GA?
HE'S VULNERABLE! ATTACK IT NOW WHILE WE CAN!
EASY, GAMES!
IT'S NOT AS IF IT WOULD BRING BACK ALL THE PEOPLE HE ATE...
BURP
THAT MIGHT, THOUGH.
HAY!
BUDDY DIDDLESPIT!

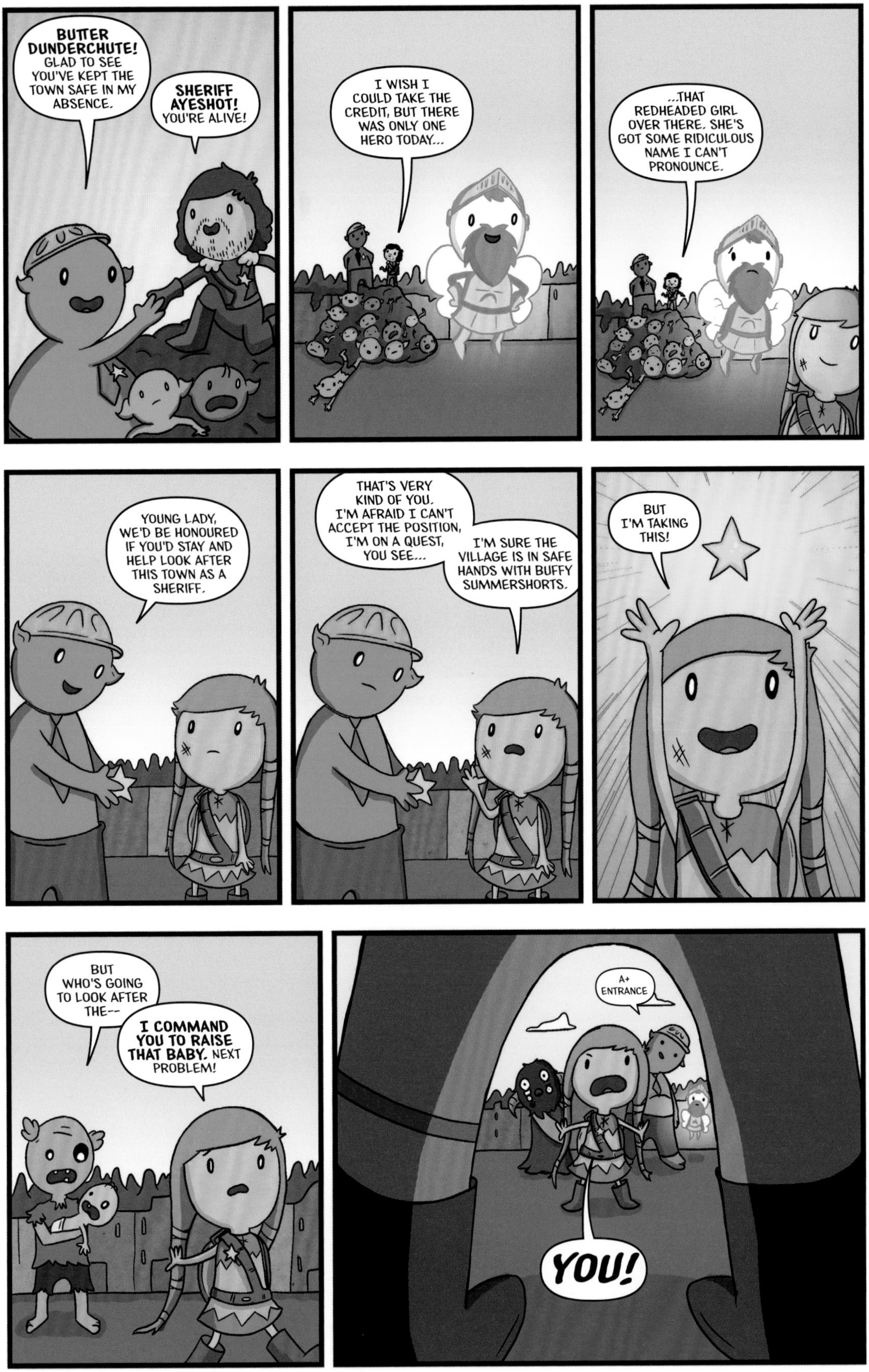
BUTTER DUNDERCHUTE! GLAD TO SEE YOU'VE KEPT THE TOWN SAFE IN MY ABSENCE.
SHERIFF AYESHOT! YOU'RE ALIVE!
I WISH I COULD TAKE THE CREDIT, BUT THERE WAS ONLY ONE HERO TODAY...
...THAT REDHEADED GIRL OVER THERE. SHE'S GOT SOME RIDICULOUS NAME I CAN'T PRONOUNCE.
YOUNG LADY, WE'D BE HONOURED IF YOU'D STAY AND HELP LOOK AFTER THIS TOWN AS A SHERIFF.
THAT'S VERY KIND OF YOU. I'M AFRAID I CAN'T ACCEPT THE POSITION, I'M ON A QUEST, YOU SEE...
I'M SURE THE VILLAGE IS IN SAFE HANDS WITH BUFFY SUMMERSHORTS.
BUT I'M TAKING THIS!
BUT WHO'S GOING TO LOOK AFTER THE--
I COMMAND YOU TO RAISE THAT BABY. NEXT PROBLEM!
A+ ENTRANCE
YOU!

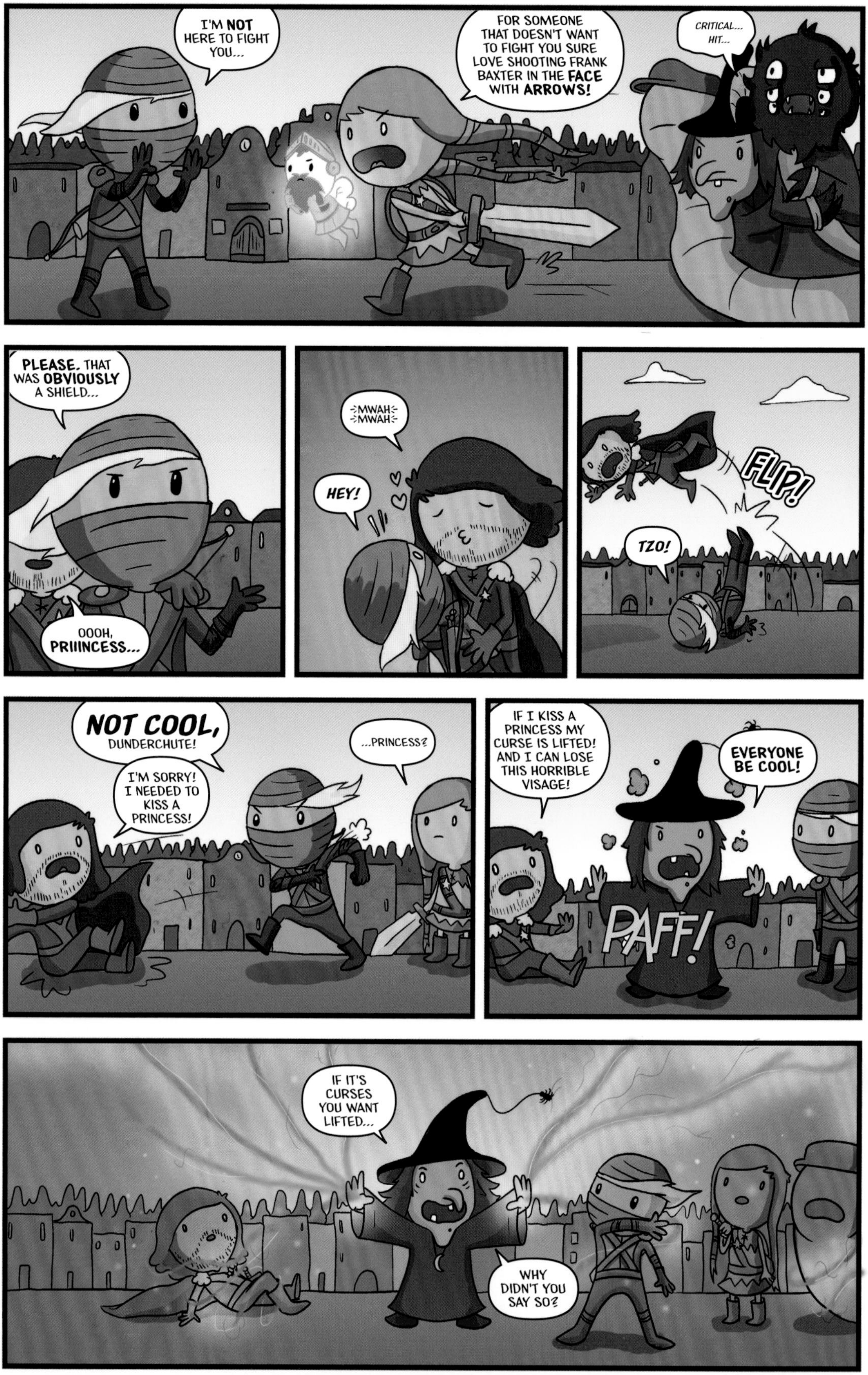
I'M NOT HERE TO FIGHT YOU...
FOR SOMEONE THAT DOESN'T WANT TO FIGHT YOU SURE LOVE SHOOTING FRANK BAXTER IN THE FACE WITH ARROWS!
CRITICAL... HIT...
PLEASE. THAT WAS OBVIOUSLY A SHIELD...
OOOH, PRIIINCESS...
MWAH MWAH
HEY!
FLIP!
TZO!
NOT COOL, DUNDERCHUTE!
I'M SORRY! I NEEDED TO KISS A PRINCESS!
...PRINCESS?
IF I KISS A PRINCESS MY CURSE IS LIFTED! AND I CAN LOSE THIS HORRIBLE VISAGE!
EVERYONE BE COOL!
PAFF!
IF IT'S CURSES YOU WANT LIFTED...
WHY DIDN'T YOU SAY SO?

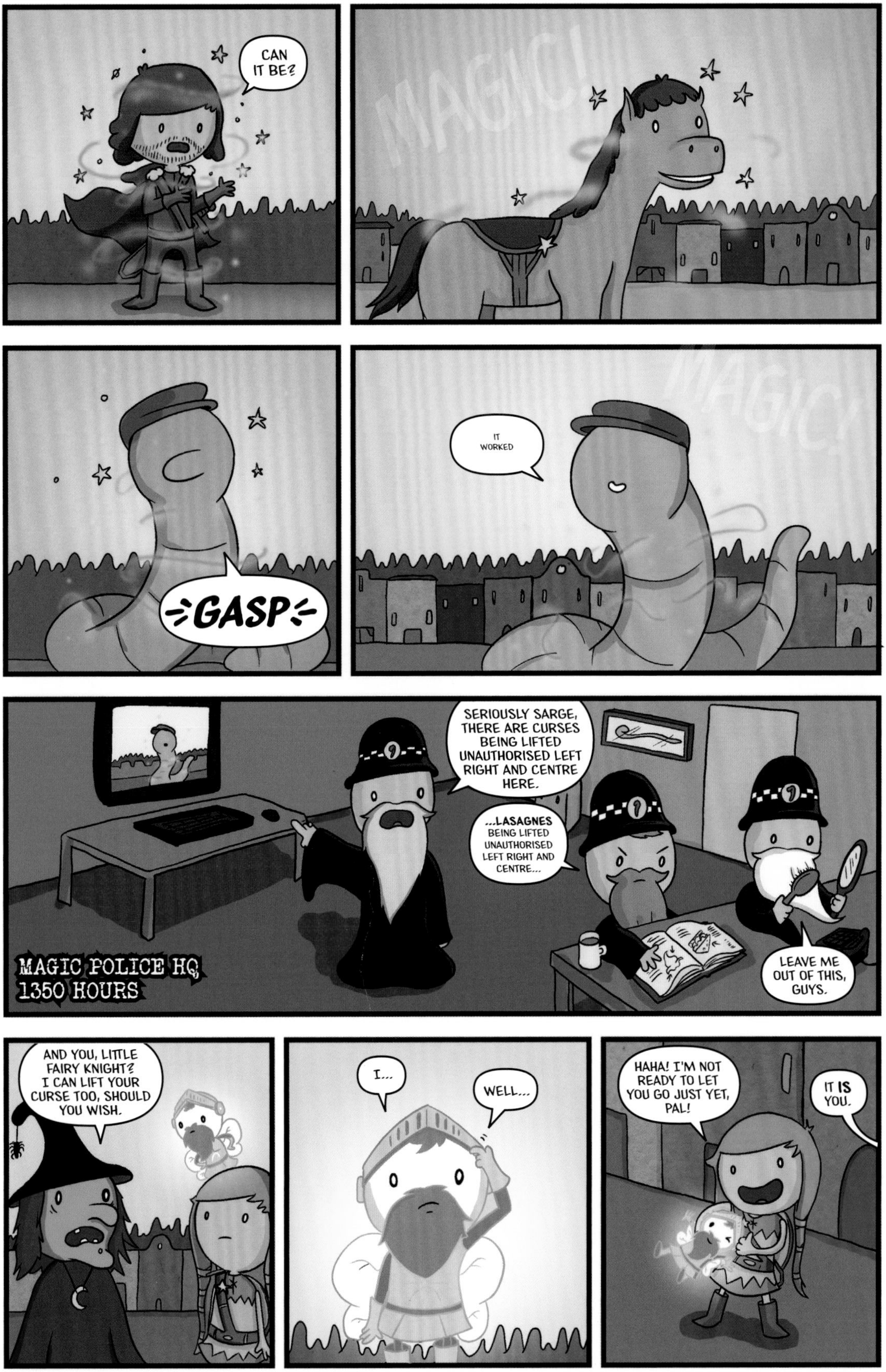
CAN IT BE?
MAGIC!
GASP
IT WORKED
MAGIC!
MAGIC POLICE HQ
1350 HOURS
SERIOUSLY SARGE, THERE ARE CURSES BEING LIFTED UNAUTHORISED LEFT RIGHT AND CENTRE HERE.
...LASAGNES BEING LIFTED UNAUTHORISED LEFT RIGHT AND CENTRE...
LEAVE ME OUT OF THIS, GUYS.
AND YOU, LITTLE FAIRY KNIGHT? I CAN LIFT YOUR CURSE TOO, SHOULD YOU WISH.
I...
WELL...
HAHA! I'M NOT READY TO LET YOU GO JUST YET, PAL!
IT IS YOU.

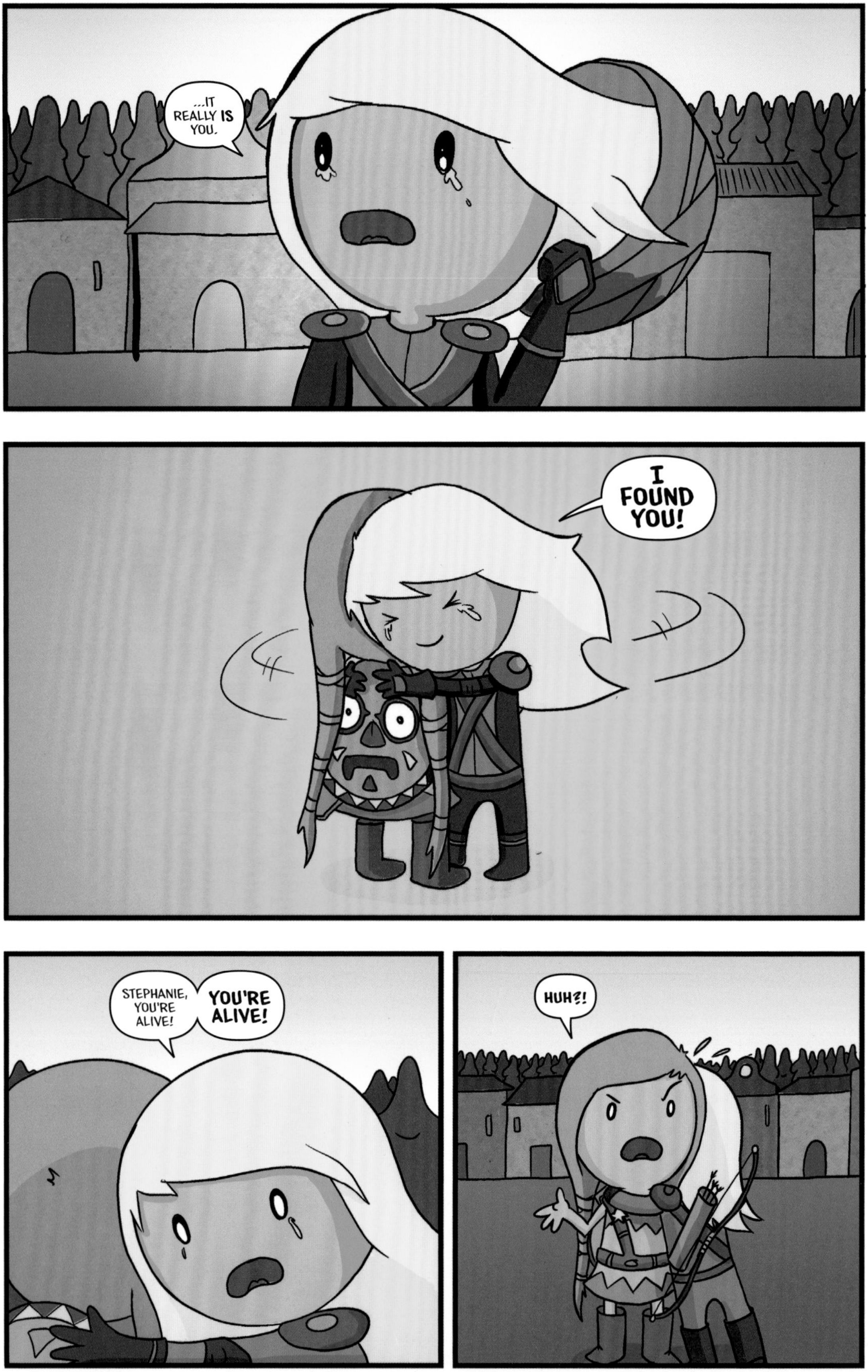
...IT REALLY IS YOU.
I FOUND YOU!
STEPHANIE, YOU'RE ALIVE!
YOU'RE ALIVE!
HUH?!

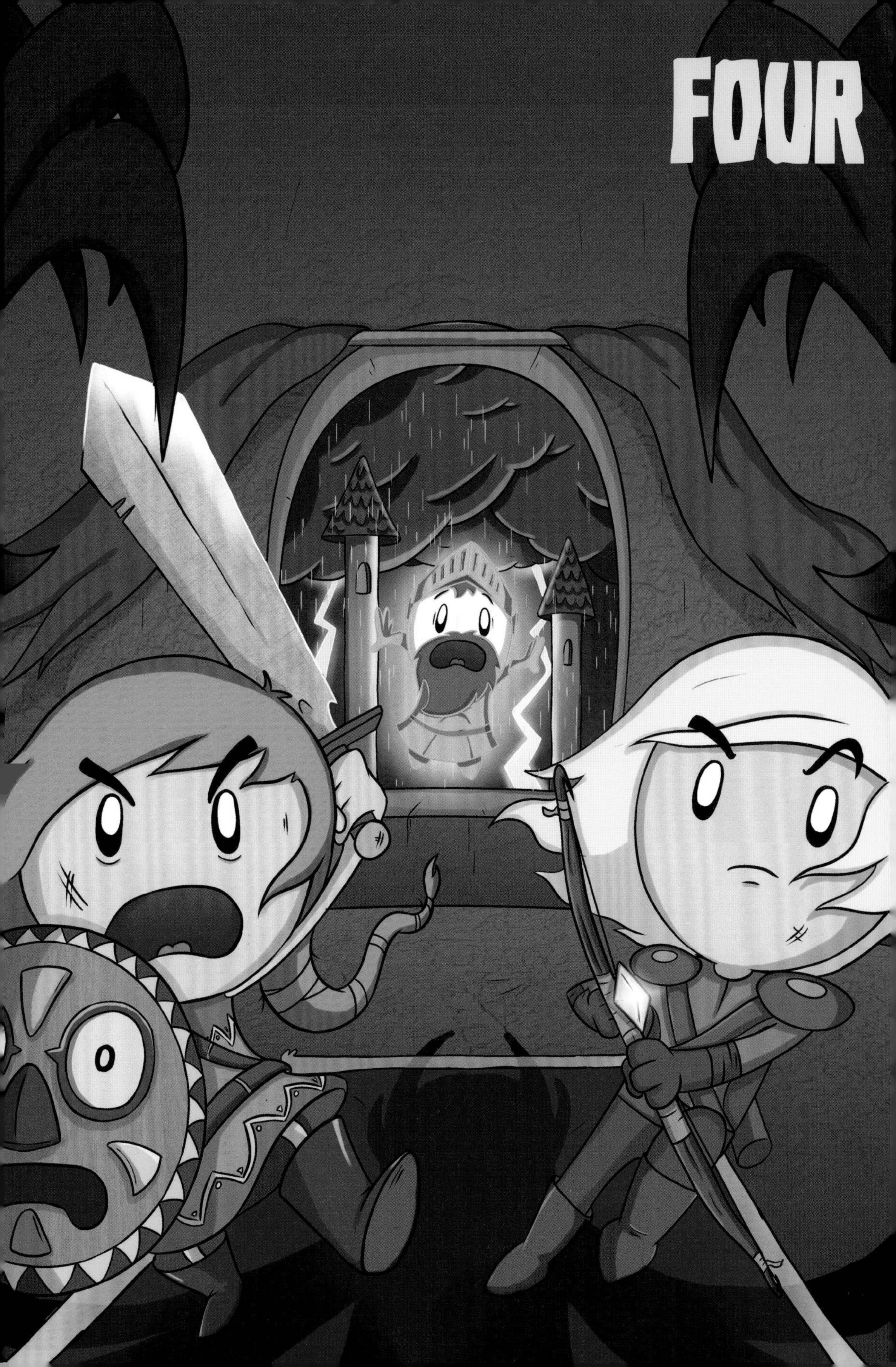
FOUR

"WE'RE ABOUT TO LEVEL UP."

THIS IS A STORY OF A GIRL AND HER SWORD.

I ALREADY TOLD YOU THAT?

OH, COOL.

SORRY TO BORE YOU.

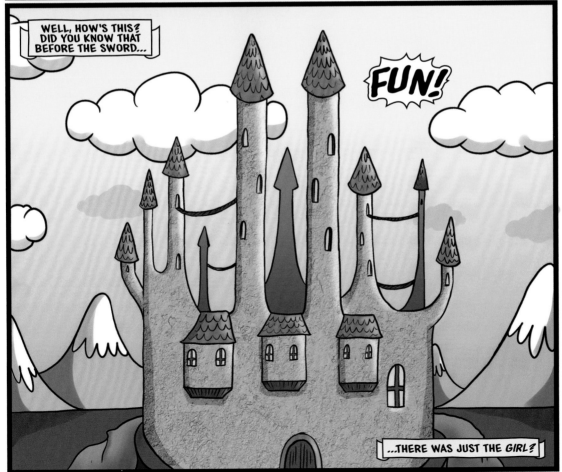

WELL, HOW'S THIS? DID YOU KNOW THAT BEFORE THE SWORD...

FUN!

...THERE WAS JUST THE *GIRL?*

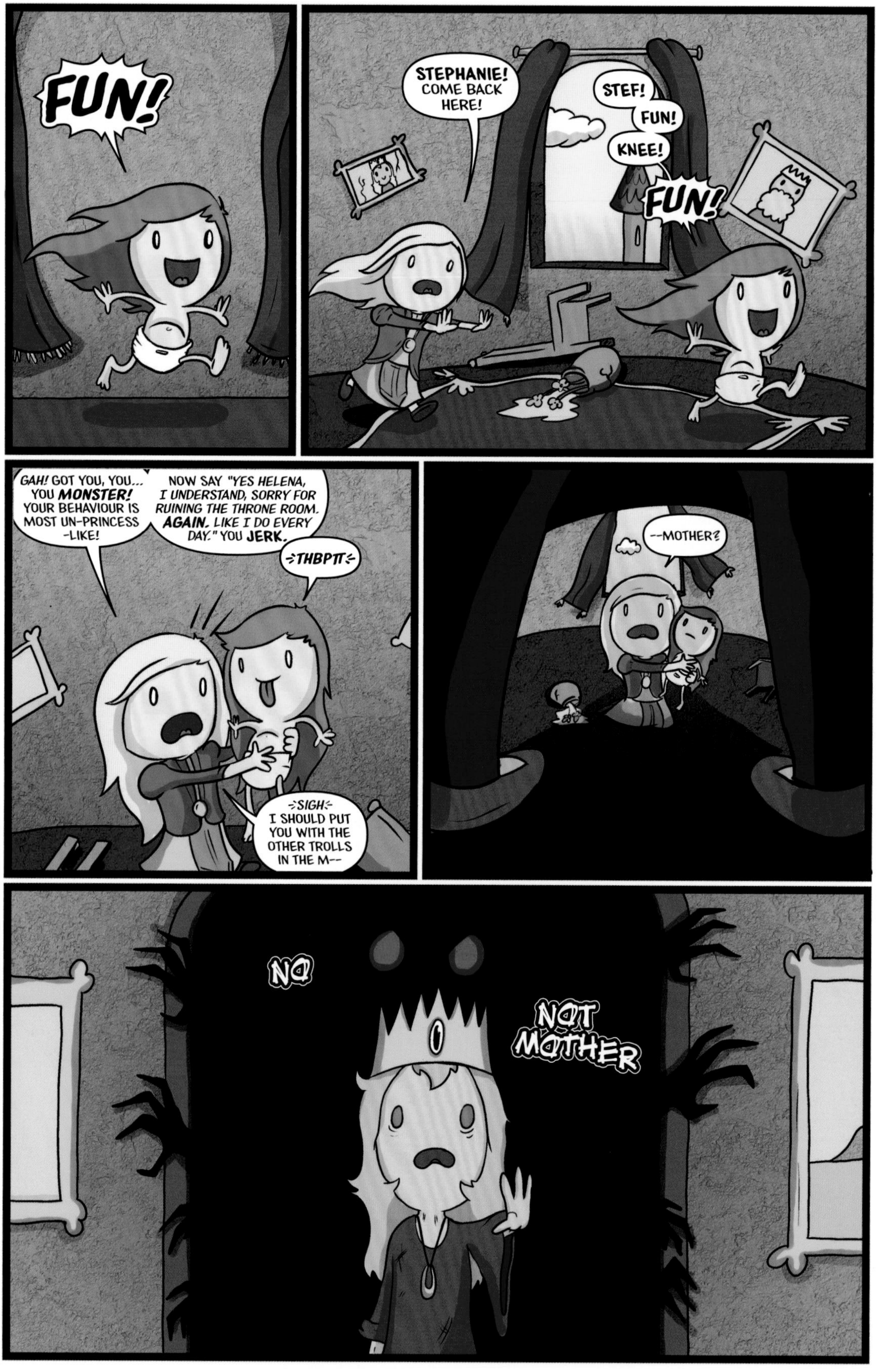
FUN!
STEPHANIE! COME BACK HERE!
STEF!
FUN!
KNEE!
FUN!
GAH! GOT YOU, YOU... YOU MONSTER! YOUR BEHAVIOUR IS MOST UN-PRINCESS -LIKE!
NOW SAY "YES HELENA, I UNDERSTAND, SORRY FOR RUINING THE THRONE ROOM. AGAIN. LIKE I DO EVERY DAY." YOU JERK.
THBPTT
SIGH I SHOULD PUT YOU WITH THE OTHER TROLLS IN THE M--
--MOTHER?
NO
NOT MOTHER

≂HNNG≂

WHAT **ARE** YOU?

YOU WILL LEARN OF US

YOU ARE OF USE

FUN?

THIS ONE

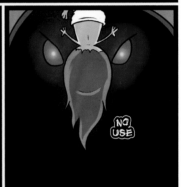

NO USE

NO! DON'T HURT HER! IF YOU WANT MY HELP, **DO NOT HURT HER.**

WE WILL NOT HARM THE CHILD

THE FALL MIGHT

NO!

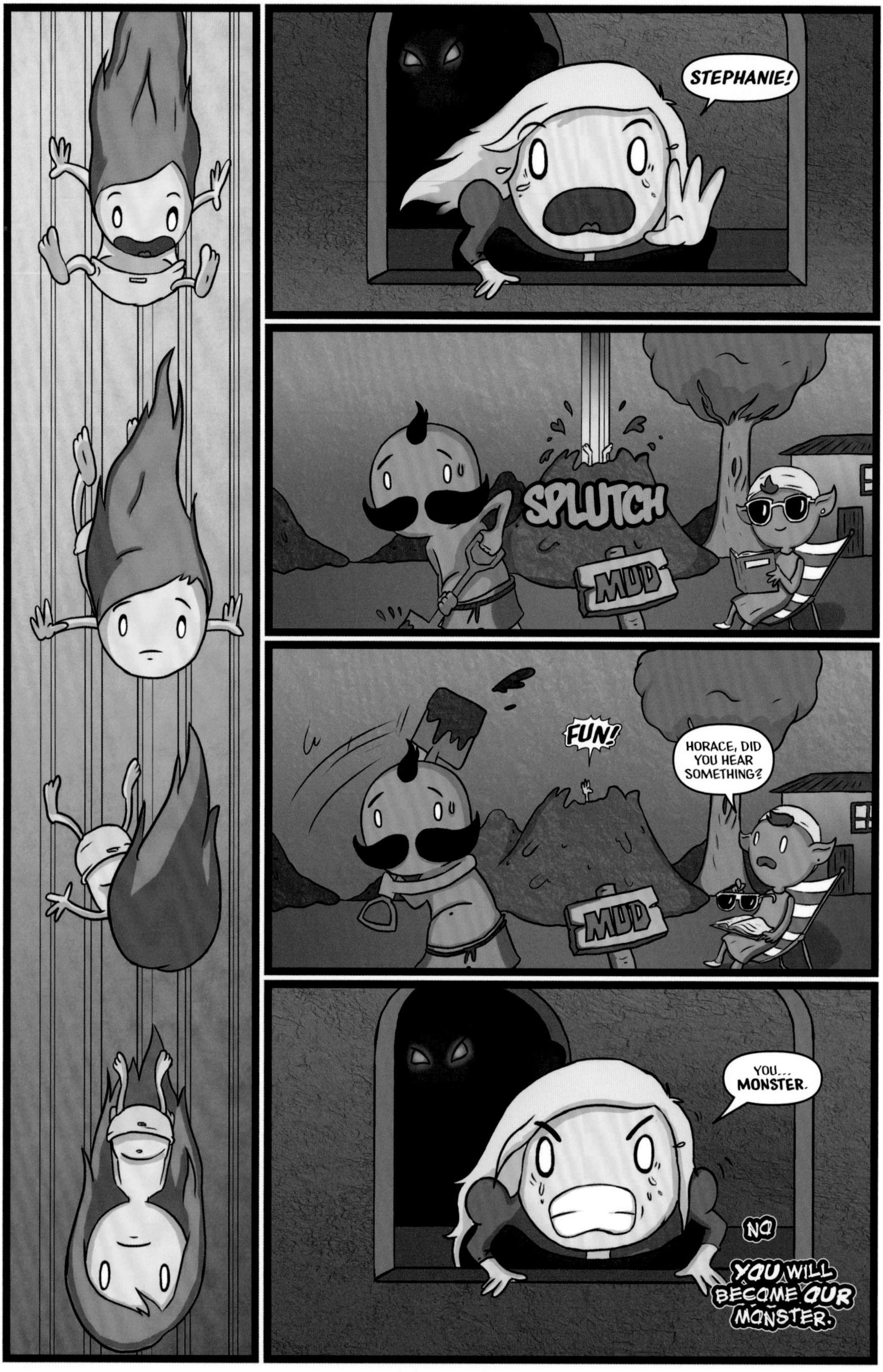
STEPHANIE!
SPLUTCH
MUD
FUN!
HORACE, DID YOU HEAR SOMETHING?
MUD
YOU... MONSTER.
NO
YOU WILL BECOME OUR MONSTER.

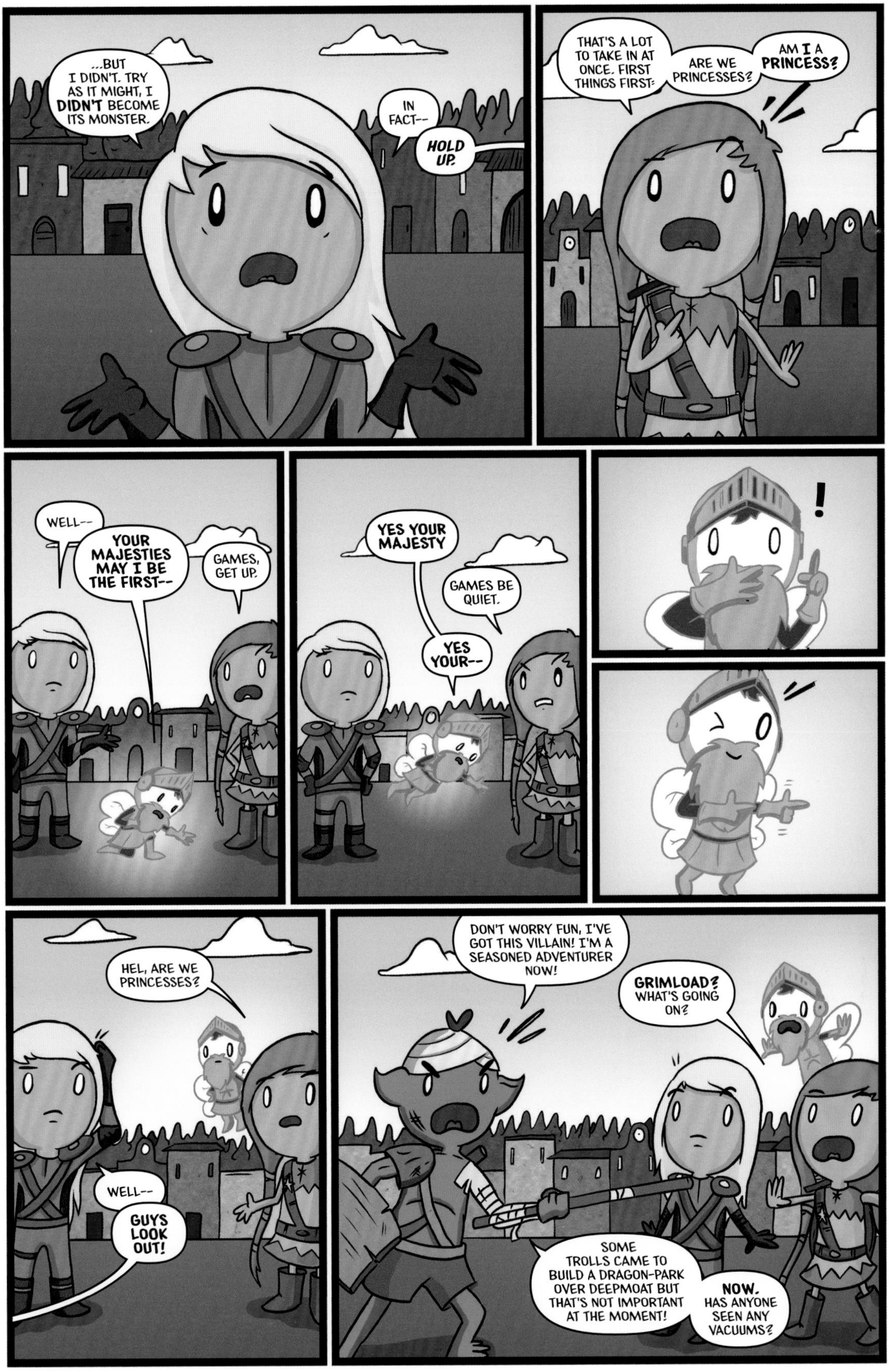
...BUT I DIDN'T. TRY AS IT MIGHT, I DIDN'T BECOME ITS MONSTER.
IN FACT--
HOLD UP.
THAT'S A LOT TO TAKE IN AT ONCE. FIRST THINGS FIRST:
ARE WE PRINCESSES?
AM I A PRINCESS?
WELL--
YOUR MAJESTIES MAY I BE THE FIRST--
GAMES, GET UP.
YES YOUR MAJESTY
GAMES BE QUIET.
YES YOUR--
!
HEL, ARE WE PRINCESSES?
WELL--
GUYS LOOK OUT!
DON'T WORRY FUN, I'VE GOT THIS VILLAIN! I'M A SEASONED ADVENTURER NOW!
GRIMLOAD? WHAT'S GOING ON?
SOME TROLLS CAME TO BUILD A DRAGON-PARK OVER DEEPMOAT BUT THAT'S NOT IMPORTANT AT THE MOMENT!
NOW. HAS ANYONE SEEN ANY VACUUMS?

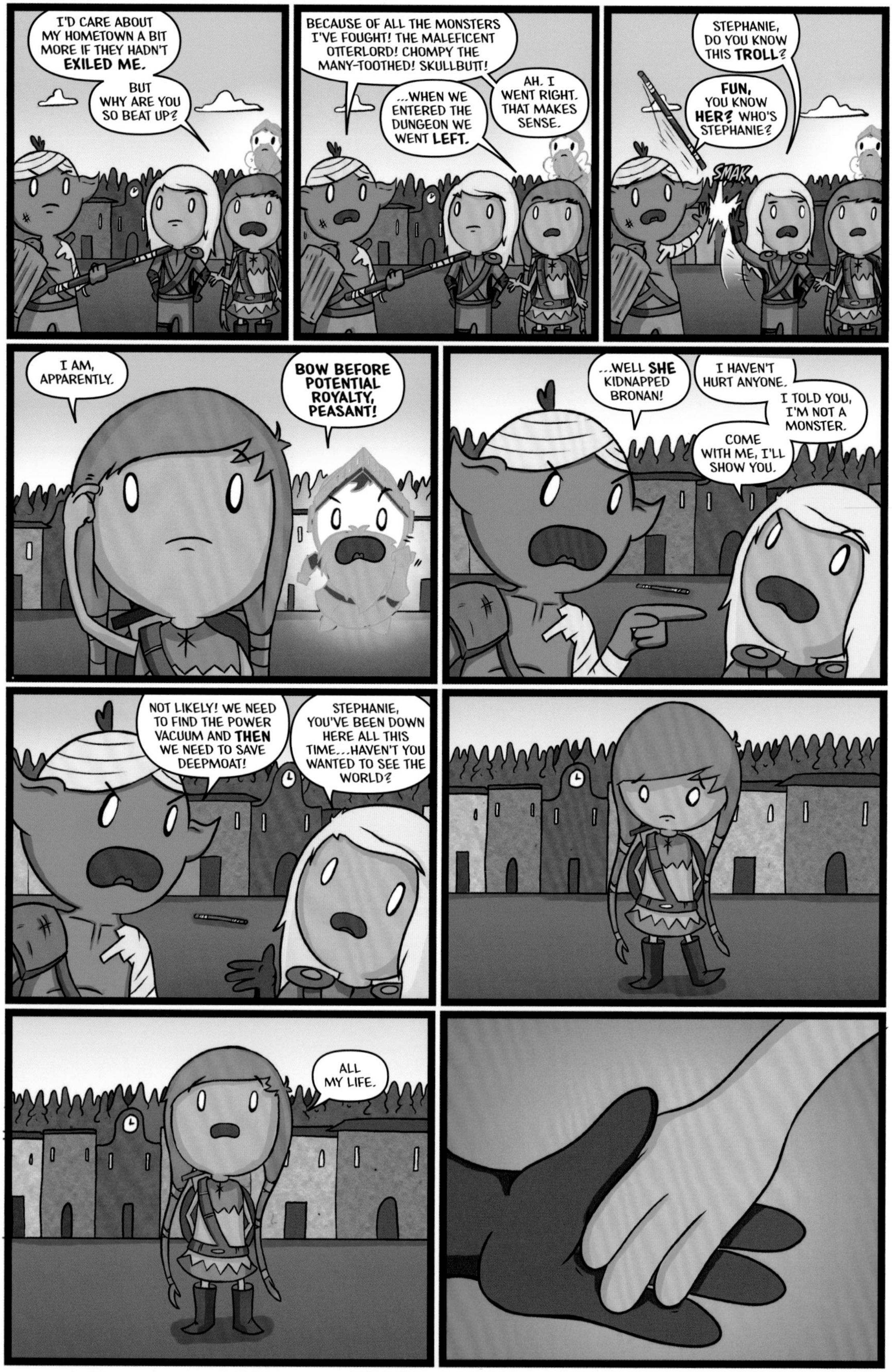
I'D CARE ABOUT MY HOMETOWN A BIT MORE IF THEY HADN'T EXILED ME.
BUT WHY ARE YOU SO BEAT UP?
BECAUSE OF ALL THE MONSTERS I'VE FOUGHT! THE MALEFICENT OTTERLORD! CHOMPY THE MANY-TOOTHED! SKULLBUTT!
...WHEN WE ENTERED THE DUNGEON WE WENT LEFT.
AH. I WENT RIGHT. THAT MAKES SENSE.
STEPHANIE, DO YOU KNOW THIS TROLL?
FUN, YOU KNOW HER? WHO'S STEPHANIE?
SMAK
I AM, APPARENTLY.
BOW BEFORE POTENTIAL ROYALTY, PEASANT!
...WELL SHE KIDNAPPED BRONAN!
I HAVEN'T HURT ANYONE.
I TOLD YOU, I'M NOT A MONSTER.
COME WITH ME, I'LL SHOW YOU.
NOT LIKELY! WE NEED TO FIND THE POWER VACUUM AND THEN WE NEED TO SAVE DEEPMOAT!
STEPHANIE, YOU'VE BEEN DOWN HERE ALL THIS TIME... HAVEN'T YOU WANTED TO SEE THE WORLD?
ALL MY LIFE.

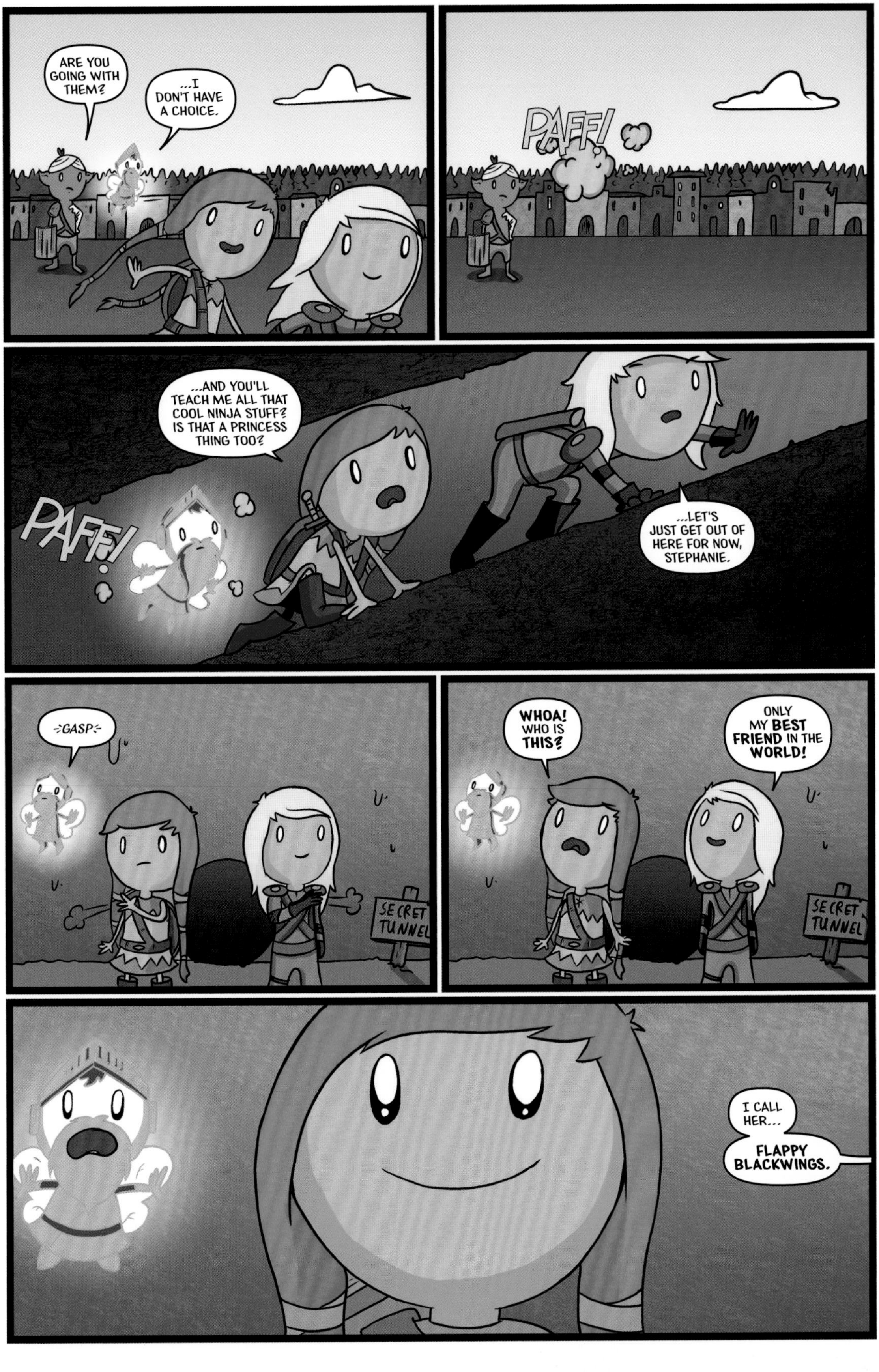
ARE YOU GOING WITH THEM?
...I DON'T HAVE A CHOICE.
PAFF!
...AND YOU'LL TEACH ME ALL THAT COOL NINJA STUFF? IS THAT A PRINCESS THING TOO?
PAFF!
...LET'S JUST GET OUT OF HERE FOR NOW, STEPHANIE.
GASP
SECRET TUNNEL
WHOA! WHO IS THIS?
ONLY MY BEST FRIEND IN THE WORLD!
SECRET TUNNEL
I CALL HER...
FLAPPY BLACKWINGS.

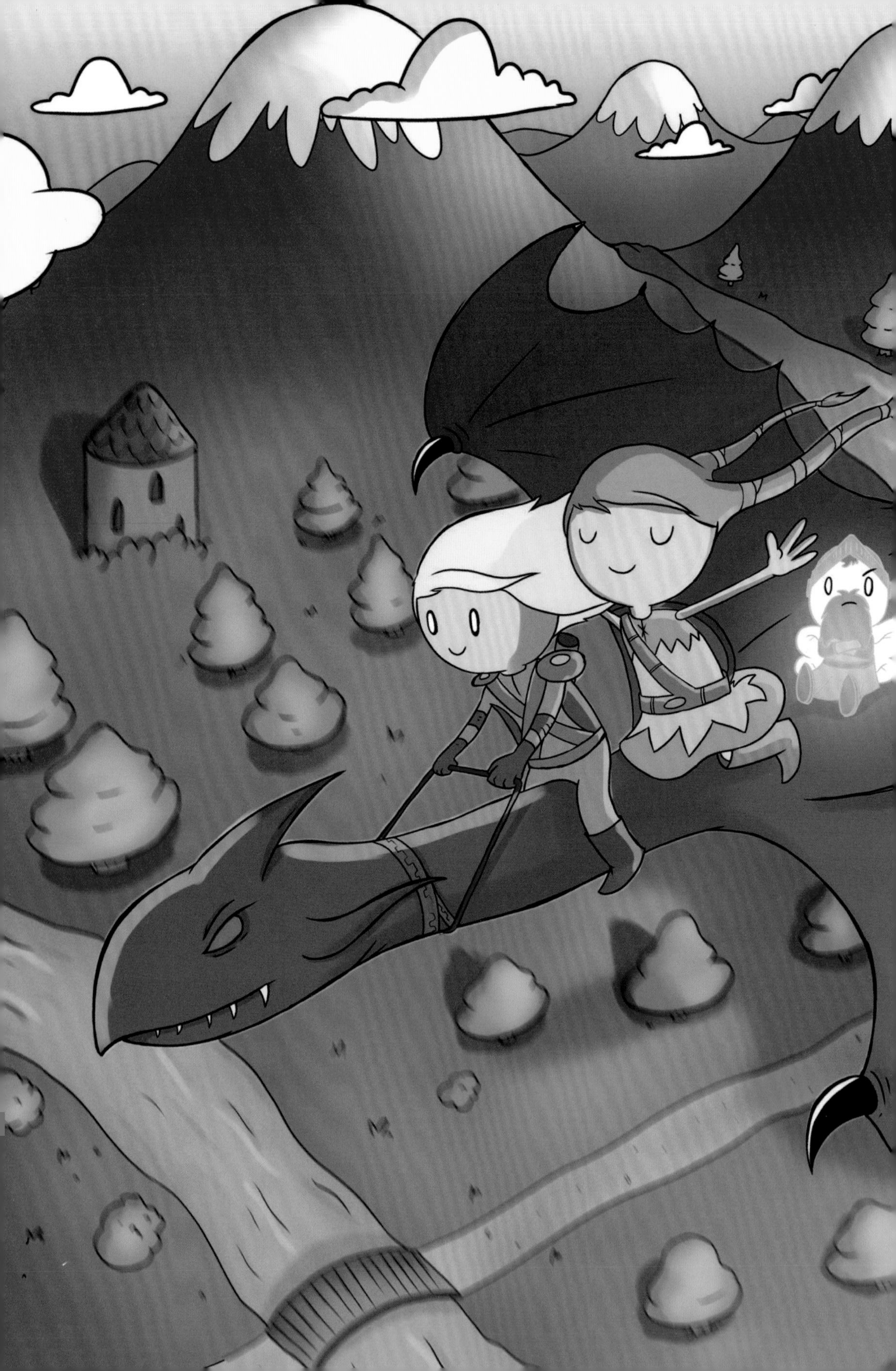

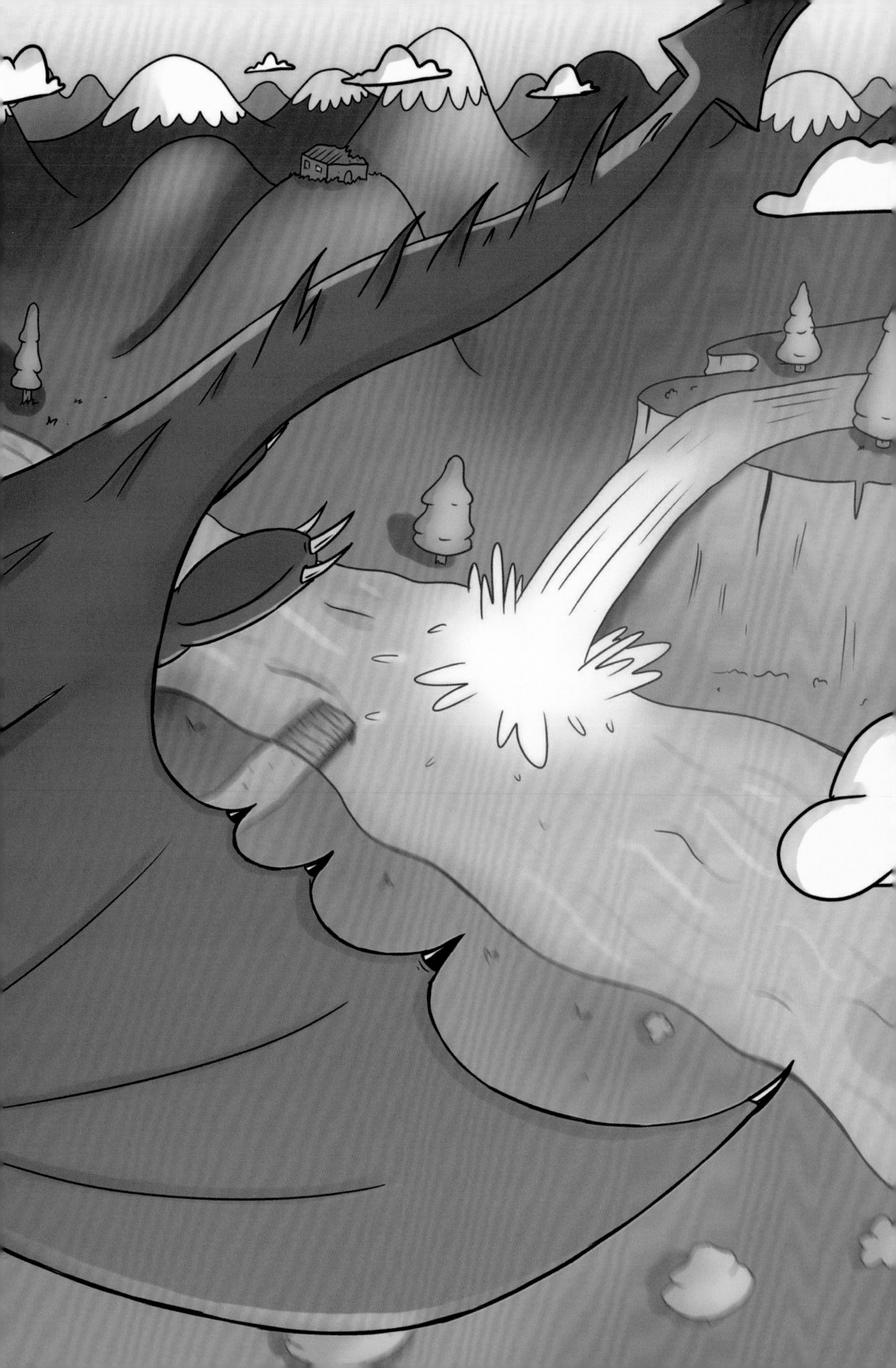

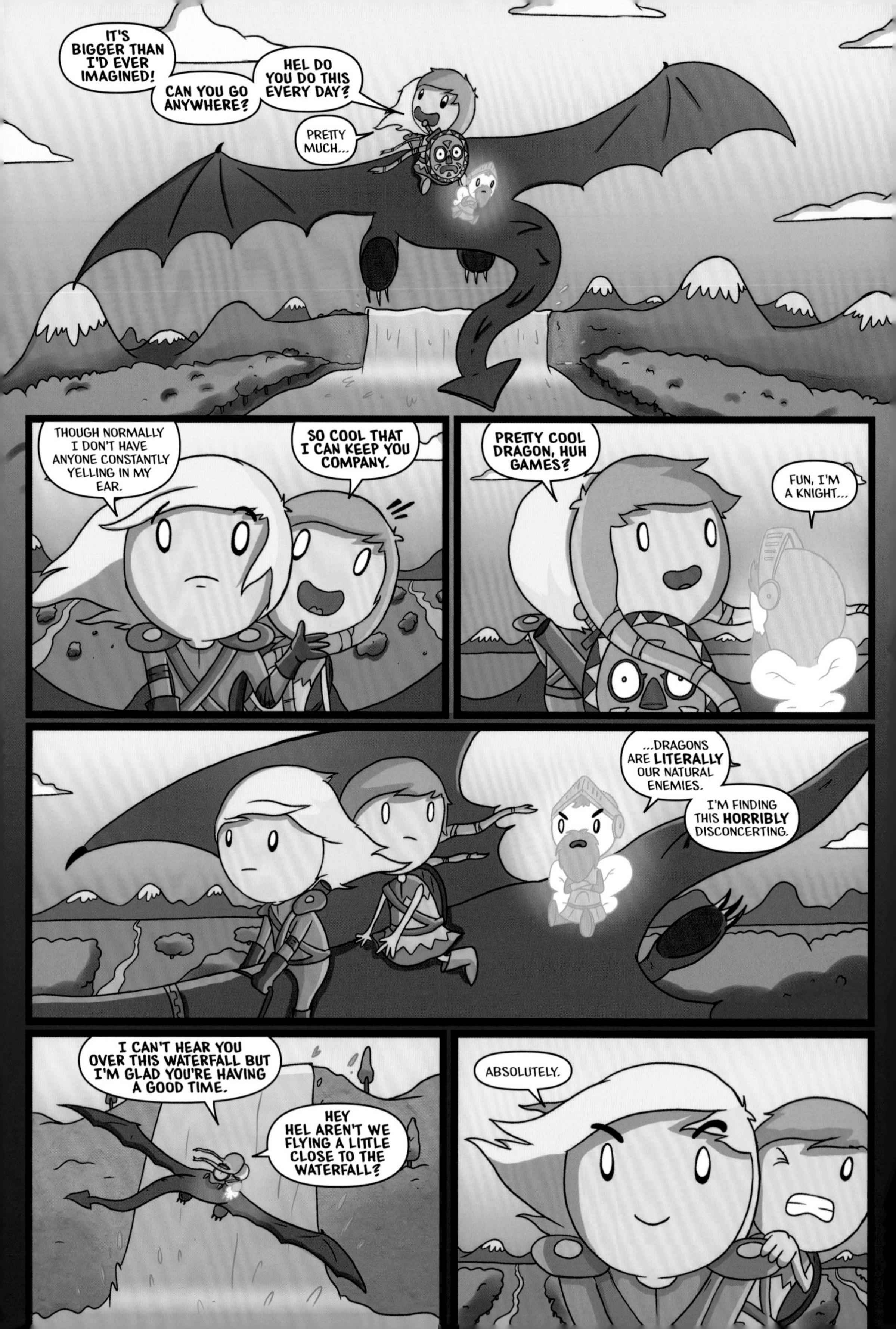
IT'S BIGGER THAN I'D EVER IMAGINED!
CAN YOU GO ANYWHERE?
HEL DO YOU DO THIS EVERY DAY?
PRETTY MUCH...
THOUGH NORMALLY I DON'T HAVE ANYONE CONSTANTLY YELLING IN MY EAR.
SO COOL THAT I CAN KEEP YOU COMPANY.
PRETTY COOL DRAGON, HUH GAMES?
FUN, I'M A KNIGHT...
...DRAGONS ARE LITERALLY OUR NATURAL ENEMIES.
I'M FINDING THIS HORRIBLY DISCONCERTING.
I CAN'T HEAR YOU OVER THIS WATERFALL BUT I'M GLAD YOU'RE HAVING A GOOD TIME.
HEY HEL AREN'T WE FLYING A LITTLE CLOSE TO THE WATERFALL?
ABSOLUTELY.

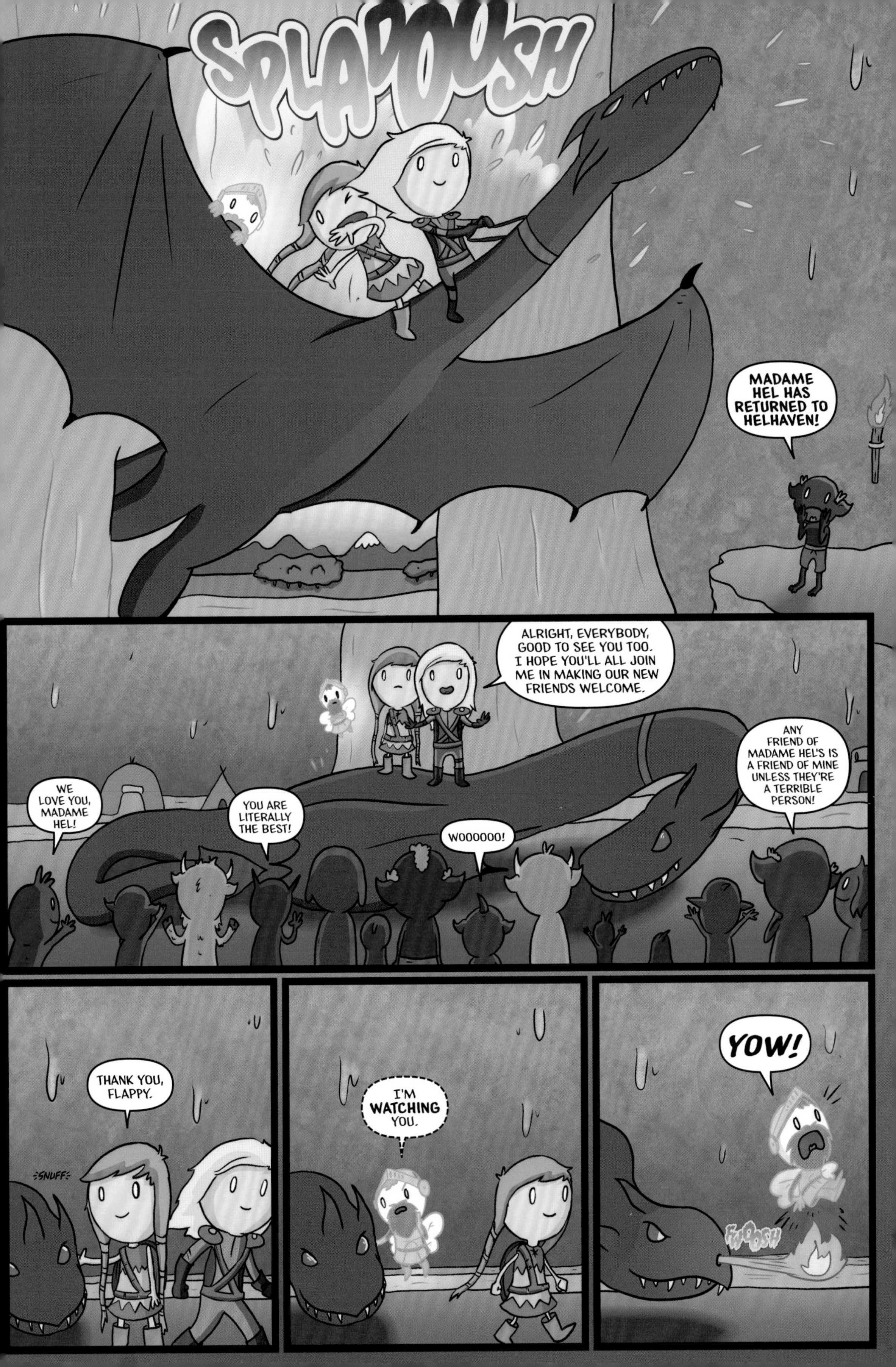
SPLADOUSH
MADAME HEL HAS RETURNED TO HELHAVEN!
ALRIGHT, EVERYBODY, GOOD TO SEE YOU TOO. I HOPE YOU'LL ALL JOIN ME IN MAKING OUR NEW FRIENDS WELCOME.
WE LOVE YOU, MADAME HEL!
YOU ARE LITERALLY THE BEST!
WOOOOOO!
ANY FRIEND OF MADAME HEL'S IS A FRIEND OF MINE UNLESS THEY'RE A TERRIBLE PERSON!
SNUFF
THANK YOU, FLAPPY.
I'M WATCHING YOU.
YOW!
FWOOSH

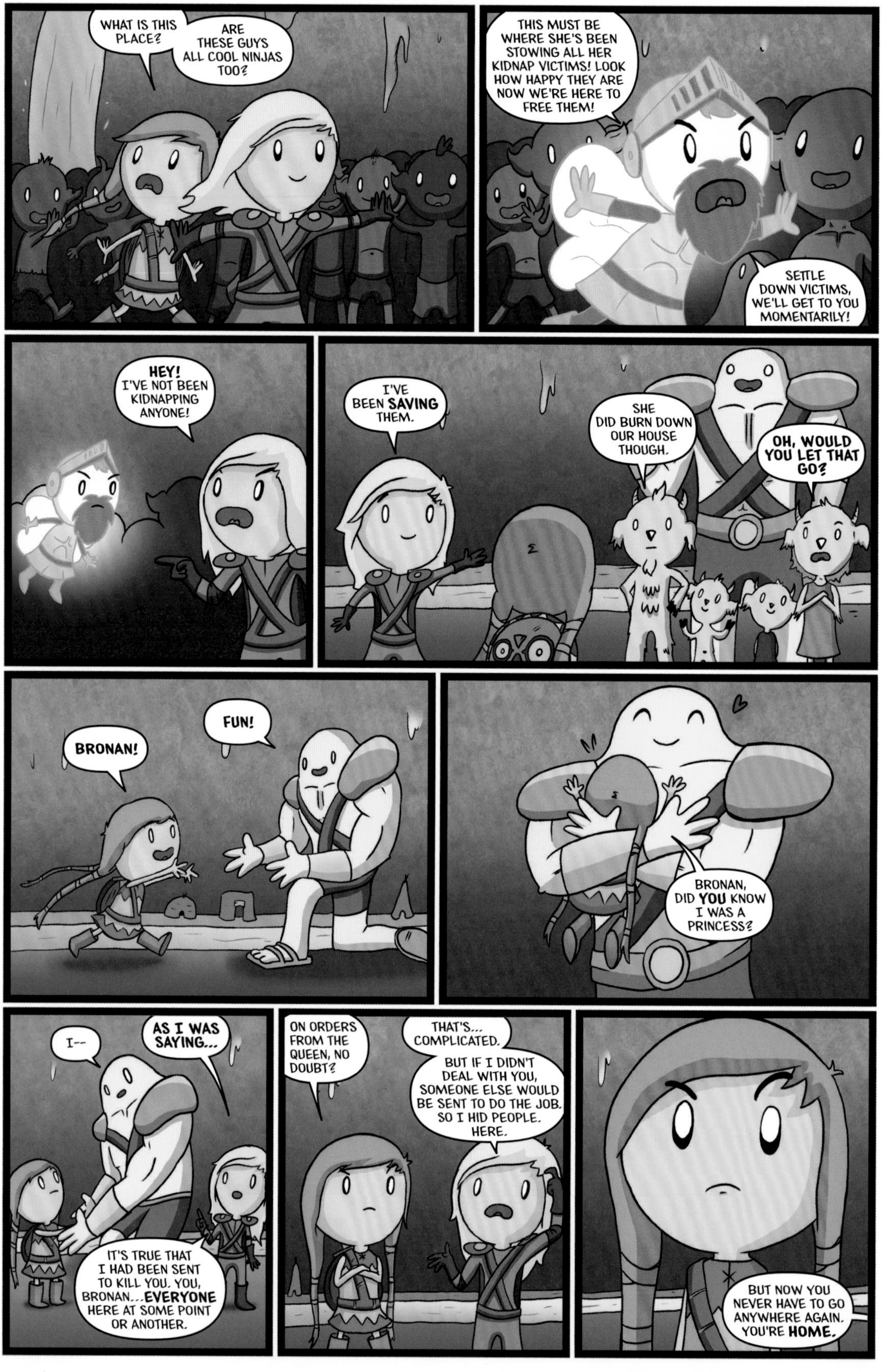
WHAT IS THIS PLACE?
ARE THESE GUYS ALL COOL NINJAS TOO?
THIS MUST BE WHERE SHE'S BEEN STOWING ALL HER KIDNAP VICTIMS! LOOK HOW HAPPY THEY ARE NOW WE'RE HERE TO FREE THEM!
SETTLE DOWN VICTIMS, WE'LL GET TO YOU MOMENTARILY!
HEY! I'VE NOT BEEN KIDNAPPING ANYONE!
I'VE BEEN SAVING THEM.
SHE DID BURN DOWN OUR HOUSE THOUGH.
OH, WOULD YOU LET THAT GO?
BRONAN!
FUN!
BRONAN, DID YOU KNOW I WAS A PRINCESS?
I--
AS I WAS SAYING...
IT'S TRUE THAT I HAD BEEN SENT TO KILL YOU. YOU, BRONAN... EVERYONE HERE AT SOME POINT OR ANOTHER.
ON ORDERS FROM THE QUEEN, NO DOUBT?
THAT'S... COMPLICATED.
BUT IF I DIDN'T DEAL WITH YOU, SOMEONE ELSE WOULD BE SENT TO DO THE JOB. SO I HID PEOPLE. HERE.
BUT NOW YOU NEVER HAVE TO GO ANYWHERE AGAIN. YOU'RE HOME.

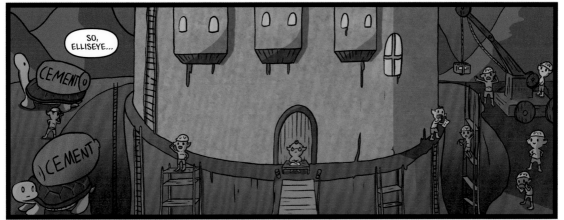

SO, ELLISEYE...

I GUESS YOU'RE GOING TO TELL ME YOU SAW THIS COMING?

...YES!

I SEE ALL!

IT'S KIND OF MY THING!

BUT IT'S OKAY! FUN WILL--

OH, **ENOUGH** ABOUT FUN! YOU PINNED ALL OUR HOPES ON THAT POOR GIRL! AND FOR WHAT? NOTHING!

SHE'S NOT COMING. SHE'S NOT GOING TO SAVE US.

MY BOY WILL!

WELL.... AS LONG AS ONE OF US IS RIGHT.

MUM?

WHAT ARE YOU TWO DOING H--

AW, I WENT THE WRONG WAY.

I WONDERED WHY I WAS FIGHTING EVERYONE TWICE.

IT'LL HAPPEN. SHE'LL COME BACK.

PLEASE HAPPEN.

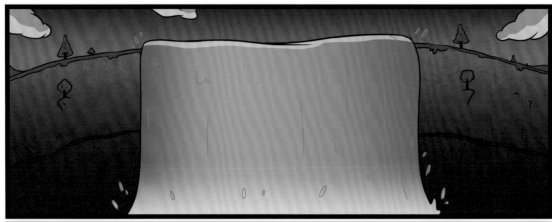

THIS IS NICE, ISN'T IT?

ALL OF US HERE.

SAFE IN THE DARKNESS OF THIS COLD, DANK CAVE.

HEL... WHAT IS IT THAT YOU'VE GOT US ALL HERE HIDING FROM?

IS THE QUEEN SOME KIND OF **MONSTER?**

WHAT? NO.

THE QUEEN'S MY **MOTHER.**

SHE'S JUST A LITTLE... **POSSESSED** BY SOMETHING.

KUMMERSPECK.

IT'S THE **KUMMERSPECK.**

A CREATURE AS OLD AS TIME ITSELF!

KUMMERSPECK

'kUm-ir-shpek

A DEMON CONSTRUCTED OF SHADOWS THAT SUSTAINS ITSELF ON THE FEELINGS OF GRIEF AND MISERY FROM THOSE AROUND IT!

MAINTAINS A SYMBIOTIC RELATIONSHIP WITH A HUMAN HOST--WILL DIE WITHOUT ONE.

TOO BAD NONE HAVE GOT NEAR ENOUGH TO KILL IT!

SO THIS THING DELIBERATELY KEEPS EVERYONE MISERABLE TO KEEP **ITSELF** ALIVE?

THAT MUST BE WHY DEEPMOAT'S BEING DEMOLISHED!

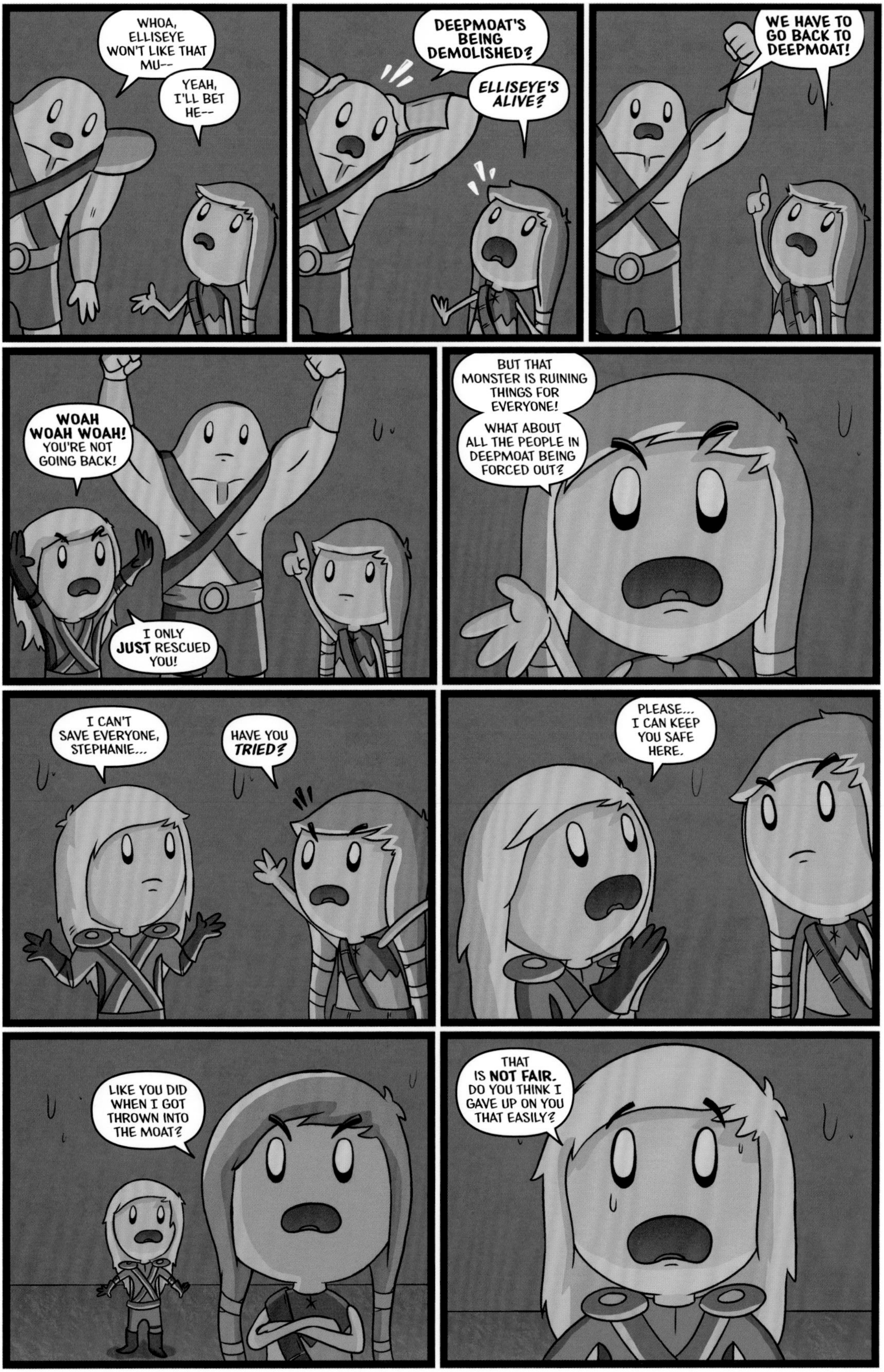
WHOA, ELLISEYE WON'T LIKE THAT MU--
YEAH, I'LL BET HE--
DEEPMOAT'S BEING DEMOLISHED?
ELLISEYE'S ALIVE?
WE HAVE TO GO BACK TO DEEPMOAT!
WOAH WOAH WOAH! YOU'RE NOT GOING BACK!
I ONLY JUST RESCUED YOU!
BUT THAT MONSTER IS RUINING THINGS FOR EVERYONE!
WHAT ABOUT ALL THE PEOPLE IN DEEPMOAT BEING FORCED OUT?
I CAN'T SAVE EVERYONE, STEPHANIE...
HAVE YOU TRIED?
PLEASE... I CAN KEEP YOU SAFE HERE.
LIKE YOU DID WHEN I GOT THROWN INTO THE MOAT?
THAT IS NOT FAIR. DO YOU THINK I GAVE UP ON YOU THAT EASILY?

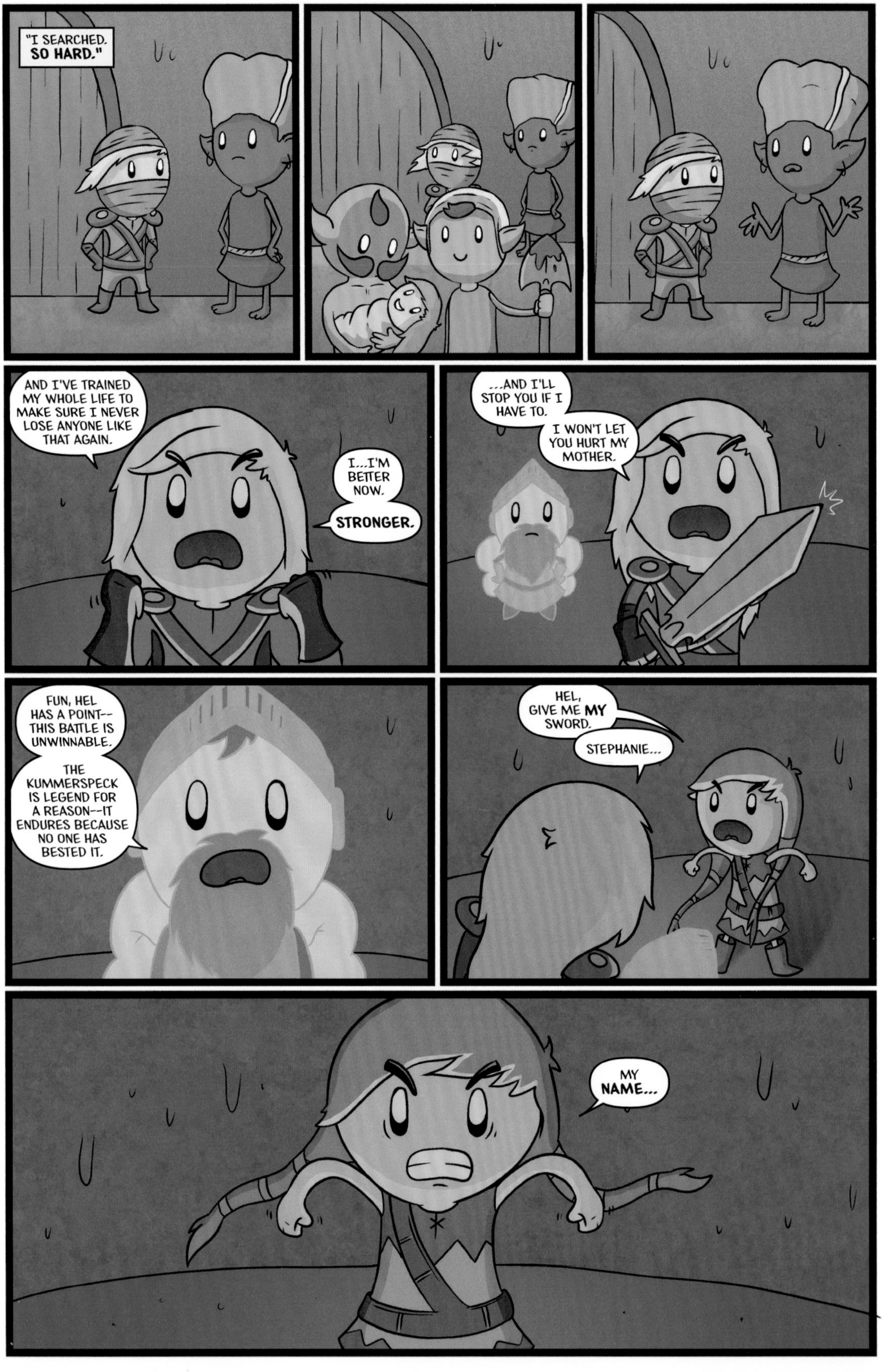
"I SEARCHED.
SO HARD."
AND I'VE TRAINED MY WHOLE LIFE TO MAKE SURE I NEVER LOSE ANYONE LIKE THAT AGAIN.
I...I'M BETTER NOW.
STRONGER.
...AND I'LL STOP YOU IF I HAVE TO.
I WON'T LET YOU HURT MY MOTHER.
FUN, HEL HAS A POINT-- THIS BATTLE IS UNWINNABLE.
THE KUMMERSPECK IS LEGEND FOR A REASON--IT ENDURES BECAUSE NO ONE HAS BESTED IT.
HEL, GIVE ME MY SWORD.
STEPHANIE...
MY NAME...

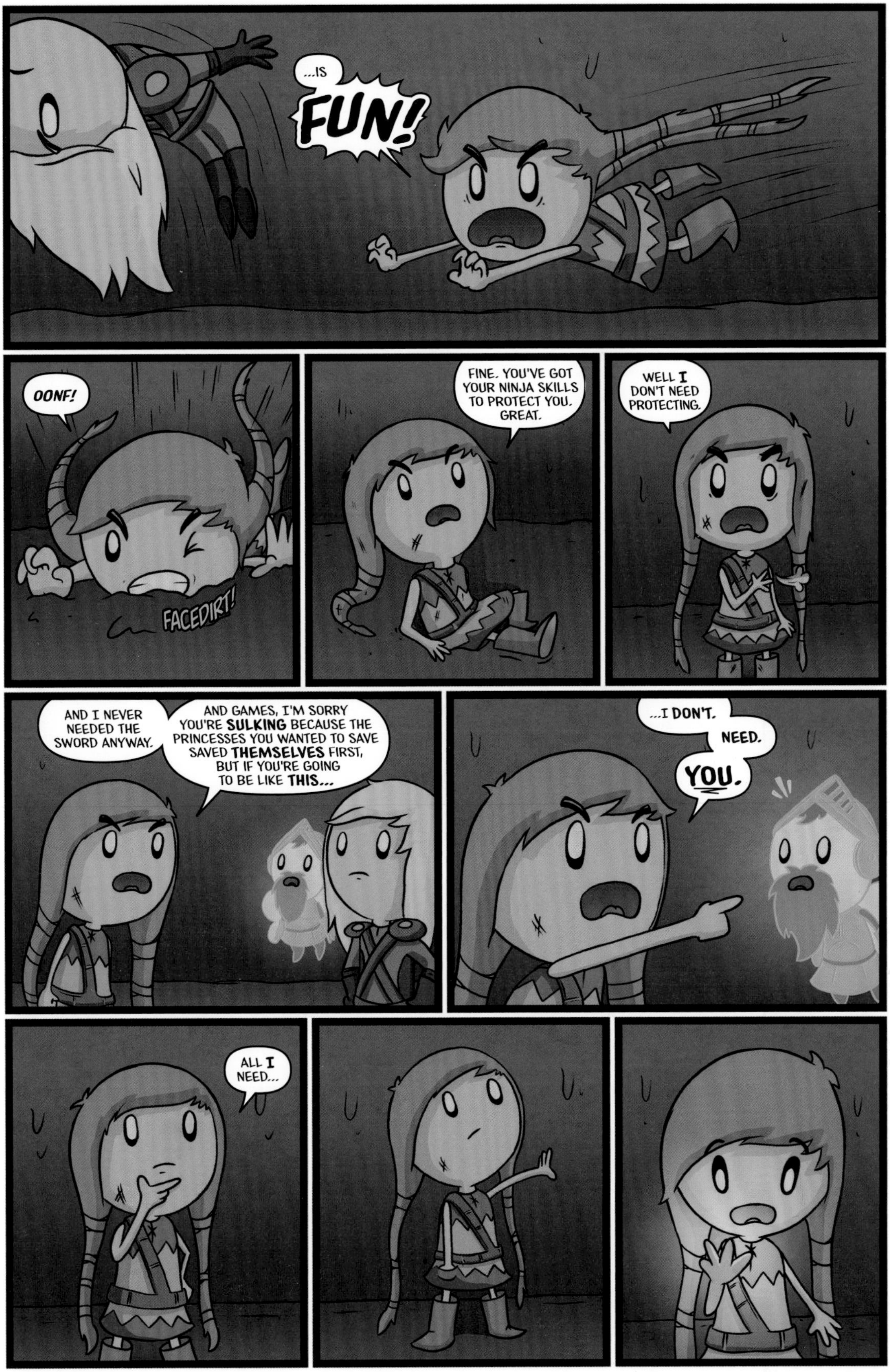

...IS
FUN!
OONF!
FACEDIRT!
FINE. YOU'VE GOT YOUR NINJA SKILLS TO PROTECT YOU. GREAT.
WELL I DON'T NEED PROTECTING.
AND I NEVER NEEDED THE SWORD ANYWAY.
AND GAMES, I'M SORRY YOU'RE SULKING BECAUSE THE PRINCESSES YOU WANTED TO SAVE SAVED THEMSELVES FIRST, BUT IF YOU'RE GOING TO BE LIKE THIS...
...I DON'T.
NEED.
YOU.
ALL I NEED...

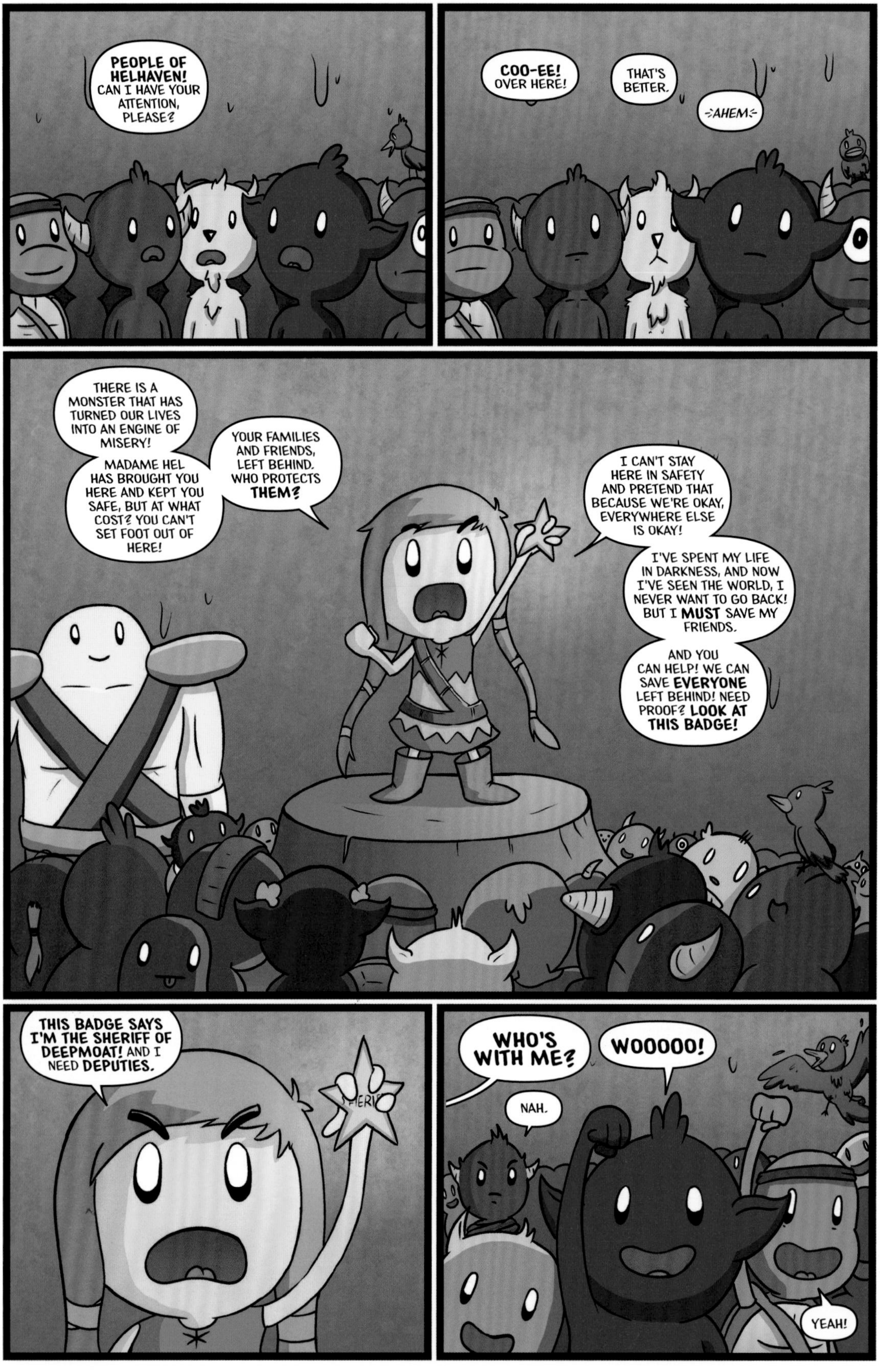
PEOPLE OF HELHAVEN! CAN I HAVE YOUR ATTENTION, PLEASE?
COO-EE! OVER HERE!
THAT'S BETTER.
AHEM
THERE IS A MONSTER THAT HAS TURNED OUR LIVES INTO AN ENGINE OF MISERY!
MADAME HEL HAS BROUGHT YOU HERE AND KEPT YOU SAFE, BUT AT WHAT COST? YOU CAN'T SET FOOT OUT OF HERE!
YOUR FAMILIES AND FRIENDS, LEFT BEHIND. WHO PROTECTS THEM?
I CAN'T STAY HERE IN SAFETY AND PRETEND THAT BECAUSE WE'RE OKAY, EVERYWHERE ELSE IS OKAY!
I'VE SPENT MY LIFE IN DARKNESS, AND NOW I'VE SEEN THE WORLD, I NEVER WANT TO GO BACK! BUT I MUST SAVE MY FRIENDS.
AND YOU CAN HELP! WE CAN SAVE EVERYONE LEFT BEHIND! NEED PROOF? LOOK AT THIS BADGE!
THIS BADGE SAYS I'M THE SHERIFF OF DEEPMOAT! AND I NEED DEPUTIES.
WHO'S WITH ME?
WOOOOO!
NAH.
YEAH!

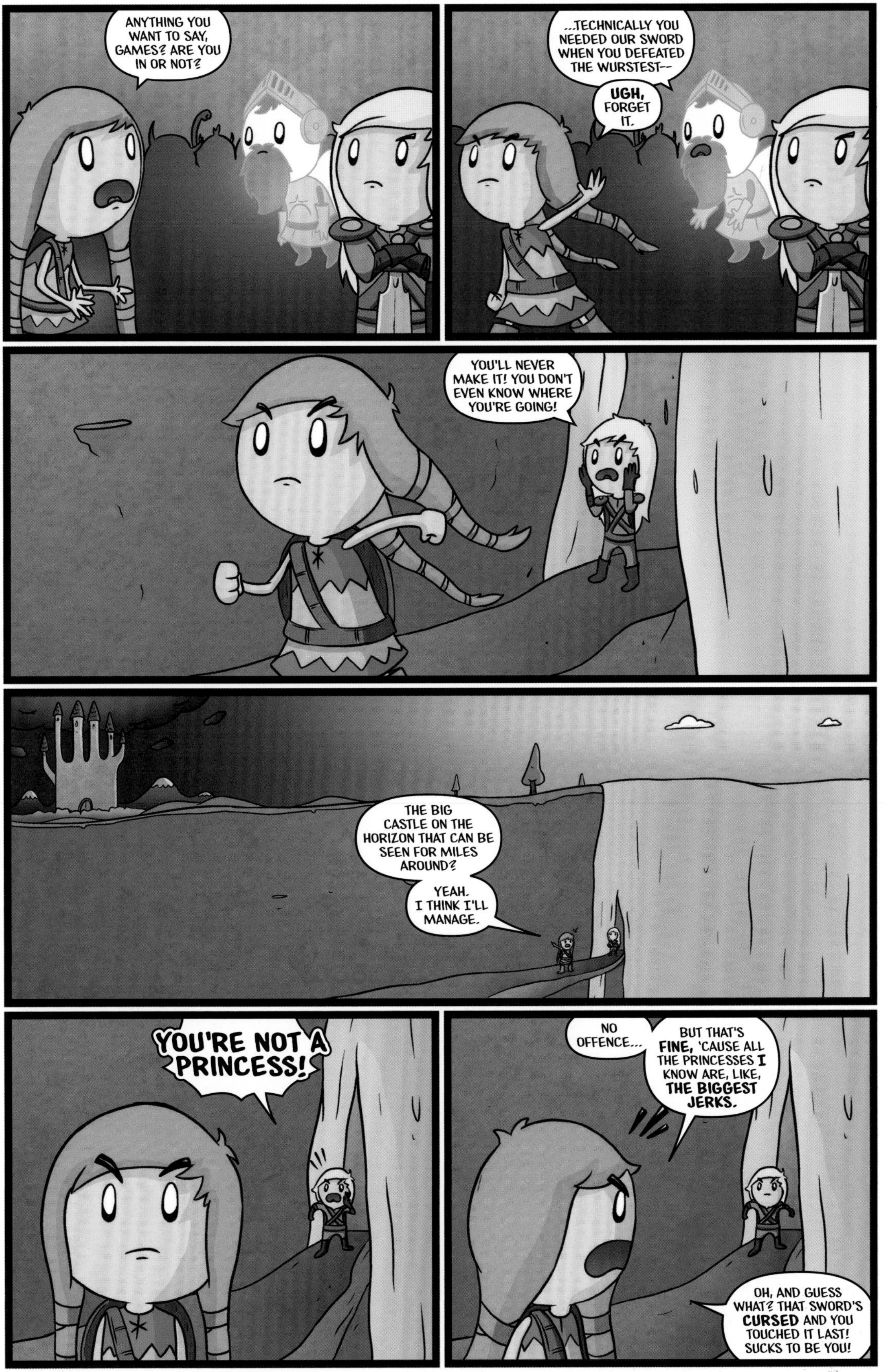

ANYTHING YOU WANT TO SAY, GAMES? ARE YOU IN OR NOT?
...TECHNICALLY YOU NEEDED OUR SWORD WHEN YOU DEFEATED THE WURSTEST--
UGH, FORGET IT.
YOU'LL NEVER MAKE IT! YOU DON'T EVEN KNOW WHERE YOU'RE GOING!
THE BIG CASTLE ON THE HORIZON THAT CAN BE SEEN FOR MILES AROUND?
YEAH. I THINK I'LL MANAGE.
YOU'RE NOT A PRINCESS!
NO OFFENCE...
BUT THAT'S FINE, 'CAUSE ALL THE PRINCESSES I KNOW ARE, LIKE, THE BIGGEST JERKS.
OH, AND GUESS WHAT? THAT SWORD'S CURSED AND YOU TOUCHED IT LAST! SUCKS TO BE YOU!

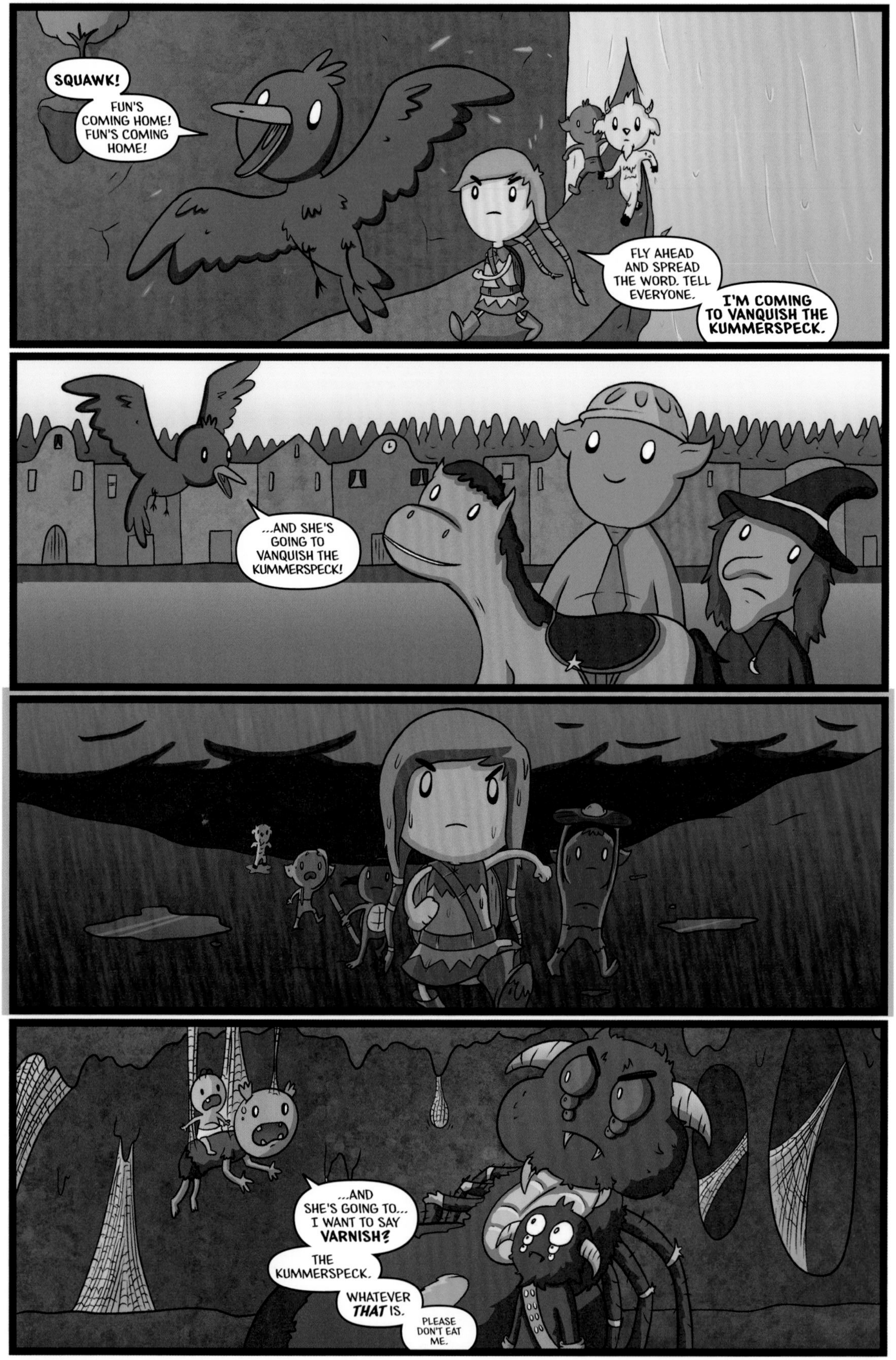
SQUAWK!
FUN'S COMING HOME! FUN'S COMING HOME!
FLY AHEAD AND SPREAD THE WORD. TELL EVERYONE.
I'M COMING TO VANQUISH THE KUMMERSPECK.
...AND SHE'S GOING TO VANQUISH THE KUMMERSPECK!
...AND SHE'S GOING TO... I WANT TO SAY VARNISH?
THE KUMMERSPECK.
WHATEVER THAT IS.
PLEASE DON'T EAT ME.

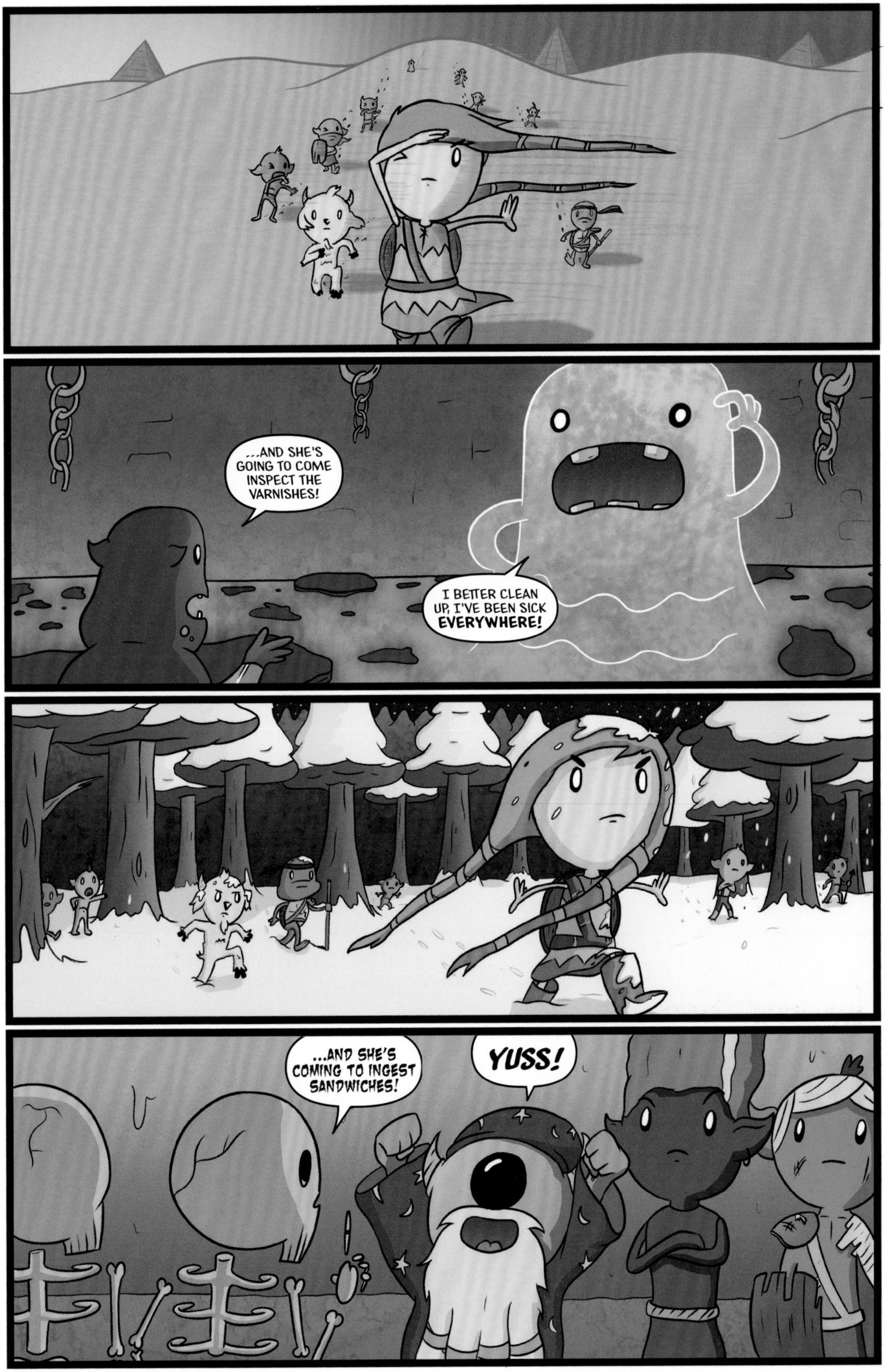
...AND SHE'S GOING TO COME INSPECT THE VARNISHES!
I BETTER CLEAN UP, I'VE BEEN SICK **EVERYWHERE!**
...AND SHE'S COMING TO INGEST SANDWICHES!
YUSS!

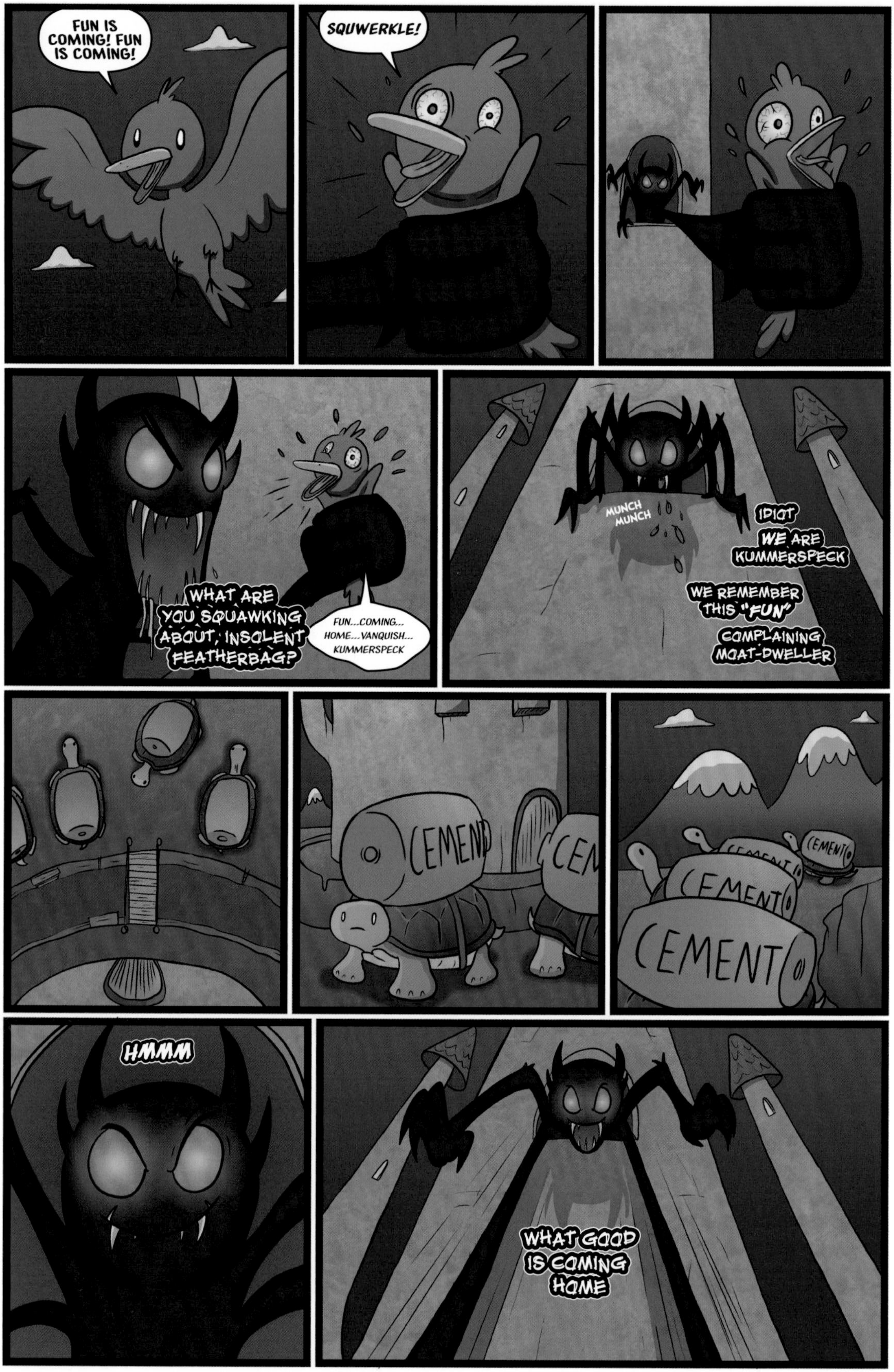
FUN IS COMING! FUN IS COMING!
SQUWERKLE!
WHAT ARE YOU SQUAWKING ABOUT, INSOLENT FEATHERBAG?
FUN...COMING... HOME...VANQUISH... KUMMERSPECK
MUNCH MUNCH
IDIOT
WE ARE KUMMERSPECK
WE REMEMBER THIS "FUN"
COMPLAINING MOAT-DWELLER
CEMENT
CEMENT
CEMENT
CEMENT
CEMENT
CEMENT
HMMM
WHAT GOOD IS COMING HOME

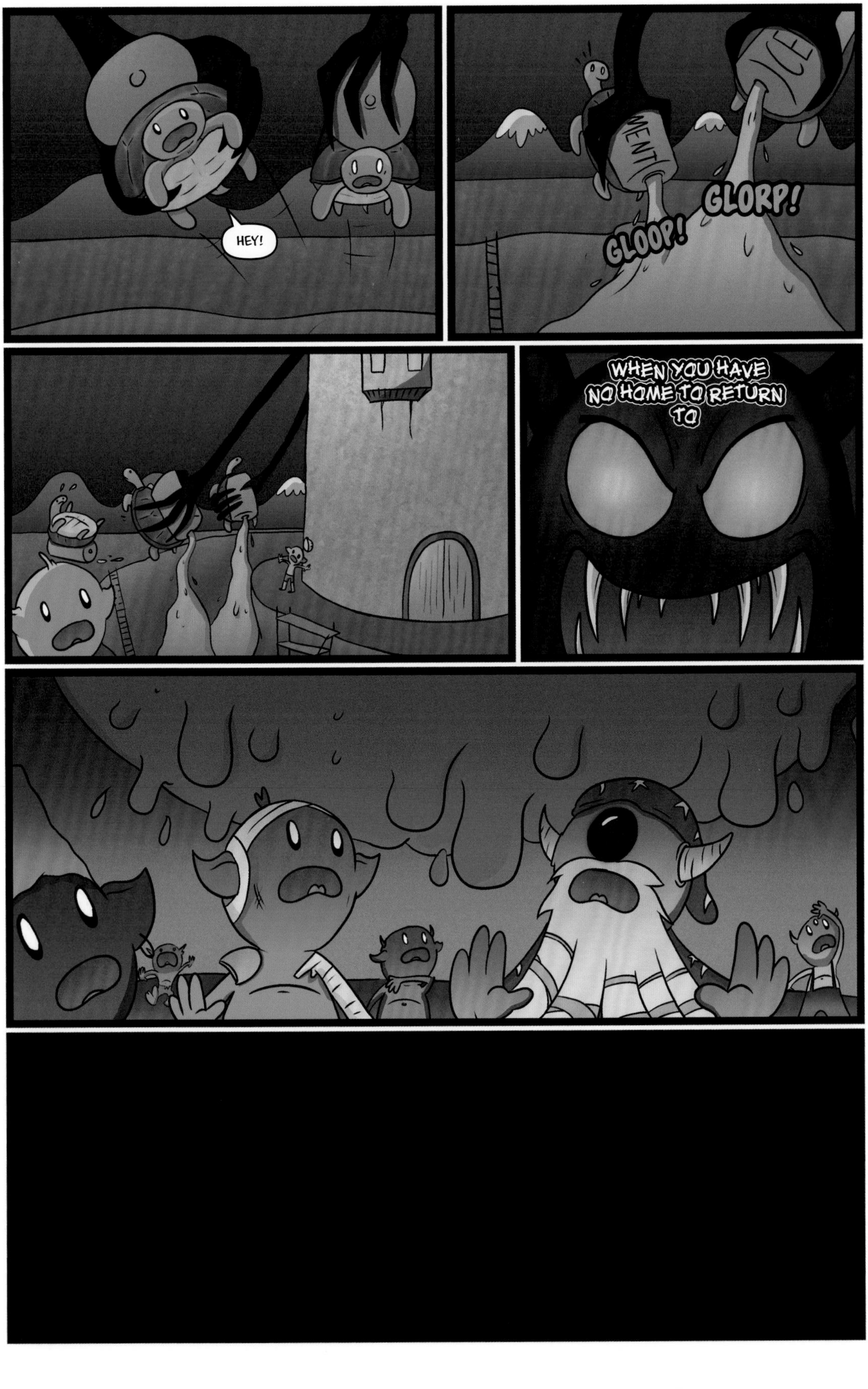
HEY!
GLOOP!
GLORP!
WHEN YOU HAVE NO HOME TO RETURN TO

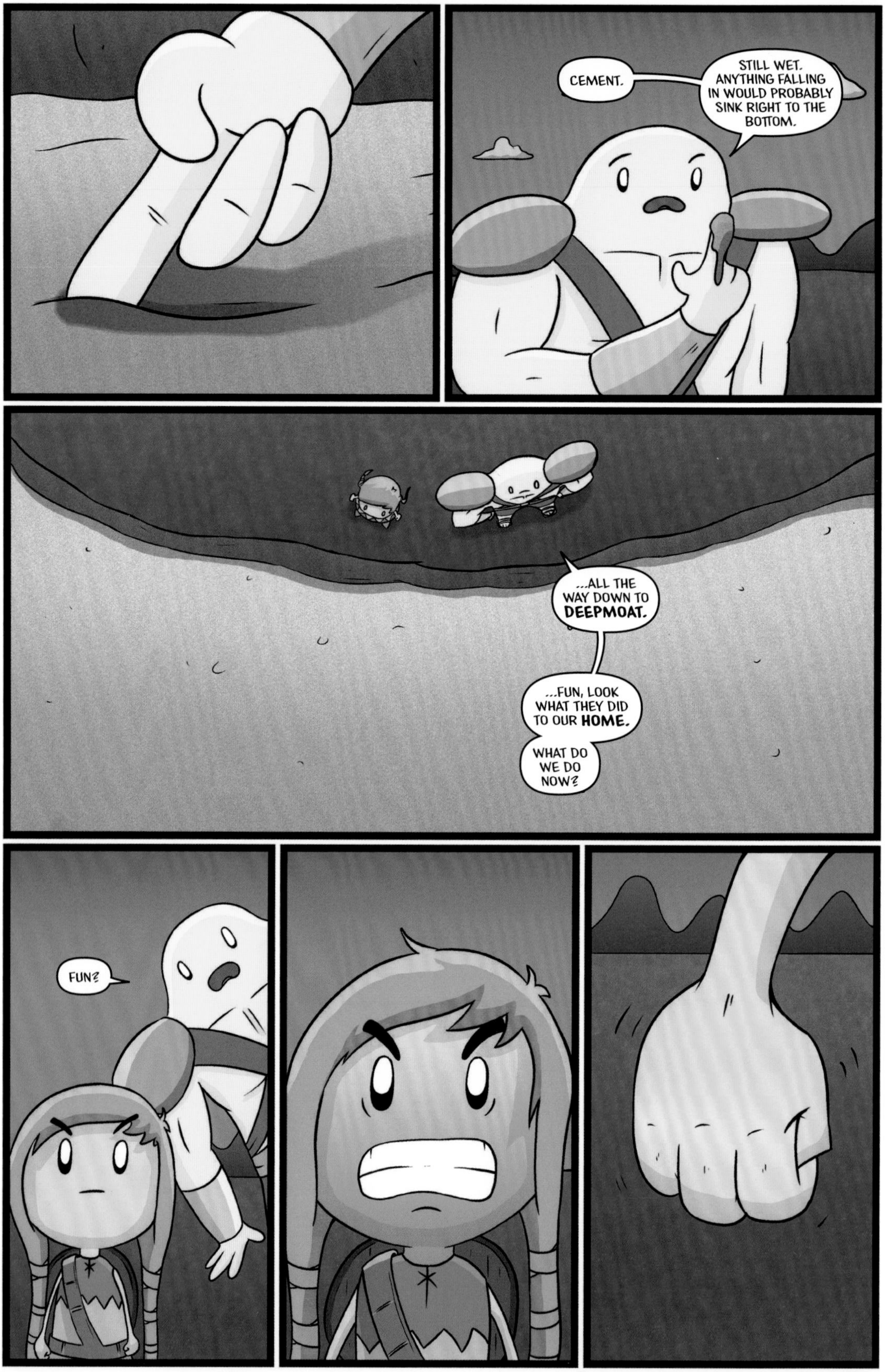
CEMENT.
STILL WET. ANYTHING FALLING IN WOULD PROBABLY SINK RIGHT TO THE BOTTOM.
...ALL THE WAY DOWN TO DEEPMOAT.
...FUN, LOOK WHAT THEY DID TO OUR HOME.
WHAT DO WE DO NOW?
FUN?

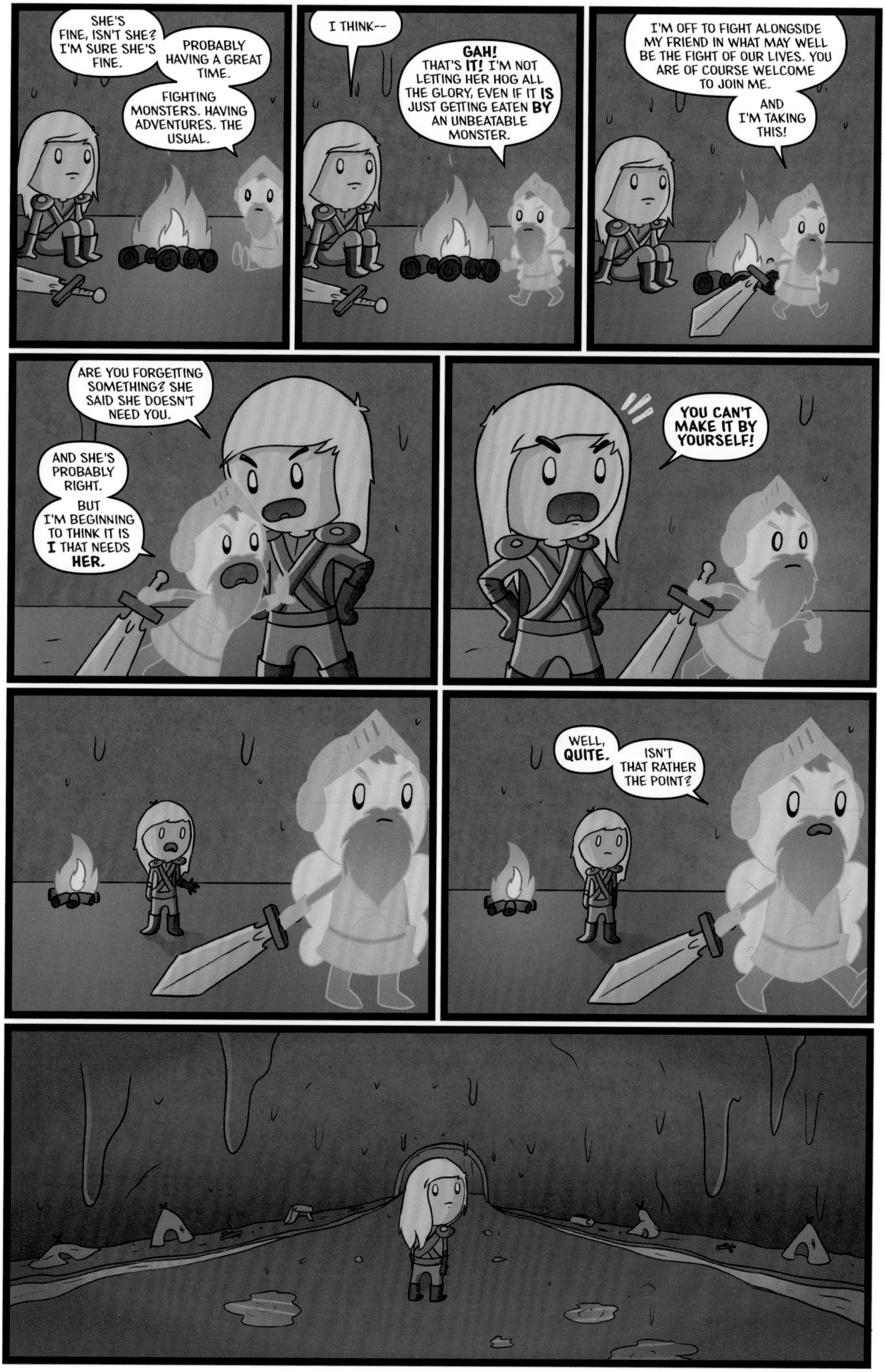
SHE'S FINE, ISN'T SHE? I'M SURE SHE'S FINE.
PROBABLY HAVING A GREAT TIME.
FIGHTING MONSTERS. HAVING ADVENTURES. THE USUAL.
I THINK--
GAH! THAT'S IT! I'M NOT LETTING HER HOG ALL THE GLORY, EVEN IF IT IS JUST GETTING EATEN BY AN UNBEATABLE MONSTER.
I'M OFF TO FIGHT ALONGSIDE MY FRIEND IN WHAT MAY WELL BE THE FIGHT OF OUR LIVES. YOU ARE OF COURSE WELCOME TO JOIN ME.
AND I'M TAKING THIS!
ARE YOU FORGETTING SOMETHING? SHE SAID SHE DOESN'T NEED YOU.
AND SHE'S PROBABLY RIGHT.
BUT I'M BEGINNING TO THINK IT IS I THAT NEEDS HER.
YOU CAN'T MAKE IT BY YOURSELF!
WELL, QUITE.
ISN'T THAT RATHER THE POINT?

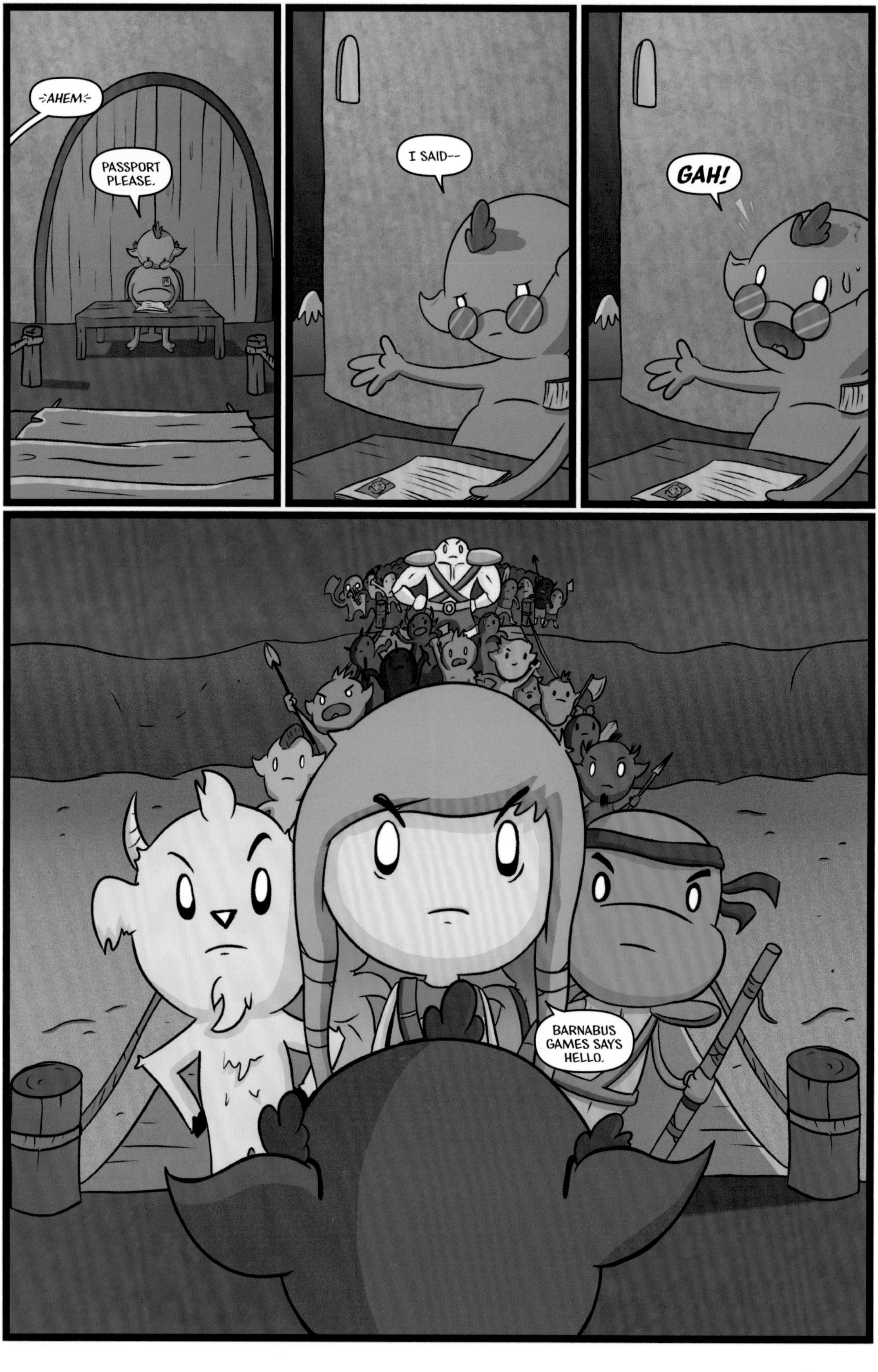

-AHEM-
PASSPORT PLEASE.
I SAID--
GAH!
BARNABUS GAMES SAYS HELLO.

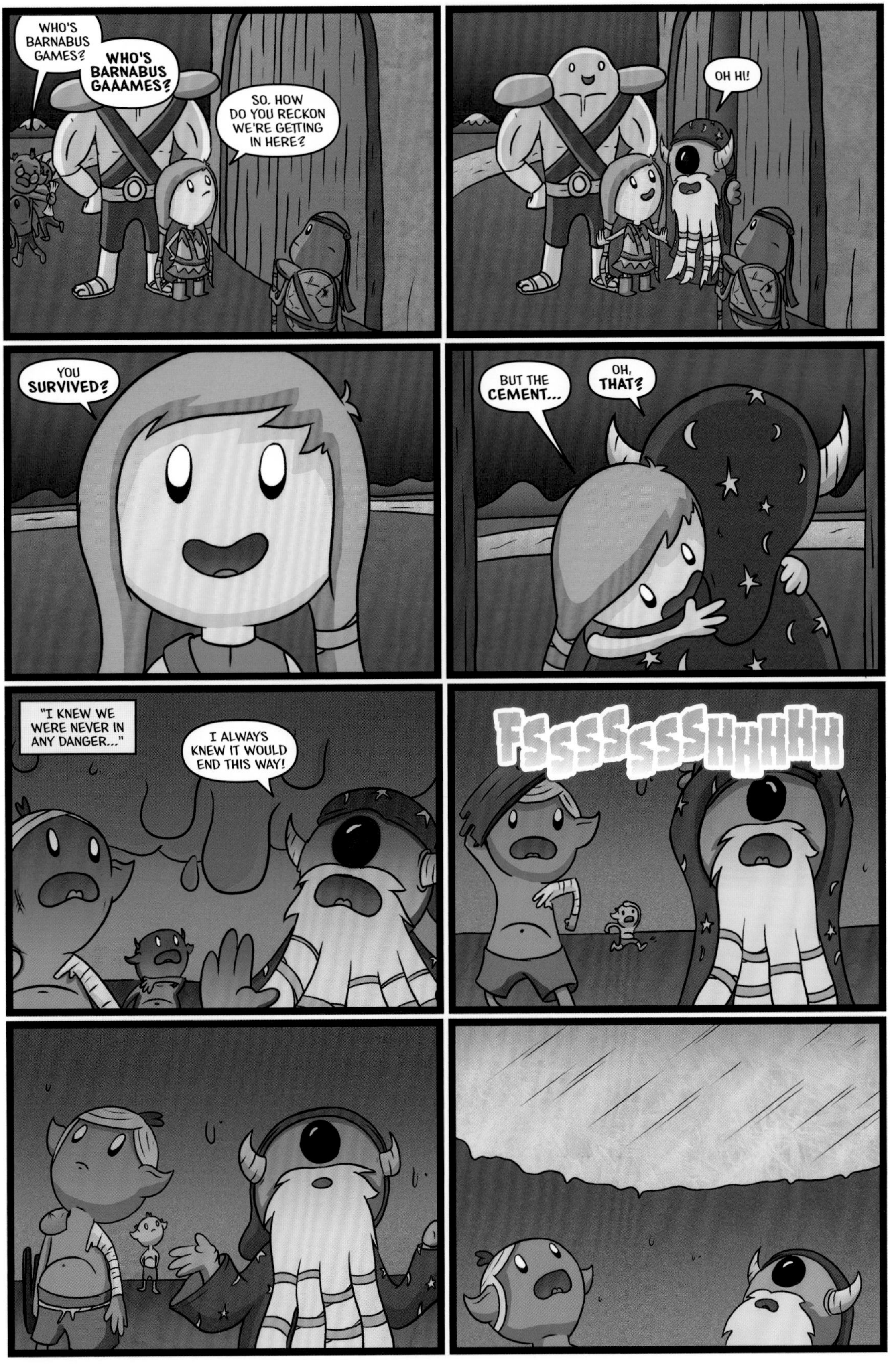
WHO'S BARNABUS GAMES?
WHO'S BARNABUS GAAAMES?
SO. HOW DO YOU RECKON WE'RE GETTING IN HERE?
OH HI!
YOU SURVIVED?
BUT THE CEMENT...
OH, THAT?
"I KNEW WE WERE NEVER IN ANY DANGER..."
I ALWAYS KNEW IT WOULD END THIS WAY!
FSSSSSSSHHHHHH

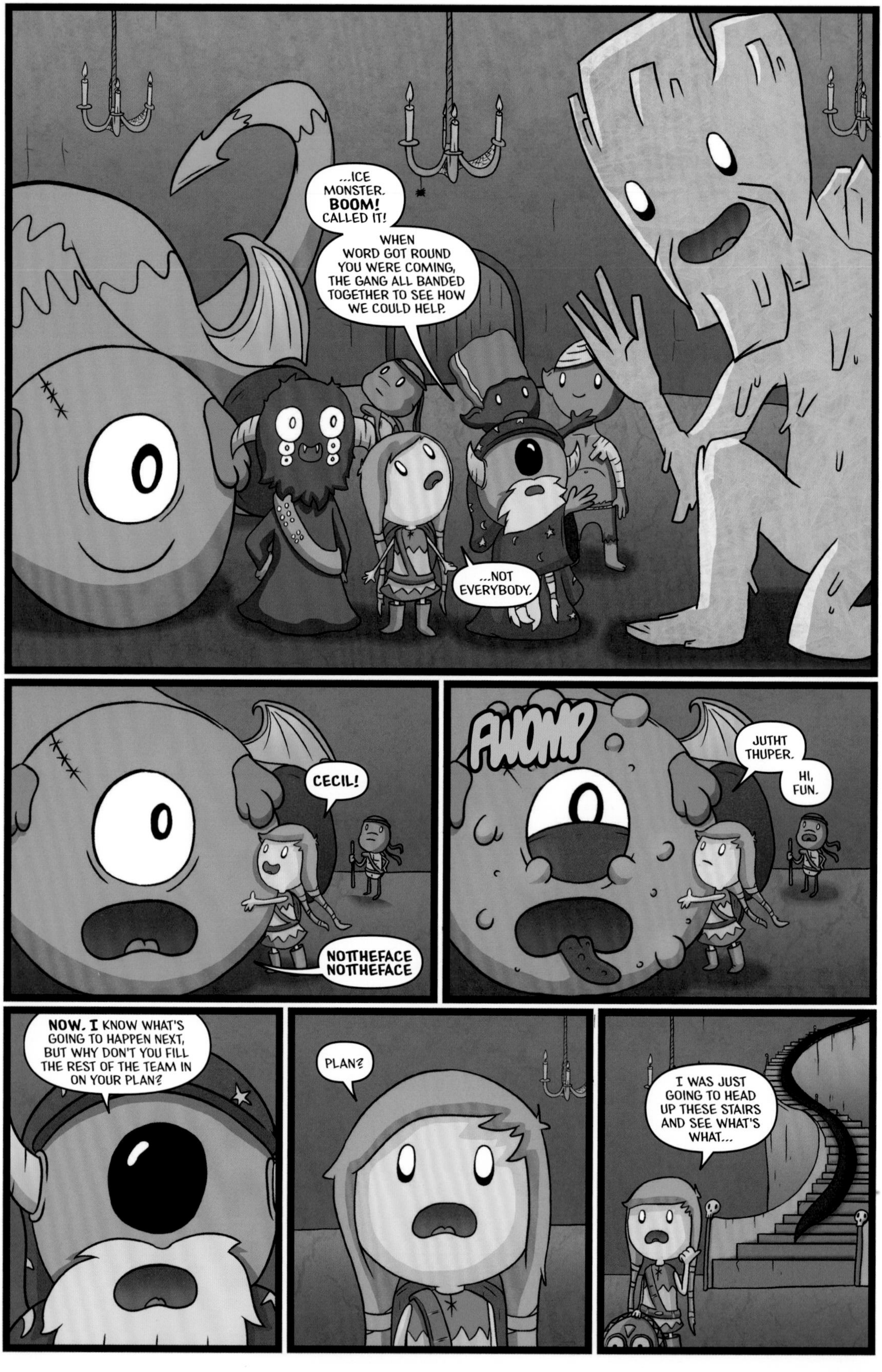

...ICE MONSTER. BOOM! CALLED IT!
WHEN WORD GOT ROUND YOU WERE COMING, THE GANG ALL BANDED TOGETHER TO SEE HOW WE COULD HELP.
...NOT EVERYBODY.
CECIL!
NOTTHEFACE NOTTHEFACE
FWOMP
JUTHT THUPER.
HI, FUN.
NOW. I KNOW WHAT'S GOING TO HAPPEN NEXT, BUT WHY DON'T YOU FILL THE REST OF THE TEAM IN ON YOUR PLAN?
PLAN?
I WAS JUST GOING TO HEAD UP THESE STAIRS AND SEE WHAT'S WHAT...

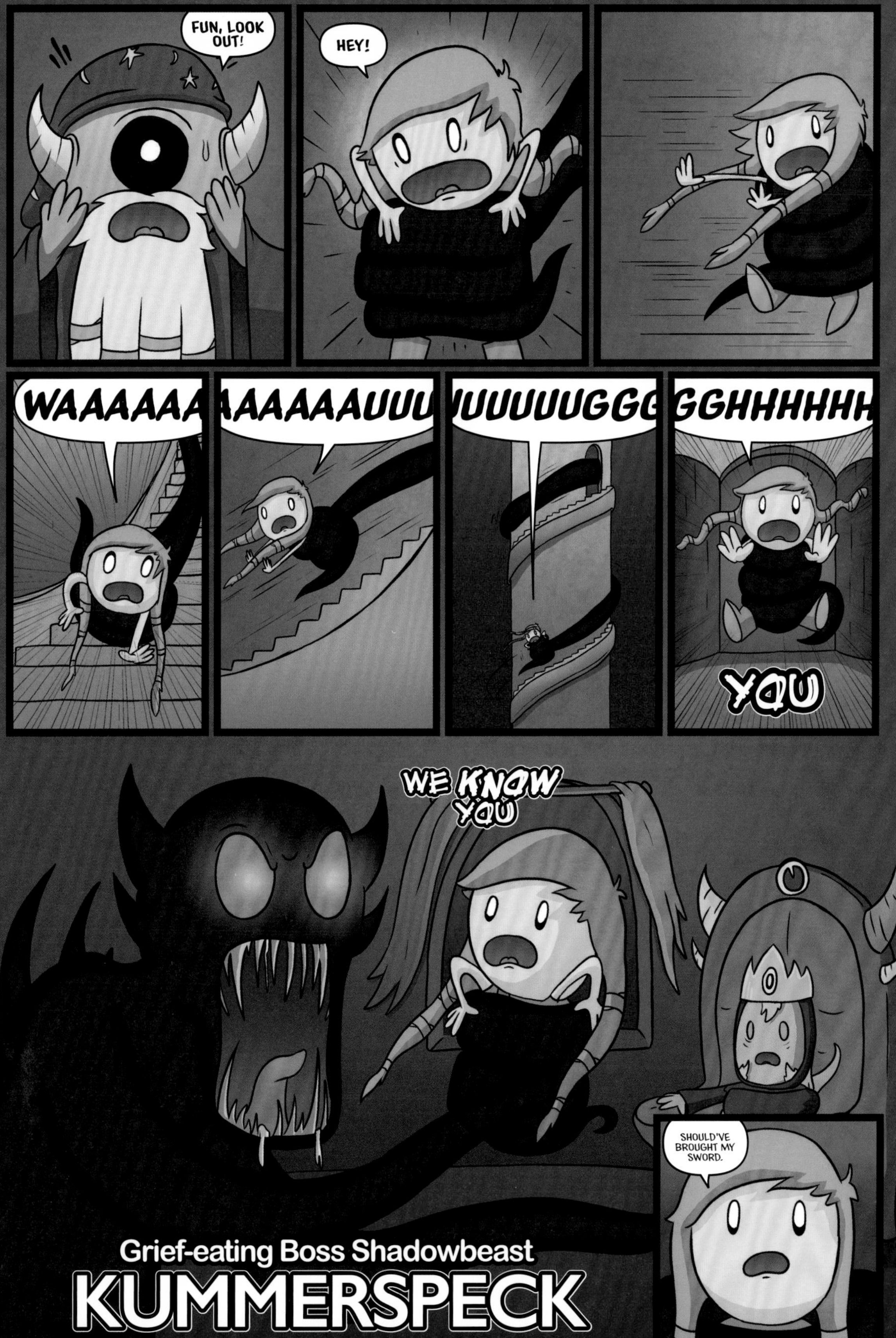
FUN, LOOK OUT!
HEY!
WAAAAAAAAAAAAAUUUUUUUUUGGGGHHHHHH
YOU
WE KNOW YOU
SHOULD'VE BROUGHT MY SWORD.
Grief-eating Boss Shadowbeast
KUMMERSPECK

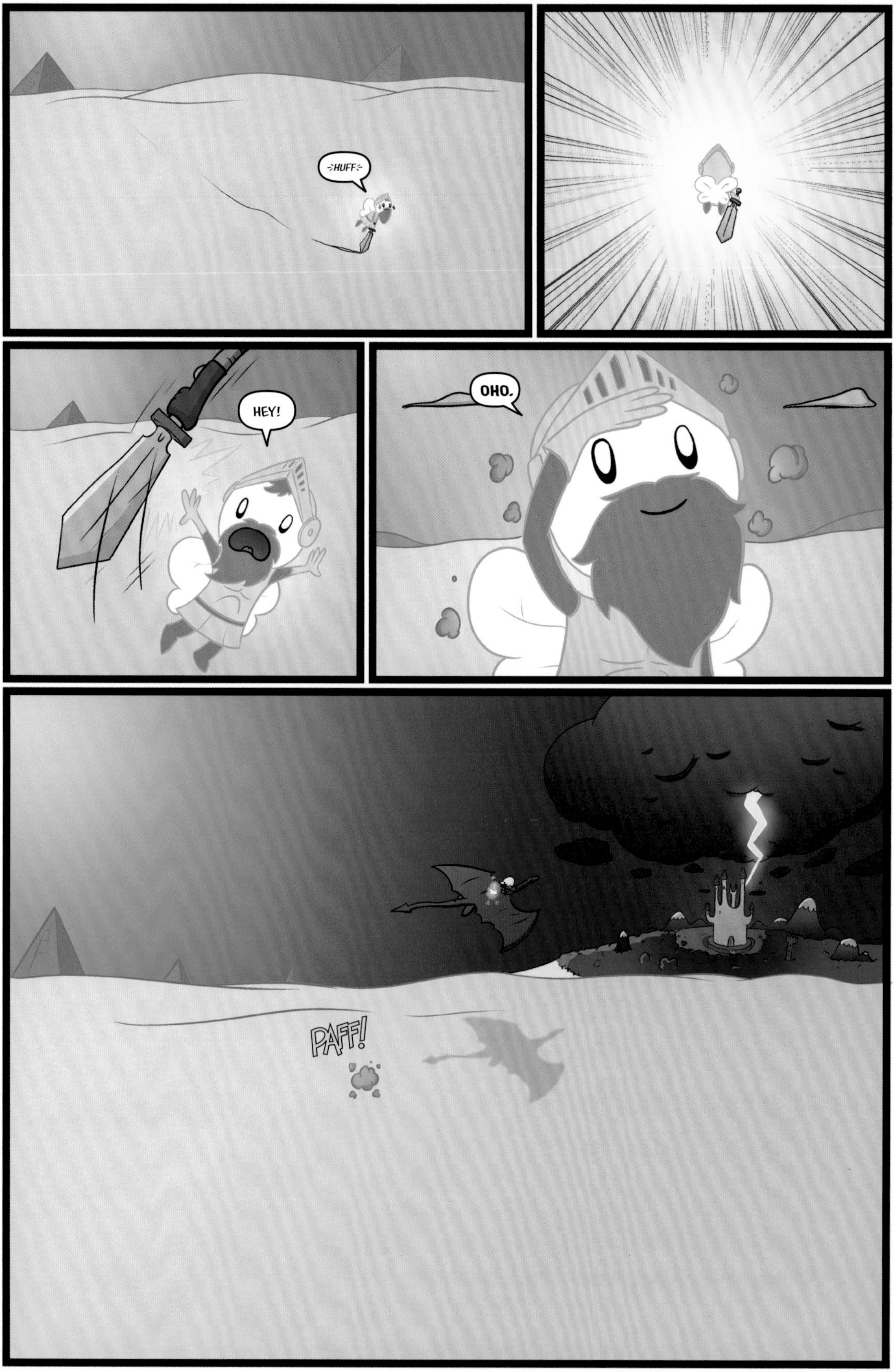

HUFF
HEY!
OHO.
PAFF!

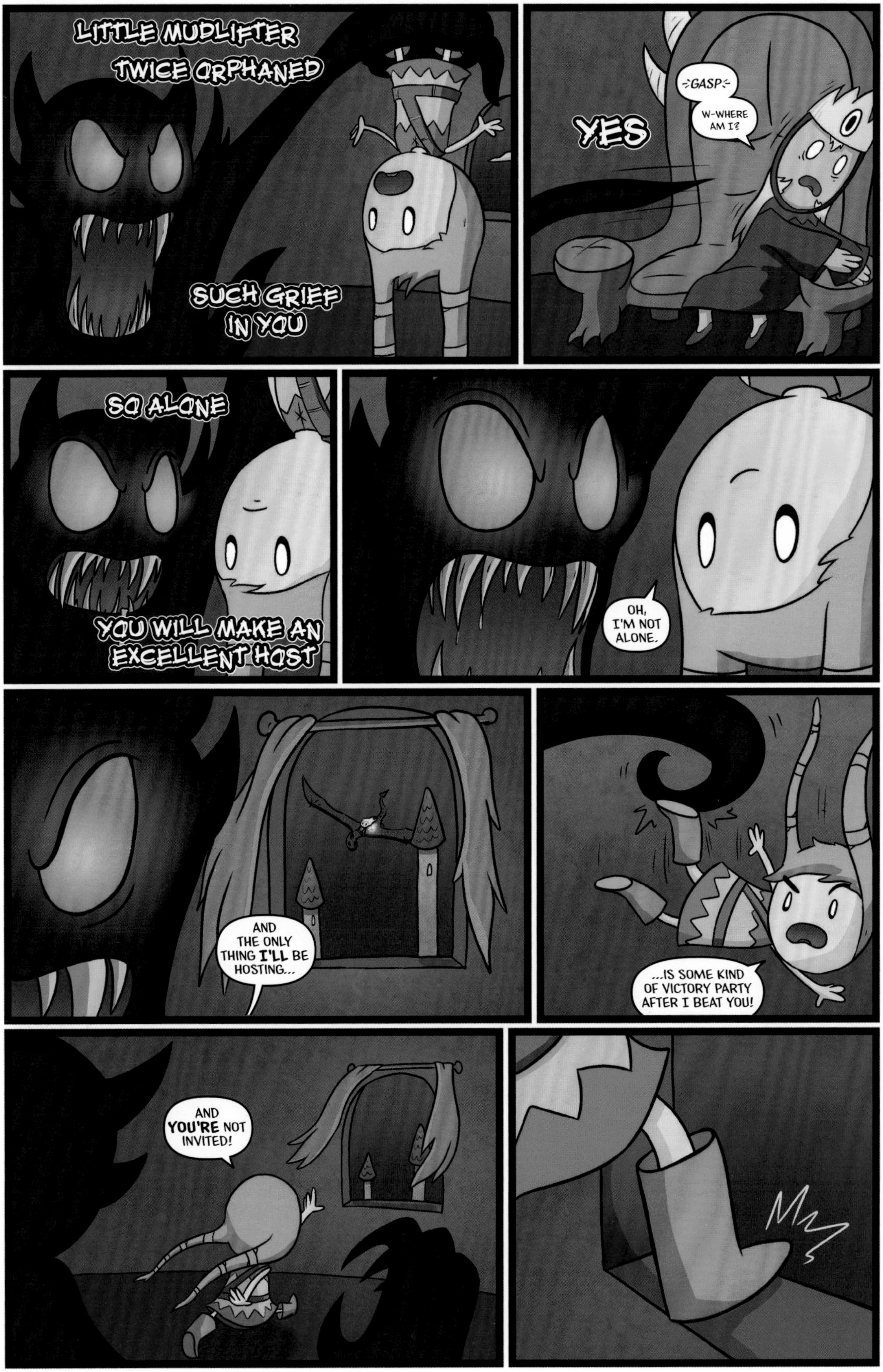
LITTLE MUDLIFTER
TWICE ORPHANED
SUCH GRIEF IN YOU
YES
-GASP-
W-WHERE AM I?
SO ALONE
YOU WILL MAKE AN EXCELLENT HOST
OH, I'M NOT ALONE.
AND THE ONLY THING I'LL BE HOSTING...
...IS SOME KIND OF VICTORY PARTY AFTER I BEAT YOU!
AND YOU'RE NOT INVITED!

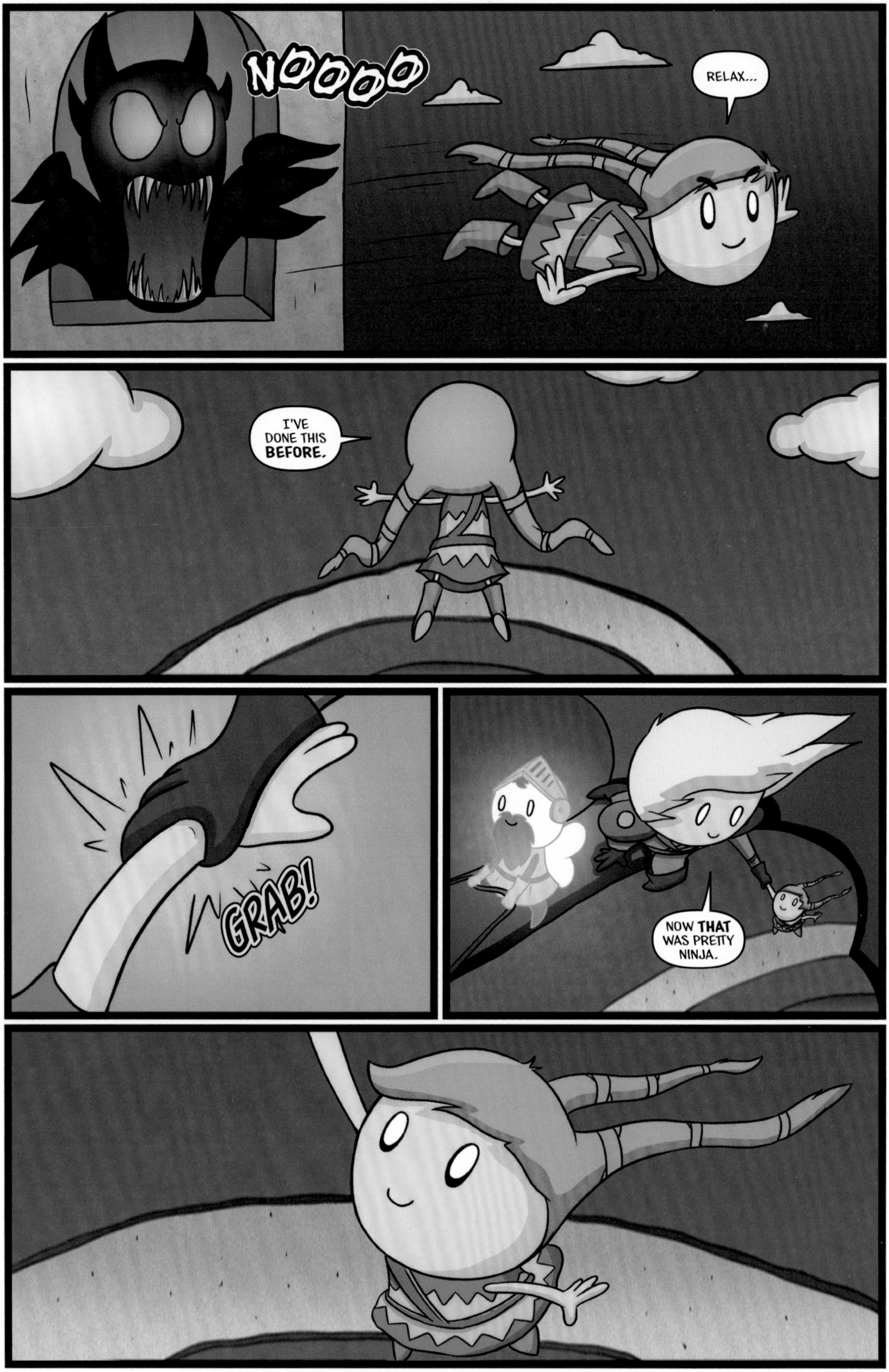
NOOOOO
RELAX...
I'VE DONE THIS BEFORE.
GRAB!
NOW THAT WAS PRETTY NINJA.

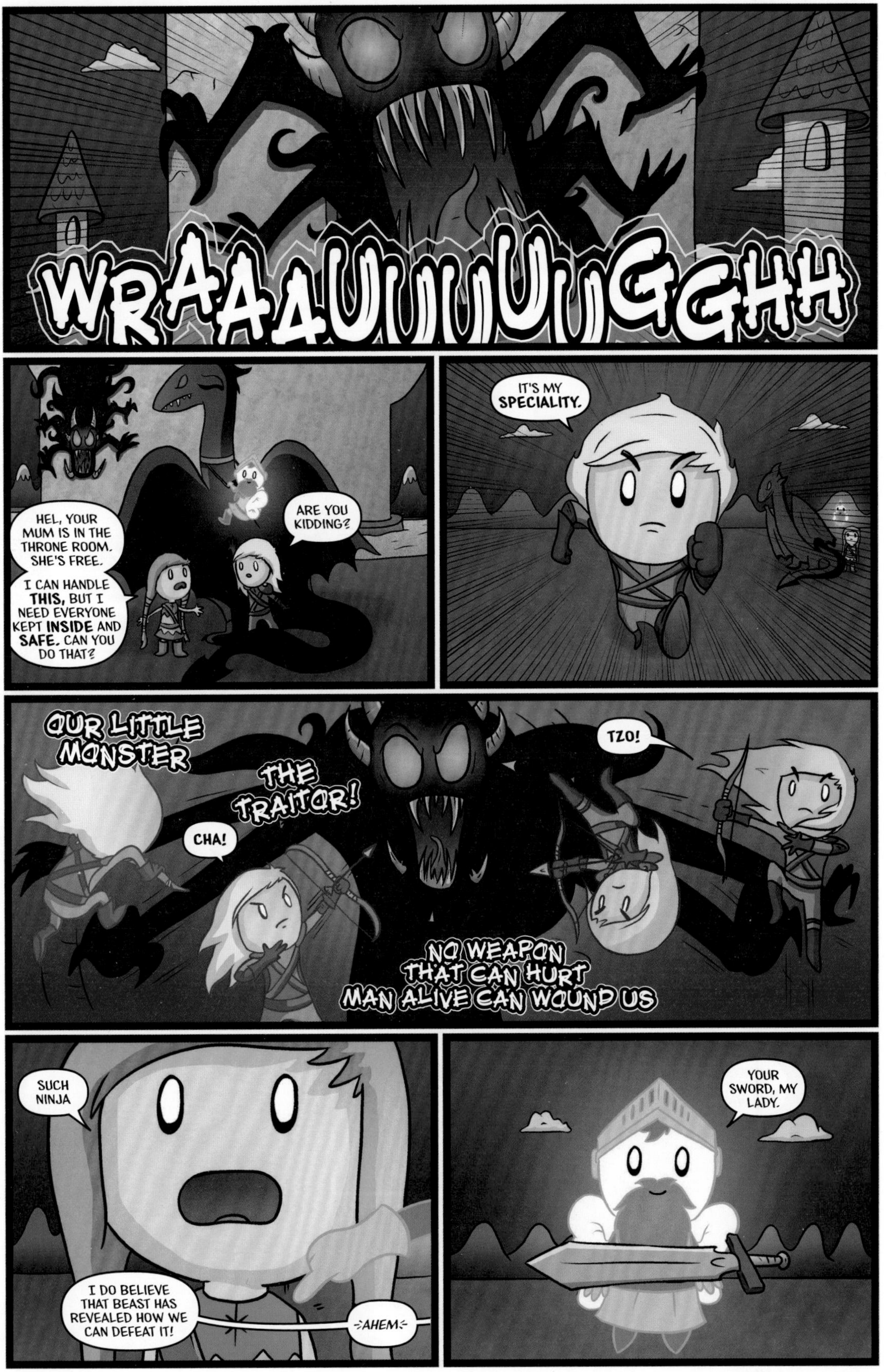
WRAAAUUUUUGHH
HEL, YOUR MUM IS IN THE THRONE ROOM. SHE'S FREE.
I CAN HANDLE THIS, BUT I NEED EVERYONE KEPT INSIDE AND SAFE. CAN YOU DO THAT?
ARE YOU KIDDING?
IT'S MY SPECIALITY.
OUR LITTLE MONSTER
THE TRAITOR!
TZO!
CHA!
NO WEAPON THAT CAN HURT MAN ALIVE CAN WOUND US
SUCH NINJA
I DO BELIEVE THAT BEAST HAS REVEALED HOW WE CAN DEFEAT IT!
AHEM
YOUR SWORD, MY LADY.

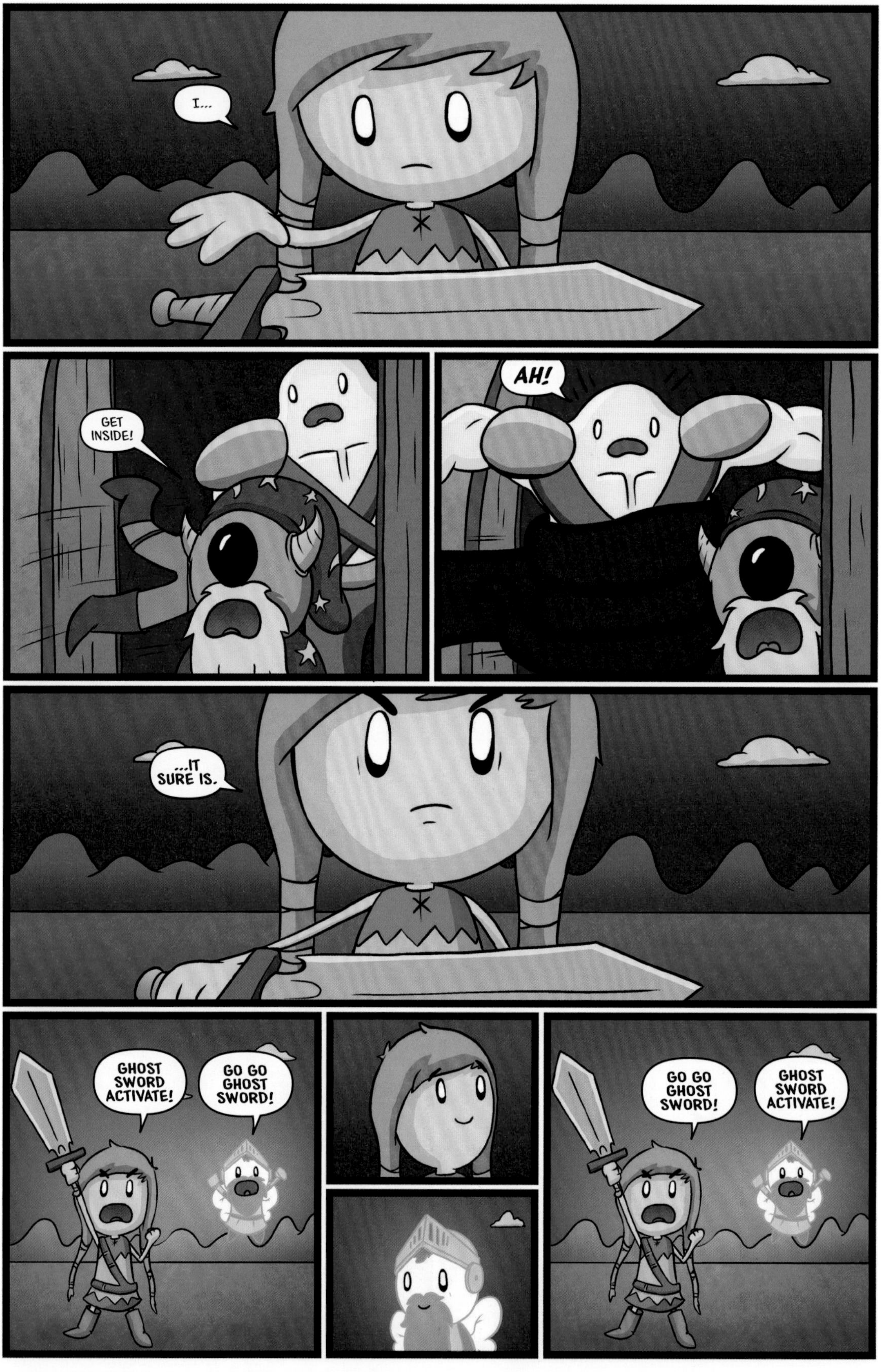
I...
GET INSIDE!
AH!
...IT SURE IS.
GHOST SWORD ACTIVATE!
GO GO GHOST SWORD!
GO GO GHOST SWORD!
GHOST SWORD ACTIVATE!

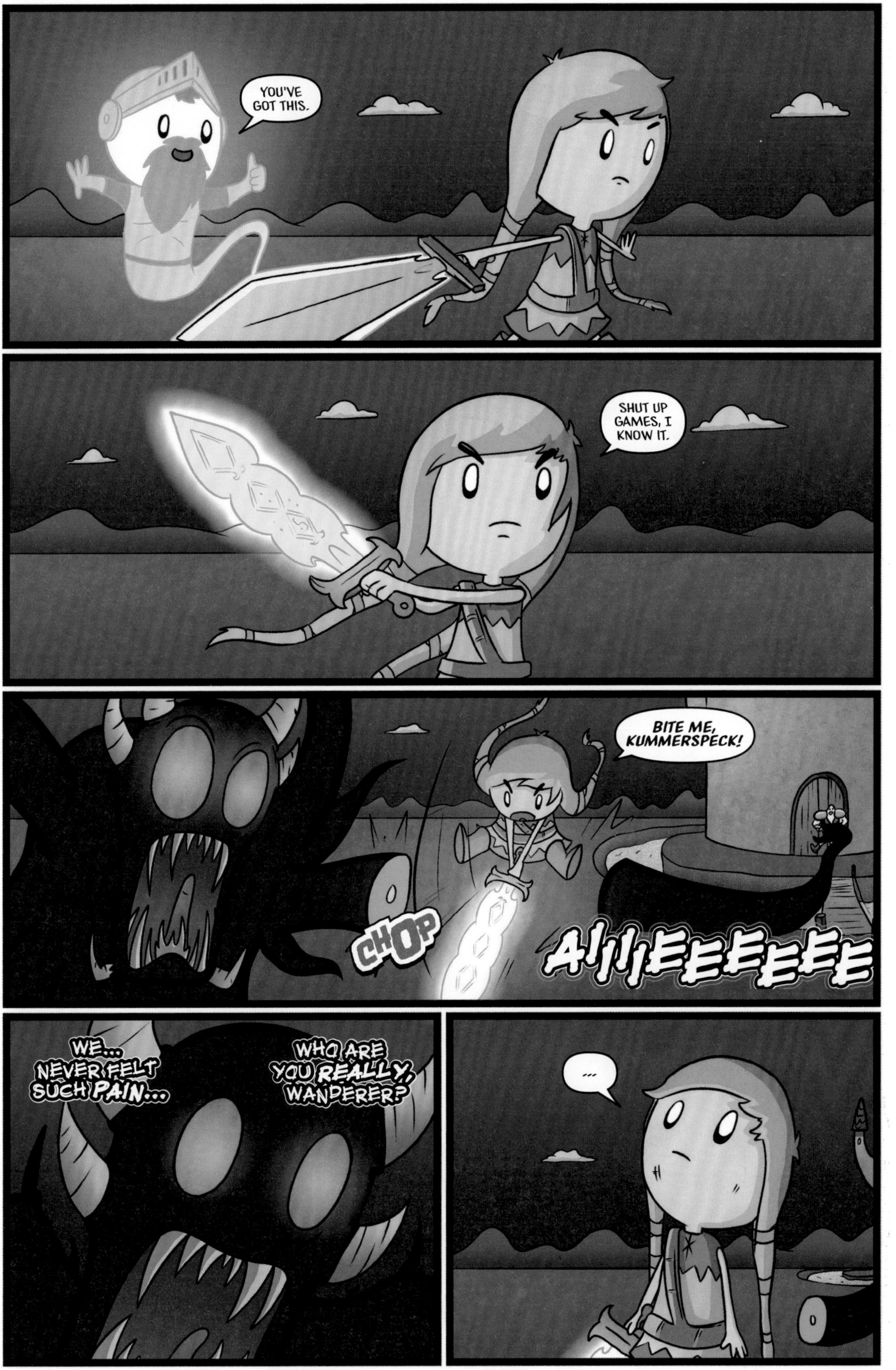
YOU'VE GOT THIS.
SHUT UP GAMES, I KNOW IT.
BITE ME, KUMMERSPECK!
CHOP
AIIIIEEEEEEE
WE... NEVER FELT SUCH PAIN...
WHO ARE YOU REALLY, WANDERER?
...

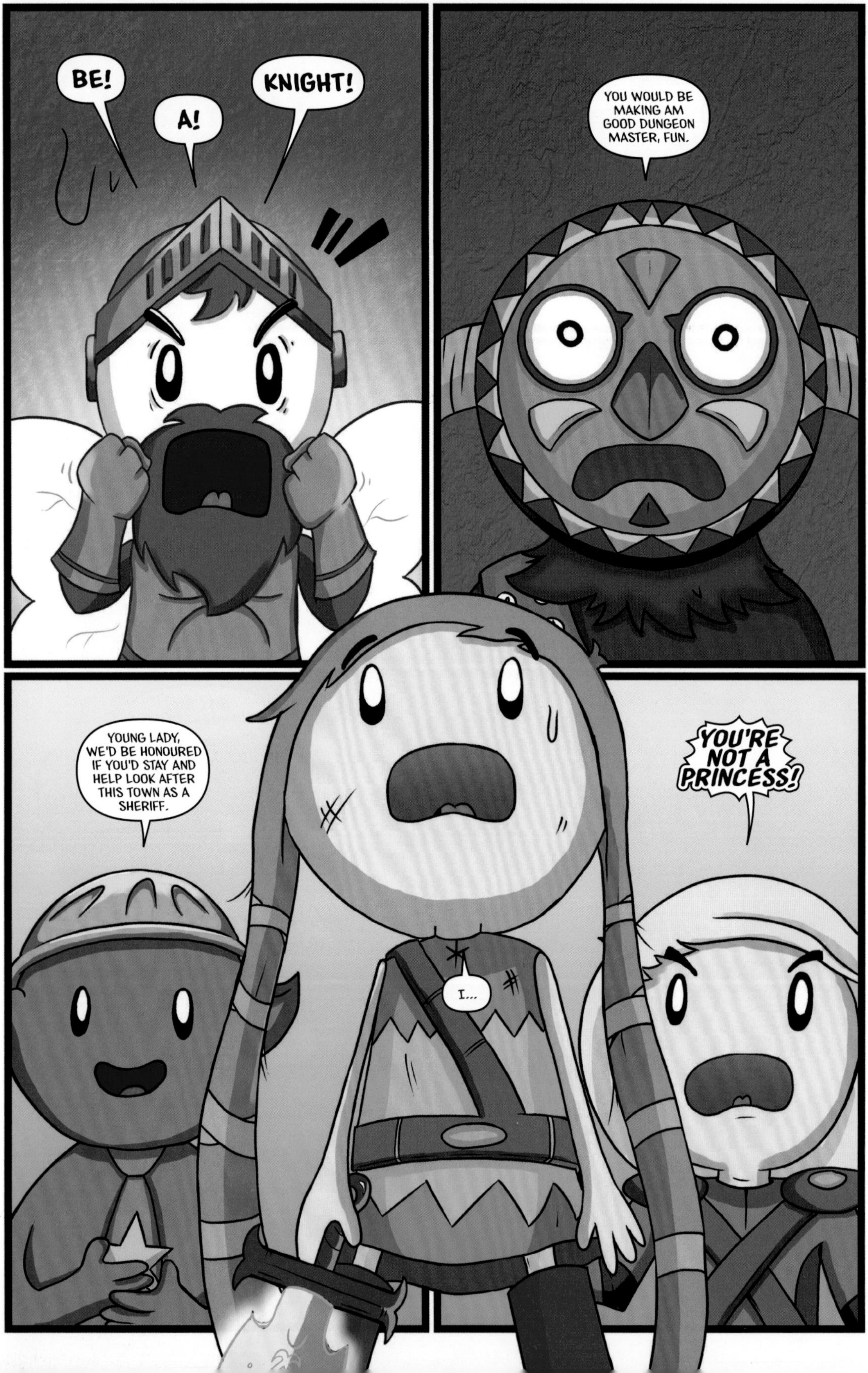
BE!
A!
KNIGHT!
YOU WOULD BE MAKING AM GOOD DUNGEON MASTER, FUN.
YOUNG LADY, WE'D BE HONOURED IF YOU'D STAY AND HELP LOOK AFTER THIS TOWN AS A SHERIFF.
I...
YOU'RE NOT A PRINCESS!

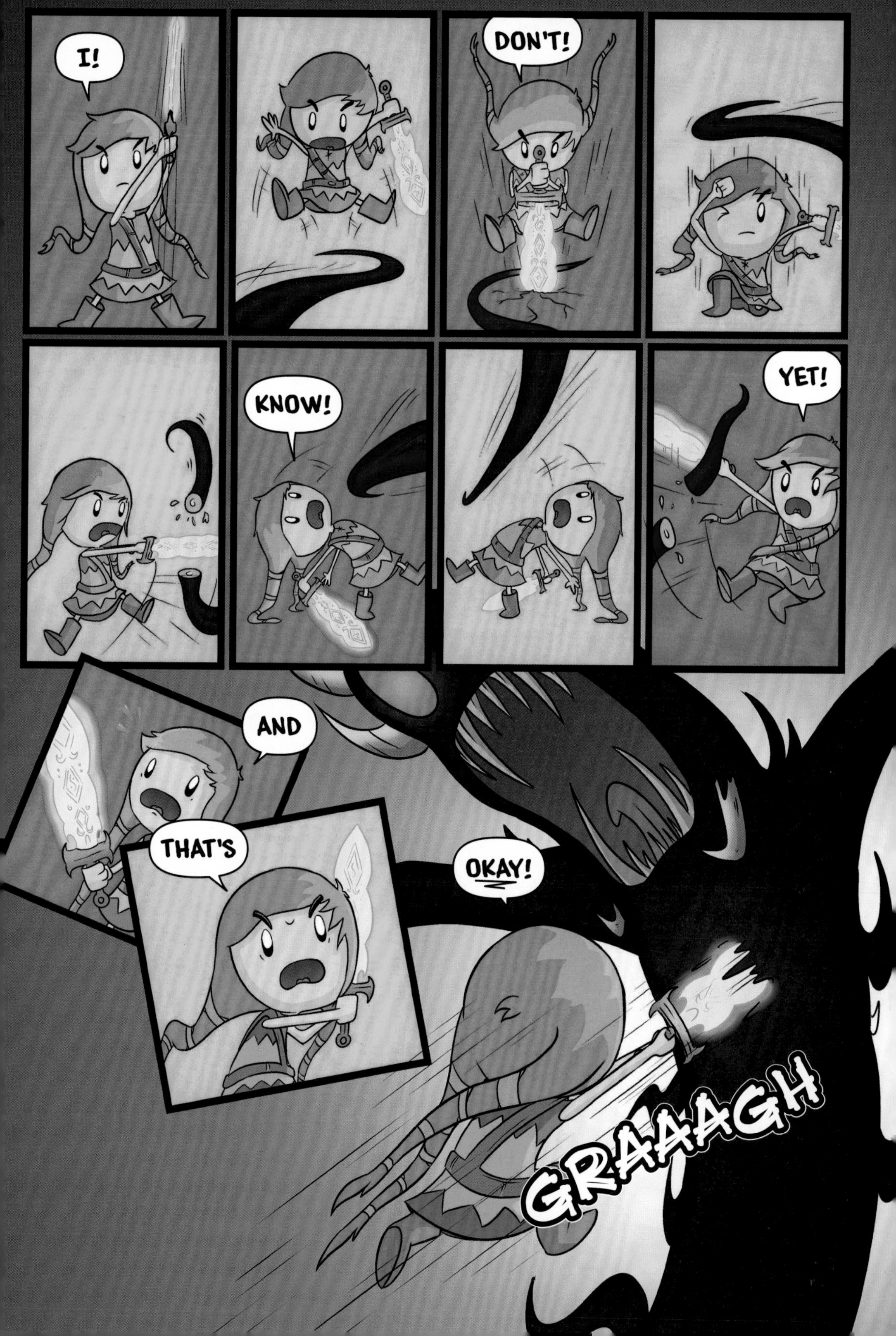
I!
DON'T!
KNOW!
YET!
AND
THAT'S
OKAY!
GRAAAGH

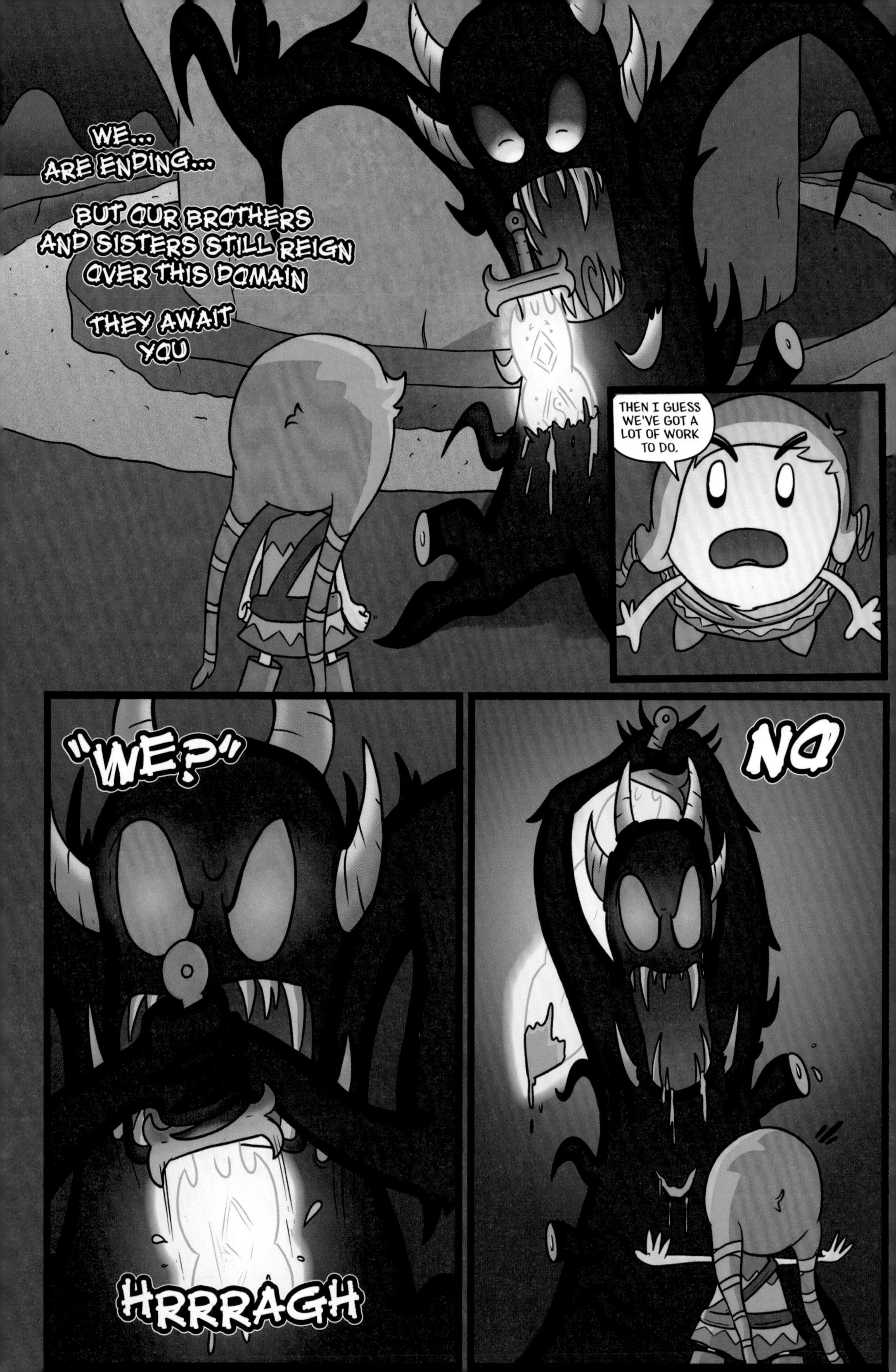
WE... ARE ENDING...
BUT OUR BROTHERS AND SISTERS STILL REIGN OVER THIS DOMAIN
THEY AWAIT YOU
THEN I GUESS WE'VE GOT A LOT OF WORK TO DO.
"WE?"
HRRRRAGH
NO

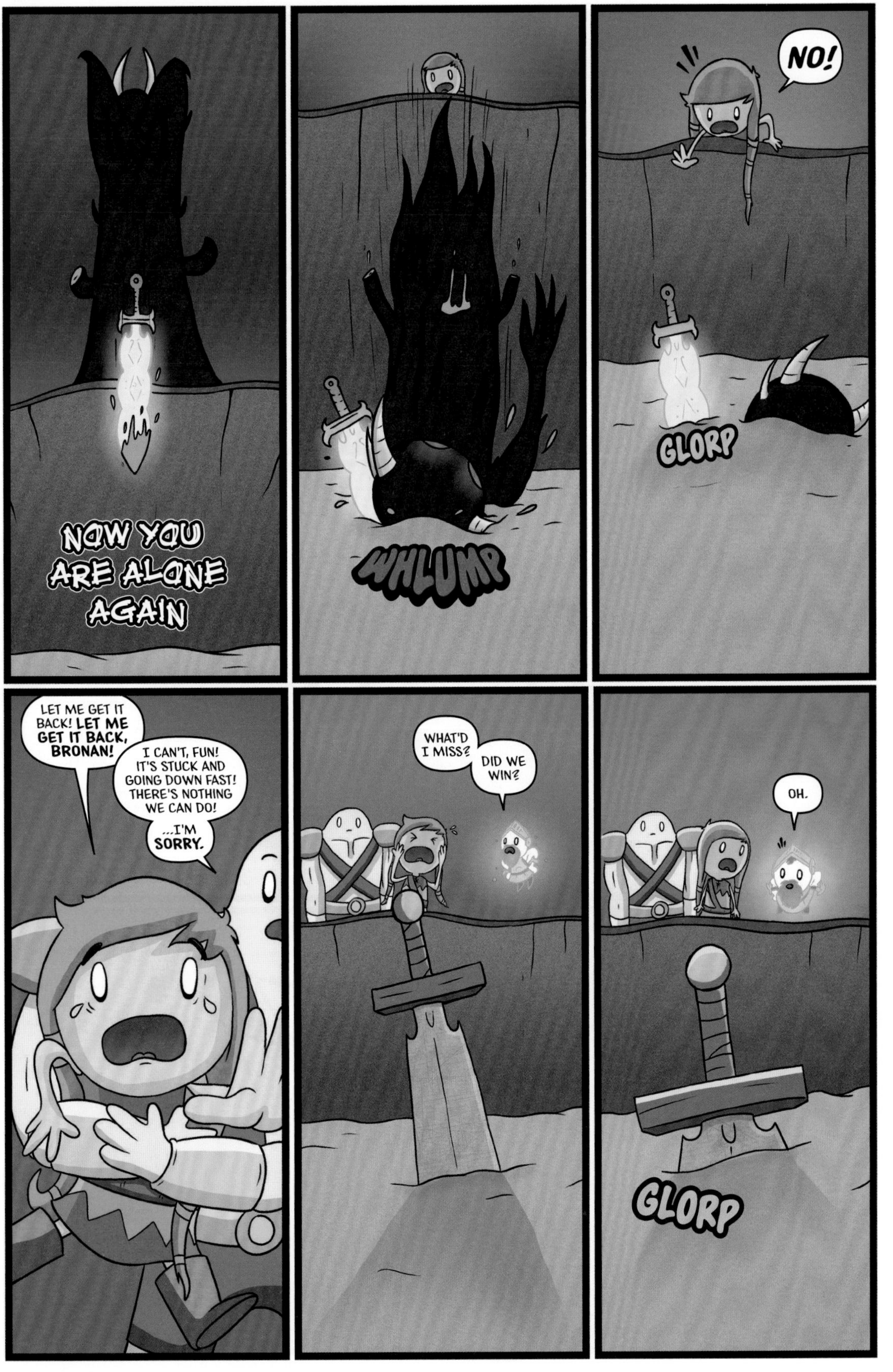

NOW YOU ARE ALONE AGAIN
WHLUMP
NO!
GLORP
LET ME GET IT BACK! LET ME GET IT BACK, BRONAN!
I CAN'T, FUN! IT'S STUCK AND GOING DOWN FAST! THERE'S NOTHING WE CAN DO!
...I'M SORRY.
WHAT'D I MISS?
DID WE WIN?
OH.
GLORP

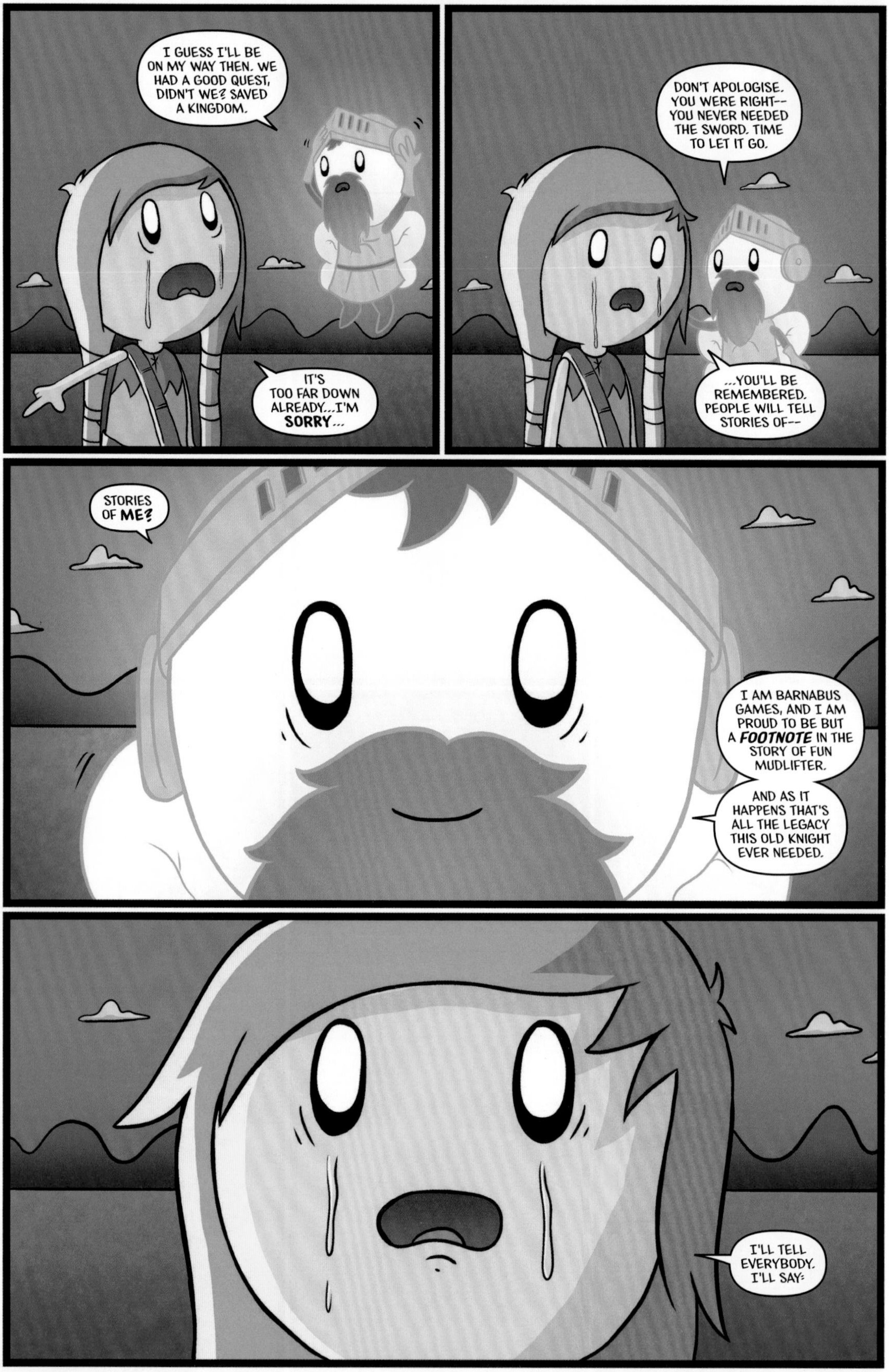
I GUESS I'LL BE ON MY WAY THEN. WE HAD A GOOD QUEST, DIDN'T WE? SAVED A KINGDOM.
IT'S TOO FAR DOWN ALREADY...I'M SORRY...
DON'T APOLOGISE. YOU WERE RIGHT-- YOU NEVER NEEDED THE SWORD. TIME TO LET IT GO.
...YOU'LL BE REMEMBERED. PEOPLE WILL TELL STORIES OF--
STORIES OF ME?
I AM BARNABUS GAMES, AND I AM PROUD TO BE BUT A FOOTNOTE IN THE STORY OF FUN MUDLIFTER.
AND AS IT HAPPENS THAT'S ALL THE LEGACY THIS OLD KNIGHT EVER NEEDED.
I'LL TELL EVERYBODY. I'LL SAY:

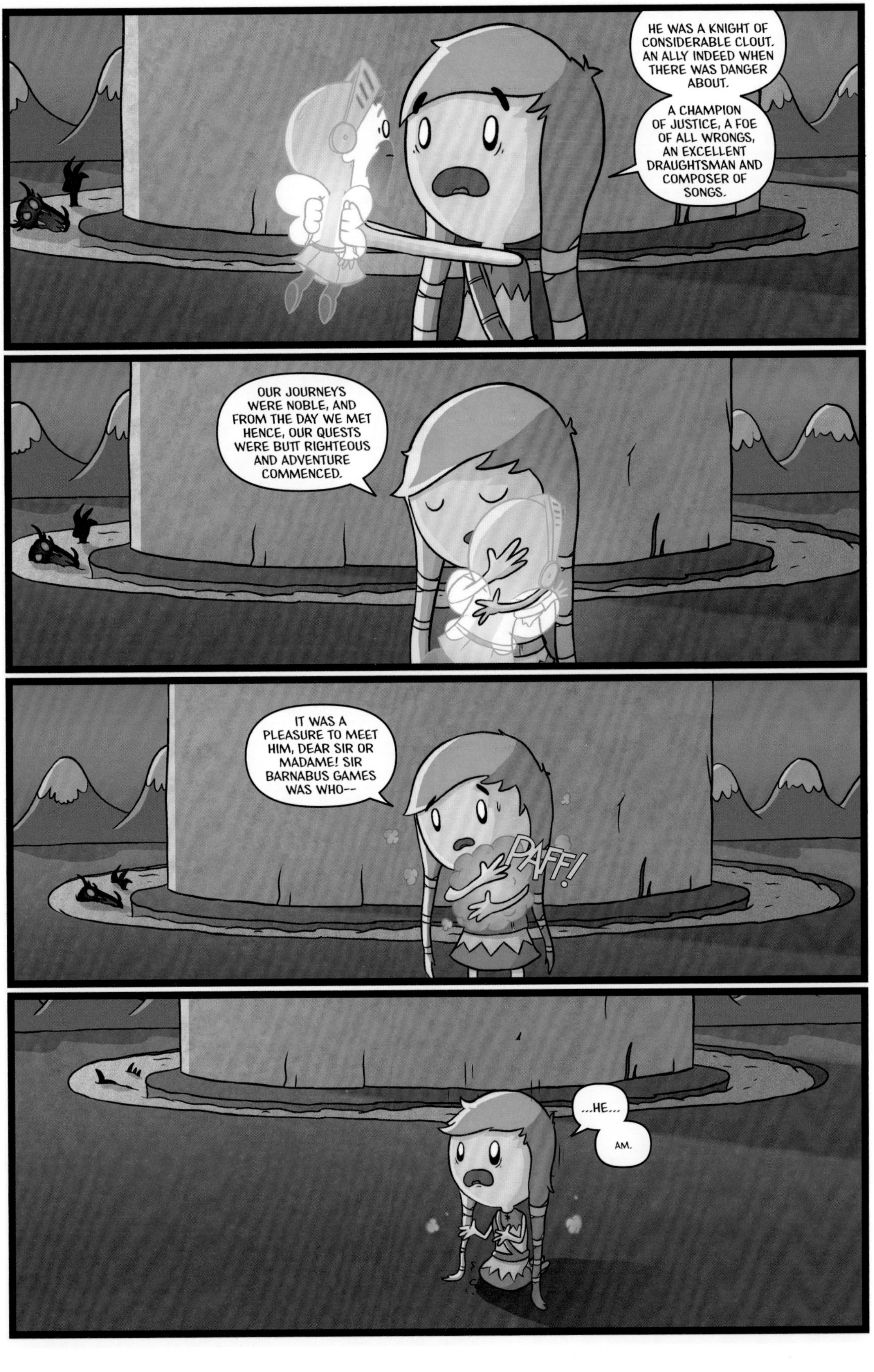
HE WAS A KNIGHT OF CONSIDERABLE CLOUT. AN ALLY INDEED WHEN THERE WAS DANGER ABOUT.
A CHAMPION OF JUSTICE, A FOE OF ALL WRONGS, AN EXCELLENT DRAUGHTSMAN AND COMPOSER OF SONGS.
OUR JOURNEYS WERE NOBLE, AND FROM THE DAY WE MET HENCE, OUR QUESTS WERE BUTT RIGHTEOUS AND ADVENTURE COMMENCED.
IT WAS A PLEASURE TO MEET HIM, DEAR SIR OR MADAME! SIR BARNABUS GAMES WAS WHO--
PAFF!
...HE...
AM.

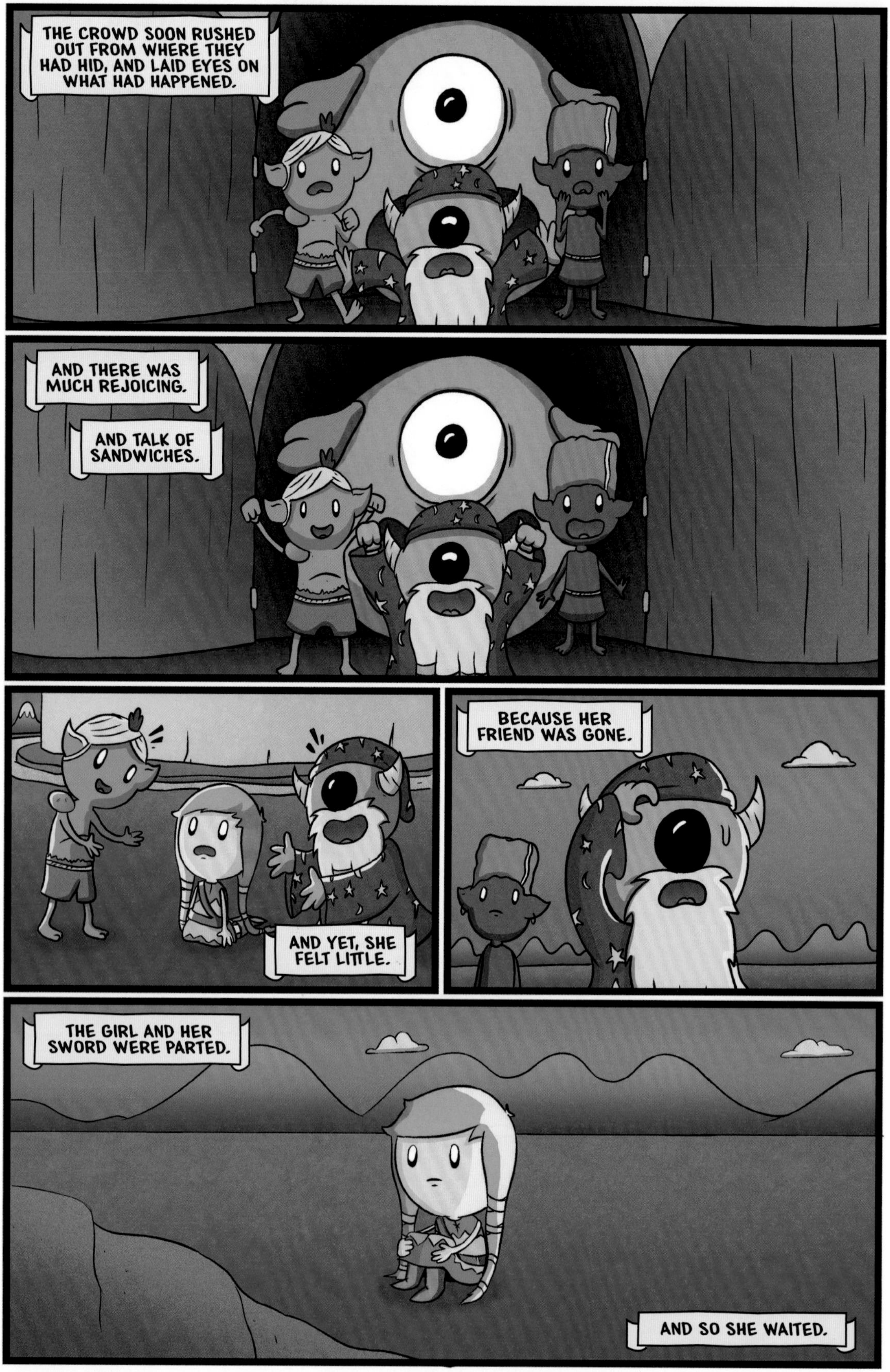
THE CROWD SOON RUSHED OUT FROM WHERE THEY HAD HID, AND LAID EYES ON WHAT HAD HAPPENED.
AND THERE WAS MUCH REJOICING.
AND TALK OF SANDWICHES.
AND YET, SHE FELT LITTLE.
BECAUSE HER FRIEND WAS GONE.
THE GIRL AND HER SWORD WERE PARTED.
AND SO SHE WAITED.

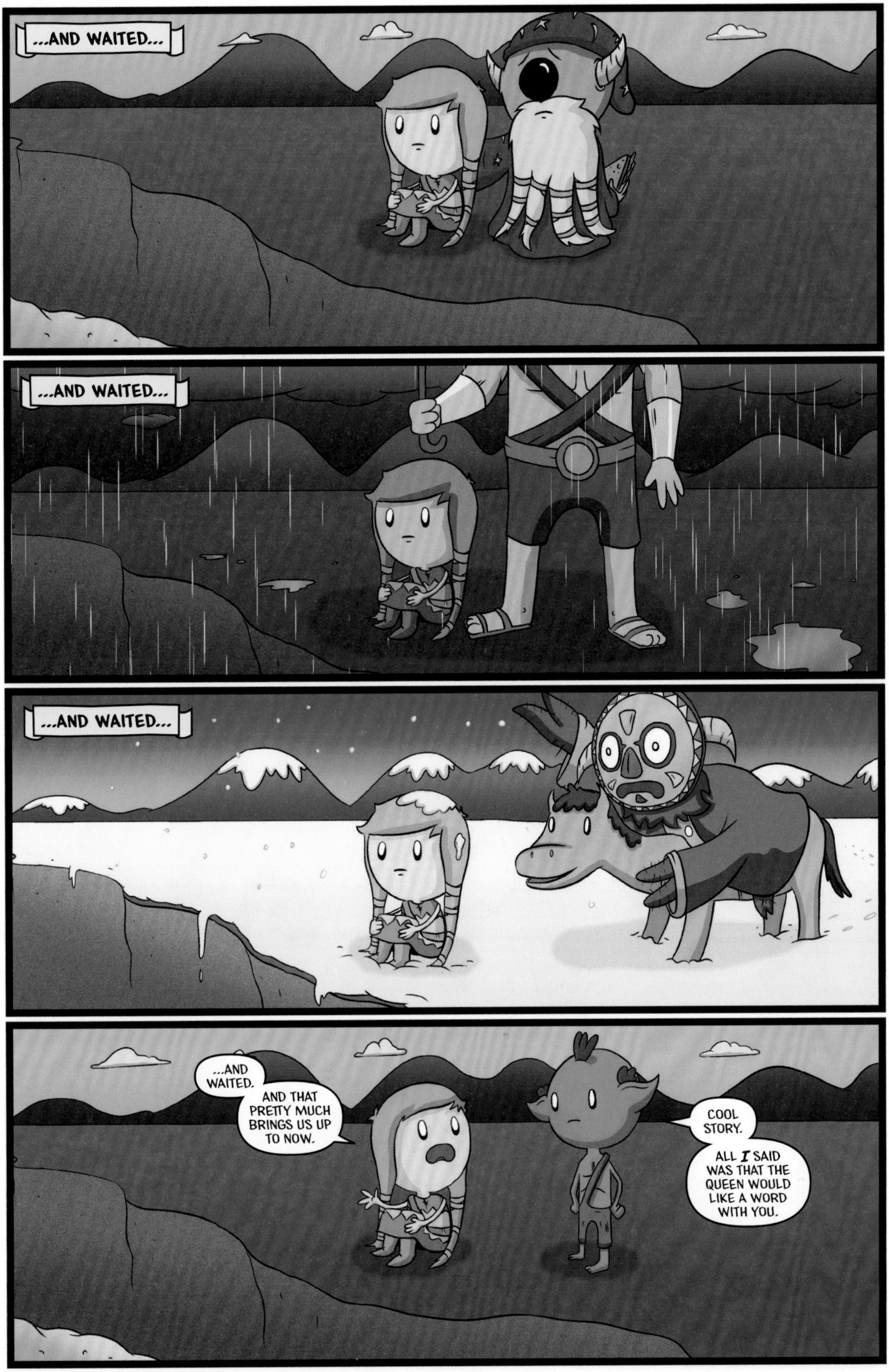
...AND WAITED...
...AND WAITED...
...AND WAITED...
...AND WAITED.
AND THAT PRETTY MUCH BRINGS US UP TO NOW.
COOL STORY.
ALL *I* SAID WAS THAT THE QUEEN WOULD LIKE A WORD WITH YOU.

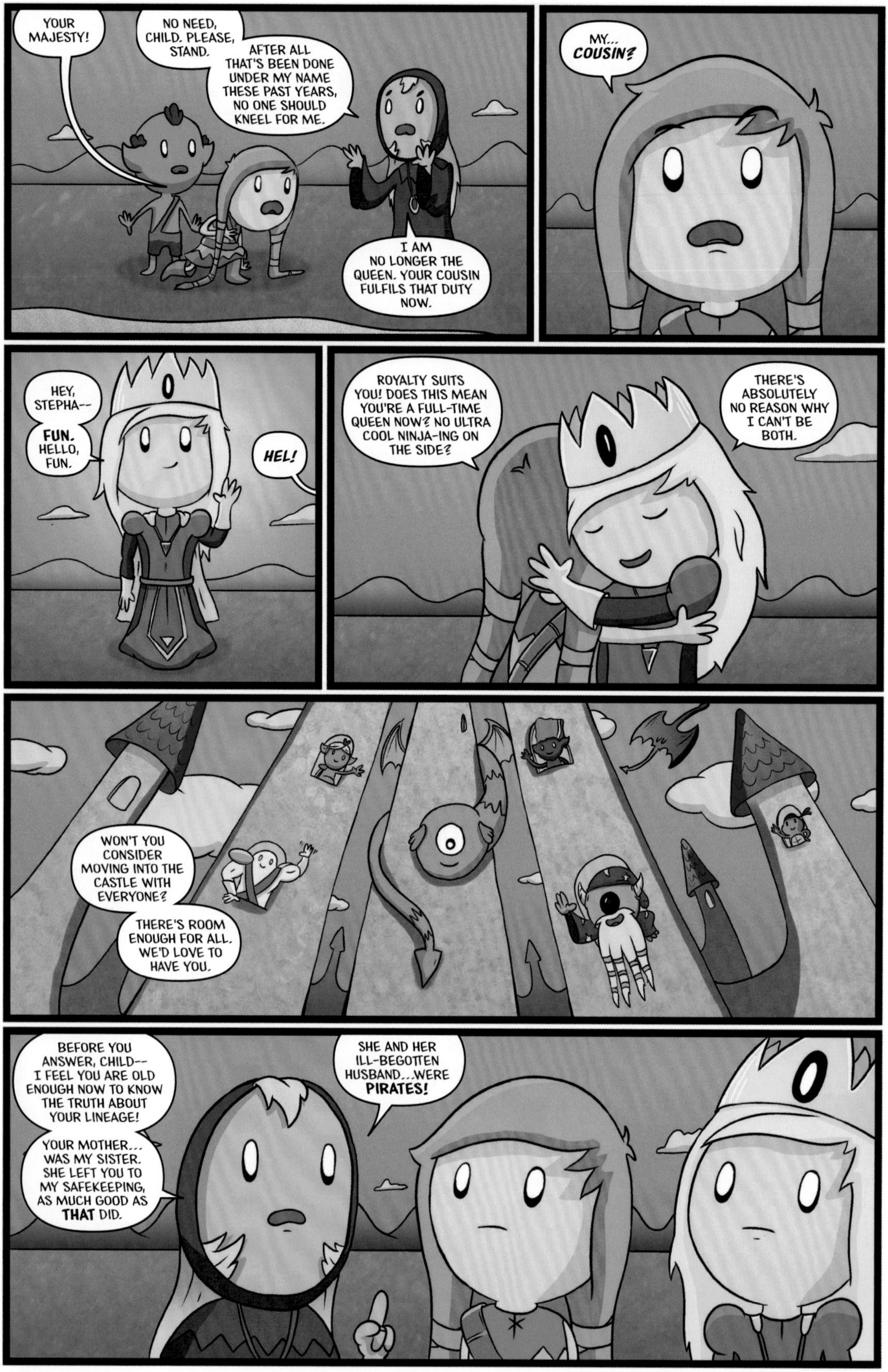
YOUR MAJESTY!
NO NEED, CHILD. PLEASE, STAND.
AFTER ALL THAT'S BEEN DONE UNDER MY NAME THESE PAST YEARS, NO ONE SHOULD KNEEL FOR ME.
I AM NO LONGER THE QUEEN. YOUR COUSIN FULFILS THAT DUTY NOW.
MY... COUSIN?
HEY, STEPHA--
FUN. HELLO, FUN.
HEL!
ROYALTY SUITS YOU! DOES THIS MEAN YOU'RE A FULL-TIME QUEEN NOW? NO ULTRA COOL NINJA-ING ON THE SIDE?
THERE'S ABSOLUTELY NO REASON WHY I CAN'T BE BOTH.
WON'T YOU CONSIDER MOVING INTO THE CASTLE WITH EVERYONE?
THERE'S ROOM ENOUGH FOR ALL. WE'D LOVE TO HAVE YOU.
BEFORE YOU ANSWER, CHILD-- I FEEL YOU ARE OLD ENOUGH NOW TO KNOW THE TRUTH ABOUT YOUR LINEAGE!
YOUR MOTHER... WAS MY SISTER. SHE LEFT YOU TO MY SAFEKEEPING, AS MUCH GOOD AS THAT DID.
SHE AND HER ILL-BEGOTTEN HUSBAND...WERE PIRATES!

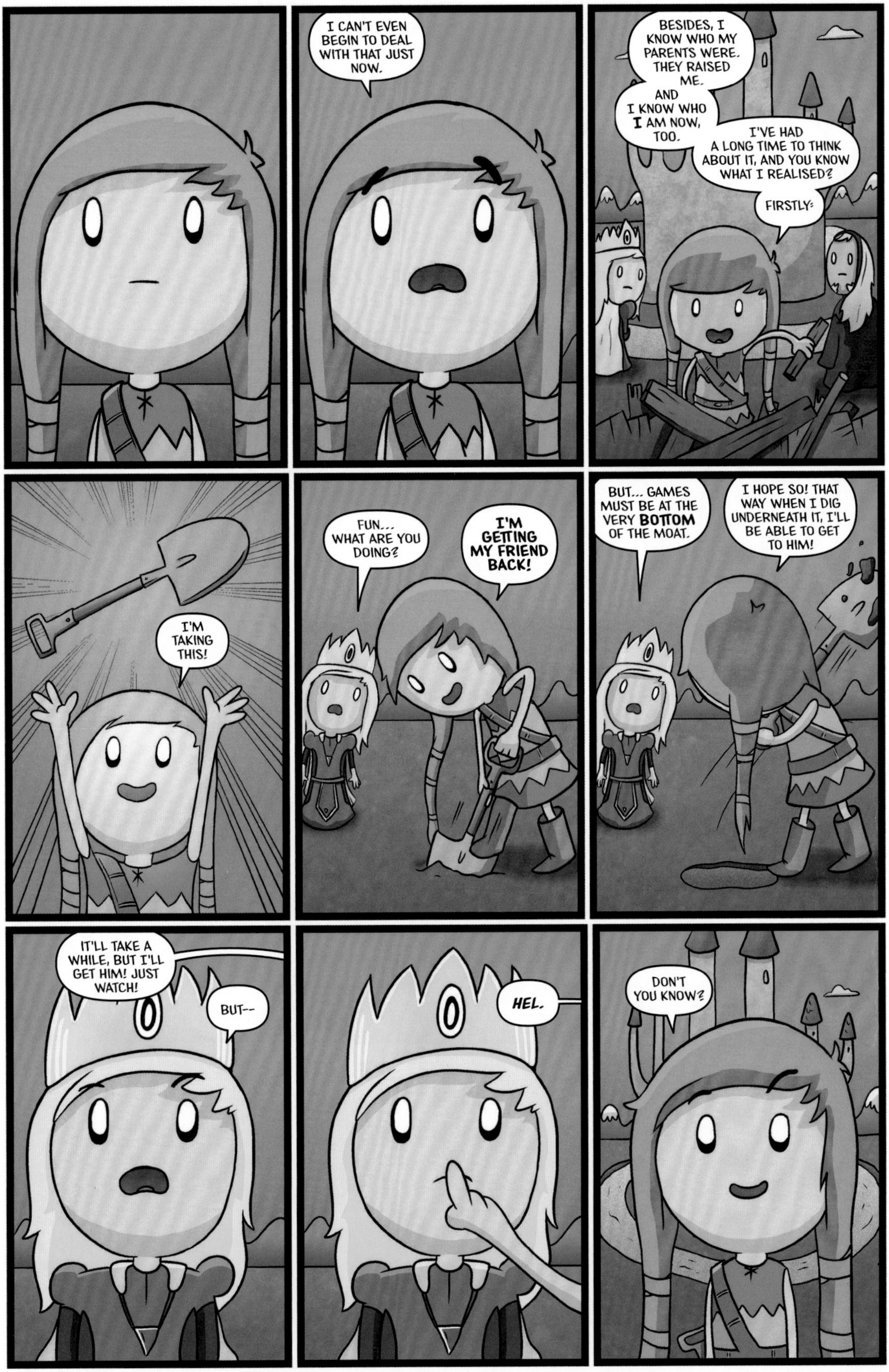
I CAN'T EVEN BEGIN TO DEAL WITH THAT JUST NOW.
BESIDES, I KNOW WHO MY PARENTS WERE. THEY RAISED ME.
AND I KNOW WHO I AM NOW, TOO.
I'VE HAD A LONG TIME TO THINK ABOUT IT, AND YOU KNOW WHAT I REALISED?
FIRSTLY:
I'M TAKING THIS!
FUN... WHAT ARE YOU DOING?
I'M GETTING MY FRIEND BACK!
BUT... GAMES MUST BE AT THE VERY BOTTOM OF THE MOAT.
I HOPE SO! THAT WAY WHEN I DIG UNDERNEATH IT, I'LL BE ABLE TO GET TO HIM!
IT'LL TAKE A WHILE, BUT I'LL GET HIM! JUST WATCH!
BUT--
HEL.
DON'T YOU KNOW?

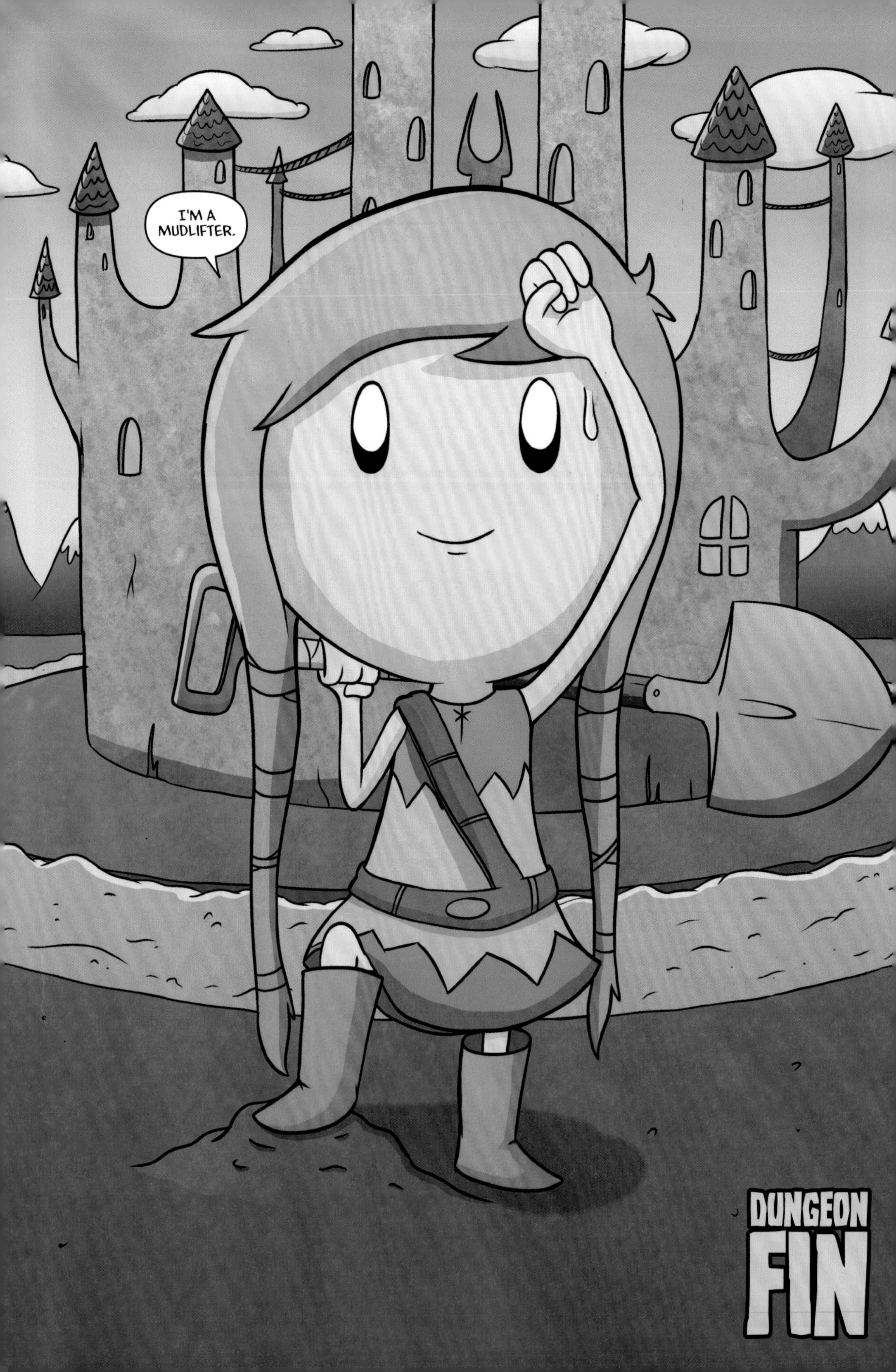
I'M A MUDLIFTER.
DUNGEON FIN

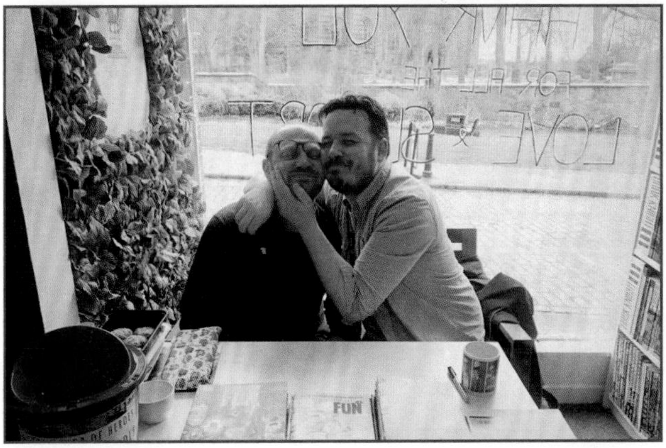
FUN

ABOUT THE AUTHORS

NEIL SLORANCE

NEIL SLORANCE IS A GLASGOW-BASED ILLUSTRATOR AND COMIC ARTIST. HE IS BEST KNOWN FOR HIS WORK ON THE AWARD-WINNING ALL-AGES COMIC **DUNGEON FUN** AS WELL AS HIS WORK ON **DOCTOR WHO** COMICS WITH COLIN BELL.

NEIL HAS BEEN ILLUSTRATING AND SELF PUBLISHING HIS OWN COMICS FOR 10 YEARS AS WELL AS WORKING AS A POLITICAL CARTOONIST FOR STV AND THE NATIONAL NEWSPAPER SINCE 2015.

NEIL HAS WORKED WITH SUCH CLIENTS AS THE BBC, STV, TITAN COMICS, THE NATIONAL AND HACHETTE CHILDREN'S GROUP

COLIN BELL

COLIN BELL IS A COMICS WRITER AND LETTERER. IN ADDITION TO DUNGEON FUN, HE HAS ALSO WRITTEN FOR TITLES SUCH AS **DOCTOR WHO: THE TWELFTH DOCTOR** AND **2000AD**. HIS LETTERING HAS APPEARED IN TITLES FROM MANY PUBLISHERS, INCLUDING BOOM! STUDIOS, IMAGE COMICS AND DARK HORSE COMICS.

HE LIVES ON THE OUTSKIRTS OF GLASGOW WITH HIS WIFE AND DAUGHTER, WHOSE INFINITE PATIENCE AND SUPPORT MADE THIS BOOK POSSIBLE.

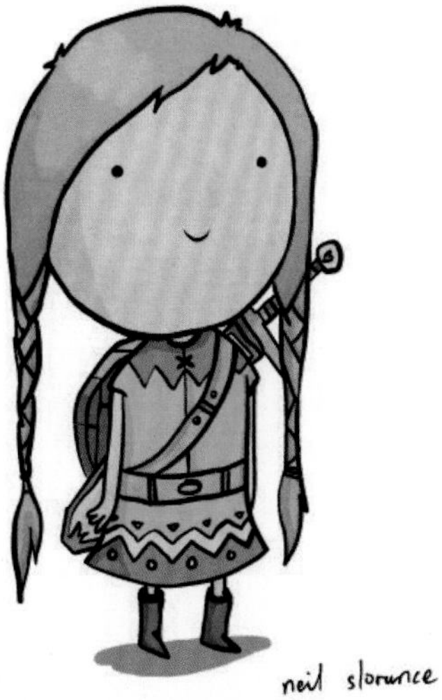
neil slorance

BHP COMICS

JACK LOTHIAN :: SHA NAZIR
LAPTOP GUY
FOREWORD BY
JOHN WAGNER

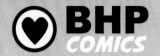

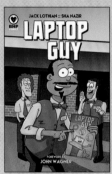

GN | 84 pages | Full Colour
£7.99 UK | $10.95 USD
ISBN: 978-1-910775-00-4

BHP COMICS
COMIC INVENTION
THE WORLDS FIRST COMIC, EVERYTHING BEFORE, AFTER AND FRANK QUITELY

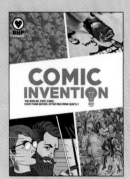

GN | 180 pages | Full Colour
£29.95 UK | $43.00 USD
ISBN: 978-1-910775-03-5

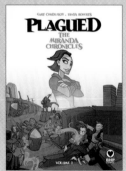

PLAGUED
THE MIRANDA CHRONICLES
VOLUME 1
BHP COMICS

GN | 64 pages | Full Colour
£8.99 UK | $13.00 USD
ISBN: 978-1-910775-19-6

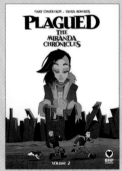

PLAGUED
THE MIRANDA CHRONICLES
VOLUME 2
BHP COMICS

GN | 48 pages | Full Colour |
£8.99 UK | $13.00 USD
ISBN: 978-1-910775-14-1

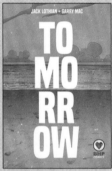

JACK LOTHIAN + GARRY MAC
TO MO RR OW
BHP COMICS

GN | 48 pages | Full Colour
£7.99 UK | $10.95 USD
ISBN: 978-1-910775-05-9

FROM THE CREATOR OF JUDGE DREDD
BHP COMICS
ROK OF THE REDS
John WAGNER
Alan GRANT
Dan CORNWELL

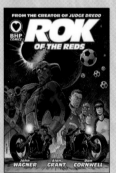

GN | 144 pages I Full Colour
£18.99 UK | $26.95 USD
ISBN: 978-1-910775-11-0

FRANK QUITELY
DRAWINGS + SKETCHES
BHP COMICS

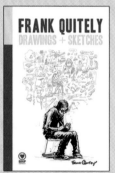

GN | 128 pages | Full Colour

Hardback
£18.99 UK | $26.95 USD
ISBN: 978-1-910775-09-7

Softback
£9.99 UK | $14.95 USD
ISBN: 978-1-910775-18-9

FULL COLOUR
A GRAPHIC ANTHOLOGY
BHP COMICS

GN | Black & White |
£8.99 UK | $13.00 USD
ISBN: 978-1-910775-15-8

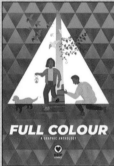

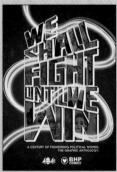

WE SHALL FIGHT UNTIL WE WIN
A CENTURY OF PIONEERING POLITICAL WOMEN.
THE GRAPHIC ANTHOLOGY.
BHP COMICS

GN | 64 pages | Full Colour
£9.99 UK | $15.00 USD
ISBN: 978-1-910775-16-5

WARREN PLEECE • SHAZLEEN KHAN • ROBIN JONES
FREEDOM BOUND
ESCAPING SLAVERY IN SCOTLAND
BHP COMICS

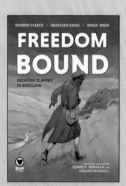

GN | 144 pages | Full Colour

Hardback
£19.99 UK | $27.95 USD
ISBN: 978-1-910775-12-7

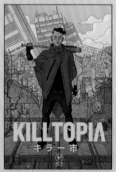

KILLTOPIA
キラー市

GN | 48 pages | Full Colour
£8.99 UK | $13.00 USD
ISBN: 978-1-910775-17-2

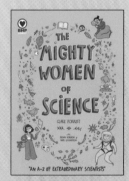

BHP
The MIGHTY WOMEN OF SCIENCE
CLARE FORREST
"AN A-Z OF EXTRAORDINARY SCIENTISTS"

GN | 48 pages | Full Colour
£9.99 UK | $14.95 USD
ISBN: 978-1-910775-06-6